Beneath the Surface

By Jeremy Clayton Birkey

ISBN: 9781983383151

Jeremybirkey1988@gmail.com

Contents

Acknowledgements

I'm grateful for the friends and family who expressed an early and sustained interest in my writing. Special thanks to Benjamin and Gabriel for their insight, and Cheryl for her encouragement.

Part One: Collapse

Chapter 1

Desertion. The word is nearly synonymous with cowardice; with treachery. The complete antithesis of duty. Nothing will tear an army down quicker.

—*Sovereignty General Jadaro Sahn*

Desertion. Marina had been losing sleep, consumed by the idea, and she expected that her restlessness would continue in the long nights that awaited her.

But not tonight. On this evening a mix of fear, anxiety, and adrenaline drove out her shame. Marina knew she was risking death to a degree well beyond any danger she had endured during her two years in the service. If caught, her execution was probable. Or she would be caged and displayed as a despicable failure for many years to come; the press department would have a field day with her trial, sentencing, and imprisonment. Both possibilities seemed equally appalling.

She had second thoughts about having come to the lounge. She sat alone at a small circular table. A fiddler performed across the room to a jeering crowd of his squad mates. She recognized the young man from her unit but didn't remember his name. Her eyes darted about the room as she kept her head propped casually with her arm. She spotted a few familiar faces but no one she was particularly close to. *Does anyone notice me?* she wondered. *What if they try to strike up a conversation and*

I sound as nervous as I feel? They might suspect that something is up... Perhaps she should have stayed in her cot and pretended to be sick until the designated time. But as she looked through the softly lit warehouse that served as the unit's informal gathering place, she saw nothing but smiling faces, competitive games, and hearty meals brought in from the mobile kitchen parked outside. Her stomach twitched at the sight of the steaming tin bowls being brought in, but she was much too anxious to eat. Although the building had been recently converted to a recreational space for the troops, it already felt worn-in. The relaxed atmosphere reminded her of some of the taverns she had visited located in the sleepy corners of the galaxy—the kind with wood paneling and fireplaces, where one could reasonably expect to meet interesting strangers and hear the latest scuttlebutt. The space smelled of peanuts, savory stew, and spilled beer.

She guessed there were perhaps eighty army staff crowded around the room, sitting on crates, leaning against the long counter at the edge of the room, or milling around the pair of tilted pool tables bolted into the concrete floor. As soldiers crisscrossed the room, their shadows danced under the three strands of lantern-style lights hung low across the middle of the room, fastened precariously with wire from the rafters and casting a soft, orange tint. Whimsical evenings like this caused her to question her plan to desert. But she had made up her mind— she was leaving it *all* behind—so she was not in a proper state of mind to appreciate the night's festivities. Marina knew that for most, tonight offered a rare chance at rest and recreation, and was quite possibly the calm before the storm. No one was wasting time brooding or scrutinizing fellow soldiers. If her anxiety was visible and somehow gave her a less-than-patriotic aura on their eve of victory, no one in this room would notice.

Marina wasn't alone in her purpose—but whereas she had spent the evening perched away from the other soldiers, lest her stress become too evident—Titus, her partner-in-crime, had treated the night like any other. He joked with the others in their unit, threw a few drinks back after he was invited into the makeshift officer's lounge, and was by all observations his usual jovial self. Titus's steady, sonorous voice projected confidence, and the man backed it up with no shortage of relatable stories that never failed to end in laughter. Marina could always count on his humor; it was probably one of the reasons they had become friends in the first place. Far more than just blending in, Marina was convinced that Titus was truly enjoying his last hour before becoming a fugitive.

Their four thousand-strong battalion had moved constantly over the previous three days, often on foot—their vehicular transport had been waiting for its fuel supply, at the mercy of logistics failures. After that frenetic trek, having been afforded barely a night of rest, the battalion had secured a position on this sparse land only twenty-four hours earlier, surrounding what was by all accounts a critically important mining operation. The camp they occupied was a distribution facility, conveniently dormant because it was only a seasonal operation. The Sovereignty had started the generators, airlifted equipment and prefab structures, and established a perimeter overnight: Fort Callous was born. Having gained a vital strategic position with the enemy many kilometers away—at least that is what Marina had pieced together—many of the soldiers had been finally granted time to relax.

Marina was glad that Titus was composed. His poise helped bolster her confidence. If Titus could walk out of the camp tonight with swagger, then she could at least hold herself together during their escape. Titus wasn't putting on a show; he really was being himself. *I'll never know how he can be so chill, but I'm glad he is*, she thought. He didn't seem to have any reservations about what they were going to attempt—and despite her anxiety, she couldn't help but feed on his energy, even from across the room.

The fiddler whirred a crank on the side of his instrument and then unleashed a rousing tune to the cheers of half the hall. It was a variation on the Sovereignty army's anthem, familiar to all but with a funk twist. Marina tapped her foot during the first few bars to blend in with the other listeners' energy. A nearby group of men and women laughed heartily around a long rectangular table as they played cards. One of the players lazily slid a card across the table and it fluttered off the table to land at Marina's feet. The group, thoroughly lubricated with alcohol, cackled at this development. Marina quickly scooped up the card and leaned forward to hand it back, getting nothing in acknowledgement but the briefest nods from the tipsy players, which was fine by her.

She had been checking the clock for each of the past fifteen minutes. She looked at Titus but he was still laughing with some others. *Come on, Titus...how can you lose track of time on a night like this?!* As if on cue, Titus reluctantly stood. His companions waved at him to sit back down as they pushed a bottle in his direction. Titus gestured apologetically in the opposite direction, miming some unseen task across Fort Callous that required him.

He laughed warmly, bid farewell to his new buddies, and sauntered across the room toward the exit. Midway through, he locked eyes with Marina his piercing eyes told her that he was still on point. After he left, she waited a few seconds before rising and attempting to leave in a nonchalant manner.

Titus was waiting alone in the hallway. Marina checked both ends for anyone passing through. The hearth-like feel instantly evaporated. Unlike the warehouse, which had been thoroughly converted into a lounge, the adjoining hallway was entirely sterile and utilitarian.

"Do you have everything?" Marina asked quietly. "It doesn't look like you have anything on you."

"Exactly. If we packed a giant suitcase, you can bet we would be stopped. If it looks like we're out for a casual stroll to enjoy this beautiful evening—not so much. But trust me, I've got the things that count. Besides the paperwork, of course, I brought a few things extra." Titus looked her up and down. "And it looks like you brought only what we need too. I'm sure there were a few souvenirs you wanted to sneak along. I applaud your resolve, Marina."

"Yeah, ok—keep it down. Let's get going." She patted her jacket pockets to once again check for the essential documents. "No one is expecting you back later, are they?"

"Those guys in there? Nah, we never even got around to telling each other our names. They're not exactly the nosy type, anyway."

Marina shook her head, once again amazed by Titus's skill as a social chameleon. They walked swiftly down the corridor and rounded a corner toward the double doors that led outside the building.

Although they vastly differed in their outward demeanors, Marina and Titus held a close rapport going back well over a year. Marina had found a sympathetic ear for her grumblings and dissatisfaction in the service. When Titus demonstrated that he could keep her disloyal talk to himself, she had confided more in him, and he had reciprocated. The hint of desertion emerged naturally enough. They had never called it desertion, of course. It was "getting away from all of it" or "starting fresh" or some other euphemism. But they knew no one else would characterize it so mildly once the deed was done.

Marina had joined the service two years ago and Titus had joined the year before that. Both had joined primarily for pragmatic reasons, each hoping for a springboard to a career once the standard two-year term was completed. But then the full-scale war had rapidly erupted between the Sovereignty and the Coalition. Battle lines were drawn up between governments that supported the Sovereignty movement and those that constituted the Coalition.

The central issue that had sparked the war was human cloning. Recent advances had made the technology much more efficient and available even to people of limited means. Amid streamlining of the fertilization process, more infants than ever before were surviving. Before society could come to grips with the technology and the demographic revolution it promised, a significant percentage of the population was already clone-birthed. The frontier of cloning was wildly unregulated.

While many governments threw their support behind cloning, the backlash was equally strong. The anti-cloning movement became known as the Sovereignty. For a myriad of reasons, they sought to outlaw human cloning. Through a flurry of treaties, the Sovereignty formed to oppose human cloning at the same time that the governments that would become known as the Coalition sought to protect and promote it.

"No turning back out there," Titus warned as they strode toward the exit. A muffled roar of laughter from the hall echoed in the sparse hallway. "Now or never."

"Why are you trying to talk me out of this?"

"I'm not. But the risk is real. No shame in changing your mind."

Marina didn't mask her annoyance. "I know. This is exactly what I want. I'm not turning back."

"Good. I'm glad," Titus smiled, nervously, she thought. "It's just one night, and then we're in the wind."

Neither Marina nor Titus was particularly passionate about the human cloning issue—certainly not enough to have risked their lives. They had joined the military before the Sovereignty and its anti-cloning agenda emerged. After the unexpected outbreak of the war, Marina's and Titus's obligations were extended indefinitely by the army. As the two years of war spilled over into almost every aspect of life across the galaxy's settled territories, the Sovereignty army had become increasingly comprised of true believers who opposed the cloning nations, with fewer of the pre-war recruits remaining. That Marina's enlistment had turned into conscription had troubled her, but desertion hadn't crossed her mind immediately. However, as the years dragged on and the war expanded with unrelenting ferocity, her morale deteriorated. She was weary of the chaotic skirmishes that always ended in stalemates and that left her hypervigilant for days, only to be plunged into the next war zone without warning.

As the army shipped her all over the galaxy for battles that accomplished nothing except attrition on both sides, she envied the possibilities of civilian life: the plentiful sleep, the privacy, and of course the personal freedom. Human cloning was here to stay, she thought, and in any case, soldiers were now chiefly used in power plays that went far beyond the stated objectives of the war. She wasn't a particularly good student of history, but the grueling course of this war reminded her of the ancient First World War, now centuries past; she had learned about it in school and couldn't remember the names of the mythical-sounding nations involved, but the tales of grand armies fighting from miserable trenches over small tracts of land using increasingly brutal tactics resonated with her as the Sovereignty conducted similarly slogging campaigns.

She could have anticipated her waning loyalty when she first joined, of course. Indeed, perhaps part of her had known—but if so, she had refused to acknowledge it. She had always been more of the creative type and also had quickly shifting interests. As a child, she had changed her favorite color constantly, and had a revolving door of best friends. As an academy student, she had changed her discipline during three consecutive semesters, each time after losing her initial passion.

But she knew that her discontent ran deeper. She was perpetually unfulfilled by too much of the same thing. She had broken up with several steady boyfriends over the years, simply because she thought she had learned all there was to know about them. The men had been thoroughly decent, and no particular conflict or flaw had driven her away. Her passion had merely waned, and so she had cut ties—to mutually painful effect. Their confusion at the sudden break-ups had troubled her more than anything. There were a couple of false starts in her career, too: promising jobs left before she could fully learn each trade. And she had fervently pursued several languages that now languished half-learned. She had demonstrated talent in these endeavors, certainly—but it hadn't been long before her passion waned. And so it was now with her status as a soldier: a disillusioned, unwilling participant in a war with no end in sight.

Marina knew that duty had its place: if everyone were to shirk an important responsibility, society would devolve into chaos. She knew she would be despised for deserting. But her unit would move past it quickly. She and Titus were just two soldiers, and she had grown increasingly distant from her unit, especially as it became increasingly radicalized into a mentality of total war against the Coalition. Other than with Titus, she had no deep friendships in the rest of the unit—just some goodwill shared with a few acquaintances. Marina reminded herself that the unit would be far better off without her anyway—she would only drag down morale the longer she stayed. It had to be clear to them that her heart and mind wasn't with them.

She had fantasized about escaping for months now, before the current opportunity presented itself. She imagined falling back from the front line, taking a walk into a forest, and emerging into some idyllic, untouched village on the other side. The type of rustic place without rationing, conscription, or any other type of spillover from the war; a home where people took naps after a hard but fulfilling day of work, sold their goods in an open-air market, and hadn't yet been affected by cloning. In short, Marina yearned for the simpler life that was not unlike the calm, slow-moving village in which she had grown up. She pictured herself touring the coastal colonies as a musician—once she properly learned to play the *quagga*, of course. The guitar-like instrument employed a series of thick strings that amplified the musician's motions into powerful vibrations—the audience could literally feel the music in their bones. She had first encountered the quagga at five years old, and she could still recall the way the music had enveloped her little body. Despite having started lessons from time to time, she had never consistently pursued her interest in the instrument, having always been swayed to concentrate on what her elders considered to be more practical matters.

But soon she would be free to pursue her long dormant passions such as the quagga. Emboldened by the confidence she had developed in the army, she would make a successful career for herself far from Sovereignty or Coalition territory. Marina had a clear vision for the rest of her life, and the first step was leaving this failed endeavor that she had been a fool for joining in the first place. She just needed to take the plunge—and now the time was ripe.

When Marina had first learned they were to be deployed to this barren planet, she had immediately begun entertaining thoughts of desertion. She had never been to this location before, but she was pretty sure she had some relatives here: a pair of cousins whom she had not seen since childhood. She had carefully made contact with one of the cousins and through this woman had formed a plan to escape and remain undetected. The first step was to escape her unit—by far the biggest obstacle. They were going to be careful, but there were still risks of being caught. If they could sneak out of Fort Callous's perimeter, the dominoes to her freedom would fall in line, and within days she and Titus would be offworld, far from the Sovereignty. With the war escalating, they didn't think it likely that the Sovereignty could devote many resources to finding them anyway. Indeed, their gamble partly depended on that calculation.

Titus waved his hand to draw her blank stare. "Marina, you look troubled. We can, uh, wait a bit I guess, if you think that would help." But Titus sounded reluctant as he said it.

Her face flushed with annoyance: she hated her transparency. "No, let's just do this. I'm fine." The exit loomed only a few steps ahead. The weak light above the rusty doors flickered as they approached.

"Really? Because as we've been walking, your eyes have gotten this really nervous look."

"Titus, there's never going to be a time when I'm not nervous about something like this. I just express it differently than you. It's all the waiting that's agonizing—let's just go."

Titus gave her look that suggested he didn't quite believe her. Marina led the way and collided with the squeaky pushbar, and the door creaked open to a flash of light.

Chapter 2

Marina and Titus emerged into the still-warm air under a flickering light that attracted a frenzy of large, feathery white moths. She would never be nostalgic for this world. In the brief two weeks since she had landed on planet Sarabek, the land had imparted a harsh and desolate impression; filled with giant insects, harsh winds, and sparse vegetation. She had learned very little about the way of life here—but enough to know that Sarabek was afflicted with plain foods, few job prospects outside of the mining industry, and uncouth locals. It was no wonder that the prospect of visiting her cousins had never crossed her mind in past years.

However, Marina had to admit that it was a beautiful night. The stars shone brightly through a cloudless sky. A nearly full moon rose over the twin peaks of mountains, whose craggy silhouettes were clearly visible despite being over sixty klicks away. The air was crisp with a comfortable warmth. What the land lacked in culture and riches it at least attempted to make up for with occasionally startling displays of serenity. They passed a pair of technicians and grunted a greeting. Marina and Titus counted on the perimeter security being comparatively light; no known threats were in the immediate vicinity. There were a couple of places to slip out, though perhaps not totally unnoticed. Their cover would be the activity surrounding the camp. Fort Callous wasn't completely enclosed and the fences were still going up. The base wasn't intended to be long-term anyway.

To the east, large cargo vehicles and fuel tankers were refueling outside the perimeter, where there was a concrete parking lot and a pair of bulbous, 10 meter fuel tanks that were the butt of constant jokes. The swift hovercraft models could conquer tough terrain, but these were few; most of the vehicles were older, wheeled trucks. Staff regularly walked back and forth across the fuel depot and the main camp, so the wheeled gate of the fence was left open. Marina and Titus needed to slip past the vehicles and the depot crews and cross the restricted field until they escaped the sentries' line of sight. Crossing the fuel depot should be simple; the sentries at the guard posts were there to watch for outsiders—not to keep soldiers in—and Marina hadn't seen any guards on the ground. The depot crews would probably see them; the trick was to play it cool and lose their attention long enough to slip away into the night while avoiding any commanding officer who might scrutinize their motives for trying to step beyond the fence. A valley with a dry riverbed wound around half of Fort Callous, less than half a klick from where they now stood. The riverbed's many jagged tributaries cut deep into the rock, forming many narrow canyons that would provide excellent cover as they fled the camp.

They walked casually across the courtyard that led to the fence and the open gate. It was a comfortable night after a week of grueling heat and many of the army personnel were taking a stroll between Fort Callous's widely spaced warehouses. Where the tower lights didn't reach, the bright moon lit the gravel-filled yard. The flicker of campfires glowed around the corners of several buildings, followed by the laughter of the soldiers tending them. Marina wasn't sure how they had obtained the wood—she had seen only a few sparse clumps of trees since they had arrived. The campfires smelled simultaneously smoky and savory; perhaps there was a little barbeque action going on too. *Maybe there are things on this planet worth eating after all.* Though she had eaten some canned rations a couple hours ago in preparation for their escape, she wished they could swing by and taste the slow-cooked meat. She hadn't eaten proper barbeque since the war began. The shadows of the soldiers danced around the courtyard. *A beautiful night to desert.*

Marina slowed down. "Listen." She refrained from pointing toward the fuel depot and instead nodded. There were shouting and laughter outside the gates; obviously the crew was not on high alert. "I'll follow your lead if they challenge us, like we discussed."

"We might encounter some assholes, but I've seen all sorts of personnel on the other side of that fence these past couple days. Some of them might have had a purpose, but many were out for a stroll. And not one of them deserted. At worst, the sentries will be annoyed; not suspicious. We're going to be fine, Marina."

Marina tried to channel his confidence again but came up short. No time to dwell on their plan. They were only a few steps from the gate. She looked back across the courtyard for the last time, and instantly regretted it. She had a sudden urge to run back to her barracks, disappear into her bunk, and curl up in her cot. But it was too late: she would have hated herself if she reversed course now, abandoning the many promises she'd made to her future.

She swiftly followed Titus through the gate and toward the first of three fuel tanker trucks in their chosen trajectory, on the opposite side of the giant fuel tanks. On reaching the vehicle, they slowed down. By now, they were within the line of sight of one of the eastern guard posts. Titus forced a grin and wrapped an arm over her shoulder.

One of the soldiers came around the front of the truck. His face registered surprise. He looked them up and down and smirked. "What are you guys up to?" he asked. He was on the young side and neither Marina nor Titus recognized him.

"None of your business," Titus said with rude indifference. He looked back longingly at Marina, who conjured a warm smile in return.

"The hell it isn't. We've been refueling all night, so if you weren't sent to help, then get out of here. There are plenty of other places you can be to have fun."

"Listen, cadet." Titus spat the words through gritted teeth and pointed forcefully at the four stripes on his own chest which indicated his significantly higher rank of corporal. "I'm out for a little fresh air with this lovely lady, and had a very long day myself. Much longer than yours, I can guarantee." Turning away from the young man, he gazed back at Marina, and gripped her rear. *That* part had not been rehearsed.

Marina choked back her protest and instead rubbed Titus's shoulder in her own toned-down attempt at improvisation. It seemed to be working: the soldier was backing away, muttering under his breath.

"What was that, cadet?" Titus let go of Marina and glared daggers.

The man faced them again, but his eyes were downcast. His face was visibly red even in the moonlight. "Uh, my apologies, sir. I'll leave you be." With that, he returned the way he had come, slinking around the fuel truck.

Wordlessly, they walked to the next fuel truck. No one accosted them as they were briefly visible between the two trucks. Black crickets hopped between clusters of grass poking out of the pavement as they walked alongside the long, cylindrical body of the tanker.

"Stop," Marina hissed, then grasped Titus around the neck and pulled him close.

"Marina, this isn't the time." Titus said with a nervous smirk as she pulled his warm, grizzled cheek against hers. "What's up?"

"The east sentry sees us. Don't look. He isn't saying anything yet. Maybe he doesn't feel like shouting tonight. He's probably checking us out, so we need to convince him not to worry."

Titus leaned back slowly against the tanker and Marina joined him, this time putting her arm around his shoulder. "And what if he gets jealous and decides to give us a hard time?" he said into her ear.

Marina didn't know how Titus was able to perform so coolly in these circumstances, and she was downright perplexed that he could joke on such occasions. *He has to be overcompensating for nervousness,* she thought. *He has to be...*

Still facing Titus, Marina peered at the sentry out of the corner of her eye and saw him raise a radio to his mouth. His rifle remained lowered. "Shit. He's calling us in."

"OK, let's get going." He led Marina around the truck, out of sight from the sentry. *Hopefully they aren't interested in us enough to cause a commotion just yet,* Marina hoped.

They headed for the last truck, this one parked at the very edge of the pavement of the fuel depot. As they quickly covered the gap between the two tankers, Marina stole a glance toward the cluster of soldiers tasked to refuel the trucks. A few leaned against a moth-covered lamppost as the rest wrestled a thick hose across the concrete. Although they had a clear line of sight, they either didn't notice or didn't care about Marina and Titus. The two reached the cover of the truck cab and gasped in relief.

The crackle of a radio gripped Marina's attention. "Sure...Yes, I'm looking now—what did they look like?"

There was no time to find better cover. The man with the radio came around the far side of the tanker and shone a flashlight directly at them. "Never mind, I see them. I've got this." He hastily holstered the radio. He wore an officer's uniform and a stern scowl. He approached several more steps while shining the flashlight into their faces.

"Excuse me, can you stop trying to blind us?" Marina protested.

"Excuse yourself," the officer said. "What are you two doing out here?"

"Just out for a stroll, like half the base does on their time off," Titus said. "Didn't mean to bother you guys—we'll get out of your hair."

"I don't care what half the base does. It's against protocol, and we're in a state of war. You could be shot." He looked closer at Marina with a disturbing smirk. "Out for a roll in the hay, huh? Don't act innocent: I know why people are always trying to head to the southeast corner."

"Well, you know—it's been a while." Marina tried a disarming grin, but the man just frowned. "Can we help you for your troubles and be on our way?"

The man tilted his head back in forth in a pensive expression that Marina interpreted as cooperation. She looked to Titus, and he held out several large bills. The officer lit them with the flashlight for several long, breathless seconds. *C'mon, take it. Don't be an asshole.* Then he shone the flashlight right back on their faces.

"You are mistaking me for a weak-willed worm or a common whore. Either way, I'm not buying any of the excuses you're peddling out here. Both of you are coming back—right now."

Marina took a tentative step toward the camp as instructed, but Titus halted her with a hand on her shoulder. "Aren't you too old to be playing hall monitor?" he asked, exasperated. *Stop goading him,* Marina thought. The man reached inside his jacket, placing a hand on a holstered weapon. "All right, all right. We're going back," Titus said, and he and Marina lurched forward, walking quickly. She glanced at him. He rolled his eyes at her, as if this were merely an irritating setback. "Another time..." he whispered. Marina slowly exhaled and resisted the urge to glance back at the confrontational officer.

They heard the crackle of the radio back at the tanker. "Jones again. Those pricks you saw—yeah, I'm bringing them through the gate. Meet me there. Okay." Jones holstered the radio. "Hey, stop!" he ordered.

They hesitated, then complied. As they stood motionless, still facing Fort Callous, Marina bit her lip, trying to vanquish her rising panic.

The officer strode in front of them, his stern expression now even more hostile.

"Geez, what *is* it?" Titus said.

"The more I think about it, the more I'm convinced that you two weren't just exploring for a nice spot to get frisky with each other." His voice was tense with aggression, as if each barked word were trying to outdo its predecessor.

Titus spread his hands in a compliant gesture. "Look, we're sorry for causing a problem. It's just that—"

"I know your type!"

"Huh?"

"You're done." Jones snarled. "I think we're going to find a lot of cash on both of you along with some very...interesting paperwork. And it looks like you have an extra layer of clothing on underneath. For when you turn your back on your uniform."

"Hey, you don't—"

"You're deserting. And you screwed it up," Jones said, his confident smile disturbing Marina more than ever.

Marina opened her mouth to refute him, but the words wouldn't come. Her face had already betrayed the truth and Jones had seen it; she had looked away far too late. She peered toward the camp to see two soldiers, weapons drawn, jogging through the gate. One of the guard posts swiveled a spotlight in their direction, and Titus and Marina squinted under its blinding assault.

"Were you going to meet someone from the mine—or maybe catch a ride at that shithole of a town?" Jones spat.

"Titus..." Marina whispered. He looked back at her, and she saw the same panic in his eyes.

"Don't be even more stupid..." Jones hissed. He reached under his jacket again. But Titus moved fast and shoved into him, knocking the handgun to the pavement. The cash that had been offered as a bribe fluttered to the ground.

"Marina, run!"

They darted past the tanker trucks and bounded into the open grass field. They heard multiple voices shouting behind them, including Jones as he screamed at the nearby refueling crew to help. *I can't believe this. We're already fugitives.*

"Straight ahead! The valley's right there!" Titus shouted.

They ran side by side. Marina stole a glance back and saw the officer starting to lose ground and other soldiers scrambling from around the tankers to join in the chase. The Another look, and the officer was already puffing, slowing further still. Marina looked ahead and saw the rim of the valley looming up ahead. *Almost there. We can lose them.* Suddenly, gunfire crackled right past them. Marina jumped straight up and nearly tripped, even though part of her had been bracing for the sound.

She heard a gasp from Titus, who stumbled even as he tried to keep moving forward. "Titus!!" she screamed. She tried to brace him as they reached the grassy edge of the valley, but he lurched forward and knocked them both over the edge, spilling out onto the embankment. They came to a rest against an outcropping of shrubs that prevented them from sliding farther.

Marina scurried over to Titus on her hands and knees. He struggled to get up, then gasped and slumped onto his back. “Where are you hit?!” Marina reached over his body, unable to see clearly in the limited moonlight. “Come on—we’ll patch you later." She tugged on his arm, but Titus stiffened.

“I-I’m not good...Marina,” he gurgled. His shaking hand was pressed against the side of his neck, glistening with blood. His belly was also soaked with it.

“No, no. This is all wrong." Marina crouched and peeked over the embankment. The officer had stopped in a crouch in the tall grass, perhaps 30 meters away. The other staff were slowing up behind him, taking up cautious positions. It was hard to see which direction the officer was facing against the backdrop of one of the spotlights. *Can he see me?* Just as Marina noticed his outstretched gun-hand, he fired a shot that whizzed by her head.

She dropped back to Titus. He looked dire. He realized it too: she could see it in his wide eyes. *I can’t leave him like this, can I?* But she knew she could do nothing for him. More important, she admitted, acknowledging her motives for fleeing—he could do nothing more for her. She couldn’t depend on him any longer. “I’m sorry, but I gotta leave you." Her voice quaked.

“Do you really have to?” he asked feebly. It was killing her to see him reduced to this.

“I-I can't get caught. They'll kill me. That officer didn't seem too interested in taking prisoners once we ran."

His eyes widened in even greater agony, and then a sad calm settled in. Acceptance, perhaps? *Please understand. I need to leave.* Titus nodded weakly, resignation beginning to cloud his previously piercing eyes. "I know, I know—yeah. I'm a goner." He feebly raised his head to look at his blood-soaked abdomen. "Pretty sure anyway."

There was no doubt in her mind. Marina looked down the valley and saw a deep gorge no more than 15 meters away that would provide cover far into the valley. She was confident that she could lose her pursuers if she could reach it. She looked back at Titus but couldn't hold his glassy-eyed gaze.

I've got to be practical. I've still got a chance. She eyed Titus's trousers. Avoiding looking at his face, Marina quickly fished into his pockets and wrestled the cash out of them, along with the carefully folded documents intended to aid in Titus's long-term escape. She had to lean forward to reach all the way down his pockets, and in doing so leaned against his abdomen, causing him to groan. "Sorry. I need these," she said between tears. "I'm really sorry this happened to you." She rose into a crouch, feeling strongly pulled to escape.

"Marina, please..." Titus gasped. He still gripped his neck wound tightly.

"I'm going to get away...for both of us." The others would appear over the bluff any moment. *No more time.* She wanted to amend her final words to Titus, but not knowing what else to say, Marina feebly shook her head before scurrying away from him and breaking into a sprint for the cover of the gorge.

Chapter 3

One day before.

Lizby and Sabos Sasquire had invested considerable effort and expense to imbue their cramped apartment with a sense of charm. The couple had made the mass-produced unit as much their home as possible, first hanging warm string lighting, then placing inviting antique wooden furniture, and gradually affixing all manner of earth-toned decor to the plaster walls. That they had any decor at all distinguished them from their utilitarian neighbors. The furnishings had been difficult to come by—they were so far from major shipping lanes and major retail outlets. The investment had certainly been worth it: their space had a warmth and tranquility that was rare in their bleak neighborhood. It served as a quiet refuge from the mine's incessant industrial activity and the gloom that spilled over into Haast, the company mining town.

"It would be a lot more money," Sabos said. "Imagine where we could be next year—no more mining for either of us. No more spending half our time underground."

"Are you kidding? I love working for the mine," Lizby said. "I've already pledged my soul to the company.'" She broke into a grin as she placed a hand over her heart.

"Seriously, babe—what do you want to do?" Sabos stopped folding the laundry and looked across their tiny apartment at her.

Lizby pursed her lips, still fighting a smile. “I thought we basically decided last night. We’re going to stay and work,” she said as she crossed the room to him.

“I don’t think we decided for sure.” Sabos smiled mischievously. “We didn’t fully finish that conversation, remember? We got...busy.”

“Oh, yeah." Lizby flipped her hair back flirtatiously. “I guess we stopped using our words.”

“The talking got boring.” Sabos leaned forward expectantly but Lizby ducked his embrace.

She took her spare mining uniform from the laundry basket and began folding. “I think that at this point in our lives, we need to go back into the mine, hon. I honestly don’t think it’s a serious matter of safety. The war wants nothing to do with the miners. We’ll be left alone." She sighed deeply, rubbing her forehead. “We need the money; we need every penny if we’re going to get offworld during the next migration window. And if we take a break and leave the mine now, who knows when we’ll get a ride back here—or even if our jobs will be waiting for us?”

Sabos nodded, slowly picking up the laundry again. “I gotta admit, the double-time that OreLife is paying is enticing. I just wanted you to know that we would leave in a heartbeat if you felt the threat was solid. The money isn’t worth our lives. I would never risk your safety.”

“Thanks for being the protective husband, but we’re in this together—and we are going to be fine.”

“OK. Glad we’re on the same page.”

Lizby crossed the room. She admired the strands of her air that were attached on a board hung on the wall leading into the kitchen. It was a local tradition: she had attached a new strand every year since she was five. The length of the hair samples got much longer for the first five years and then stayed consistent. Lizby's hair had started very light in color, then gradually darkened. Most of the girls and women from the region participated in the practice. Sabos had yet to get used to the custom, along with so many of the traditions of this isolated region. He had been here for years already but still felt no closer to becoming a local, despite having married one.

"Staying now will show that we're committed," Lizby said. "Believe it or not, ambition eventually gets noticed around here. Normally, it's all about well-placed connections, but out here who you know means nothing—you've got to be a good cog in the OreLife machine."

Sabos nodded again. "Carmenta told me the same when I asked her if she was going to leave. She's definitely staying, and she'll work any shift available while this double-time continues." Sabos's older sister Carmenta also worked in the mine. She lived in an identical apartment building a few blocks away. "But it wouldn't surprise me if she was hoping to see some action from the war, probably observing from close range."

Lizby managed a smile at the thought. Her impulsive sister-in-law preferred things to be interesting rather than safe, so she was inevitably drawn to danger. "Yeah, Carmenta would probably make a war documentary if she had a chance. You know, I didn't see her yesterday at the mine. And she hasn't been coming by here lately, at least this week."

"She mentioned on Monday that she was going to some of the evening events at the Fire Nights Festival this week."

"I hope so. I'd hate to think that she is just sitting in that depressing apartment after work."

"She hasn't been one to mope around lately, Liz. I'm sure she's up and about."

"I'll probably run into her in the mine today."

"Any word from your family? Can't imagine your folks are pleased that we're still here, and much less so when they find out we're choosing to stay on as part of the voluntary skeleton crew." Sabos had hesitated to broach the topic of her family; lately they had been a topic of frustration. Despite his wife's outward attitude, including her quirky humor and the spring in her step, it was subtly evident to Sabos that the last few months in the mine had been weighing heavily on her spirit, as they had on his. Their occupations as miners would always be a source of friction between Lizby and her family: her father had worked long in the mine so that his three children wouldn't have to. Sabos had been trying to triage his wife's many stresses, but he felt that the topic shouldn't be avoided any longer.

Lizby sighed. "Yes, we chatted for a little while yesterday morning. Dad was freaking out, of course. He warned about reports of deserters leaving the front ahead of the armies. He thought we'd get robbed, kidnapped, bombed—you name it. I told him and Mom that we're fine here, but they're still going to tear their hair out. Oh, and Mom wanted to know if we'd be back in the village for the Water Festival. I told her I didn't think it was likely." Lizby used the filter by the kitchen sink to pour a glass of water. Clearly already done with the subject, she gazed admiringly at her hair band on the wall, one of the many adornments they had arranged to combat the sparseness of their OreLife-leased apartment. Lizby had spent her entire life in this land surrounded by family. Her generation was leaving to make better lives, and although Lizby and Sabos liked being close to her family, they both knew that migration was the inevitable next step toward achieving their goals. Lizby's parents knew it too: they no longer asked if she and Sabos would return to her home village. Lizby loved them dearly, and she knew Sabos did, too—but there was no going back. OreLife was the very last game in town. There was nothing else for them here.

Lizby glanced out their only window toward the dwindling sunset. She snapped her fingers at a sudden thought. "I wanted to stop by the shop tonight to get some insecticide. We're almost out of the old stuff. I've heard that the bug storms might come back early this season; something about excessive soil moisture causing them to hatch." She made a grotesque face at the mental image. "Did you want to come?"

"Sure; I can finish the laundry tomorrow," Sabos said. In truth, he was exhausted from a full day of work underground so the prospect of going to the store was not appealing, but he cherished every moment with his wife during the busy work week. "Probably a good idea for me to join you anyway in case you get attacked by a particularly bold horde."

Lizby smiled, but Sabos was not entirely joking: the bug storms were a seasonal menace, capable of overwhelming small animals or occasionally even vulnerable humans. It had been a couple years since someone had been seriously injured in Haast, but the locals all knew of pets that had been consumed by the insects and the stories of homeless, elderly, or juvenile residents in the countryside that had gone missing only to be suspected as victims of the bug storms. The large insects couldn't flutter more than a few meters at a time, but they crawled in groups of thousands that blotted out the ground. Each weighed 100 grams; more than most of the local birds, bats, or rodents. The insects hatched mostly in the badlands, but it wasn't uncommon for them to migrate many kilometers into the mining town. When the hordes came to the settlement this year, Sabos and Lizby wanted to be stocked with insecticide in case some bugs found their way to the apartment building.

Lizby opened the door to the persistent quiet whoosh of the mining operation. Haast was centrally located within a natural bowl-shaped geological feature, about 5 kilometers across with slopes so steep that it was difficult for some vehicles to scale them. The bowl was surrounded by plains with minimal tree cover: just sparse prairie dotted with small ponds. Although there were occasional storms, annual rainfall was light enough that flooding was a rare problem for the Haast residents. The noise from the non-stop mining operation to the west traveled to the town and swirled around in the bowl shape of the land; its hum seemed to come from all directions. It wasn't the worst sound in the universe, but it almost never stopped. Lizby wondered what it would be like to live where she could open her door and hear nature, or children playing, or even silence. Anything but the industrial drone of the mine that followed her home.

Wanting to travel with the fading sunlight, Lizby and Sabos hustled down the rusty stairs of their second-floor apartment toward the OreLife-run general store. Parts of Haast were ancient, dating back hundreds of years to when residents had used far more primitive mining techniques and had chipped their homes out of the stone. Nearly half of the town's real estate was OreLife-owned, including most businesses and many apartments. Most of the company properties were recently constructed but depressingly utilitarian, featuring minimal use of windows, landscaping, amenities, or anything that could be considered charming. They looked more like cargo containers than architecture.

The route to the store took them by Carmenta's apartment building, and they both glanced at her window hoping to see if she was home. The room was dark and the street around them was also deserted.

"Where do you think she is?" Lizby asked as they continued along the street.

"Well, there's not too many options in Haast," Sabos said. "If I was a gambler, my money would—"

Suddenly they heard Carmenta's voice as she walked around the corner of the apartment building. "...but it's not. And I don't think it's safe to stay here." Her voice was rushed and anxious. She wore workout clothes. She held a phone against her face with her shoulder. She fumbled for keys in her pocket and carried a gym bag with her other hand. "I understand. I'm not trying to," Carmenta said irritably. Her eyes narrowed at the other's response. "Uh-huh. I realize that, and I'll do my part. Just trust me." Carmenta finally fished the keys and started walking up the exposed stairwell to her apartment. Just then, she finally noticed Lizby and Sabos; her eyes widened and she almost dropped her phone in surprise.

"Oh! Hey guys," Carmenta said sheepishly, blushing. "Let me wrap up this phone call and take this bag in and I'll be right out."

"OK, no problem," Sabos said, sharing an inquisitive expression with his wife as Carmenta slipped inside. "What was that about? And what was she saying it about it not being safe here?"

"I don't know, but I'm not going to ask her," Lizby whispered. "Are you?"

Sabos looked at the ground. "No. If she wants to talk about it, then she'll bring it up." They stood together in silence, looking around the neighborhood, but the courtyard was empty save for some plastic bags snagged on the weeds. When Sabos glanced over, a curtain moved in the window of an apartment across from Carmenta. A fussy baby was crying in one of the buildings. Though most of Haast was aesthetically offensive, Carmenta's street was particularly unwelcoming.

Carmenta emerged from her apartment less than a minute later. She trotted down the stairs and joined them. "What's up?"

"Not much. We're walking to the store and were going to see if you were home," Lizby said. "How have you been?"

"Tired, but not too bad. I've been working extra hours to take advantage of that bonus now that we are reduced to a skeleton crew in my department too," Carmenta said. She now sounded composed. "I'm probably going to take some time off when this is all over."

"Good," Sabos said. "You should. The mine will suck your soul if you let it."

Carmenta grinned slightly. "Yep. But don't worry; I won't lose my soul or my sanity for this extra pay."

Sabos raised his eyebrows. “Oh, I’m definitely insane. And I didn’t even get that much money from the sacrifice.”

Carmenta gave her brother a knowing roll of her eyes.

“Has everything else been okay?" Lizby asked, sensing that Carmenta was troubled despite her relaxed manner.

“Yeah, nothing too dramatic," Carmenta said. “I went to some of the Fire Nights Festival events this week. Opening night was fun; they front-loaded the best music that night. But overall it has kind of sucked this year because so many people are gone. Hardly any out-of-town acts. I guess the war is scaring some away.” Carmenta fidgeted and leaned slightly toward her apartment stairwell.

Lizby nodded. “Sounds like we shouldn’t regret missing this year." She hesitated, but then decided to acknowledge her simmering concern. “Hey, we couldn’t help but overhear your phone call." Sabos sighed next to her and Carmenta stiffened. “It sounded intense, but I know it’s not our business. I just wanted you to know that you can always share anything with us, big or small.”

“Thanks for your concern, but it’s really nothing. Just an old friend from school. Our talks always get a little...passionate," Carmenta said evenly. She looked away, but then met Lizby’s gaze head-on. “You should know I would confide in you; it’s just that there’s nothing to share." A frown flickered across her face, but she continued. “Things are stressful with work, but I’m pushing through. It’s just the usual toil; nothing too complicated.”

"OK, glad to hear..." Lizby trailed off awkwardly but then her expression brightened. "Maybe we can get lunch tomorrow? Or at least dinner after work?"

"Um, I don't know about lunch because the shift is going to be unpredictable tomorrow. But we should definitely do dinner if we can. Message me if I don't run into you in the Pit."

"OK, will do," Lizby agreed. "Well, off to the store we go. Hopefully we won't get jumped by some bugs in the dark."

They exchanged farewells and Lizby and Sabos walked toward the store. A small dog yipped through a window at them, the harsh sound echoing among the closely spaced apartment buildings.

Lizby, sensing that her husband was about to speak, beat him to it. "I think she's lying, Sabos," she stated, and then braced herself for his reaction.

"Seriously?! Based on what?" Sabos asked, his arms spread in exasperation. "That was so uncomfortable; why did you pry?"

"Because secrets aren't good. And your sister has one. I can tell from her body language."

"You know, sometimes people are anxious or just a little awkward at times. It doesn't mean they're concealing a deep, dark secret," Sabos reasoned.

Lizby questioned her instincts for the briefest moment before shaking her head. "Sometimes, yes. But I can always tell with her. Plus the phone call was suspicious and sounded like trouble no matter how you try to interpret it."

"Even if that were true, we've got to give Carmenta her distance."

"Look, I won't press the subject any more. I let her know we are here for her and backed off. We're all good."

"Lizby, it's not just this little thing. It's everything that came—"

"OK, can we just drop it? I'll keep offering an open door to your sister, but I won't be too nosy either."

"It's not curiosity that's the problem. Carmenta is proud, and you have a way of insinuating that she's overly vulnerable with your—"

"I asked you to drop it," Lizby snapped, uncharacteristically heated. "Let's get this bug shit and get home before it gets totally dark."

"Fine," Sabos muttered. They walked on in silence as the sun fell below the hills and passed its torch to a brilliant moon. A few street lights flickered to life with a grating buzz, as if reluctant to illuminate the drab buildings of the street.

Chapter 4

The frontline reports of morale are not encouraging. We still have the public's support, but the troops feel distant from the cause. Sovereign choice, the right to genetic destiny—these terms mean little to them when their lives are so constantly placed under fire.

—*Sovereignty General Jadaro Sahn*

Marina ran perhaps harder than she had ever in her life; beyond even the grueling pace of basic training in the Sovereignty. She continued to press on even though she suspected that her pursuers had given up the initial chase early on. The sentries would probably regroup and then there would be a more organized effort to recover her. Marina and Titus had expected this. They doubted that the guards would stumble out into the wilderness on so little information, and probably wouldn't assemble a search party at any point during the night. She herself had nearly broken her legs several times while blazing through the rough terrain with unpredictable rocky formations interspersed among deceptively soft sand pockets. Even in daylight, much of the terrain's features would be concealed by tall weeds.

As her adrenaline finally subsided, she allowed herself to slow. No, the Sovereignty wouldn't risk a hurried, unorganized pursuit across the wasteland, she knew. She certainly wasn't worth mobilizing aircraft for, either. Instead, the Sovereignty would wait for her to resurface among civilization—or at least what counted for it in this region—and then they would use their information networks to guide their field agents. Or at least she hoped they would wait. She also counted on the agents being too occupied with the war to worry much about a single deserter right now. She could be careful enough to follow the plan in order to avoid showing up on their radar. She was confident of that. However, the thought of professionals in active pursuit was gut-wrenching. She doubted the Sovereignty had the manpower to spare, but if she was wrong about that assumption, then it could cost her dearly.

Her panicked run through the maze-like structure of the valley had caused her to lose her sense of direction. She knew the general direction of Haast, the mining town, and was confident that the lights would guide her when she was several kilometers away. For now, the sole visibility came from the moon's illumination; even the lights from Fort Callous were gone. Soon the ground sloped downward and the rough terrain evened out. Marina tromped through a sparsely vegetated plain comprised of a smooth rock that was pocked everywhere with countless small yet deep pools of water. She had to constantly zig-zag to avoid stumbling into the pools, each one a mini oasis for a variety of creatures, including larval insects and slender jumperfish. Her panic had subsided enough for her thirst to become prominent. She had lost her water bottle during her escape but did not dare drink from the pools. Even the region's groundwater was full of microbes—Fort Callous had to boil water for its drinking supply and showers. The stagnant surface pools would surely harm her.

Marina thought about having to leave Titus behind and was haunted by the memory of his eyes when she had seen his hope die. *I can't stop thinking about it. He was so surprised, and then so sad, so devastated...*With his death tonight, her enthusiasm for a better future had deflated, and she was driven by fear alone.

The only thing that twisted her heart more than the memory of her friend's demise was the dread of facing her former Sovereignty comrades as a deserter. Loyalty was everything in the Sovereignty war machine, she had learned. You didn't need to be a brave soldier, or even a good soldier. As a cog in the machine, you needed to be loyal, first and foremost. The Sovereignty was molding all types of people into soldiers, but before building the skills of a warrior, the Sovereignty vetted its recruits all manner of disloyal tendencies. Accordingly, desertion was considered just as bad as espionage; maybe even worse. At least a spy was loyal to a cause. She knew the unit would despise her, but she had made her peace with that by believing she would never see them again. Now that she had escaped the camp, she would probably become someone's long-term recapture project. Although the officer in the refueling area had shot to kill, less impulsive minds would probably plan to take her alive and make a spectacle of her court martial and subsequent sentencing. Marina imagined what might happen. She had heard about deserters either being shot on sight or dropping off the face of the universe once captured. She also recalled the media circus that surrounded some of the other captured deserters—when the Sovereignty deemed it necessary to make an example out of them. *Oh god, what would that even be like? They would probably hologram the whole trial, if they have one. Children would use my image as a piñata. The Sovereignty would dig up my old friends and family and shame them. No—stop thinking about that!*

Consumed by her frantic worries, Marina stumbled on the edge of one of the steep pools. She fell backward as her boot slipped on mossy residue and she skidded halfway into the dark water. A cool shock jolted through Marina as her warmed-up body submerged into the pool up to her waist. The startled eel-like jumperfish splashed out of the water, soaking her even more. One of the creatures streaked out of the water and onto her throat, where the slimy fish writhed about before falling free. True to their name, the other jumperfish twisted their lithe bodies and then reversed the motion to propel themselves into the surrounding pools several meters away to escape.

Not this; not now! She scooted out of the pool. Her legs were soaked. *Great, my papers are probably messed up.* She reached inside her hip pocket and confirmed her worry; her cash and documents were completely wet. Probably not ruined, but their damaged appearance would not grant her any favors in any transactions she attempted. Fortunately, her forged ID with her fake miner alias was unharmed. She thought of the microbes that were probably teeming in the pool and shuddered. She stood up and the water drained down, saturating the inside of her boots. She knew her wet feet could become a huge problem; even disabling. This had been apparent in the harsh environments where the Sovereignty had taken her unit, in which even the most strapping young soldier could be brought down by improper footwear. But she needed to keep going. It hadn't been recommended in her training, but she had no choice: she took off her boots and socks, gripping them in one hand, and continued walking barefoot. She prayed that there weren't any venomous critters in her path.

She took a deep breath and reminded herself that the plan was still intact. Although their desertion had become known almost immediately and Titus had been lost, she would find refuge by the morning and escape offworld within the week. Yes, the Sovereignty would love to capture her, but they couldn't allocate many resources in the midst of such a critical time in their campaign.

Marina was also confident that the Sovereignty didn't know about her ties to the region. No one in the camp had known besides Titus. Her cousin in Haast would see her through. There was no one remaining on planet Sarabek whom she trusted more than her cousin, though that wasn't saying much.

The ground was rough under her bare feet but not painful. Her damp pants were already starting to chafe, but she decided that removing them was not an option in such an unfamiliar and potentially lacerating environment. She also felt a twinge of prudent modesty, even out in this uninhabited wilderness. *Who knows, maybe there's a goat herder up ahead. I wouldn't want to surprise him while wearing no pants.* Marina guessed that she had run and then walked a total of 10 kilometers. She was well over halfway to Haast by her estimation. As she walked among the pools, she had to admit that the moonlit landscape was serene and like no other place she had seen. The water sloshed slightly as the jumperfish hunted insects or engaged in mating frenzies. Crickets chirped softly and hopped underfoot. The stone formations that rose between the pools were smooth and bulbous and layered with different hues of sediment and moss. The vast collection of water pools glistened from the moonlight's reflection, creating a dazzling honeycomb of light orbs that stretched far in every direction. The whole scene looked alien, yet on some other night, it might have been soothing.

She trudged up a gradual rise in the ground and gained a better vantage point of the horizon. She sighed deeply in relief as she saw the glow of lights in the distance that hopefully indicated the Haast's location. She guessed that the town was no farther than 5 klicks away: less than an hour's walk. *I can do this,* she encouraged herself. She shed her despair, willing to believe that sanctuary was near.

Chapter 5

Human cloning, once a mere concept in science fiction, has claimed its inevitable place in society at blinding speed, ushered in by the visionary, and vilified by a new breed of Luddites.

—Professor Ella Socarin, Genetics Department, University of New Seattle

One day before.

Gerund groggily opened his eyes underneath cloudy water. Opaque, green-tinted lights glistened from beyond the water and he realized that his entire body was submerged. But he did not panic. *Am I drowning?* he thought, oddly peaceful at the possibility. But then he exhaled and felt some of his own hot breath come back at him. A mask was fastened to his jaw with a pair of hoses jutting out in opposite directions. *What the hell?*

An intravenous line full of a teal liquid was strapped into his right arm. Gerund tried to lean forward, but his chest was secured by a thick strap. A plastic-covered device was attached in the middle of his chest—perhaps a medical monitor. He was otherwise naked. The water was uncomfortably cool. He could see only right in front of him; there was a confusing blur of lights and moving shapes beyond the pane of glass that surrounded him like a cocoon. He raised his legs and felt the resistance of gravity. *I'm laying down, strapped in a giant fish tank—this is a little strange,* Gerund thought analytically, without a trace of fear. He looked at his feet. That end of the tank ended in a grate with several pumps underneath. *Where is everyone? Where is my—*

Then the memory came flooding back to him. He had entered suspended animation for an extended journey along with the rest of his unit. It had been Gerund's third time traveling in suspended animation, but the longest he had hibernated before was 40 days. The Coalition had told them 6 months this time—the trip would take them all the way across the war's theater. There had been no room in the spacecraft for so many soldiers if they were awake and moving around, let alone the supplies needed to sustain them. And even if there had been enough room, suspended animation was still the best option. As much as the soldiers had dreaded the induced hibernation, it was still preferable to a long, mentally taxing journey across empty space while confined to tight quarters.

With a swift *whoosh*, the water around Gerund was sucked through the grate at his feet. The capsule emptied within seconds and the cloudy glass case cracked open with a small hiss.

"Hand me a towel, please?" a male voice said on the other side.

The glass case swung fully open, flooding Gerund with bright light. A man and woman in lab coats stood before him. Several other staff worked in the background within the narrow confines of the transport ship's hold. They assisted other nearly naked soldiers as they groggily emerged from their capsules.

The smiling man passed him the towel, which Gerund used to wipe his face and torso before wrapping around his waist. “Good morning, Corporal Williams. I trust you slept well?" the man asked with a self-indulgent smirk.

“Uh, yeah, I guess,” Gerund managed. The formality of the man’s greeting was unnerving. *I’m naked, so you might as well call me Gerund. Corporals aren’t naked.* He tried to lean forward, but the harness held him back.

“Oh, just a moment. I’ll disengage everything," the woman said. “Do you think you can stand? Be honest. Many soldiers don’t realize how unsteady they are after such a long sleep,” she cautioned with a hint of condescension, as if he was a clumsy child.

“Yes, I’m good to stand,” Gerund declared. The memory of the weeks leading up to the hibernation came back to him: the intrusive medical exams, strenuous physical conditioning, and anxiety building up to such a dangerous journey. To aggravate matters, Gerund’s former unit had disbanded the month before the hibernation with its personnel scattered to different units, so that Gerund was with a new unit of mostly untested men and women he barely knew. He missed the soldiers with whom he had trained and fought with during the preceding years. There just hadn’t been enough time to bond with his new unit, and now they were thrust into a frontier mission together, dazed and weakened from 6 months of suspended animation.

The woman toggled a switch on the case, and the harness with its medical monitor and the intravenous line retracted. Gerund stepped out of the case and steadied himself against the wall, ignoring the hands offering stability. He looked around the hold, trying to remember everyone who had been stored in the chamber with him. He could see almost all of them from his vantage point. Half were still unconscious in their tanks; the rest sat groggily on benches as medical staff checked their vitals and tested their senses. Men were located in one portion of the hold, women in the other. Nothing separated the groups, however. This war had torn down notions of privacy. The names of his new squadmates came flooding back to him, but details were elusive.

"What day is it?" he asked. "Were we suspended for the full duration?"

The woman smiled knowingly. "A bit longer than expected, but only by a week. 189 days total. I'm sure you have a lot of questions, corporal. We are here to help orient you as smoothly as possible and to ensure that you are physically stable. You are safe here, and we'll take as long as needed. The commanders will be able to answer any questions of a more military nature in greater detail."

"OK, I guess I'll wait." Gerund was still disoriented but starting to fit some pieces together. He looked to his right and noticed that the capsule was empty. He did not see Jonas recovering nearby. It looked as if the medical staff were waking everyone else at the same time, so where was Jonas? "Hey, the guy to my right, where is he?"

The two medics looked at each other indecisively, and the man frowned.

"Hey, just tell me. He's my friend; we're in the same unit," Gerund said. It wasn't quite true. He didn't have a lot of true friends in the unit yet and had only known Jonas briefly, but he was a decent fellow and Gerund wanted to know what had happened to him.

The male medic finally spoke: "Your friend woke up 60 days early, in the middle of a dose transition. His mental state was not good; he was, uh...he had trouble perceiving reality and entered psychosis within hours of waking up."

Gerund shook his head in disbelief. "You're saying he went nuts."

"He's still undergoing treatment. He's confined to the clinic, but I understand that he's much more stable now."

"That's just peachy," Gerund mumbled sarcastically. He sighed, realizing that the medics shouldn't be faulted for serving as the messengers. "Thanks for letting me know." He wasn't sure if he wanted to see Jonas anytime soon. He had seen hibernation madness once before, and it wasn't pretty. Often the patient was perpetually suicidal and had difficulty constructing any sort of meaningful reality. The Coalition always insisted that the hibernations were overwhelmingly safe—as well as a necessary means of overcoming some logistical challenges of the war effort. However, this was Gerund's third significant hibernation, and something had always gone wrong in a few of the capsules. He was tired of the spin his commanders put on the situation, just as he was sure that they would try to minimize the fuss over Jonas's situation.

The woman motioned to a folding chair. "If you'll please have a seat, then we'll perform our cursory exam and validate that you are stable enough to leave." Gerund did as instructed and gave her a quizzical look. "Physically stable, I mean. We don't suspect any mental illness," the woman added, blushing a bit.

"There was something we were wondering about." The man flipped through a clipboard and pointed to a chart but didn't bother to provide Gerund with a clear angle. "Our data showed you had a minor fever accompanied with dreamstate activity about a month ago. The fever lasted about a week and your detailed physiological signs were otherwise normal. We didn't pull you out of hibernation because nothing met our criteria for a serious health risk."

"You two were on the ship? That must have been a boring wait."

"It's part of the job. Like I was saying, your vitals were within limits. But we're interested in any dreams you may have had associated with this persistent fever. It may have been a response to your mental state. Do you recall any dreams from your suspended hibernation?"

Gerund frowned, and the woman glared at her colleague. Apparently, it was too soon for such a taxing question. "Only if you remember off the top of your head," she added. "Really, this is more academic curiosity than anything else. We suspect your fever was a minor episode with no ill long-term effects."

Gerund contemplated a bit more and shook his head. "Sorry, no dreams that I can recall." The woman placed a blood pressure cuff around his arm as the man checked his eyes and other cranial features. They proceeded in silence for several minutes as they conducted the routine checks, apparently finding everything checked out as expected. Gerund struggled to remain facing forward while the medical staff continued to process other soldiers just a few meters away.

The conflict had been deteriorating when Gerund had been induced into hibernation. The Coalition had been abandoning its recruitment campaign in favor of conscription, a practice that the Sovereignty had already instituted. Propaganda was demonizing on both sides and tactics increasingly more reckless. Gerund had worried that their transport ship might not even survive its journey through the no-man's-land of open space. Just before they had shipped out, they heard reports that one of their troop transports had been bombed while carrying a full load of sleeping soldiers. "What's been happening with the war? With the universe in general?" He wasn't trying to make conversation; he suddenly craved to know what he had missed.

"Uh, you'll be debriefed shortly. Until then, we really can't say anything," the man said with a shrug.

Gerund didn't hide his annoyance.

"The planet is still spinning, and our forces are in control," the woman said, smiling to assuage his frustration. "We are probably not the best informants anyway; we were mostly in the dark on the ship, too. The readings from your monitor were good, but we need to take a blood sample now, just to be thorough, OK?"

"Yeah, sure," Gerund murmured. He watched her take out a needle from a plastic pouch along with a vial for his blood. But he felt nothing but curiosity.

Wait—I'm terrified of needles. At least I used to be. He watched as she cleaned the skin of his arm with a swab and then pressed the long needle into ready position while flipping down a face-shield. *But this isn't bothering me at all...*

The man looked up from his clipboard and must have noticed Gerund's quizzical expression. "Is everything okay, sir?" The woman paused with the needle against Gerund's skin and looked over at him.

Gerund furrowed his eyebrows but nodded. "Yeah, I'm still a little foggy, but I feel calm. It was like this the other two times I woke up from hibernation."

"OK, just making sure."

The woman inserted the needle into Gerund's vein, causing a small spurt of blood across the surrounding skin. The pain was initially sharp but immediately subsided. Next, she attached the vial against the port on the other side of the needle. The sight of the blood rapidly squirting and filling the vial would have made Gerund nauseated before, but now it did not trouble him in the least. *What is going on? They used to have to practically tie me down in years past before they got a needle anywhere near me.* Once the vial was filled with his warm blood, the woman retracted the needle and placed a small adhesive bandage over the puncture site. "Keep it on for two hours," she advised.

"Excellent, corporal. All your vital signs read strong," the man said, sealing the blood vial in a bag marked with his name and ID number. We'll test your blood for any irregularities but don't anticipate any problems. You are free to exit—there will be someone waiting in the next chamber with your uniform and gear. They'll direct you to where you will receive further instructions."

"Good luck, sir." The woman once again smiled.

"Thanks." Gerund wrapped the towel tightly around his waist and walked past them toward the exit, looking over his shoulder to get a last glimpse at some of his comrades. But it was hard to see anyone through the swarm of medical personnel, and it probably wasn't the best setting to gawk, especially since the women were emerging from the same suspended animation cases in minimal states of clothing. Gerund blushed. *If anyone saw me right now they would probably think that I'm a pervert.* Wartime necessity had required unprecedented female participation on the front line and had broken down a lot of gender norms. Almost 40 percent of front line personnel were women. There simply wouldn't be enough men to go around otherwise. Men and women lived and served in close proximity to each to other. But some boundaries were strictly enforced by the Coalition. The Coalition had to be very vigilant about sexual harassment with so many men and women tossed in together in close-knit community. Satisfied that his innocent stare down the cargo hold hadn't been misinterpreted, he exited the chamber.

Gerund thought again of the needle insert and his astonishing calm about the whole process. He knew his past fear had been disproportionate to any risk and therefore unreasonable, but that didn't make it any less real and powerful in its primal hold over him. But he had just woke up from a major hibernation. *I do feel a bit foggy. I'm just not myself just yet.* With this rationalization, Gerund gave his full attention to the staff member awaiting him in the next room.

Chapter 6

We strongly recommend relocating mine assets offworld at earliest opportunity. The risk of Coalition or Sovereignty takeover has grown too great as the war has seen neutrality and internal law increasingly violated. A fully equipped mining operation may be too tempting a resource to either faction.

—OreLife Board memo to investors

Lizby and Sabos woke early the next morning. The tension from the previous evening had dissipated, and they were both eager to get their double-pay work day under way.

Sabos was finishing the mound of laundry that he had started the previous evening. Lizby was putting together the finishing touches on a breakfast she had cobbled together from their depleted pantry. She folded the burritos but frowned at the rips in the tortilla covering, which was bursting with fresh greens, mushrooms, and lab-grown chicken. She shrugged at the presentation and took a few bites of her own while placing Sabos's burrito on a plate. She nodded in approval. Many of Haast's stores favored convenient food items over health. It was hard to have anything approaching a culinary experience in the mining town. Even though it was difficult to get premium supplies, Lizby and Sabos had made a concerted effort to eat well and to slow down from their busy days to enjoy meals together. The fresh greens and mushrooms had been carefully cultivated by a local farmer who priced it at top dollar, but it was a superior product to the packaged goods that most of Haast's populace settled for. And although Lizby preferred naturally birthed chicken, this lab-grown alternative was high-quality nutrition, too.

"I'm probably going to have a short shift, based on where we left off yesterday," she said. "The ore veins in the current tunnels are barely worth running the rig on. What do you expect on your end?"

"Right—the boss mentioned a slow day also, so I expect to get done around the same time as you. Very likely we'll be able to eat dinner together at a reasonable hour," Sabos hoped.

"Yeah hon, we'll see." Lizby said. They were fortunate to have been granted similar hours, considering that the mining operation normally raged on around the clock. Lizby was a monitor: she guided the path of drilling rigs from a workstation at the bottom of the mine and entered the tunnels to diagnose the machines when they malfunctioned or encountered an irregularity in the bedrock. On other worlds, her pay would have been exceptional, but on Sarabek's frontier, it was merely adequate and very hard to prosper on.

Sabos was in a similar situation. As a mechanic who serviced the conveyor belt systems, Sabos was vital to mine operations and in theory should be very hard to replace. But with OreLife continuing to find discount workers from other worlds, the competition for even skilled positions was fierce, and the locals had few viable options in education except to train for work in the mine. As a result, OreLife granted no favors to Sabos and the other mechanics. They were replaceable, and paid accordingly.

Because Lizby and Sabos depended on the mine for housing and many other basic necessities, OreLife swallowed much of their earnings, making the option of saving their way to a better future a slow, arduous prospect. Sabos's debt to OreLife complicated their situation further. Even though he and Carmenta had been refugees at the time of his recruitment, they had enough mechanical skills to pique OreLife's interest, so they were flown in, set up, and trained to work in the mine. In return, Sabos and Carmenta were paying for the passage and training through aggressive garnishment of their paychecks.

Sabos's situation was not unlike that of indentured servitude; although OreLife had spun the opportunity as both philanthropic on their part and lucrative for him. Sabos claimed he didn't lose sleep over it and would easily do it over again—he certainly had come from a horrid situation—but OreLife applied interest and made it very difficult for those who defaulted on their loan to get other work or even a passport.

Early in their courtship, Sabos had disclosed his OreLife debt to Lizby, wholly expecting her to part ways because of the burden. Lizby, for her part, had anticipated this debt, knowing Sabos's refugee origin. She vividly remembered that cool autumn night three years ago: they had walked the park, Sabos nervously wringing his hands and quieter than usual. She had known something was going on. When he revealed his status as indentured debtor, she was relieved to find that this was the extent of his baggage. She embraced him after his uneasy disclosure, and their relationship had continued with new-found hope. Nine months later, they married.

Lizby looked at the clock, sighed, and then joined Sabos to help put away the laundry. Sabos reached for her wrist and grasped her hand. "I've got this: I have an extra 30 minutes. You should get ready and finish eating. I'll be done in a little bit and then I'll get ready too."

Lizby smiled through her apprehension. She kissed him and was reluctant to leave his embrace. She then went to prepare for another arduous day in the mine.

Lizby's rotation that week had been proceeding as expected. Expected wasn't necessarily good, but the problems that did emerge were surmountable. Harsh rain, broken-down equipment, software glitches: these were standard problems that miners employed by a logistically challenged mining operation on the frontier had become adept at overcoming. The miners managed by creatively repurposing old tools and strategically disregarding protocol to keep things moving. Lizby wished a whole day would run smoothly—just once. She left the apartment that morning thinking of the extra cash they would earn today. The next step in their future was that much closer.

The walk to the shuttle was cool, dark, and lonely. Lizby always took the main path between the apartments—it was a common-sense approach that minimized danger, and she had promised Sabos that she would. The deteriorating pavement led nearly a kilometer to the shuttle shelter at the edge of the mining town. Streetlamps illuminated pathetic patches of gravel and shrubs that were spaced between the drab gray apartment exteriors and the narrow roadway. Ahead, she could see other miners assigned to the 7th hour shift walking toward the shuttle.

An apartment door creaked open just a few steps ahead. Lizby detoured toward the center of the street as a shifty man with hollow eyes leaned out. “Need a pick-me-up today?” he rasped. He spread his fingers just enough to reveal the vial of tiny purple pills in his palm. Lizby didn’t look at him as she quickly shook her head. Up ahead, another man leaned against a streetlamp, making it clear that he, too, had product to sell. Lizby drifted further to the left to avoid him as well. Normally the drug peddlers simply moved on to the next passerby when rejected, but some of them could be persistent—and nasty. Until something truly awful happened, though, the authorities were unlikely to respond with a patrolling presence to prevent such encounters. Lizby agreed with the rest of the residents that the Haast security team, funded by OreLife, was a joke. Their top priority was protecting mine assets, with violent crime coming in a distant second. The petty theft and drug activity that saturated Haast was not their concern. Drug-addicted employees, who inevitably missed work, were quickly replaced: there was no shortage of new recruits, shipped in from even more desperate worlds. Rumors of corruption among the security division were constant, and Lizby had seen enough firsthand to know that the suspicion was well founded.

She felt reasonably safe, though, if only because there were so many witnesses along the path right before a shift. She told Sabos that she never walked this route alone in the off hours but rather always waited to go with a group of their neighbors to the store or the gym. This was mostly true, but occasionally convenience had overridden safety, and she had gone down the road when activity had died down. Sabos would have a fit if he knew about these occasions, and he would be justified. The mining town had never been a great place to live, but lately it had become even more desolate and squalid. Lizby and Sabos had no shortage of daily reminders of why they wanted to leave this place and migrate offworld.

Lizby reached the waiting shuttle bus a few minutes before it was scheduled to depart for the short 5-kilometer ride to the mine. Normally, there would be two or three shuttles, but after recent developments, only one bus was running per shift. Beyond the bus stop was a derelict warehouse and beyond that a rock-strewn plain pocked with pitiful shrubs and tufts of grass. The vegetation was littered with plastic food cartons and other trash. Small birds fluttered and swooped as they picked the whole field over, examining the trash for any scrap of nourishment or engaging in territorial displays interspersed with mating songs. The birds' energy infused the otherwise bleak scene with vibrant life. Lizby climbed into the shuttle, stepping around the bits of trash that spilled into the aisle. She squeezed all the way to the back of the creaky vehicle, hoping to not have to share one of the bench seats, but to no avail. She slid in next to a friendly face, an older woman she didn't know very well but had occasionally chatted with on past commutes. They nodded at each other and mumbled a good morning but didn't say anything else. It was early yet for small talk.

Within minutes, the rickety shuttle lurched away from the half-circle onto the winding road leading to the mine. The roar of the overworked engine merged with polite chitchat, the occasional wheezing cough, and the groans of those still hung over from the night before. The sun was just rising. It pierced across the barren landscape, interrupted by the occasional ridge, shrub patch, or derelict mine equipment.

Lizby was pulled forward as the bus rolled down a sudden incline. The shrubbery and prairie grass gave way to barren rock. She could see the huge outline of the Pit ahead through the windshield. It never failed to take her breath away: the sheer size of it, steeped in history and leading to the most extensive network of tunnels ever developed. The mine had a fascinating structure; epic in scale, and widely known throughout this sector of the galaxy. The massive Pit ended in a sprawling network of tunnels. It had been dug 600-meters across in the dense yet brittle bedrock, narrowing to 300 meters after dropping an incredible 1,000 meters. On a cloudless day, people said, the mine could be seen from orbit.

The bottom was a staging area for collection of the raw ore that was brought up via a series of large conveyor belts for processing at surface facilities. In some cases, the tunnels burrowed kilometers into the rock. Between the bottom and the rim that marked the surface were transport lifts, conveyor belt systems, scaffolding, and conduits. Rising several stories above the mine's rim was a network of walkways, control towers, equipment sheds, and additional conveyor belts that spilled over to the barren plains that surrounded the mine. This infrastructure was suspended by beams from embankments on the mine's rim or from a network of trusses from the mine wall.

A security gate slid open, and the bus passed through. On reaching the mine parking lot, the miners lumbered out and headed toward the arched walkway that took them from the edge of the Pit to the main employee lift. Although Lizby had made the passage hundreds of times, crossing the walkway over the deep chasm was always visually exhilarating. The rim of the Pit was a breathtaking 600 meters across. Looking down, the early sunlight was quickly swallowed by darkness that enfolded the machinery below. Hundreds of meters farther down, that darkness gave way to the brilliant lights that marked the ground floor of the mining operation. Nothing in the haze was identifiable from this distance, and the light sources twinkled like distant stars.

Lizby looked up to the sound of high-pitched chirping. Hundreds, and perhaps thousands, of long-tailed bats were making their morning quest for breakfast. The bats were said to be endemic to this region and perhaps even the mine itself; they had resided here well before the ancients had begun to mine the Pit. Accordingly, they were said to exhibit some unique traits, although scientists had never been allowed in the mine for close observation. OreLife had tried to eliminate the bats from its operation: they sometimes nested in equipment and shat all over the Pit on their way out of the mine. But the branching tunnels went deep, and the spots where the bats could roost in the depths were beyond count. Lizby wondered where the bats flew during the early morning, but so far everyone whom she had asked had been unable to provide a convincing explanation.

Because the mine was running on a skeleton crew, gone were the sounds of crude joking, mirthful mining songs, or even the complaints of those miners who tried to subject others to suffer with them in their drudgery. Lizby approached the lift checkpoint. A single armed guard checked in everyone who entered the mine. Normally there were two, but his companion, like so many others, must have taken his leave. Lizby scanned her ID badge, then passed through with only a half-hearted nod. The guard, so often the jokester, seemed to pick up on her reserved mood and didn't attempt his usual banter. He lazily waved his wand over Lizby and moved her on. As she walked toward the lift, Lizby glanced nervously toward the horizon.

At first, Lizby had disregarded the rumors of an encroaching battle front as tabloid whispers, but the rumors were given more credence when OreLife began posting travel advisories, just a week before both factions had landed on another of Sarabek's continents. A mere three days ago, OreLife had declared attendance at the mine optional and granted leaves of absence to mine employees wishing to seek safety. Many availed themselves of this option, traveling to the northeast coastal towns until the uncertainty calmed down.

In her two years of marriage to Sabos, they had persevered through ceaseless toil and many disappointments, yet generally Lizby felt that momentum was on their side and contentment soon to be within reach. However, recently the mood had soured: it seemed as if they were just holding on in the midst of an encroaching war—a conflict that the locals had cared little about when it was formerly so far away. Her dream since childhood had been always to leave Sarabek. She knew her family wished her the same. They had worked the mine for many generations and, like almost all the locals, were mired in perpetual squalor. Beyond the security of her family, there was no future here. The only people who came to the region were desperate transients or refugees, like Sabos.

Occasionally a local did manage to leave—and sometimes even prosper on an offworld city. But more often than not, migrants struggled in their new locations.

Lizby's grandfather had left 50 years ago, only to return to the mine within a couple years because he hadn't found steady work and had been alienated in his new environment. Subsequent generations had not had much success in leaving, either. One of Lizby's cousins had cut ties with the family and had managed to move to another frontier world, but it was an open secret that she resorted to prostitution to get by. At first, Lizby's aunt and uncle had gone to great lengths to conceal this truth, but soon everyone in the village knew, and now the aunt and uncle callously referred to their daughter as if she were dead to them on the rare occasion she came up in conversation at all. Lizby was aghast that they saw their daughter that way.

In recent years, pimps and madams had come by the region looking to recruit, but they, like most visitors, stood out and were usually forced out by the community, who were well aware of the dead ends, sometimes literally, that awaited the women on the other side of such ventures. Lizby suspected that she and Sabos would find a way to succeed in a new locale, but they wanted to be as prepared as possible before they took the plunge and made the journey. OreLife's garnishment of Sabos's wages was almost over, and they soon would have enough saved to relocate. The timing would be critical.

A blast of air disrupted these thoughts as she waited for the lift doors to fully open before stepping across along with a dozen other crew members. One of the techs stood right by her, and they nodded a polite greeting to each other. Like half the crew, he looked as if he hadn't slept last night. The doors slid closed once all were across the threshold. A miner hit the green button, and the lift began its kilometer descent to the bottom of the Pit.

The lift quickly accelerated to its top speed, a brisk 8 meters per second. The light showing through the grate panels of the cage quickly dimmed, and soon the blue light of the lift's overhead panels was all that illuminated the ride save for the occasional ambient light coming from floodlights embedded in the wall of the Pit. The tech scrolled through his tablet with a grimace during the whole descent, no doubt backed up with many service requests because of the recent employee departures, which had reduced his department's ability to respond to equipment glitches and failures.

Two minutes later, the lift smoothly stopped at the bottom of the mine. It was significantly warmer down here, not unlike a stuffy summer day, as they were closer to the Sarabek's molten core. The lift platform was brightly lit and crowded with activity. The walkway branched off with stairs in four directions. Nestled against the side of the Pit were several pieces of drilling equipment. Floodlights posted above the platform illuminated a surprisingly open area. Thick beams stretched up into the darkness, as did the ore conveyor belt that wound along the Pit's edge at a sharp slope. An automated system of OreLife's drone robots was suspended on rails above the miners' heads, often piggybacking on the conveyor belt system to save space. One of the boxy robots whooshed by overhead, beeping out its status, its arms tightly retracted against its body. The floor of the Pit was damp, and water pooled within some of the larger depressions of the smoothed stone surface. The recent rainfall had trickled all the way down from the open surface of the mine, a kilometer above.

A two-story administrative building was located near the center of the Pit floor. It housed break rooms, high-end electronics, and communications equipment, and the bottom-level control room on its second floor. Lizby was still a bit early. She ascended the stairs leading to one of the control room doors. She clocked in upon entering the crowded climate-controlled room. Employees sat at workstations around the computer-dominated space. Large screens took up the entirety of the height of some of the walls, displaying machine analytics as well as live feeds from various points in the Pit and the tunnels. She headed toward the opposite side of the control room to sign out her equipment.

"Hi Lizby—so good to have you down here. I'm always glad to see more of one of my best workers," her supervisor, Darius, said. He stood behind his console along the wall.

"Good morning, Darius." Lizby saw Darius as condescending much of the time, yet polite enough that she was content to just shrug it off. She looked years younger than she really was, and she suspected this was part of the reason people like Darius didn't seem to take her seriously or seemed surprised when she could consistently manage and master significant responsibilities within the tunnels.

"As you probably know, we're short on monitors, so you'll be maintaining the digs in tunnel CH and the Christmas Tunnel." Darius motioned to the screens showing live feeds from the dusty tunnels, with idle drills waiting for action. One of the tunnels, CH, was lit by the standard yellow-white embedded lights that OreLife used throughout the mine. The other, nicknamed the Christmas Tunnel by the miners, was illuminated by green and red lights on opposite sides of the passageway floor.

"Got it. Are we expecting any backstops on the extraction feed?"

"No, you're good on that front. Seismic reads are all clear, too, so no delays expected for once."

"OK, I'll get to it." Lizby said. Darius swiveled his chair to address a tech's inquiry, and Lizby walked toward the equipment locker.

"Oh hey, Lizby—I thought I heard your voice," Carmenta said as she peeked out from a utility alcove. She wore the burnt-orange mining jumpsuit and jacket, although she had added shiny knee-high boots as a personal touch. Dirty hydraulic cables were draped over her slender shoulder.

Lizby, who had nearly jumped at Carmenta's sudden appearance, smiled warmly. "Hi! How's it going with you?"

"The dig has stalled out in the east sector tunnels. Looks like I'll be hauling these bastards back and forth all day, replacing connections." Carmenta patted the bundle of cables and twirled her ratcheting tool with her free hand. Beneath Carmenta's nonchalant posture, Lizby still sensed that something wasn't quite right. Carmenta looked extra tired—as if she hadn't slept all night. Beyond the physical tiredness, her eyes had a worried hollowness to them. If Lizby didn't know better, she might suspect that her sister-in-law had become addicted to drugs. Although she didn't think that was the case, just a little doubt had crept in.

"Sabos is supposed to arrive a little while after me today. Like we said yesterday, maybe we can all eat lunch together if the breaks overlap," Lizby said, scanning her sister-in-law's face for a reaction.

Carmenta stared toward the wall, her mind clearly preoccupied. "Yeah, maybe," she said doubtfully. She walked toward the back exit and motioned for Lizby to follow.

Lizby walked with Carmenta to the landing of the stairway outside. Carmenta rested the hydraulic cables on the railing before taking out her handheld device and showing the screen to Lizby. "See the fire and the smoke on the left? Someone took this picture last night just west of Mullhon Station. They said it was hit by artillery." Carmenta pointed to the area of the screen where a fire blazed about a destroyed ore transport truck. "People are reporting that the driver got out and that it was most likely a case of mistaken identity."

Lizby nodded. "Looks like the war isn't just passing through. Makes me think that the outbound operation is going to shut down for a while."

Carmenta's face blanked as she was again gripped by whatever was worrying her, but she snapped out of it just as quickly. "Oh, if you check your login, you'll see that OreLife has posted another dozen security memos. I'm sure Darius is going to gather everyone around soon to go through them."

"What fun," Lizby muttered. She wondered what Carmenta really wanted to say. How long would the tension continue? It was uncharacteristic for her sister-in-law to beat around the bush.

Lizby had an up-and-down relationship with Carmenta. When she had first started dating Sabos, Carmenta had been vocal in her suspicions about the local girl dating her younger brother. Carmenta had considered Sabos to be vulnerable to manipulation and had misjudged Lizby's intentions. This, of course, was off-putting to Lizby as well as Sabos. It wasn't until the week of the wedding two years earlier that Carmenta relented and they had been able to find some healing in their relationship—it had been right before the rehearsal dinner that Carmenta had pulled Lizby aside to give her blessing. The timing now seemed too convenient—as if Carmenta had finally caved in to social pressure and fallen in line with the rest of the family when it became clear that the marriage was unstoppable. But at the time Lizby had thought that the blessing had been sincere. Carmenta and Sabos had fled dismal conditions as refugees, and both tended to live life with chips on their shoulders; it seemed to Lizby as if Carmenta had envied her brother's newfound stability in his marriage, which had happened to coincide with an OreLife promotion. Still, Carmenta seemed to have gotten beyond such feelings, diving into her ever-increasing responsibilities with OreLife with enthusiasm.

Unfortunately, her contentment had been fleeting thanks to a decision that had been easy to criticize after the dust had settled. Carmenta had become the girlfriend of an older man who promised to leave the continent with her: he was coming into an inheritance that would allow them to start a new business in his home region. 6 months later, Chuck had seemed poised to deliver on his promise to whisk Carmenta away with him. However, he vanished one weekend, taking only a few essentials and leaving his apartment in disarray. Both Lizby and Sabos had suspected, and indeed secretly hoped, that Chuck had simply left town without bothering to break up with Carmenta. Lizby had never been fond of the man; he had quick wit and a silver tongue but no foundation of character to back up his charm. She took his sudden departure as a surprise but was secretly relieved. But local rumor, later confirmed by the police, had it that Chuck had fought with another local woman to whom he had also made promises, had stabbed her, and had then fled the region ahead of the authorities. The other woman survived her ordeal, but Carmenta never heard anything from the police about her ex-boyfriend's whereabouts.

Understandably, the highly gossiped incident had shattered Carmenta's trust and left her humiliated. In the aftermath, she became aloof, cynical, and prone to bouts of heavy drinking. She referred to herself as a "sad cliché" to anyone who would listen long enough to her alcohol-fueled venting. Lizby and Sabos gradually saw progress in the months afterward as Carmenta cooled down and dialed back her pessimism—but she remained listless outside of work. Based on late-night talks with her sister-in-law in the tiny apartment, Lizby believed that Carmenta had become truly wiser through the disappointment. If there were another silver lining, it was that Lizby had forged a closer bond with Carmenta through this fire. She had stuck with Carmenta through it all, and although her sister-in-law still seemed troubled, they had a foundation of trust to build on as Carmenta took one day at a time.

"Anyway, I was wondering..." Carmenta put away her handheld and cleared her throat. "Has Sabos said anything about me and the money this week? He's been giving me a weird vibe, but he won't come out and say it to my face." Carmenta's expression was subdued, but the underlying frustration in her frayed voice was evident.

Lizby was surprised that this was what had been troubling Carmenta. She had thought it was something...deeper. She wanted to voice her suspicion: *Aren't we past this? What's really going on with you?* Instead, she said, "No. We haven't talked about it lately."

Carmenta furrowed her brow. "Really?"

"Yes, we've had other things on our minds," Lizby said, a bit defensively. She paused as she built up her words. "Does this have anything to do with yesterday?"

"What? No! Totally unrelated," Carmenta snapped, then softened a bit. "I told you: that was just a little argument with my friend from school. An asshole friend, really."

An asshole friend? Whatever... "Right, of course," Lizby said, sounding less convinced than she intended. "Sorry," she added, although she instantly regretted apologizing to Carmenta yet again.

"It's just that the last few times I brought up my situation trying to explain myself, he wasn't very gracious. He didn't want to listen. And during those times, he always has this expression at the end of our conversations, like 'Is that it?' Like he wants *me* to bring it up. But I don't take the bait. I have nothing more to explain until I pay back the rest of it."

"We know you're good for it. And we're okay in the—"

"Look, Lizby—I get it. I know you both are getting by fine, but it's more important to me that you can trust that I'm going to come through for you guys," Carmenta insisted. She loosened, leaning low against the railing. "When he—when Chuck left, he took nearly everything. And I was a nasty person for a while right after. I realize that now. But I know I was already a fool long before that. To fall for it in the first place, and for all those months!" Carmenta sighed. "I'm trying to forge a new path, Lizby."

Lizby hesitated, then placed a reassuring hand on Carmenta's arm. "I've told Sabos I'm okay with things between us. I can talk with him tonight. But there has been a lot of stressful stuff going on; just give him some time." She scanned Carmenta's face for a reaction.

Carmenta nodded but was apparently deep in thought as she gazed at the Pit's intensifying operations while tapping the railing. Lizby had the oddly distinct feeling that Carmenta brought up the money issue as an excuse for why she was rattled. It was subtle, but Lizby could tell that her sister-in-law was especially uneasy today. And she sensed that Carmenta knew that she could tell—hence the act with the money. Unfortunately, Lizby had no idea what the real source of Carmenta's unease was, and she knew from experience not to press the issue.

Carmenta straightened to attend to her handheld computer, which was flashing insistently, buzzing notifications. She glanced at the screen, then holstered it. "Liz, I've got to get down there. Probably can't make lunch. Thanks for the talk—I'll try to swing by your apartment later today. But first, when I get home, I have a few calls to make with OreLife about my electric bill, and I'm not sure how long that will take." She hoisted the cables back onto her shoulder.

"Have fun with their customer service," Lizby said, knowing how likely that was.

"I know, right?"

"OK, we'll be home."

"See you—and don't work too hard."

"Goodbye, Carmenta." Lizby watched her sister-in-law dart toward the tunnels on the other end of the Pit. Then she, too, went to retrieve her equipment and begin the shift.

Chapter 7

Before we even had the language to discuss human cloning, the critics hurled their stones. They have never relented in demonizing the geneticists, policy-makers, and the clones themselves in the Sovereignty movement.

—Professor Ella Socarin, Genetics Department, University of New Seattle

"Okay, corporal; I'm finished."

The sensor-laden hood was lifted off Gerund's head and his ears were left ringing after enduring 15 minutes of the continuous hum of the headgear. Gerund blinked as his eyes adjusted to the bright room.

"Yes, there is no doubt," the doctor said. His face remained expressionless behind his archaic spectacles as he read his sleek diagnostic datapad instead of meeting Gerund's eyes.

Gerund stared at the doctor for a long moment, waiting for him to elaborate. The middle-aged man hovered over him, less than a meter away. His office was cramped and filled to the brim with cabinets and paperwork, with little else besides the bench upon which Gerund sat. "Wait, what is it called?"

"Urbach–Wiethe disease," the doctor said without any gravity. "There have only been about a thousand cases diagnosed in all of history. Unfortunately, it's incurable."

Damn, he needs to work on his bedside manner. This sounds...fatal. "Oh god," Gerund gulped, and then found his voice again. "And you are sure?"

"Yes. Your blood sample strongly suggested it, and the brain scan confirms it. The disease may be rare, but it has been thoroughly documented."

"What's next?"

The doctor studied the printed test results too long before answering. The moment was agonizing. *Just tell me, fool!*

"Urbach–Wiethe is not life-threatening. You're going to be fine—more or less."

Why didn't you lead with that? Gerund almost blurted. "That's...such a relief," he said instead, finally able to unclench his fists. "But you said something was calcified—how can that be fine?"

"Right. During your hibernation, hardening of brain tissue in your medial temporal lobes occurred in about an almond-sized area. You are genetically predisposed to such a result, and the difficulty of hibernation must have triggered your condition. The medial temporal lobes are tied almost exclusively to the instinct of primal fear and all its responses in the body. What you told me about your sudden lack of fear of needles is consistent with the disruption of this area of the brain. Simply put, you now lack the capacity to feel fear."

"Are you kidding? It can't be that simple."

"No. As I said, it's not a common disease, but there have been a few very well-documented cases."

"OK...so what does this all mean for me?"

"Urbach–Wiethe is not progressive beyond the initial calcification, and you won't be restricted in your daily life. I anticipate that you can continue your duties without delay," The doctor smiled while delivering this prognosis. "Just remain aware of your behavior; you won't have the same risk-assessment skills that came so naturally before."

Have you any idea of what we do for the Coalition? Risk assessment is critical on the battlefield, which I may enter any day. But Gerund just nodded.

"I'm giving you the full clearance to proceed with your duties, but I'm scheduling a follow-up in three weeks. There are a few medication options, but they mostly just dance around the symptoms, so I'd like to avoid prescribing them to you if possible. This isn't really my area of expertise, so if you need a more in-depth scan, or perhaps a psychological assessment in the future, we'll need to connect you with a specialist when we get back to real civilization. But I'm certain of my basic diagnosis based on your symptoms and the scan. Any questions?"

Certainly, the army's physicians had many people left to process, but Gerund was astonished that his radically altered brain tissue was being treated with the same nonchalance as a mild allergy. Of course he had questions—but they swirled together all at once and failed to materialize. "Uh, no—I guess I'll know more about the new me in three weeks."

"Good luck," the doctor said without turning to see him walk out. Gerund heard him call out to his assistant for the next patient's file.

Gerund walked out of the shoddy prefabricated structure that served as the unit's hospital and meandered across the yard toward his barracks tent. He was both stunned and relieved by the doctor's diagnosis. He had felt odd since being brought out of hibernation. Part of that was a routine reaction to the sudden immersion into Coalition life after the extended rest, but there was something else. He had felt innately different and been unable to articulate why. Even a night of natural sleep hadn't helped. Now the strange feeling had a name: Urbach–Wiethe. *I am fearless.*

The man without fear... It sounded so absurd. Who would believe this? *Maybe this guy is a quack.* The Coalition had a reputation for hiring less-than-stellar medical staff, especially during the rapid escalation of the war.

Gerund altered his path toward a 50-meter steel tower with a radar dish slowly rotating on top. The height of the tower did not intimidate, nor did the prospect of getting caught. *Caught doing what, exactly*? Gerund wasn't sure.

He gripped the attached steel ladder and looked around, seeing no one close by. He began climbing. The ladder wobbled slightly, but he trusted it to hold. Without further hesitation, he climbed all the way to the top in just under 2 minutes. He looked down at the distant ground with nothing more than curiosity. *OK, this confirms it all.* He imagined himself falling off, the air rushing by as he lost control, moments away from violent death. Still no reaction—no fear.

Gerund knew intellectually that he didn't want to fall from the ladder. He knew it would kill him, of course, and he very much wanted to continue to exist. His body wasn't telling him that, however. The palm-sweating, heart-thumping, pupil-widening sensation that told him he was in danger was completely gone. He had never been unreasonably afraid of heights, but he knew he would have previously been guardedly fearful if he had climbed a 5-meter ladder, and much more so a 50-meter ladder with nothing but skull-shattering concrete at the bottom.

Gerund certainly didn't want to fall off the ladder. He didn't want to die. The idea of ceasing to be made him feel...*anxious. That's the word.* But his apprehension was much more abstract and didn't make him react in the same way as primal fear. It didn't put his body on alert, and it didn't cloud his judgment.

Gerund slowly blew out his breath. *This is beyond strange. But I can manage this. Actually, this is kind of incredible.* He hung loosely from one hand.

A soldier ran up to the base of the tower. *Shit, I'm in trouble.*

"Gerund? Gerund! What the fuck are you doing up there?"

Good question. Finding the new me, I guess. He was relieved to recognize the perplexed soldier from his unit. "Nothing—just getting a bird's-eye view of camp."

His comrade seemed unsatisfied with this answer but didn't press the issue. "Well, come on down. We're mobilizing for the field."

"What?!"

"New intel. We're moving on the mine—now."

"I'm coming down."

There would be no time to ease into this new way of being; no time to plan. Gerund was about to enter the fray as a soldier incapable of fear.

Chapter 8

Marina stared at the assortment of paperwork arranged on the table in front of her. Or, rather, she gazed beyond the forms into her memories from the day before: Leaving her life in the Sovereignty behind. The sound of the gunfire streaking over her head. The mad dash for freedom toward the valley. Abandoning Titus—and the look on her friend's face as death began to take him.

Marina shook her head as if to knock the haunting memories out of her mind, then checked off another box on her current form. She sat in a training room. Several tables were arranged around a large video screen fastened to the wall at the front of the room. OreLife had filled what had once been a spacious cavern with various administrative rooms. She surmised that the area fulfilled a purpose that wasn't already accomplished in the offices at the surface. The training area probably allowed for a quicker transition between the classroom instruction and hands-on learning in the tunnels without having to travel all the way down from the surface.

The cluster of office space was recessed into the stone, at the edge of the Pit. It was odd sitting in such a brightly lit, sterile space with plastered walls and tiled ceilings so deep underground. The space felt safe and boring—such a contrast with last night.

With several important adjacent tunnels leading further into the mine, the office space was a highly trafficked area, even with OreLife operating at reduced capacity. She sat alone at the desks, but mine employees walked past the wide glass windows that lined one side of the room. She got some curious looks but no one stopped to talk to her. She imagined Sovereignty agents charging in any moment: if they did, she would be trapped in the training room.

Marina was exposed, but that was the idea: she was hiding in plain sight, posing as a new employee getting a head start on the excessive health insurance forms. She had a fresh ID badge and had rehearsed enough to come across as a bored and bewildered recruit who was sent aside to complete paperwork on her own. Marina had always felt squirmy while sitting at desks at school or a work setting, and the falseness of the sedentary task made it even more monotonous.

Marina felt the weight of the immense stone above her, a thousand meters thick. Tucked into a little pocket in the rock, she couldn't believe that people had blasted this deep into Sarabek's crust. It was a claustrophobic, unnerving feeling. So much lay between her and the sky. There was no way to tell if the sun was out. Marina's time in the Sovereignty had exposed her to many dangers, but nothing that made her feel so powerless as the layers of stone that engulfed her. She already didn't even like entering windowless basements—and this discomfort was on an entirely new level.

A knock on the open door startled her. Her cousin Carmenta strode into the room and took a seat next to her. Marina was still looking at the door to see if anyone else was coming. Finally satisfied that they were alone, she faced Carmenta in a long moment of silence. Her savior attempted a smile that soured into a grim grin, and for the first time,

Marina felt the full weight of the imposition that she had placed on her cousin.

Indeed, imposition was putting it mildly. Carmenta had placed her job on the line, possibly even her life—all by responding to a last-minute plea for help. Certainly Marina's request had been a desperate plea; there was no way to misconstrue it. Her call had been an appeal to their shared bloodline and a tenuous connection that both women had allowed to atrophy in their years apart. For whatever reason, Carmenta had not turned her away but had instead heeded her call, reluctantly agreeing a week in advance of Marina's planned escape. As planned, Carmenta had met her by the brightest lamppost on the outskirts of Haast. Carmenta was aghast to learn that Titus hadn't made it—and that Marina's exodus had not gone at all as planned.

But there had been little time for questions. Carmenta had whisked her away to her apartment. However, on their way up the stairs, at least two neighbors had seen them. Carmenta's imagination had taken flight: the neighbors would gossip, certainly, or at least spill the beans if any investigator crossed paths with them. It was settled: hiding Marina in her apartment was not an option lest some ambitious bounty hunter come by and question the neighbors the next day, break into the apartment, and haul Marina back to the Sovereignty. Marina thought this unlikely, but Carmenta insisted that the Sovereignty had eager ears even in this formerly forgotten frontier mining town. Marina would have to go with Carmenta into the relative security of the mine. Haast was far too exposed, even for one day.

Carmenta had given her a spare mining uniform and dry boots, a hot meal, and even her bed in which to catch a few hours of rest, but Marina had barely slept. Early this morning, they had arrived at the mine after a nervous trek through the town; and to their great relief, Marina's forged ID had granted her access to the mine. With that, Carmenta was plunged into the middle of her cousin's desertion; there was no turning back now. Marina hoped that Carmenta didn't feel that her trust was taken for granted—Marina would do her best to make it up for her.

"How's it going in here? Did anyone bother you?" Carmenta was out of breath, as if she had just run across the Pit.

"Fine—I'm just getting a little restless after a couple hours of completing paperwork that will never be used." Marina studied her cousin's face closely—Carmenta seemed more stressed than she herself was. Lowering her voice, she added, "And no one is suspicious—don't worry. All the miners have left me alone." Marina tried to place a comforting hand on Carmenta's shoulder, but her cousin recoiled and looked fearfully through the window. However, no one was watching.

Carmenta sighed. "It's really hard to do my work this morning. I keep imagining someone getting nosy and figuring out that your hire is fake, then calling security on you. Or some Sovereignty agent or bounty hunter making it past security and scooping you up. Or even the chance of Lizby or Sabos walking through and seeing a family member whom they didn't even know was on Sarabek...I can't even begin to fathom how they would react."

"Then don't," Marina scolded, instantly regretting her tone. "Look—I'm really thankful that you have stuck your neck out for me. I know how stressful this has been. But last night was the worst of it—believe me, I'm lucky to be alive. Today will be fine, trust me. And if everything falls in place this evening, I can be out of your hair by tomorrow."

"I agree that it's much safer down here than in the town, especially after my neighbors saw you come in last night. But I think the Sovereignty may have eyes even down here. And that's not just paranoia: they have no jurisdiction over OreLife, but that hasn't kept them from meddling with the operation in the past. Security chased some guy out only two months ago: it turned out that he was a mercenary under contract with the Sovereignty."

Marina opened her mouth to downplay this possibility but then paused. She had to admit that the idea of Sovereignty plants in the mine had crossed her mind also. "Yes, but I just left last night. If the Sovereignty had any sympathizers here, it's possible they haven't even heard about it. It's not something they like to advertise—desertion being bad for morale and such. They wouldn't be able to find me, and even if they did, they couldn't really do anything about it when I'm down in the mine."

"I don't know about that, Marina," Carmenta replied, running her hands through her hair anxiously. "But hey, I can't stay. I need to get back to my tunnels. I just wanted to check on you; I'll be back in about two hours to bring some lunch. Be smart, be careful."

"Of course. I know what's on the line. I'll see you soon, Carmenta. And thanks once again."

Their fates had intertwined after years of minimal contact, she thought. Carmenta had changed so much throughout the years. Marina's strongest memories were all from childhood when they had lived in the same apartment building. She remembered Carmenta as the spoiled eldest of their generation, though only a year older than Marina. Carmenta had been spunky and seemed to always lead the next activity among the many cousins, whereas Marina had been more of a follower. But that had been more than 15 years ago.

She could still see some of the same expressions on this older version of Carmenta, but the face was more world-weary. Carmenta was still a strong woman—who else would have stuck her neck out for Marina?—but there was also bitterness behind the resolve in her cousin's eyes.

Marina recalled a similar look from their childhood. Carmenta had had a reputation as the best artist in their neighborhood. Others drew and made crafts, but none of their enthusiastically simplistic efforts came close to Carmenta's talent. But when a boy moved into the neighborhood to stay with his relatives one summer, his skill had surpassed Carmenta's—and he was not shy about marketing his artwork. Within a week of arriving, he had painted pictures for all the neighbors in the building. The apartment hallway was practically a gallery for his undeniable talents. Carmenta made snide remarks about the boy to the other children at every opportunity. Little Marina hadn't understood why. The boy was outgoing and pleasant to Marina; he drew her animal pictures whenever she asked. Then, when the boy's art collection was found torn and ripped throughout the apartment hallway, there was no doubt who was responsible. Marina didn't remember anything having been done about the vandalism, but no longer did any of the children's artwork adorn the hallway. Marina remembered her cousin remaining bitter and withdrawn throughout that summer, even after the boy had left.

Carmenta had perhaps not been so petty in subsequent years, and Marina's memory was selective, but she remembered her cousin having had a restless, wounded spirit. Now, all these years into adulthood, she thought she still perceived it. But it was subtler, and after all the years they had spent apart, it wasn't Marina's place to root out the source of that bitterness. Besides, she was occupied with her own challenges.

Chapter 9

In the event of simultaneous main and emergency power failures, remain where you are. This will help maintenance move about the mine more easily to fix the problem. In a prolonged outage, emergency crews will make their way to each dig site. It is imperative that miners remain at their workstations in this situation. If a miner is in a level D depth tunnel, they must exit immediately. Without air conditioning, temperatures can exceed 60 degrees Celsius.

—OreLife management memo to staff

Lizby had entered the Christmas Tunnel to check on the massive drill rig, deep into the bedrock, nearly half a klick from the Pit. Some tunnel entrances were higher up, near the surface, but most of the active tunnels radiated outward from the bottom of the Pit like spokes. From there, most of the tunnels gradually sloped down. Some of the tunnels went so deep into the planet's crust that intolerable heat radiated from the molten core and prevented miners from entering the farthest reaches, leaving them to rely on remote-controlled equipment. OreLife had tried to apply air conditioning in such deep tunnels, but malfunctions with the units had caused deadly incidents with overheated miners. Lizby had been in one such climate-controlled tunnel when the units had failed and the air temperature quickly soared to over 55 degrees Celsius. She had been close enough to the entry point that she was able to escape unharmed; sweating profusely but otherwise okay. One of her colleagues had not been so lucky; he had died of heat stroke. She had wanted to quit—she had risked her life to check on some lousy mining equipment. But she and Sabos had needed the money then, and they still needed it now.

Lizby had been with the roaring rig in the Christmas Tunnel for 10 minutes. She continually checked the readings on the rig's rear panel, behind the safety of the thick rock shield. The readings were fine. But since the measurements were available from the control room, her true purpose was a visual inspection. Careful not to get too close to the spinning drill shaft and crumbling wall of fractured rock, she inspected the conical drill head from several angles. The rock dust filled the air, pebbles vibrated over the stone floor, and the chug of the engine and crunch of rock dulled her hearing. It was easy for a miner's thinking to grow fuzzy under such disorienting conditions. That's where the real danger lay. Lizby kept her focus and her spatial awareness as she stepped parallel to the drill head. She saw no signs of valuable ore yet, but the drill was operating smoothly and pulling itself along a predictable track. The rock debris was collecting in an orderly line on the side of the tunnel, for collection and eventual processing.

The thick dust spouting from the debris was illuminated by the red and green lights embedded in the floor of the tunnel. She thought of the Christmas holiday and tried to imagine the dust instead as a fine cloud of snow illuminated by strings of bright bulbs, but she couldn't quite convince herself with the illusion. *Christmas—wow. It's been a while since*

I had a real one. Out in the frontier, the ancient holiday of Christmas was fading into distant cultural memory. The village where Lizby had grown up still made a concerted effort to celebrate—far cheerier than Haast—decked out with lights on all the main streets and residential neighborhoods, swarming with shoppers, and filled with the strange yet festive music associated with the holiday period. Hardly anyone had celebrated the occasion this past year in the OreLife-run mining town. Out here, people primarily toiled and survived, too lethargic to participate in any festivities or clubs, let alone the arts. Lizby needed more than a life with only marginal prosperity, dominated by the relentless rhythm of the OreLife mine. She felt like she had been born on the wrong planet.

Suddenly the rig bit into a vein of denser stone. The sensors still read within acceptable bounds, but Lizby relied on her refined miner's senses. The sound was deafening, and she felt the strong vibration reverberating through her feet and into her knees. Per OreLife procedure, Lizby used her remote to shut the rig down: the expensive equipment could be crippled in seconds if it encountered the wrong mineral in thick enough concentrations. The rig sputtered to a halt, and its floodlight shut off. The red and green lights illuminated the pale haze of dust that hung in the stagnant air. The sound was still deafening, but now the roar wasn't choppy like the cutting surface, nor was it the raging thrum of the drill's powerful engine. It was a steady, shrill howl: *The alarm.* But which one? *Shit—I should have paid attention more in that training session.* Lizby didn't know whether it was a general safety alarm or it signified a specific danger, such as a fire. Regardless, procedure dictated her response: she quickly headed back toward to the Pit. Bottom-level miners were supposed to go to the most secure area of the lower Pit: the two-story command center. The glowing ground lights became a blur as Lizby broke into a run. The harness holding her tools whipped against her shoulders. She had always been fast; in her youth she had dominated most of the local track events. Although regular training didn't fit with her lifestyle as a toiling miner, her natural ability let her fly through the tunnel at an exhilarating pace. Soon the brilliant illumination from the Pit floodlights crept around the gradual bend in the tunnel. As she burst into the main chamber, a distracted miner almost collided into her. He mumbled a perfunctory apology before darting under a suspended walkway. She blinked in the sudden brightness and breathed deeply, partly because she had just plowed through a half kilometer but also because she was free of the stagnant, dusty air of the Christmas tunnel. The extensive conveyor belt system had been shut off, as had the rest of the Pit's machinery. Employees swarmed in and around the command center. Lizby clambered up the stairs to reach the second level when she met a colleague on the way down.

"Roman, what the hell is going on?!"

"Surface Control called in—they said that we've been breached. We're locking down." the man said. He searched the gathering crowd before finally looking back to Lizby.

"What do you mean—breached?" Lizby asked, not understanding the chaos around her.

Roman raised his voice to be heard above the alarm. "The Coalition and Sovereignty armies snuck up on us and surrounded the mine. The alarm has been blaring since we spotted them, and now Surface says that soldiers have headed down to the Pit in lifts."

"Holy shit!" Lizby dashed up the remainder of the stairs and into the control room.

The room was surprisingly calm. Darius directed the staff with swift gestures, who responded with composure behind the lines of computer consoles. He quickly glanced up at her. "Lizby, you need to get down to the garage for safety. Just stay there so we know where everyone is."

"Have you seen Sabos?"

"Who?" Darius struggled to hear over the blaring alarm.

"My husband?!"

"Not my job to keep track of him. Just get to the shelter zone with the others." Darius turned his back on her.

Lizby huffed and flew back down the stairs. She scanned the Pit's floor. *Where would he have gone? I need to find him. Carmenta, too.* She caught a glimpse of a mechanic's uniform out of the corner of her eye. It flashed past the corner. She sprinted in pursuit and swung around to the opposite end of the control hub, only to see that the mechanic wasn't Sabos. The man threw a switch on a panel and then bounded past her. She looked up at the walkways, some of which were 50 meters above. There were no soldiers—just a few techs running between equipment consoles.

"Sabos!" she shouted. The surprise of the situation was wearing off, and now, as she thought things through, she became deeply troubled.

Shouldn't he have come down with the others? And Carmenta is always stationed at the bottom—so where did she go?!

A passing tech, alerted by her shouting, motioned for her to come toward the garage. Lizby swatted away his hand when he tried to tug her sleeve along with him. *Asshole.*

"You can't be wandering around out here. Seek shelter—we've been breached."

"I know," she scowled. "Have you seen a mechanic by the name of Sabos? Sabos Sasquire?"

"Don't know him. Did you check the shelter location?" the tech said in an annoyed tone that echoed her own.

Lizby followed him toward the garage—a sturdy, beveled building used to store ore trolleys and the like, but with plenty of room for people to take shelter under its thick frame, too. Cutting across the center of the Pit, the blue garage building was visible from over at the command center; the lift and walkway ladders lay in between. One of the beeping robots whirred by two meters above their heads on its overhead track, still carrying out its tasks. Seeing more miners passing under the garage's arched entrance, they quickened their pace. Lizby heard the whine of lift's brakes, and the lift dropped into view. It came to a noisy stop on its platform, and as soon as there was enough clearance, twelve soldiers rushed out of the doors, brandishing rifles. *Too late. They're here.* The commotion was deafening. Employees pointed and shouted while the soldiers barked out orders. Darius came out of the control room onto the second-floor walkway landing. On spotting the soldiers, he scrambled back inside.

The soldiers wore Coalition uniforms. They were well equipped and clearly focused as they descended the lift platform stairs and formed a perimeter in the center of the Pit. Oblivious to the situation, one of the rail-bots clattered into the area. It stopped and chirped a high-pitched warning while pointing its laser all over the place. The soldiers instinctively raised their weapons, and Lizby expected them to obliterate the noisy robot. *Go bot, get lost! Stupid drone.* Lizby had always hated the bots: they swooped across critical areas of the Pit, startling her, and they were very meddlesome, observing the miners and protesting what they perceived as breaches of protocol. If Lizby took her hard hat off anywhere in the mine, even when heading into a restroom, a passing bot would chirp loudly and point its laser at the safety violation; in that case, her head.

One of the men identified the bot as a non-threat and the soldiers lowered their weapons. The bot's lights pulsed in a multicolored sequence corresponding to its mission as it started winding around the control hub building and then chose the track that curved steeply toward the surface.

Frozen in place until this moment, Lizby began to gingerly sidestep toward the way she had come, heading for the cover of the control hub building. She needed to get away from these intruders. But one of the soldiers had other ideas: he shouted at her and hefted his rifle in his arms, almost pointing it at her. *Oh my god! What does he want?!* He wore a well-worn utility vest, a black helmet with translucent goggles strapped across the top, and a beige uniform made of a fabric that glistened at close range. The soldier's mouth curled in a snarl, but Lizby couldn't make out what he said.

"What? What do you want?" she shrugged. "OK, I'm stopping." *Who does he think I am?* Lizby looked around for help. The miners who had not yet found shelter lingered at the edges of the center area of the Pit. They kept their distance as the squad expanded their perimeter into a larger oval. One of the soldiers, wearing a distinctive captain's cap, emerged from the control room, leading Darius out with a firm grip on the man's forearm. Darius grimaced with a mixture of annoyance and fear, suppressing a protest.

"Did you hear me?" the soldier in front of Lizby asked.

"No. It's too loud in here." Lizby widened her arms in exasperation, careful to keep them still raised. She couldn't help but be aware of a day's worth of odor under them. She also had the strong urge to curse the man. How dare they come down here, breaking so many interplanetary laws, and rudely demand cooperation from the end of a rifle barrel? But Lizby held her tongue: she couldn't change the situation; she had to wait for the right moment.

With a loud creak, the doors of the main lift shut as it was hauled upward again. No one had set it in park mode, so it was automatically headed toward the surface. The soldiers all turned toward the new commotion, but the lift was already rising out of view into the canopy of darkness. The soldier who had stopped her had his back turned to her. He had a handful of large beads, intricately shaped to resemble human skulls, woven into short strings connected to his shoulder pad. He wore Coalition insignia also, but the decorative skulls unnerved Lizby.

Something about the men's specialized gear and demeanor deeply unsettled Lizby beyond the surprise of their arrival. *Could they be mercenaries?* Lizby almost mumbled this thought out loud as the soldier spun back to face her, his matte black rifle still in ready position.

"You need to give us space. Now!" the soldier barked at Lizby.

"OK," Lizby said, confused. She took a couple steps back and relaxed her arms as the soldier lowered his weapon. She worried about what Sabos might have impulsively done if he had seen the exchange. For being among civilians, the soldiers were wound awfully tight. If they were indeed mercenaries, perhaps they were less concerned about disrupting—or worse—the lives of civilians than Coalition regulars would be. *I need to find Sabos*, she thought once again.

The alarm had finally stopped. The captain forcibly tugged Darius toward the garage shelter entrance. Two soldiers were already there, trying to get the double doors open. They were failing miserably, one swearing and the other falling after his attempt to leverage the doors apart slipped and caused him to lose balance. Loud voices from the inside answered their attempted intrusion, but the thick doors muffled the words.

"Get them to open it from inside," the captain said, evenly but loudly, so that his voice echoed across the space. Lizby, no longer deemed a threat, walked alongside the control hub building to get a little closer, straining her ears to hear.

"I can try, but why?" Darius stammered. "It's just my miners in there."

"I don't need a reason. Open it." The captain used an elbow to prod Darius toward the door.

"Actually, I can probably do a keypad override..."

"By all means—please." The captain frowned as Darius hesitated at the keypad. The mine manager's fingers froze over the buttons. "We're not going to bother your people. We're looking for others. Just let us do our job." He motioned for the pair of soldiers to flank the door, putting Darius between the two tensed men.

"OK, OK—it's just very surprising, is all," Darius said.

Lizby became increasingly worried about Sabos and Carmenta. *What if they're in there? What do these guys want?*

Darius fumbled at the keypad. He paused once more, glancing back at the soldiers. He peered beyond them toward the control hub and met Lizby's gaze. His eyes registered resignation, then he looked back at the double doors. He steadily brought his hand up to the keypad to complete the entry code.

The screech of the descending lift commanded everyone's attention. The squad faced the platform in anticipation as the cables screeched again, perhaps still 100 meters above. The captain's face drained white as he ordered several of the men to position themselves against cover. Their fear was palpable. Lizby backed away and stood behind one of the thick beams supporting the overhead walkways.

Movement in her peripheral vision drew her attention. To the right, in the direction of the east tunnels, a hooded figure emerged with arms extended. Lizby recognized the burnt orange mining jacket and trousers but not the unfamiliar equipment in the man's belt and hands.

Even when she saw what the man held, her brain didn't quite process it: she was frozen by indecision, unsure whether to run or to keep a low profile by staying still. The lift came into view, decelerating rapidly. But before the lift reached the platform, a gunshot rang out, followed by five more jolting blasts in quick succession. Lizby, shocked, could only watch as the shooter continued his barrage. She fully expected to be shot next.

One of the soldiers collapsed in a heap. The others reacted quickly by seeking cover but didn't seem to see the assailant. Lizby suppressed the urge to point at the shooter, who was silently and methodically lining up another shot. She was witnessing a man who didn't move like a miner but rather as a trained killer.

Lizby, hearing the crunch of loose stone behind her, glanced over her shoulder as she lowered herself to the stone. Another hooded man loomed mere meters behind. At this much closer range, she unmistakably saw the pistol he carried. His hand was soot-stained and muscular. The gun was small and thin with a dull gray, but with a long barrel and unusual, artistically curved design. Lizby risked a glance at the man's face, but his hood was stretched far forward, with just enough light seeping in to hint at younger features and a grim expression. The barrel of the gun was barely an arm's length away, but she was immobilized by panic, and the gunman towered powerfully above her. *No!* Lizby didn't have time to process another thought. The gun discharged with a dizzying blast, the explosion right above her ears. She covered her throbbing eardrums as the gunman continued to fire. She looked up from her crouch. The attacker was on the move, firing wildly. But now there was a volley of return fire. The bullets whizzed above her head and clanged off steel. Lizby ducked, now completely prone.

She couldn't see any other miners. *I'm all alone...*

She heard a roar, this one much deeper and sustained than the gunfire. *Please...what now?!* It hadn't been the lift, either, which had completed its descent and was now motionless at the platform. Lights on the outside of the lift flashed green, giving the all-clear to exit.

Another loud roar came, so powerful that it overpowered even her diminished hearing. The soldiers were interrupted from their barrage and compelled to look up. Another crash came, this one with greater resonance than Lizby had ever felt, and became a continuous clamor of crashes and crunches. Wreckage pounded the stone floor—steel beams and panels, ore chunks, machinery strewn with loose cables. The lift doors slid open slowly, and Lizby glimpsed polished military boots and long rifle barrels. The captain's face tremored with surprise at the sight, and he swung his handgun at the lift.

More debris fell, some of it engulfed in flame. An unknown liquid spattered to the ground and drenched a nearby soldier, who recoiled in surprise. A steady stream of the liquid gushed from above, adding to the furious roar.

Lizby smelled fuel. Fully panicked, she scooted between a pair of thick beams. The floodlights faded to blackness as the sound became deafening, drowning out even the lingering gunfire. *Not like this... I can't go out like this,* she thought, despairing. Something enormous crashed nearby, so hard that it shook the stone beneath her. *Sabos!* She pictured her love's face. She would give anything not to be alone in this moment.

She covered her head with her arms and cried out. Suddenly she felt intense pressure on her back and lost her breath with a sharp gasp. Consciousness left her.

Chapter 10

First there was darkness, and unnerving silence. Then a sensation of motion: a nauseating swinging feeling. The motion halted and was quickly followed by a glimpse of sprawling metal suspended over an abyss of unnerving dark depths. The vision faded back to black. The swinging repeated, followed by the same scene except with a hint of more clarity; there was movement on the metal structure below, which was some sort of scaffolding. Another round of the motion and it became apparent that the movement consisted of several people, clearly distraught, scurrying across the yellow beams of the scaffolding, which was supported on beams so tall that they faded from sight below. The sickening motion repeated, the vision slowed down to become more coherent, and now the silence gave way to disorienting clamor.

He grimly understood that he was witnessing impending death.

The vision became brighter and the noises were revealed as a mix of peoples' voices and crashing metal. The people were trapped on the scaffolding, which was erected to an incredible height. There was a vague impression of structures below and a dark hole even further beneath.

The men and women clinging to the scaffolding seemed familiar, although he knew he had never met them. Before they had been just silhouettes clinging to the metal, but now they appeared before him in stark detail. Their eyes darted around in panic, and they tried to scamper farther up the scaffolding. The fires far below blasted acrid smoke that smothered their tangled screams. The man closest to him met his gaze before letting go of the scaffolding and dropping into the abyss. A frantic woman grasped in vain for an out-of-reach beam. She strained one last time, and then her exhausted shoulders slumped in despair. The others braced themselves as best they could, but what happened next was inevitable: the tower materialized out of nowhere in his vision and crashed into the scaffolding with a tremendous, howling crash. The bodies were crushed and destroyed in excruciating detail; he sensed their bones snapping, their organs rupturing, their breath extinguishing as the palpable, sharp fear finally left their bodies. The scene seared his soul, replaying on an unstoppable loop that mutated on each replay with increasing grotesqueness. His head spun beyond the worst drunkenness, and then the vision steadied; he was again forced to witness.

Each recurrence drove his torment to previously unimaginable levels. He tried to will himself to escape the vision; there had to be a way out. The first versions of the vision had been unsettling but not terrifying. By the time it became clear that this group of familiar, yet unknown people was meeting an untimely end, he began to yell out. As the details increased, so did the intensity of his futile cries to end it. Now, in the fully felt horror, he screamed endlessly. The replay mutated one last time: now the people stared through the black smoke directly at him. Somehow, he saw into each of their eyes simultaneously. This was not how they had expected it to end. The reasons that brought them here vanished as their expressions tried to convey thousands of yearnings for which no time remained. As the roar of the tower cast a menacing shadow over the scaffolding, they cried out to him in misery as they died. This final development in the vision jolted it to an end. As the scene dissolved into black and his mind stopped spinning, it felt much like he was resigning himself to a long-awaited, merciful death.

Chapter 11

The enemy looks, talks, and—more often than not—acts like us. It's the Coalition's fervent, perverse spread of human cloning that must remain at the forefront of our troops' thoughts as they battle a foe that often hails from the same homeland. The stakes couldn't be higher. More than the Sovereignty movement, it is the very soul of humankind that our intrepid men and women fight for.

—Sovereignty General Jadaro Sahn

Marina froze in her chair when she heard the alarm and the ensuing commotion. The blaring was not unlike the air raid sirens that she had heard in documentaries about the wars of old. She considered if this mayhem were some sort of drill. *Stay calm—this probably happens all the time. It's probably an overreaction to some sensor reading or something.* But as she watched the miners quickly stride past the training room's windows, it was clear that their confusion was genuine and that something was horribly amiss. Soon the miners were running, all in the same direction: deeper into the mine. Then came a few loud pops. *Was that...gunfire?* She thought she heard it coming from the center of the Pit. *Time for me to go, too.* She trotted out of the office space as the last few miners trickled her way. Carmenta had led her directly into the training room from the Pit, risking no sightseeing, so she was unfamiliar with what lay in this direction. There were a trio of tunnels in ahead of her, but Marina didn't know which the miners had entered. She entered the widest of the tunnels, the center one, labeled "Power Division." Large conduits led out along this tunnel's edges and branched off in all directions along the cavern's ceiling.

What's going on? Where's Carmenta? Please let her be safe... She thought about running back to the training room to leave a note. As she paused amid the continued echoes of gunfire, a miner nearly toppled over her as he scrambled into the tunnel. He didn't even look back to see if she was okay. Just then she heard a roar so loud that it drowned the gunfire and sent tremors through the stone like an earthquake shock. The lights flickered, and her indecision vanished with them. She dashed down the tunnel and did not hazard a glance over her shoulder until she reached the first bend. A gray plume of dust billowed underneath the scaffolding and conveyor belts that led into the heart of the Pit. *What the hell?!*

As Marina raced into the tunnel, the overhead lights died completely. Her eyes struggled to adjust to the dim glow of the backup lights along the tunnel floor before, seconds later, those also faded out.

Chapter 12

We are seeing consequences far beyond the intentions of the first-generation cloners. Athletes and celebrities are selling their genetic code, a few prominent men and women have been replicated thousands of times already. Governments are initiating large-scale fertility programs. Families replicated dead loved ones. We're well beyond the incremental corrections in genetic health that these first scientists sought.

—Professor Ella Socarin, Genetics Department, University of New Seattle

Gerund had lasting memories of times when he woke up completely disoriented. Sometimes he had regained consciousness in a strange, unfamiliar place in which he didn't remember falling asleep, either after surrendering to exhaustion during one of the never-ending Coalition patrols or after having way too many drinks during an evening on leave. His military career often required him to wake at irregular hours of the day that initially threw off all sense of time, but the worst confusion he had experienced was caused or enhanced by a hangover or delirium from the effects of fever. In most instances, a few sequences of thought usually clarified the situation quickly. His senses would spread out, and the mystery was steadily deconstructed.

The first sensation to emerge into Gerund's consciousness was pain. It seemed to be coming from everywhere at once. The pain cycled over and over again, but he could not seem to get his body to respond; in his hazy thoughts, he sensed that this powerlessness was related to the horrible dream he had just endured. This troubling idea brought him into full consciousness.

Gerund fully opened his eyes, scanning in every direction. Nothing but darkness. *What the?!* He felt cool, rough stone beneath. He couldn't remember why he was there and thus had no idea which direction he should be looking. He tentatively reached up to his tender face. It was freshly wet, bleeding from gashes across the top of his head and down across his eye. He winced at the touch, and imagined all the grit from his hands irritating the throbbing wound. His eyes ached, and that worried him. He had a scratched cornea as a child, and that had been very uncomfortable, but this felt worse. He worried about what that meant for his eyesight.

Where am I, and what am I doing here? Several stabilizing deep breaths later, a few key memories returned. Gerund started to make sense of his trouble. He was a soldier in the Coalition—there had been a battle. Images from the chaotic vision he had had while unconscious provided further insight. *The mine...we were fighting above the mine. It must have collapsed,* Gerund surmised, sighing as the confused memories began to collate into a complete picture of his predicament.

He raised his head, then moved his arms above him to see if they met any obstruction. Nothing. He caught a few more breaths and tried to sit up but quickly slumped back down. A sharp pain suggested that his right leg was sprained or perhaps even fractured. His left side was propped up on metal sheeting; his right rested on a smooth stone surface. He moaned, and this time leaned to his left while propping himself up. He again reached all about him while looking from side to side. Still nothing: complete darkness. *Am I blind?* he wondered. *What would that even feel like?* He considered this possibility calmly, but the thought of losing his sight was indeed sad. He had been revived only two days before after his long state of suspended animation. Before that, he had been cycled through the gray and dreary battlefields of the front for almost two years without respite. He missed the colors of the world. Gerund thought back to his rural upbringing in a forested mountain valley, where time passed slowly but where he had constant access to a visual feast of flora and fauna whenever he stopped long enough to take it all in. The threat of never seeing nature again, the smiles of friends and family, or anything at all was beyond disheartening.

He remembered his unit doctor's diagnosis from yesterday morning: Urbach–Wiethe disease. Now circumstances that should have terrified him—darkness, unknown injuries, the loss of his rifle and comrades, the potential of an enemy ambush—were merely processed with cold calculation. As he had discovered by climbing the communication tower yesterday, his brain was incapable of responding to these threats with primal fear. *It's true,* he realized. *I'm not afraid. I'm starting to think clearly already.* But that didn't mean he felt comfortable about the situation. The very real probability of his death was, of course, unsettling.

He listened intently. Silence. He lifted the end of his shirt to his face and tried to dab the excess blood from his face. *How long have I been here? Where is everyone? How did I even survive the fall?* Then he remembered the moment of disaster. All the memories came flooding back to him:

He was entrenched along the vast edge of the mine surface with dozens of fellow soldiers and support personnel, seeking cover among the walkways and conveyor belt system that stretched over the dark maw of the Pit. The Sovereignty was also entrenched a few hundred meters on the other side. Bullets, artillery rounds, and reconnaissance drones streaked across the space in between. It was a battle of slow attrition and a logistical nightmare for any commander trying to funnel forces through the quagmire of the mine's complex infrastructure.

The mine was a long-term strategic asset, perhaps the highest priority on the entire continent. At first the Sovereignty had seized territory surrounding the mine, but then Gerund's side, the Coalition, had snuck in from an unexpected direction, making a push for the unaffiliated mining operation. Although both armies were exhausted, spread far too thin, the commanders pushed their forces hard into the unfamiliar area, refusing to give any ground.

Gerund and the other front-line troops fought for control of the mine across the complex of conveyor belts, lifts, suspension wires, and scaffolding interspersed between the various buildings on the surface of the mine. The view was breathtaking. Except for the support frames, the buildings gave way to mostly open space below. There were some ledges and tunnel entrances partway down, but the bottom of the mine appeared only as fuzzy lights from the surface. Several men and women had fallen down this great depth during the morning's battle. Their screams had echoed through the funnel of the main pit.

Soldiers from both sides tried to get closer via the maze of paths and buildings in the center of the mine's surface, but they were killed or stranded before closing with the enemy. The battle almost immediately became locked into a defensive engagement with no resolution in sight. Neither side could mobilize overwhelming numbers or heavy equipment to the remote location on such short notice; it was difficult enough just to transport all the soldiers there, and more challenging still for either army to overwhelm its enemy. Moreover, neither side wanted to damage the mine by using heavy weapons; it would be an incredible asset to whoever could commandeer it.

To break the stalemate, both the Coalition and the Sovereignty flew in troop transports. Gerund and the rest of his fellow soldiers cheered as their dropships had appeared through the thick clouds a thousand meters above and started to descend toward the mine's edge. The dropships—massive aircraft, yet surprisingly agile—each carried a hundred troops for rapid unloading. The cheers on the ground died, however, when a pair of Sovereignty transports raced over the horizon to deploy their troops first. With only a few hundred personnel at the mine beforehand, the arrival of the ships would be the deciding factor in the fight for the mine.

Both groups of ships converged over the mine, circling to assess the situation and find the best spot to unload their soldiers. As all five ships descended to within 200 meters to find space to unload, Gerund saw two opposing ships veer toward an open lot on the edge of the mine, farther up the embankment. The pilots either didn't notice each other or refused to give up the airspace, and the distance separating the ships quickly vanished and it was clear that a collision was imminent. Small arms fire harassed each ship, further hastening their frantic descent. The enemy ship's engines bellowed as the pilot rolled his craft at the last moment, but it was too late. The massive ships screamed as metal grated together, ripping panels free and exposing the innards of both vessels. Cargo spilled out of the gash in the cargo hold, punching holes in the buildings below. Some of the Coalition passengers were exposed to the open air; they waved their arms in alarm as they were jerked against their harnesses.

The Sovereignty ship was deflected as its wide front connected with the protruding bulkhead of the Coalition ship, which wobbled but managed to regain control. The Sovereignty ship, however, sharply veered toward the ground, accelerating as its engines struggled in vain to regain control. When the ship struck the ground, it plowed through several small sheds on the mine's embankment, then rolled onto the equipment and walkways suspended over the mine, crushing some of the soldiers who had set up positions on the walkways; Gerund wasn't even sure whose side they were on. The dropship's engines continued to propel it, sustaining the craft's momentum as it slammed into the base of the control tower near the center of the mine. To Gerund's horror, the tower snapped and crushed dozens of soldiers perched on the scaffolding underneath.

Gerund remained in cover as he watched the destruction. When he realized that he was in the rolling ship's chaotic path, it was too late. Breaking free of the tower's ruins, the massive ship took one final dive downward as Gerund stood and sprinted across the walkway, rifle and gear still in hand. He hurtled over a woman too dazed to move out of her crouch. He leapt into one of the lift cages that led to the mine bottom just as the ship snapped the structure supporting the lift, flipping it into the air while Gerund slammed against the floor. He was slammed against the side of the lift as the cables tensed and whiplashed the loose lift back toward the cable track. He caught a glimpse of steel beams crumpling below him and flames streaming out of the dropship's undercarriage as it lurched down the maw of the Pit.

Gerund frantically grasped for anything solid as the lift, straining heavily against the cable, fell among the debris. He saw the crumpling and sliding metal below him through a smoky mist, but he viewed the chaos dispassionately, feeling no fear but rather an uneasy curiosity about what would happen next. The lift cage descended so quickly that it felt like free fall, and he pulled his body close to the lift's mesh wall. That was his last memory: when the cage jolted, he had been slammed to the opposite side and had lost consciousness as the lift cage descended. Its cable must have generated enough friction to slow the cage's momentum just enough before it hit the bottom.

Now, at that bottom, Gerund had only one question: *What now?* Amid the vast destruction, it was clear that no one from the surface, friend or foe, would be trying to reach him any time soon. They probably didn't even have the ability to reach the bottom of the mine any longer. *I need to find out what I have with me*, he decided. *This could be a long wait*. He carefully picked through the pile of rubble that was behind him. There was a rectangular frame of crumbled metal draped with loose cable: it must have been the remnant of the lift cage in which he had plummeted. He guessed that he had tumbled out when the lift had reached the end of its cable track and hit bottom.

Gerund wondered whether there was an emergency light somewhere, or perhaps a glowing panel or switch. *Maybe I'm trapped in a small space*, he considered. *Either I'm nowhere near even a shimmer of light, or I'm blind. Great.*

Gerund sighed and began to slowly crawl around the abyss.

Chapter 13

When Lizby woke, she was confused and sluggish. She gradually gained consciousness and pieced together details about her surroundings. In this way, her impression of her environment brought a pang of danger when her mind fully emerged from its enshrouding fog.

She widened her eyes and groaned. She guessed she had been out for a while—perhaps an hour. Her muscles were painfully stiff. She could see very little; a light source from behind illuminated just a few meters around her. Collapsed walkways, beams, and rocks surrounded her. Lizby was stuck, but she couldn't tell by what—she felt pressure from multiple angles. Movement caught her eye. A pair of men were crossing the wreckage. She saw camouflaged uniforms; they were soldiers. Their long rifles were deployed in ready position, but she could discern few other details about them. She didn't know whether they were Coalition or Sovereignty, and it wouldn't have made a difference to her.

She had a clear glimpse of one of the men as he climbed over a large mound of rubble: he had a look of determined fury on his face. Lizby had the strong urge to make her peril known, but hesitated. *I don't know if I can trust them—they look dangerous. Where are they going?* Another person scurried out of what must have been the ruins of the garage in which the miners had hid from the soldiers. *I don't have the luxury of waiting around for an ideal rescuer.* "Hey, over here!" she called. However, this survivor ignored her and disappeared into the tunnels opposite the soldiers. With a shudder, Lizby noticed the body of another soldier in the garage ruins. Only his waist and legs were visible. The rest was pinned under the fallen wall from a maintenance building. *What the hell?! Was there a bomb? Oh, my god, I hope Sabos was far away from all of this.*

Lizby tried to wriggle free from the wreckage, gasping at the deep pain. Her arms were free, and her legs were able to reach out far enough to gain a bit of traction on the ground, but her waist was firmly pinned. She reached down and felt the steel I-beam that had pinned her against another support, this one in its proper place. She looked to where the collapsed beam ended: one corner rested on the stone floor, and the other perched precariously against a battered walkway. She wondered whether she could nudge it but worried that it might swing back toward her rather than away, crushing her. She languished over the thought of whether she already had internal damage; her side throbbed painfully beneath the pressure.

Lizby saw yet another figure move at the edge of her vision. "Hey! Please help!" she yelled. The figure barely paused to take note of her and then quickly moved along out of sight.

She strained her neck to look behind. She saw fire—frighteningly close—and gulped a panicked breath. *No!*

"Hey! A little help here!" she yelled again.

The flames extended in a curved line farther into the cavern. To her horror, the fire seemed to be spreading nearer, feeding on the remains of the conveyor belt tread. It crackled, soft and menacing. The smoke was minimal so far, drifting straight up, but the flames licked the edge of the intact support beam against which she was pinned—it was already uncomfortably warm against her waist. Less worried about which way the collapsed beam would slide, Lizby braced herself, pulled in a deep, smoky breath, and then pushed away with all her might. The beam wobbled a little but otherwise stayed put. She glanced behind her. The fire was significantly bigger and now fully illuminated her.

"Help!" Lizby screamed. "I'm trapped near this fire! Please, help!" She tried pushing again, harder than she thought possible, but to no avail. She collapsed against the imprisoning beam as her breath gave out from the effort.

Lizby felt herself losing control. She had always thought of burning as the worst way to suffer. It was such a primal force, yet so intense in the agony it could cause to its victims. When Lizby was eight, the next-door neighbors' home had burned down. As she and her family had exited their own home, the intensity of the roaring fire had scorched them. The blaze had traumatized her the rest of that summer, and the hellish heat infiltrated her nightmares to this day. There was nothing elaborate about the pain from burning—just searing, all-encompassing torment. *This is going to be so awful...*

She heard Sabos's voice in her mind, encouraging her to keep trying. It was too soon to give up. There was too much to lose. *Yes, babe,* she thought. *I'm trying.*

She twisted her torso and tried to push from another angle, but this time the beam didn't even wobble. *Where are all the miners?* She looked around for anything she could use as leverage. She patted down her pockets for anything of use. Nothing.

Her eyes adjusted to the light. She could see the silhouette of the control building. The top floor was almost completely collapsed, and the bottom floor walls buckled under the immense weight from above. She looked for a miner or soldier—anybody.

The flames spread to her right, approaching her from two sides. She tried to kick away the rubble underneath her, including the conveyor belt tread that made a discouragingly good kindling, but the debris merely flapped against her feet, being as pinned by the beam as she was. She tried to remove the debris beneath her torso using the arm that could reach it, but nothing budged. Despair again threatened. *No—stop.* She shook her head in an attempt to thwart her morbid imagination's visions of the ways her body might combust.

The smoke started to envelope her. It stung her eyes, causing them to well up with protective tears. She absurdly thought of her eyes tearing up enough to soak her body and surroundings in enough water to halt the spread of the fire. Refocusing, she scanned the edge of the increasingly bright aura created by the fire for help. *This can't happen. I'm not ready.*

She saw someone coming out of the buckled door of the maintenance building. "Hey!" she screamed. This time, the man not only noticed her, but maintained eye contact. His perplexed eyes reflected in the firelight.

"I'm stuck! Please get me out before—before the fire–" Lizby spoke too quickly and coughed on fumes.

The man looked around the cavern as if eager to find someone else. He hesitated, then looked back at her with a perplexed expression.

Oh, god, no. What are you waiting for!? She fanned her hand in front of her face to indicate the intensity of the heat.

The man snapped out of his uncertainty and strode toward her. *Yes—come on!* He seemed to glide over the barriers in his way. "Hold on!" the man shouted. Lizby was relieved to the depths of her soul, invigorated by a renewed hope that she would make it out alive.

The man crouched at her side, and she pointed at the edge of the beam that had compressed her waist. The man wore soldier's camouflage—different from what the other soldiers had worn, though—and had a submachine gun strapped tightly behind his shoulder. His uniform was dusty and his hair disheveled, but otherwise he appeared intact.

As he grabbed the beam, Lizby held up a hand. "Let me help." She quickly twisted to get both hands against the edge of the beam. "Okay."

The man still seemed to be in shock from the collapse. When he looked at her, his eyes were unfocused and distant.

When he gave no sign of regathering his strength, Lizby grasped his arm. The fire was singeing the bottom of her trousers, but she did her best to keep the panic out of her voice. "Hey! Let's do this, OK?" She placed reassuring pressure on the man's forearm.

He blinked and refocused his attention on her predicament, stooping low beneath the beam. Then they both pushed up and out with all their strength: the beam lifted, and Lizby slid out as the soldier dropped the beam to the ground once more.

"Thank you! Yes! I can't thank you enough!" She crawled away from the beam. The man coughed and leaned out of the smoke's path.

Lizby tried to get to her feet, but her legs had not recovered enough circulation to support her. The man grabbed her arm and supported her before she fell. With effort, she kicked out each leg to wake them up and then lurched herself upright.

"Thank you so much. You just saved my life." Her eyes filled with grateful tears as she searched the man's face for a reaction, but his eyes were still darting around the cavern and only occasionally came across her. Sensing her steadiness, he let go of her hand, and Lizby stepped in front of him to get his attention. "Do you have an idea...do you know what happened?"

The man shook his head. "No. I– I don't know where..." He looked above at nothing in particular.

What is with this guy? "What's your name?"

"E– excuse me. I need to do something." He began to return in the direction from which he had come. As he turned, Lizby was astonished to see a gaping wound in the back of his head. Dark blood coated his hair, his neck, and the top of his jacket. She winced deeply. *How the hell are you still standing?! What happened to you?*

"Hey, wait! You're not well! You're hurt really, really bad," she called out, but the man stumbled over a heap of rubble before lumbering off into the darkness. "Hey!" But there was no sight or sound of him.

What task could you possibly need to complete when you are in the middle of dying? Lizby wondered. She considered chasing down her savior, but she couldn't help him. And he, like the other soldiers she had seen since waking up, was preoccupied with some unknown objective. *I need to find Sabos. And Carmenta.* She headed toward the east tunnel entrances, dark and foreboding against the glow of the firelight: they were her best guess at where her family members might be if they had been in the Pit during the collapse. And there weren't many other options she could try, anyway. She peeled a plank off a door panel and ignited the end. Makeshift torch in hand, she went to find her husband.

Chapter 14

Gerund could only guess which side had triumphed in the battle and controlled whatever was left of the surface. Neither the Coalition nor the Sovereignty had seemed to have the upper hand before the ships had crashed. *Does it even matter? The collapse might have wiped out both sides. I may never get out of here.* There was a glimmer of hope, though: his leg felt more intact than he had initially suspected, allowing him a degree of mobility despite its continued tenderness. Searching his immediate surroundings, Gerund recovered some of his belongings, which were in his trouser pockets or scattered nearby on the stone floor. He was thankful to find a concentrated ration bar, which helped alleviate his gnawing hunger. He picked all the grain crumbs out of the wrapper and sighed after the final swallow. *That's it—no more food.* A half-liter canteen of water would last him only a day or two, but he hoped things wouldn't come to that. He clutched his combat knife with relief on finding it nearby, still in its sheath. The knife wouldn't do him much good in the dark or against firearms, but its familiar pressure against his leg was reassuring. He found his datapad beside the knife, too. But when he tried to turn on the device, nothing happened. Perhaps it was broken, or its battery was drained. His rifle, however, was nowhere to be found; Gerund last remembered clutching it when he had run into the mine lift, just before the aircraft hit.

Gerund realized that he could be isolated for the foreseeable future. He called on his discipline and training to remain focused. He thought about his diagnosis: although he didn't fear his prospects, neither was he at peace with the situation or unable to recognize the gravity of the dangers awaiting him in the mine. He didn't have to the means to tend to his wounds, even on a rudimentary level. And he was totally disoriented, with no idea of where to go next. *No choice but forward. Just wish I knew which direction to begin with.*

After spending 10 minutes gathering his wits, Gerund felt his composure return, along with some measure of control over his pain. He began to explore the edges of the wreckage that surrounded him. He kept his knife ready and listened intently for any unsuspecting Sovereignty soldiers who might have also tumbled into the Pit or who perhaps had already been lying in wait. After a few minutes into his tedious exploration, Gerund had a better feel for the space. He could stand in many spots, but it was necessary to bend over and crawl to get very far. Overhead obstacles in the form of cables and folds of conveyor belt track jutted out from above, and the ground was littered with steel beams, drywall chunks, and ceramic tiles; these must have been the obliterated remains of the surface buildings. Gerund reached out in search of any drops or tripping hazards, flailing his arms upward as well to avoid further injury. These precautions, unfortunately, slowed his progress considerably.

Gerund rose from his crawl, trusting his leg with a little more weight. Pain stabbed his thigh, but it held up. He smelled acrid smoke, but it was faint, as if from a long-extinguished fire. He suppressed the urge to call out for other survivors. *How am I going to reach the surface? I must be hundreds of meters below if this thing is as deep as they say it is.* He tried to imagine what a large-scale mining operation would look like so far beneath the surface. Was there a crowded maze of machinery, or would he find railing or some other guidance to follow? He wondered if there were ways other than the elevator lifts of getting to a higher level. From what Gerund had understood from the much-too-brief mission briefing, the Pit was enormous even at this depth and accessed dozens of tunnel entrances. Gerund hoped to stumble on a completely new area created by the wreckage. Perhaps such an area would have a light source and other Coalition or even civilian survivors. He walked slowly, his arms in front, and felt dust drifting down onto his arms and face. He closed his eyes and heard a loud crunch from above, perhaps from settling wreckage.

"Shit!" he hissed, much louder than he had intended. When the debris made no further noise, Gerund walked onward—and almost immediately stopped on hearing footsteps. *Did I hear that right? Did they hear me?* He suppressed his breathing even as his heart raced. He wondered whether the sound had come from the front or from his right.

Gerund heard a crunch of rock and then breathing—it was unmistakable. He reached down and removed his knife from his sheath, steeling himself for a confrontation. *It could be anybody...* He considered if it was a miner, or perhaps even someone from his squad. *Do I dare speak?*

Another set of steps, but this time there was no attempt at stealth. The breathing rasped mere meters away. Gerund held his knife outward. "Wh–who?" he croaked out from his parched throat. No further words would come.

Suddenly Gerund was hit from the front. As heads connected, Gerund saw a white flash behind his eyes. The other person gasped. *Whump!* The jarring impact sent Gerund toppling backward, but he flailed his free hand in an attempt to grab the arm of his assailant. The other person, also off balance, fell atop him with a loud grunt. As his attacker rolled off, Gerund connected with a swipe of his knife. The yell was at first surprised, then full of pain. It sounded like a man. Gerund thought he had slashed across an arm—probably not a fatal wound. The man punched Gerund in the neck while he was still on his back. Gerund's breath escaped in a gasp and his eyes watered, but he had the presence of mind to keep fighting. He stabbed with his knife, but the blade swished empty air.

Gerund rose into a crouch and lunged forward. His knee pinned the man's elbow, and he grappled for the wrist of the man's free arm. Gerund's knife hand, however, was free. He raised his arm to prepare for a strike.

"Please!" the man gasped. Gerund hesitated, the knife still high above his shoulder—ready for a deadly plunge. The voice from this other human brought him back. *What am I doing?* The man, still struggling under his grip, sighed in defeat.

Gerund pushed off and leapt back. He heard the other rise, too. Gerund's leg throbbed in pained protest. He held his knife in front and widened his stance.

But another charge didn't come. Instead, he heard retreating footsteps. Gerund maintained his defensive stance long after the footsteps trailed off. Finally, he put the knife back in its sheath and rubbed his sore neck. *What the hell? Who was that?* Gerund wanted to shout the questions. *That escalated quickly. I almost killed him, whoever he was.* Another thought occurred to him, and this one gave him hope. *He couldn't see me, either...which means it's pitch black down here; my vision may be all right after all.*

Gerund continued to wait for the man's return. But that seemed unlikely. It was time to keep walking, but Gerund was now unsure of direction from which he had come. *This has been a waste.* There were no markings, nothing his senses could detect to tell him whether he was back-tracking or not. There was only randomly scattered debris. Dejected, Gerund started moving, at the mercy of the unknown path in front of him.

Chapter 15

Sabos and Carmenta had been working in the same sector of the mine when the alarm started blaring, warning of the arrival of the battle above. Sabos had been diagnosing one of the faulty coolant systems of the conveyor belt at the time, and Carmenta had been deep within one of the tunnels, working on the hydraulic systems of an ore lifter. With the mining staff reduced to a skeleton crew, they had both been working alone. Sabos, unsure if Carmenta had heard the alarm, had ventured within the tunnel to retrieve her, intending to seek Lizby as soon as they exited the tunnel. To his relief, Sabos had found Carmenta coming his way after only a couple hundred meters. She had been fine but, like him, had been bewildered by the commotion. As they approached the tunnel exit, they had seen a hooded man brandishing a gun, waiting in the exit corridor. He had worn a miner's uniform but hadn't looked like any of the workers assigned to the area. He had either not noticed them or paid them no mind; Sabos and Carmenta had hung back against the tunnel wall, not wanting to encounter him.

Soon the man had left. With increasing concern for Lizby, Sabos had insisted that they enter the Pit immediately, right on the heels of the gunman. But as they had begun to approach the exit again, gunfire had erupted from the main Pit chamber. The flashes had erupted just in front of them, and the reverberating blasts had forced them to seek cover. They had retreated just beyond the curve of the tunnel as the stream of gunfire continued. Shortly after, the roar of the collapse had pushed them back farther into the tunnel—right before the tunnel ceiling had collapsed near the exit and everything had gone dark.

Sabos's senses were smothered in the surreal moments that followed. He felt dizzy and was enveloped by complete darkness. He lost balance and fell backward as a swell of hot air swept over him. On the way down, he hit his head.

Am I buried? he pondered weakly, absurdly disoriented. But then he felt the unyielding stone of the tunnel wall behind him. He was slumped against it. *Not dead yet.* Sabos rose unsteadily to his feet. His eyes stung, and his ears rang. He fumbled for the flashlight clipped to his waist and nearly dropped it in his haste, but managed to secure his grip and click the button. The light revealed swirling dust so thick that visibility was cut to barely a meter. The particles moved swiftly through the tunnel, looking like the dizzying snow of a blizzard in headlights.

"Carmenta!?" He reached for his sister, spinning with an outstretched arm while trying to catch his bearings with the flashlight. *Please be okay.*

"Here!" She coughed. Their hands connected, and she pulled him against the tunnel wall. "We're going to be okay. I think it's over." Echoes of Sabos's childhood flashed into his mind: memories of his older sister comforting him when the lights went out during one of their home's frequent power outages.

Sabos wiped the dust from his face as best he could. The hair on his forearm trapped a thick coating of fine dust. "W–what just happened? It seemed like something exploded at the surface level."

"No clue, but I don't think it was planned," Carmenta said. "Not with how much this mine is worth to everyone." She leaned in closer to the light; the dust had already begun to settle. Her willowy frame quivered with adrenaline and her green eyes shone, alert. "We're not getting out that way."

Sabos followed her gaze and pointed the flashlight toward the tunnel exit. It had imploded near the opening, completely blocked by large slabs of stone. "I know our tunnel intersects with a lot of the old dormant tunnels. Do you know if any of those lead back to the Pit?"

"Not for sure, but it's certainly possible."

Sabos stared at the blocked exit. "Where do you think she would have gone, Carmenta?" He imagined a dismal array of deadly possibilities, ranging from gunshots and crushing beams to fire and fallen ore. "Lizby has a good head on her shoulders. She went somewhere safe, I'm sure." Her assertion sounded hollow to Sabos, but she persisted. "There was a lot of time between the alarm and the collapse."

"I know OreLife had everyone go through some drills, but I don't know if she would have followed them," said Sabos. "Maybe she stayed in one of the tunnels." In the dim light, his eyes looked watery to Carmenta. "And that gunfire—what were the soldiers doing down here? She must be so scared."

"She's got a lot of people out there to help her."

"How can you be certain? And she's probably worrying about why I can't get to her." *I should have gone to find Lizby right away*, he reasoned. *Carmenta would have been fine in here.*

Carmenta placed a reassuring hand on Sabos's shoulder, but he bristled at her touch. "I'm concerned, too," she said, "but we can only speculate at the moment. Let's find a way out first."

Sabos nodded reluctantly. He clenched his jaw and sighed deeply. "Was there anyone else farther inside the tunnel?"

"No, I'm almost positive I was the only one left. There was a sampling crew, but I saw them run out when the alarm began."

The tunnel was starkly silent. Sabos examined his flashlight, as if discovering it for the first time. "It should have a full charge; I almost never use it. But we may only have a couple hours with it. So let's get going." He nodded into the depths of the tunnel.

"Yes, and stay close. This isn't a safe place even when it's well lit," she replied. They walked resolutely into the unknown.

Chapter 16

As the tunnel dropped into complete darkness, Marina stumbled toward the panicked voices ahead. A cloud of debris roared into the tunnel behind her, and she felt thick dust lick her heels as she ran blindly. *Where am I going?* Picturing stalagmites and bottomless pits in the path ahead, she could only hold an arm out in front to defend against unknown obstacles. She strained to detect the voices of the miners but heard only the deafening screech of wreckage pushing its way into the tunnel behind her. She bounced off the side of the tunnel and scratched her arm through the sleeve of the coarse mining jacket that Carmenta had loaned her—but she remained upright, overcorrecting to the other side of the tunnel. As she did, a brightening glow began to outline the end of the tunnel. Near the exit, she heard the roar behind her finally subside but could still feel the dust billowing past.

As her eyes adjusted to the light, she proceeded cautiously into an expansive chamber. Its stone floor was smooth and polished, a stark contrast to the tunnel's uneven surface. The ceiling arched to an incredible height—perhaps 70 meters. The space was dominated by a humming three-story tower on the far side of the room. The structure was studded with transformers and heavy conduits—it served as one of the mine's power plants. Blinding floodlights running the height of the enormous cylinder illuminated the room. Several thick conduits radiated down from the tower into a large pool of water that encircled it. Other power conduits exited the water and converged at one end of the room before curving into a 2-meter-wide trench carved into the stone and running in the direction of the Pit. A single steel catwalk extended across the water pool to the tower base. A trio of miners were talking on the other side of the chamber, dwarfed by the imposing tower. They were gathered at the thin yellow railing along the water moat that encircled it in a 20-meter radius. She approached them, seeing two men and one woman, but they didn't acknowledge her presence until she was right among them.

"...maybe she knows something we don't," a middle-aged man was saying as he turned to her and waved. "Hey there—was there anyone behind you?"

"No, I don't think so. It was just me," she managed between breaths. "What's going on?"

"We're not sure. We all heard gunfire–"

"Not just heard—I saw it!" the woman interjected, meeting Marina's eyes with an eager gaze that suggested she had the story of the century. "There were dozens of soldiers that came down the elevator. Armed to the teeth—not here to make friends, either. I saw miners with their hands up—the soldiers held them at gunpoint. They were questioning some of us, and they were very nervous. I stayed on the edge of the scene, and then I bolted when the first bullets started flying. And I mean flying out of nowhere. It was chaos after that."

"So you didn't see what caused all of the crashing?" Marina asked.

"Nope—no idea. But it had to be huge," the woman said.

"I think the tunnel might be blocked." Marina said.

The man nodded glumly. "I'll go confirm, just to be sure," he volunteered. He trotted off with a flashlight.

"Be cautious, Jethro!" The woman called after him.

Marina looked at their faces. Each miner was clearly tense and wired but seemed in control of their wits. She tried to infer their roles by their clothing and the gear strapped to their belts, but it was all foreign to her. She would claim it was her first day on the job. That would have to suffice, because she didn't know what else she would say if they asked her anything beyond the most basic questions about her mining background. She hoped that the imminent threat that concerned them all would deflect any sustained interest in her.

"Is there another way out of this chamber?" the woman asked.

"No," the other miner said. "There's the equipment lift, but that looks like it's out of commission." He pointed at the darkened elevator. Marina studied his uniform closely and noticed that his chest badge read "Temeru Collins, Power Division." He looked impossibly young—perhaps just beyond high school age. "We'd better hope there's a way to squeeze through that main tunnel—otherwise it's going to be a long wait." Temeru gestured to the tunnel just as Jethro returned. Jethro crossed the open floor, panting with the exertion.

"Well?" the woman prompted anxiously. "Can we get out?"

Jethro shook his head. "The tunnel is completely blocked by a jumble of steel and rock, just beyond the bend. Looks like we're waiting for a rescue. Get comfortable."

"Shit!" Temeru hissed. "Octavia, did anyone see you come this way? I'm wondering if anyone even knows we are here."

"No, I was separated from everyone in my department," Octavia lamented. "No one knows where I went."

Temeru pointed at Marina. "You new here? You've got no gear on you. What's your name?"

"Marina," she blurted. *That* wasn't what she had planned. *Shit, what if they ask for my ID? It definitely doesn't say Marina...I guess I'll say that it's my nickname.* "Uh, yeah, I'm new. I started orientation this morning, so you could say this is becoming one hell of a first day for me."

"Yeah, I bet," Temeru said, nodding.

"Is this the mine's only power?" Marina asked, pointing toward the tower. *Enough about me.* "Is it the only thing that's lit up right now?"

"Well, it's the only power source down here, on bottom level," Jethro explained. "Some of the surface and upper level facilities use the main grid, but OreLife built this monster for more efficiency for the subsurface operations."

"Most likely the rest of the mine is out of main power and emergency lighting," Temeru added. "Whatever happened, too many lines were damaged. But as you can see, the power station itself is undamaged."

As if to prove her wrong, the room burst into light with a deafening blast whose pressure wave nearly toppled Marina. She instinctively crouched and covered her head. She felt an intense heat flare into the chamber and narrowed her eyes into slits. Temeru, Octavia, and Jethro were similarly cowering. Temeru pointed over to the trench in which the heavy conduits had been stored. The conduits had blasted out of the trench and were strewn in every direction. *I can't believe this! This is the worst luck.* A fiery inferno from the center of the trench stretched along the stone walls of the chamber, already scorching the sides of the tower.

"Oh my god!" Jethro screamed. What's going on?"

"What can we do?" Marina shouted, trying to hear herself over the ringing in her ears.

"I don't know what happened! I– I don't–" Temeru stammered.

Octavia started backing away, and the rest followed suit.

"I think....I think this has something to do with the cardone gas." Temeru said. His face flashed with realization, but Marina was haunted to see shock there, too. "The coolant line in the trench somehow got ignited. All the failsafes, they—uh—failed. No stopping it now."

"Gas? We're being gassed?" Octavia cried in disbelief, covering her mouth.

"No—it isn't harmful to breathe!" Temeru shouted above the roar of the flames. "But it's a dense gas. This fire is only going to grow." His eyes bulged as the gravity of their plight dawned on him. "The smoke from the other burning debris is also going to be a problem. This is basically the worst-case scenario they told us about in training."

"What was the training solution?" Jethro asked.

"Uh, there was none," Temeru said, his voice flat.

"What are you saying?!" Octavia wailed, gesturing wildly. "We're screwed?"

Temeru didn't respond, but Marina saw the answer in his eyes. *No*, she thought. *Not after the week I've had. This can't be!*

Marina heard a screech and looked up to see a trio of long-tailed bats flutter frantically in the smoke-filled heights of the cavern. The bats swooped down to the tunnel to find relief but seemed disoriented on finding their escape blocked. Within seconds, the first succumbed to the smoke and crashed to the ground, twitching. The other two did the same moments later.

"You don't have a fire extinguisher in here?" Jethro said.

"It was in the equipment lift, but it wouldn't do much against this blaze, anyway," Temeru said with a sigh.

By now they were back up against the wall in intense heat. The flames continue to wrap along the walls, rising above them. Octavia's eyes were wild with panic and Jethro seemed dazed and resigned to his fate, but Temeru was scanning their surroundings for a solution.

They all seemed to eye the pool of water at the same time.

"The water!" Octavia shouted. "But..."

"But we still have to breath," Jethro finished. "It may protect us from the flames, but not the smoke if this whole chamber keeps filling with it. And we would be right under the tower, and that's basically lining up for death." As Jethro said this, the tower clanked horribly, and the floodlights attached along its side brightened.

Marina would have given anything to turn the clock back a day and return to her bunk at Fort Callous. She wouldn't care where the Sovereignty sent her or what they ordered her to do. Titus would still be alive, and she wouldn't be facing what increasingly looked like a grisly death. *I've been such a fool. Look what I've gotten myself into.* She longed to go all the way back, before she had even joined the Sovereignty. For the first time since she had embarked on her latest and longest attempt at self-realization, she regretted having left home. She had insisted on blazing her own trail, but she had failed miserably, and now it was all about to end. She wanted to dial back the years and return to her homeland, her family, and all that was familiar. She had been estranged from her parents when she left and hadn't talked to them since joining the Sovereignty. But in this moment, she knew her parents would welcome her back wholeheartedly, and she would embrace them gratefully. They were imperfect, incredibly flawed people, but they loved her unconditionally, she knew. She couldn't believe how easily she had shrugged that off and ended all contact over what seemed so petty now. *There will be no reconciliation,* she thought mournfully. *I won't get the chance.*

Temeru's face brightened. "There *is* something we could try…The water coolant pool is deep, but it leads to another chamber under the rock. It's worth a try."

"Huh? How far?" Jethro asked, snapping out of his despondency.

"Could we even fit?" Octavia leaned over the railing to investigate the pool. Thick pipes circulated through it, and lights illuminated the deep pool from the bottom. Along one side of the tower's base, a dark opening near the pool's bottom indicated the passage Temeru had described.

"I– I've never been down there. The techs put on wetsuits and do a check once a week." Temeru said rapidly. "They use oxygen tanks, though they usually aren't underwater long. And the techs don't swim all the way through. The tanks and masks should be in one of the equipment lockers." *Please, please be in the locker.* Marina allowed hope to swell up inside her amid all the fear.

"What's on the other side?" Jethro asked.

"There's a reservoir—I'm not sure how big. It connects with some other tunnels."

Temeru bounded to the wall that contained the equipment lockers. The inferno sent out another plume of rolling flame and searing heat. Through the dark smoke, Marina saw Temeru take out cylindrical tanks and heard the clank of metal on stone. *This is happening. We've got a way out!*

The three gathered at the railing. "I hope we don't get electrocuted," Jethro said.

Octavia shook her head vigorously. "That is one of the last things on my freaking-out list right now." She looked with apprehension at the inferno and then into the water of the pool, which seemed calm by contrast.

Temeru sprinted over with the equipment. Right away Marina could see a problem. There were only two oxygen tanks and two respirator masks.

"So how do we do this?" Octavia asked, glancing over her shoulder at the fireball not more than 10 meters away. "I–I can't swim, either."

Marina let a frown break through her intensity. "Really? It's just moving your arms and legs around. Let instinct take over." Octavia ignored her.

"So how are we going to get through with only two sets of equipment?" Jethro asked.

"We're going to share, and we're going to take it slow," said Temeru. "My light rod works underwater: stay close and follow me so that you can see." Young Temeru was perhaps not accustomed to being in a position of such authority, but this was his division, so he continued to function as the closest thing to a steady voice in the chaos. "It's not that far—or so I gathered from how the techs talked."

"That sounds..." Octavia trailed off, shaking her head.

"Sounds a whole hell of a lot better than burning to death," Jethro said, convinced.

Temeru adjusted the mask and goggles over his face, fumbling with the valves on the oxygen tanks. Before the others could make a move, Marina grabbed the other set and placed the mask over her mouth and nose. She twisted the valve closest to the hose connection and received a refreshing blast of oxygen. There were also a knob sticking out of the side of the mask, but it didn't seem to be adjustable.

Temeru pointed at it. "That little pump helps maintain suction on your face and even sucks out excess water." He had gotten his tank open, too. "That's going to be important when we're trading off underwater."

Jethro had already climbed down the ladder and was treading water. He struggled to stay buoyant—perhaps weighed down by his clothing. The pool was deeper than Marina expected—and it only seemed to get deeper near the base of the tower and the open passageway.

Octavia looked over the railing with trepidation. "Can't we just stay at the surface and use the tanks? That can protect us enough from the smoke. We can hold our breath in between, just like we would have to do underwater."

As if in response to Octavia's suggestion, the equipment locker closest to the conduit trench exploded into flames, and an acrid liquid flooded out on the stone floor. Marina strapped the tank onto her back using the pair of elastic shoulder straps and climbed over the railing, ready to hop down at a moment's notice. The flames flashed over the liquid and with a hiss engulfed almost the entire chamber. Even parts of the pool were aflame where some of the liquid had run into it.

"We need to do this now," Jethro said, coughing out the words. "Get in!"

"I'll lead. Just follow my light," Temeru reminded them. "I'll share with Jethro. Marina, you'll need to help Octavia." He jumped in.

Great. I get the one who can't swim.

The heat was unbearable. Octavia was frozen halfway over the railing. *You must act, girl. We don't have the time to ease you into this.*

Marina put a firm arm on Octavia's shoulder and stared into her glassy eyes. "I'll be right with you. It won't be far," Octavia, held in her steady gaze, nodded slightly. "We'll trade off every 25 seconds, but you just tap me if you need the mask even a second sooner. We can do this. You can start with the mask when we submerge." She handed Octavia the diving goggles, trying to increase the woman's confidence any way she could.

Marina could wait no longer; she felt nearly overcome by the flames and the swirling smoke. She jumped into the water. It was comfortably warm: the pool had been used to cool the tower. As soon as she surfaced, she swam toward the passage. Her clothing and boots made her motions awkward and plodding. A splash confirmed that Octavia had also jumped in. Her claims of not knowing how to swim were greatly exaggerated, because when Marina looked back, she saw Octavia clumsily yet steadily paddling toward them.

"There's no time to practice," Temeru exclaimed. "Just keep moving—and stay calm. It can't be that far to the other side. We've got plenty of oxygen in these tanks."

More oily liquid flooded into the pool, merging with the existing burning patches. Octavia yelped from the heat: the volatile patches seemed to spread across the pool almost as fast as she could swim.

Marina's heart raced. She was normally comfortable in water, being a competent swimmer, but the circumstances were hardly cooperative. The pool was still brightly lit from beneath, but only a few meters of the passage to the reservoir were visible. There was another explosive blast from across the room, but they couldn't see the source.

"Ready?" Temeru asked. "Let's go." Before Marina could voice any of the countless concerns that swirled inside her mind, Temeru motioned for Jethro to follow him, and they both dove. The flames encircled Marina and Octavia, uncomfortably close to their faces. There was nowhere else to go but under. Marina scrambled to hand the mask over to Octavia, who put it on with shaking hands. The tank stayed strapped on Marina's back.

"We've got to stay close with them so that we can see," Marina insisted. "Let's go on the count of three."

Marina counted down with her fingers while inhaling deeply. She almost coughed from the taint of smoke just as Octavia dove. Marina plunged under and immediately starting kicking to stay close to Octavia, as the hose that connected to the tank was no longer than a meter and a half.

Temeru's light revealed about four meters of his surroundings in front along a wide swath of his path, making all sides of the passage clearly visible. The sides of the stone were smooth, as if they were part of a natural formation produced by erosion, and were covered by a fine, velvety lichen. The light cast behind them was just strong enough for Marina to see Octavia. Marina's arms stretched forward slower than expected, and her booted feet met stiff resistance when she kicked out. Making the swim fully clothed might have been a very dangerous choice, Marina realized—except it hadn't been a conscious choice. Like so many other things they hadn't considered before they were forced into the water, the effects of the waterlogged clothing apparently hadn't occurred to any of them until they were in the pool.

Marina counted out the seconds and decided to hold out longer than the previously agreed-on 25 seconds: she could endure it easily, and she wanted to minimize both the time Octavia had to hold her breath and also the total number of times they would make the dangerous trade-off. Ahead, she saw Temeru hand the mask off to Jethro, who smoothly put it on. The pair was moving farther ahead with their light rod, and Marina worried that this would limit visibility for her and Octavia.

After a full 32 seconds, she still had endurance to keep going on her first breath, but she knew it was unwise to wait until her limit. She tapped Octavia on the forearm. The miner's fear was evident even in the dim light, but she took a deep breath and tugged the mask off. Marina quickly applied the mask, and the pump mechanism sucked the water out in about 3 seconds, displacing it with oxygen while maintaining a tight seal on her face. She met Octavia's gaze and tapped the mask while counting to three with her fingers, indicating the need to wait for the mask to clear the trapped water after a switch.

"Wait 3 seconds," she said, but the sound was muffled even to her own ears. She breathed deeply, trying to remain calm and recover her stamina. The passage had narrowed to about 3 meters wide. It was even darker here, and Temeru's light shone as a distinct beacon up ahead. Only 18 seconds into her turn, by Marina's count, Octavia was already tapping her shoulder insistently. *That's not good,* Marina lamented. *She's going to need it even sooner next time.* Without delay, Marina took a breath and pulled the mask off. Octavia hungrily pressed the mask to her face, nodding her thanks after it was secured.

They swam steadily, but to Marina's dismay the passage was steeply dropping, with no end to the underwater slope in sight. She heard Octavia murmur something beside her, but when she glanced over, Octavia was staring straight ahead. The light became more irregular ahead. The floor of the pool had become uneven, with large rock formations nearly pinching off the passage in a few places and even some jagged stalagmites obtruding from the ceiling. Jethro and Temeru had slowed their pace. Marina saw why: there were some tight spaces ahead.

It had been 28 seconds, by her count. She tapped Octavia, who quickly relinquished the mask this time. Marina pressed it to her face and breathed the sweet oxygen as soon as she was able, began counting toward the next moment when she would need to give up the lifeline.

"We've got this," she said, giving Octavia a thumbs-up. Octavia nodded in response. *She's holding up okay now. We've going to be okay.* The water was suspended with flaky, dust-like particles. The lichen along the walls was thicker. Marina and Octavia dipped low to clear a pair of stalagmites. Just as Marina counted to fifteen, Octavia squeezed her wrist and pointed at her mask. *What the hell? Yikes, at this rate....* Marina made the switch and felt her panic surge again, so soon after it had subsided. Surely the passage would rise to the surface soon. It had to. Octavia's endurance was quickly diminishing. Perhaps she had never had it to begin with. After all, they had begun the dive in a panic. *I've got to calm down.* But focusing on her need to stay calm only caused her heart to beat still quicker.

As they approached a large boulder, Marina gripped Octavia's tunic so that they could stay close and not put any strain on the oxygen hose between them. As they passed over the boulder, Marina spotted a spiked creature crawling down the rock into a crevice. It looked like a large crustacean and had a blotchy powder-blue pattern on its carapace shell. She glanced over to find out if Octavia saw it, too, but her companion was staring straight ahead. Marina decided against pointing out the animal; she wanted Octavia to be fully focused on moving forward.

They passed through a few more obstructions and Marina tapped for the mask after counting to only 20 seconds this time. *At least we seem to have our rhythm down.* Marina figured they would bottom out around 10 seconds each with the oxygen; she tried to assure herself that they would be good from that point onward.

Octavia was taking longer with her last breath than before, and Marina was struggling by the time she finally had the mask and the water had been sucked out. Thankfully, the passage was finally sloping upward. Their buoyancy would help them rise more quickly than they had descended.

Temeru's light was moving rapidly back and forth. The two men were stopped ahead, no more than 10 meters away. Marina squinted, trying to figure out what was happening. Jethro waved his arms in alarm, pointing at a narrow squeeze in the tunnel. As Marina and Octavia drew close, they could see the reason for Jethro's hesitation. A cluster of the large crustaceans, each about the size of a volleyball, lined the squeeze in the rock. They shook their front appendages at the light rod, and the black eyestalks on top of their heads seemed to glare at the miners. Their segmented abdomens bristled aggressively and the wicked spikes stuck out in all directions. Marina wondered if OreLife had any idea what was thriving down here between the cooling pool and the reservoir on the other side. She doubted that the technicians ever came this far. How else could this little ecosystem get so out of control?

What is Jethro waiting on? There is no choice. We have to go through! Marina thought as they too came to a halt behind the first pair. *It's just a bunch of cranky lobsters!*

Temeru pointed at his wristwatch and then to Jethro's mask. Jethro nodded and his large chest expanded as he took in a deep breath before handing off to Temeru. Octavia also indicated her turn by vigorously shaking Marina's forearm. It had been only 12 seconds this time. The lobsters, as she had begun thinking of them, scooted back and forth across the floor of the passage; a pair also crawled across the ceiling. Even the smaller specimens, no smaller than a fist, joined in the territorial display.

After Octavia frantically placed the mask over her mouth, she didn't wait long enough for the water to exit before taking her breath.

Oh my god.

Octavia choked and instinctively reached for her mask with both hands. Her eyes went wide, and Marina thought she saw all trace of rationality leave them. Marina fought a rising desire to rip the mask away and swim off on her own. *I'm not willing to do that to her just yet*, she told herself. *It can't be far; she can still compose herself in time.* Hiding her inner panic as best she could, Marina reached over to console Octavia. But Octavia, still coughing between short breaths, recoiled from her touch. Her coughing sounded awful underwater. Marina reached out again, much slower this time, and lightly squeezed Octavia's shoulder. She tried to project as much serenity as she could despite the calamity around them. She saw a flicker of hope return to Octavia's eyes, then take hold as her breath steadied. But it had already been 12 seconds, and Marina was close to the end of her own breath.

Suddenly the light became much dimmer; Marina looked over to see what Temeru and Jethro were doing with the crustaceans. Perhaps frustrated with Jethro's hesitation to pass the creatures, Temeru had decided to pass through the squeeze on his own in the middle of his turn. Jethro frantically swam after him, no doubt depleting his breath much more quickly than expected with his sudden explosion in movement. But the crustaceans were having none of this: they stood their ground, and even more defenders scurried out of surrounding crevices. Temeru tried to brush a particularly large specimen out of his way, but it instead latched onto his arm and flexed its body. Temeru cried out in shock and pain as blood streamed, quickly clouding the water. Another crustacean jetted through the water and thrust the spines of its back into his chest. This time Temeru's cry was much more guttural and he swung wildly to knock the animals away. Jethro had caught up by this time and seemed intent on the oxygen while totally ignoring the crustaceans, who all seemed still focused on Temeru. Jethro grasped for the mask as Temeru continued to swing wildly at the bottom of the passage, but all the blood seemed to obstruct Jethro's vision.

Marina could wait no longer; it had been 20 seconds, and she felt light-headed. She tapped Octavia, who looked over from the carnage unfolding mere meters in front of them and held up an index finger to indicate just a little more time with the oxygen. Marina's lungs were bursting. She grabbed for the mask, and Octavia finally relented. Marina blasted her held breath into the mask, gasping for pure oxygen as soon as she could.

Temeru continued to flounder, swirling in his own blood amid circling crustaceans. And Jethro was in trouble. Bubbles streamed from his mouth as he released the last of his breath and lunged for Temeru's mask. The mask came off. "No!" Temeru screamed, the sound garbled underwater. Despite his injuries, he fought back, grappling with Jethro's wrist. They struggled back and forth, and Jethro had the mask nearly against his mouth when Temeru struck him with a free hand. Their struggles incited the crustaceans even more; they bounded off the rocks to gouge both Temeru and Jethro in their legs. Jethro shuddered as he made one last, unsuccessful attempt to pull the mask free. Jethro retched horribly as he sucked water into his lungs while simultaneously trying to expel it in vain. He writhed in agony, and even gaped at Marina and Octavia for some sort of miraculous help. But his struggle quickly ended. Staring at his unconscious form, Marina knew that brain activity would cease in minutes. Temeru finally applied the mask to his face and sucked in several desperate breaths before feebly pulling himself along the floor through the passage and into a wider section. His clothing was shredded, and he bled from several nasty wounds. *He's not going to make it, either,* Marina thought.

Marina's and Octavia's light source was leaving, and their endurance was hanging by a thread: it was now or never. She made and held eye contact with Octavia, trying to surmise if she could be counted on. After having seen what just occurred between Temeru and Jethro, she knew there was mutual mistrust between her and Octavia. But she had to try to help Octavia make it. Marina carried the tank on her back, after all, and Octavia was going nowhere without it.

Marina had lost count of her turn and didn't question the timing when Octavia first pointed and then lunged for the mask. After Octavia had it on, Marina pointed through the bloodied and progressively dimming passage, still lined with the violent creatures, and gave Octavia her most encouraging thumbs-up. In the back of her mind she wondered if anyone would ever discover her fate if she were to die down here. What would her cousins, Carmenta and Sabos, think? Assuming they were alive themselves. And what of her parents? They wouldn't know her fate—only that she had deserted her post and gone missing. They would think she had died with a grudge against them.

Octavia plodded ahead. The crustaceans, seemingly unfocused in their swarming anger, made no move to impede their progress. However, Jethro's body had floated in the middle of the gap, and Octavia frantically pulled him back down the tunnel. Marina nearly collided with his corpse as it drifted by. She got a disturbingly close-up of his vacant expression and bloodshot eyes. Before his body had cleared, Jethro's foot snagged the oxygen hose hard and tugged the mask off Octavia's face. Octavia froze in sudden distress before desperately reaching behind her for the mask. Marina grabbed for it too, but the escaping oxygen made the mask dance through the water unpredictably. They competed for space, and Marina used one arm to hold Octavia back while reaching for the mask. A crustacean floated through the space beside them, its many legs fluttering uselessly for traction, but Marina paid no attention to the lobster-like animal. Octavia kicked off the stone wall to propel herself toward the mask, but Marina was able to reach behind and get a hold of the hose to reel it in. She quickly applied the mask and held it tight as Octavia grappled for it.

"Stop!" Marina screamed into the mask, sending the remaining water sloshing all over the plastic. "You'll kill us both!"

Octavia's eyes were wild behind her goggles. She pressed against Marina's shoulder and tried to pry the mask off with her other hand. Marina felt a rage ignite inside her unlike any passion she had ever felt. She relinquished her tight grip on the oxygen mask and clawed at Octavia's face and throat with both hands. She knew Octavia was going nowhere without the tank strapped to Marina's back. Octavia suppressed a yelp of pain as Marina tore gashes across her cheeks and the side of her neck. Octavia's eyes were now bloodshot and her lips pressed tight and thin. She raked Marina's arms and forehead with her fingernails.

Octavia made one last lunge for the mask. Marina tried to bat her hand aside, but Octavia got hold of the mask and pried it away. Octavia frantically pulled it in, but Marina shot her arms out through the bloodied water and grabbed Octavia's wrists before the other could pull it into place. They briefly made eye contact. Marina saw a mix of fear and anger, and under it all a sense of dread and resignation. In this moment, Marina felt only the demand for survival; for maintaining the spark of life. She pulled the mask free and slammed it onto her face. Octavia threw her head back as she sucked in water, making a gurgling moaning sound that Marina was certain would haunt her the rest of her days. A moment later, the mask had sucked out the water; Marina gasped for air. She wheezed deeply and her heart thudded hard in her chest. She paddled away as Octavia continued to writhe, clutching her chest as she suffocated.

A young life was ending right in front of Marina, and it was a sight she knew would haunt her the rest of her days. "I'm sorry!" she said when she had just enough breath. "I'm so sorry!" She didn't know if Octavia heard her, but couldn't imagine it would be much comfort, anyway. Finally, mercifully, Octavia stopped struggling and became limp.

Marina maintained her distance from the crustaceans as she continued to catch her breath. They seemed to be finally settling down along the rock bottom. *Better stay there, fuckers.* She noticed that Temeru's light was completely gone; her surroundings were lit only by ambient light coming above from the other side of the passage. *I've got to be almost there.*

Just as she started to feel more comfortable breathing, she became aware that something was wrong with the air hose. There was still water in her mask, and the pump apparatus struggled to filter it out. She looked for a tear in the line. It could have happened any number of ways during the struggle. But she couldn't see clearly through the water and the low light. *This day couldn't possibly get any worse*, she lamented. The mask continued to fill with water, and Marina struggled to not inhale it. She reached behind her and opened the valve on the oxygen tank more, but this made no difference. *Shit. There's no time to fix it. I need to make a break for it—now.*

Marina inhaled the very last of the air in the mask through her nose, then ripped both hose and tank off and swam toward the tight pass. There were still several large crustaceans right in the way, but she didn't hesitate. Even as a pair of them gouged her right arm and thigh with their spikes, the pain barely registered. With a few more power kicks, she was through. Her lungs already felt as if they were bursting. She followed the sharp rise in the tunnel and made a beeline for the light source glimmering beyond the surface. It seemed impossibly far ahead. She pulled herself along the bottom of the pool while she kicked. *I'm going to make it—a little more and it will be over.* The tunnel had widened and was clear of any stalagmites or boulders. Marina could see the opening more clearly now. The tunnel appeared to widen into the part of the reservoir that Temeru had told them about. Marina could only vaguely see the stone underneath her and directly to her right; on the other side, the water extended beyond her vision. The light shining beyond the surface showed small waves; the reservoir must have held a large volume. *So close...* The surface represented life itself.

Marina's furious motion had depleted the oxygen in her bloodstream. She released some of the air in her lungs and struggled to hold the rest. How far away was she? It was hard to tell. The light started to dissolve. She was on the cusp of losing consciousness. *No!* She blew out the last of the spent air and realized that she was about to drown. Before, her lungs had throbbed in pain, but now she felt only weakness and lightheadedness. *Don't stop....* As the choppy water of the surface loomed mere meters above her, Marina's vision faded, and she lost consciousness.

Part Two: Crucible

Chapter 17

After her rescuer departed, Lizby squinted under her torchlight as she tried to figure out which tunnel to enter. *No time, got to go.* The smoke from the expanding fires was becoming intolerable. Perhaps this smoke partially explained the absence of other miners—with no upward escape from the Pit floor, most miners would have scattered into the tunnels as the fires grew, probably in the several minutes she was unconscious. *And apparently all the miners that had passed me had written me off as a lost cause.* This realization hurt; the tone of apathy was set. With the exception of her savior with the head wound, she could expect everyone to behave selfishly. Well beyond self-preservation, she expected people would hoard any resources and be reluctant to help their fellow human. If she was honest, she shared this callous—if perhaps necessary—attitude.

As the smoke swept through, Lizby's eyes welled with tears and she coughed through each breath. She tried to cover her face while holding the torch straight. There was no time to carefully consider which tunnel to enter. She headed toward one labeled RA, which she was at least familiar with from an inspection a few months ago. She knew it led deep into the stone. Perhaps one of the branches it intersected would lead her close to the surface.

A few steps in and already the air was far easier to breath. She walked swiftly with the torch outstretched to her side. The flame barely illuminated the tunnel walls and gave her only a few meters of visibility.

She saw nothing of consequence; just the dizzying grooved pattern left by the huge drill rig that had originally dug out this access tunnel. The utilitarian sparseness of the access tunnels had historically been a problem; rookies sometimes got lost for nearly a day because of the lack of any identifiable characteristics, before OreLife noticed they never checked out of the mine and tracked them down. Away from the crackle of the burgeoning inferno, Lizby listened intently for human activity. She didn't hear any voices, no machinery; nothing. Her confidence in her memory of the tunnel's layout faltered now that both the overhead and backup floor lights were out. Additionally, she wasn't seeing any of the characteristics she remembered from before; the large crevices in the tunnel wall, chunks of ore left to crumble on the side of the tunnel floor, or the shallow depressions in the floor. Perhaps she was missing these details because of the poor lighting.

Lizby pushed onward, passing many intersections, and still seeing no clues that jogged her memory. She permitted herself to take a break and collapsed against the wall in exhaustion. She rested long after she had caught her breath, letting her nerves compose as much as possible under the circumstances. Lizby thought of Sabos, Carmenta, and her parents. She pledged to herself and any deity who was listening that she would seek a life of greater purpose after she got through this test. She would love deeper, seek truth, and give more of herself. The sun would shine brighter, even in this perpetually overcast climate. Food would be tastier, water would be more refreshing. *So much I've taken for granted.* She figured that she and Sabos would still leave Sarabek eventually. But until that move came, they would embrace each day instead of enduring it as a stepping stone. At least a half hour passed. Her stress finally lessened from her experience of being trapped, her muscles felt looser, and she knew that if she stayed any longer she would fall asleep. She thought of Sabos once more and rose with purpose. *I bet he's not resting right now—neither can I.*

As Lizby continued, the monotonous grooved pattern of the tunnel walls threatened to dull her concentration and give her fatigue another foothold. But after 10 minutes of travel, her path forked. In one direction, the tunnel straightened along a slight incline, ending in a hinged metal door 20 meters away. *This must be something significant.* She thought the hallway looked familiar, so she chose it, jogging up the incline with renewed energy. She hit the push bar harder than she intended. The door swung open and slammed noisily against the wall. She started to cross into the next room but stopped before she fully cleared the door. Too late; she was exposed—a dark figure was lying in wait on the other side.

Chapter 18

Marina awakened on her side, coughing violently. Water streamed out of her mouth and nostrils. She reflexively sucked in a deep breath, and then coughed again. The glimmer of the water pool beside her and rough rock beneath her reminded her that she had made it on the shore of the reservoir. *I...I'm ALIVE. But how...*

Suddenly there was a heavy hand on her shoulder. "Slow. Take it easy," It was Temeru. "I'm here to help." But Temeru didn't sound well himself. His voice tremored.

"What—" she began, before another round of coughing. When her wheezing subsided, she shook her head as if trying to clear the fog from her mind. Temeru must have dragged her out of the water right after she passed out and surfaced, she surmised. It was the only way she could have survived. Temeru sat next to her, leaning heavily toward one side. His oxygen tank and mask lay near the edge of the pool and his light lay in a dip in the stone. It must have been the light source she'd seen in her near-fatal race for the surface. Otherwise, the chamber was dark.

Temeru was clearly in bad shape. He was covered in blood from a vast array of wounds, including deep stabs and lacerations all along his torso and limbs from the crustaceans. His eyes were unfocused and his lips quivered. Marina wondered how he had enough strength to drag her waterlogged body from the water.

"It all went to shit," the young man lamented. "You saw—I didn't mean to leave Jethro like that. I had too."

"I-I know," Marina gasped weakly. She looked at her arms and legs where the crustaceans had struck her, but the minor wounds already had coagulated enough to stop bleeding. What stung more were the scratches along her neck and brow that Octavia had inflicted. She tried to lean into a crouch but her lungs expelled another spout of water. After she let her breathing acclimate a bit longer, she raised her head and looked around the reservoir. This chamber was possibly even larger than the power station. The pool disappeared around a bend and the walls extended beyond the dim light. Farther up the bank, the rock rose sharply along a craggy contour, but it seemed like there was more space, and hopefully a way out, at the higher elevation.

Temeru groaned and laid down on his back. Marina was finally breathing comfortably and knelt beside him. He was ghastly pale and her hand shook as she touched him, as if she thought he would collapse under the slightest pressure. She couldn't see the source of the bleeding; he was covered in a swirl of blood and water, obscuring the location of his wounds.

"We need to stop your bleeding," she told him. Her pulse quickened as the gravity of Temeru's dire condition overwhelmed her. His entire body glistened with the dark blood. "Do you know, uh, where the worst wound is—so I can apply pressure?"

"No, it feels about the same on all my limbs. My back too," he said weakly. "My whole body feels numb right now, honestly."

"Do you think there might be some toxin involved?" she asked, more concerned about her own wound, if she was honest with herself.

"I don't think so, Marina. Those fuckers just carved me up real good, that's all."

Marina knew he wasn't going to make it, and from the look on the young man's face, he knew it too. "Shit. I don't know what to do, Temeru." She gestured helplessly at his shredded body.

"Th-that's ok," he said, almost a whisper. "Forget me. When you crawl up the bank, I think there are..." He paused to gather his fleeting breath. "Ways out. Up there. I think so."

Marina tried not to show disappointment at his lack of certainty. "Thanks for saving me." Her gratitude sounded so paltry to her own ears. "I owe you my life. I would have drowned."

"You're welcome," he rasped. He lay quietly and his eyes began to close. Marina stoically knelt beside Temeru for the next several minutes as life left him.

Chapter 19

It didn't take Sabos and Carmenta long to find a branching path. Since Carmenta was more familiar with this area of the tunnel, she dismissed the first few intersecting tunnels as dead ends. But as they walked on, her certainty wavered. At first, a scan from the flashlight would reveal the dead ends extending only a few meters from their tunnel. But then they passed the branch that her crew had been most recently been working in. It had proven veins of ore, and she had come here often to service the rigs as they pounded through the rock.

Carmenta paused, trying to remember the mine floor plan. She had been further in the tunnel only a few times, with the last time being several months ago. But without the floor lights to illuminate the tunnel and the usual activities that served as markers, her memory of what lay ahead was hazy. They came upon a branch that Carmenta had hoped led to one of the parallel tunnels going back to the Pit, but when they rounded the first bend, the flashlight revealed that the path sharply narrowed to a point. Another dead end. Both Carmenta and Sabos sighed with disappointment; it was clear that they couldn't count on getting back into the Pit. They returned to the main tunnel in silence.

"So, what now?" Sabos's voice was nearly a whisper.

"I could have sworn...they must have recently closed it off." They leaned heavily against the slight curved tunnel wall.

"OK. What's further on?"

"I'm not sure, Sabos. I was never part of an actual dig this deep. I used to make out with a guy further down, where it was quiet, but the last time we were together was a couple of months ago. I know OreLife has been very aggressive in expanding its outer shafts. But I have no clue if anything ever leads to another part of the mine."

Sabos considered this. "So how far does our main tunnel go?"

"Not much further, but it's possible some of these branches ahead could extend for kilometers." Carmenta reached her hand out for her brother's flashlight, beckoning it. Sabos transferred it to her, and they trudged onward. "We need to explore now when we have our strength."

"So, who was he?"

"Huh?"

"The guy you had snuck off with down the tunnel, to uh, *make out* with."

Carmenta waved her hand dismissively. "Oh, he was the same as the others."

"How so? A pattern, huh?"

"He was not a very kind person," she answered in a distant tone.

Sabos would welcome a distraction during their dire night, but he sensed Carmenta's fling was not the topic to pursue. "We had been very close to leaving Sarabek, you know."

"Yeah, Lizby has mentioned a few places you guys wouldn't mind moving to one day."

"Right, but I mean we were two months, maybe three, from saving up enough to leave."

"Oh." Carmenta sounded genuinely surprised. She faced Sabos and turned the flashlight upward so they could see each other clearly. There was an eerie contrast of light and dark on each of their faces.

"We didn't want to say anything until it was more of a sure thing."

"Oh." Her face first contorted and then lapsed into disappointment. She frowned. "You know, it's not like I would have asked to tag along. Or have asked for more money."

"Of course, Carmenta—I know that. I just didn't want to give you anything else to wonder about. I know you have a full plate. And like I said; it's not a sure thing yet for us."

Carmenta turned around and Sabos followed her deeper into the tunnel. She was silent for several steps. "I have things under control." She sighed. "You can tell me these things, brother. Even if it's not a sure thing."

Sabos wanted to tell her that such issues were between him and his wife. "You're right. Obviously we got other problems right now, but I'll be more candid with you in the future," he said instead.

They trudged on without another word. They passed through another intersection, but a quick scan with the flashlight showed that both directions went nowhere. These short tunnels were filled with dusty, dilapidated equipment. This part of the mine didn't seem to have a lot of recent activity.

"I need to pee," Carmenta said and motioned toward one of the dead ends.

Sabos was left in darkness as Carmenta left to take care of her business. His thoughts were immediately consumed by Lizby. He and

Carmenta were safe for the time being, but his concern for his wife was nearly physically debilitating. It was hard for him to keep his breathing steady. He wanted to scream every few minutes. She could have been lost and alone. Perhaps held captive by soldiers, at the mercy of their savagery. Or very possibly crushed beneath wreckage...

Stop., Sabos ordered himself. *She got to a safe place. We'll find her soon. Tonight, even.*

Carmenta returned. She looked at him, and he felt naked with the turmoil on his face. She grabbed him and they continued further down the main tunnel path. They walked steadily at first, but as time wore on deep into the next hour, they trudged on in disbelief. *Many of tunnels stretch on more than a kilometer,* Sabos thought, *but this is unreal.* During normal operations, he rode swift transport carts under bright lighting when he had to traverse such long tunnels. In contrast, their dimly lit path was seemingly endless.

Carmenta conceded that she was no longer familiar with this sector of the mine. As their sense of disorientation built, Sabos's spirits sank further.

Chapter 20

A pair of eyes glimmered from just a few meters ahead, piercing through the fiery aura of Lizby's torch. She hopped reflexively and narrowly missed the door frame with her head.

A man shrieked. Lizby did too, and jumped again. She didn't recognize him. He was tall, perhaps around her age, and dressed in soldier's gear complete with torso armor and a helmet, though once again she couldn't tell which faction he belonged to based on his uniform.

"Hey!" He pointed at her. "Who are you?" he demanded. Lizby just then noticed that his other hand held a pistol at his hip.

"Lizby. Lizby Sasquire. I'm a miner." To emphasize her cooperation, Lizby widened her hands, showing that she didn't hold any instruments of war. "Do you know what went on out there?"

As the soldier assessed her carefully, sweat beaded down her forehead. *I could have been shot...I could still be shot!* Finally, he loosened his combative stance and carefully holstered the handgun. "Nah, not really. But you're safe now. You're in good hands with our squad. Where did you come from?" The soldier relaxed his posture. He looked back over his shoulder. "Hey, it's okay! We have another civilian."

"Your turn: please tell me who you are." Lizby stepped through the door, letting it close. She was in a narrow room, which tapered to a 3-meter wide point and disappeared around a corner. A collection of pull-carts and cargo lifts lined one side of the room.

"We're the good guys," he quipped. "I asked you where you came from," he added with a hint of impatience.

"Huh?" Lizby was still processing her situation. "I came from the Pit. I followed this tunnel for a while; not exactly sure where I was going. The Pit was on fire and the smoke forced me to leave."

"All right. I'm coming around," a woman's voice echoed from beyond the corner. A glow emerged around the hallway corner and the female soldier emerged, carrying a lantern that bathed the whole room in its vibrant white light. A rifle was slung over her shoulder. She stared at the pair, quickly appraising the situation. She placed a radio to her mouth. "We are all good here. No worries. We're going to bring a miner back...Yes, she's alone."

The man pointed at Lizby. "Wait, what did you say? It's all on fire?"

"Yes, the fire had grown and the smoke was awful. I was pinned under a beam and saw some people from a distance."

She clipped the radio to her waist and threw Lizby an inquisitive look. "Who else did you see?"

"Soldiers, I think—just one or two at a time. One of them helped me get free. Then he left right away."

"Were these Coalition soldiers?" The man asked.

"I don't know. I saw several different people—there could have been both sides, really. It was hard to see clearly." Lizby couldn't recall the insignia of either side, and had no idea how to tell the troops from one faction apart from the other—they spoke the common language and by all accounts shared a similar cultural identity. "Um, you guys are not

Coalition, right...?". Looking at the two soldiers more closely now, Lizby noted that their uniforms were highly specialized. Each piece was nearly pitch-black and seemed unusually personalized with badges and decorative gear such as a shimmering canteen flask and leather gun holsters. The uniforms did not have the battle-weary look she would have expected.

"Hell no!" The woman exclaimed. "Why—do you sympathize with them? Are you a clone-hugger?" She sneered.

"N-no—I just don't know much about the conflict at all. We're kind of at the edge of everything and center of nothing out here. No clones around, and neither army has been here before," Lizby said. The war had previously passed them by, and she truly only knew bits and pieces about the conflict. "Does that mean you guys are part of the Sovereignty?"

The woman glanced knowingly at the other soldier. "More or less," she said. "We work alongside the Sovereignty. We're our own professional entity."

"Sooo...you're mercenaries?" Lizby asked warily.

Another significant look between the two soldiers. "Yep, but don't be so scared of the word," the man said, pointing at one of the more prominent badges on his chest. "We're the Badgers."

Lizby struggled to recall what a badger was. She thought she had read once that a badger was a carnivorous mammal. She got closer to get a better look at the insignia on the man's chest. It indeed showed a furry creature, with a ferocious expression and bullets for teeth. The words "never back down" and "no mercy" were etched underneath the creature. Looking closer, she noticed that the badger's eyes consisted of human skulls. *Bizarre...*

"June, can you escort her back?" the man motioned Lizby to walk through. "I'm supposed to stay on the perimeter here."

"Sure, Portals. By the way, it sounded like she snuck up you. Are you sure you got this?" June mocked.

"Go, I got it," Portals shooed them onward. "She walked in without a sound; like a ninja." Portals explained.

"But with a torch, though?" June chided.

"Goddamnit, June. I saw her before she saw me. I was just surprised to see another one. And I did my job, didn't I? I raised the alarm, and I didn't shoot her."

"Just be careful. We have no idea how many Coalition clone-huggers snuck down before the mine collapsed. And they could have agents that were here before that, dressed as civilians..."

Lizby and June had started down the hall toward the next chamber, but now Portal's and June's eyes fell on her with blatant suspicion. June lifted the lantern up toward Lizby.

Lizby tried to casually lean against the wall. She laughed nervously. "Well, that's not me. I'm not ambitious enough to get into the whole espionage business." Their stares lingered on her. *Shit, that didn't sound right.* "Look at me; I'm clueless. Ask me anything." She again laughed, almost to herself.

Portals' serious stare suddenly dissolved. "Nah, I'm not worried about this one," he said while waving them along. "Good luck, Lizby."

"Thanks," Lizby murmured. She wondered how serious they were about miners serving as spies for the rival Coalition army. Were they messing with her, or were they really so paranoid? If the latter was the case, then had they really tempered their suspicions about her?

June led her past the corner to another hallway. There were men's and women's restrooms along the sides. June sensed her attention. "Do you need to go?" June asked.

"Yes, I do."

"Actually, I need to bring you to the Captain first, then you can go in a little bit. When you do, don't flush."

"Don't these restrooms still have water? And are there sinks with drinkable water?"

"They do for now, at least. But we don't know how much we got left."

"Ok, I won't try to flush, I guess."

"Cool."

They passed through another door, and the hallway opened to a large chamber. Lizby took in the depth of the room, and the mix of cave-like and man-made features, and it dawned on her where they were. It was a sort of way station for miners, a place to store equipment and sometimes excess ore, but also to rest and eat meals. The complex had a break room, supply closets, and rows of man-sized, spiral drill heads that lined the wall. It was a logical refugee for any miners trapped in this sector of the mine. She was optimistic she could find help here; at the very least, some supplies such as water and food; perhaps even Carmenta or Sabos.

There was a circle of lantern illuminating the center of the space, with the edges of the expansive chamber shrouded in darkness. Piles of unprocessed rock crowded the far side of the room. A short building housing the break room had been erected on the edge of the chamber. It looked quaint and odd against the backdrop of the cavernous stone wall that rose above it. She could see seven Sovereignty mercenaries standing amongst the lanterns, taking casual interest as she and June walked toward them. To her pleasant surprise, she saw at least a dozen miners in an area of equipment lockers that was offset into the wall as an alcove. Most were crouched against the wall and several talked casually on a bench. They had a single lantern in the center of the lockers that brightly lit their space. Lizby scanned the miners frantically, but to her dismay, saw neither Sabos nor Carmenta.

As June led Lizby into the glow of the lanterns, all eyes turned to her. The torch in her hand felt odd.

June outstretched her arm toward Lizby. "Lizby claimed to have wandered in from the Pit. She said the fires had gotten worse. She escaped and came here alone."

One of the mercenaries stepped through the center of the lanterns and offered his gloved hand to Lizby, along with a photogenic smile.

"Hello Lizby. I'm Captain Halion. I lead this bunch." His grip was overly firm. Like half of the other soldiers, he wore a cap instead of a helmet. He had a thick and neatly kept beard. She thought the gear adorning his vest appeared top-notch, some of which she couldn't even name. "We can take that torch off your hands. We have the ability to start another fire, and as you can see, we have plenty of light in the meantime."

"Sure. I kind of forgot I was even holding it," Lizby said. Another mercenary stepped forward and took Lizby's torch before extinguishing it on the stone floor.

Halion gestured diplomatically with his arms opened. "I know this whole situation is a pain in the ass for you and your fellow miners. You guys have nothing to do with this operation. But I need you to bear with us and stay here, so we can ensure your safety. We don't want to blindly run into you in the tunnels. That could be dangerous if you can imagine, right?"

"Yeah, I could see that." *I don't feel like I'm getting a choice in this matter,* Lizby realized.

"Good," Halion motioned to the locker alcove. "So have a seat and relax. We have plenty of water as well as some food from the break room that we're rationing. This will all be over soon. Just let me or one of my people know if you have a need." He started to turn away.

"Um, Captain? I've been looking for some miners."

Captain Halion turned back around, with a trace of annoyance creeping into his overly composed posture. Lizby spoke up so everyone in the chamber could hear. "My husband, Sabos and his sister, Carmenta. I'm asking if anyone has seen them." She described their appearances in detail, but none of the miners or mercenaries perked up as she spoke. By the end of her description they all just shook their heads.

"Has anyone seen the miners this woman has described?" Halion asked. Again, shaking heads and a chorus of *no*.

“Sorry, Lizby.” Halion sounded sincere. “It’s a big mine, though. Plenty of places for them to seek refuge. We’ll keep our eyes peeled, of course, and bring them in safely if we encounter them.”

“Thank you, Captain,” Lizby mumbled. Dejected, she found a spot to sit among the miners. They acknowledged her politely. Lizby took a second look at them. There were thirteen miners. She guessed that they worked in a specific portion of the mine since she didn’t recognize any of them. Most seemed very stressed or tired, but none were seriously injured. One middle-aged man met and then held her gaze with a quizzical tilt to his head.

“Hey, I recognize you. I’ve seen you around in the control room,” He extended his hand and she shook it slowly, trying to recall his face. Despite being at least 20 years older than her, his keen eyes shone with vitality, and his slightly wrinkled skin seemed to ripple with charisma. “I’m Mathias." The man smiled warmly and leaned back against one of the lockers.

“Sorry, I can’t place you. OreLife is a big outfit, you know? What’s your job?”

“I’m on the mine survey team. For the most part, I spend the day in the tunnels that have the newest digs underway. Or in the surface control room studying charts,” Mathias said.

“Oh, I see. You are part of the tip of the spear; I’m sure you see it all. I’m part of Inspections. Or Quality Control, technically." Lizby grinned. “Notice we’re using the present tense? Like our jobs will still be around after what happened today?”

"Oh, you never know. Maybe OreLife will cut its losses and move on, but with so much of the mineral down here, someone else is bound to clean things up and resume operations." Mathias took his eyes away from her and observed the movements of the mercenaries with a wary look. "So you came from the Pit, huh? I was in the tunnels when all this chaos was dumped on us. What happened out there?"

"Well, first I hear an alarm. I run out of my tunnel to find out that there is a battle closing in around the mine. Then soldiers showed up in the main lift; not even sure if they were Coalition or Sovereignty. Or maybe some others were already here by coming down the equipment lifts. But that's just me speculating. The soldiers I saw come down the main lift fanned out along the center of the Pit, and then a gunfight broke out." Lizby paused when she noticed that all thirteen of the miners and some of the closest mercenaries were listening intently. Mathias's eyebrows were stretched with intrigue, and some of the miners scooted closer.

Having the large audience was unsettling, but she had nothing to hide, so she continued. "Uh, right before the fight broke out I saw some gunmen dressed as miners. They seemed to be coming from the interior of the mine. This gunfight breaks out and I'm huddled, trying not to get shot. Then there is a huge roar as debris crashes in from above. Everything goes dark, and then I myself go dark," Lizby voice rattled at the memory, and she decided to summarize the ordeal as succinctly as possible. "I woke up trapped by wreckage. The fire was getting worse and the smoke was just..." her voice broke, as she remembered the helpless feeling of being trapped by the fire. "...intolerable. But I got free. I couldn't even see portions of the Pit because they were blocked off by wreckage. Almost everyone had scattered, most before I even woke up. So I got the hell out too."

Mathias shook his head. "That's crazy. We all agreed to be part of the skeleton crew, I know. But there was nothing to suggest that the battle was coming inside the mine, of course. The only warnings I heard from OreLife were about our supply lines being disrupted and travel being restricted."

Lizby nodded. She anticipated more questions from Mathias, but he sat silently. When the mercenaries who had drawn close to listen walked away, he finally spoke quietly. "I don't like this setup we have with the mercs, Lizby. None of us do. They insist on escorting us to the restrooms; they've restricted our access to the break room and the other exits. This cramped equipment locker area is what we're confined to." Lizby raised an eyebrow in concern. Mathias continued with a tone appropriate for whispered conspiracy. "They're pleasant enough right now. But that's because they feel like they're in control. The shared supplies have yet to be squeezed, and no one is complaining–yet. But just watch."

"It's not ideal, I guess. But you really think it's going to get nasty with these guys?" Lizby missed Mathias' initial calming presence.

"I hate to predict doom and gloom; I really do. I like to envision the best in people and then pursue that," Mathias' eyes held steady with conviction. "I don't know these mercenaries really well, but I do know people. And I know the situation we find ourselves in, and it's not good.

It's just a matter of time before all of these people, in these circumstances, succumb to a state of nastiness."

"I don't know. They seem quite reasonable to me."

"Because they have no reason not to be. Yet."

"So why not leave?"

"No one has pressed the issue yet, but as you heard Captain Halion say, they aren't too keen on us wandering around the mine."

"Do you think they would stop us from leaving? As in shoot us?"

"I doubt it would escalate to that extreme right away. But they would probably respond with some sort of force." Mathias reflected for a bit, and then lowered his voice so none of the other miners could hear. "Of course, you have this need to find your loved ones. But if you seem too eager to bolt right away, these mercs will be suspicious and watch you like hawks. I recommend you stay and wait for a bit, at least while things are still civilized. That's what I'm going to do. You are more than welcome to join me at the opportune time. If we wait until they sleep, then maybe we can slip away before—"

"Hold on, I don't know if that's—"

"Lizby, I've talked to most of these miners and they all seem willing to put their fate in someone else's hands. But I've survived through ordeals out in the frontier far worse than this war, if you can believe it. I know better, now. Don't be like them. You need to plan for when things fall even further apart." Mathias crossed his arms with a confidence that suggested that the case was closed.

Lizby was flustered. "Hey, don't get ahead of me here. You've only been here maybe a couple of hours, right? And you are already inciting distrust in the wake of this disaster? The soldiers aren't here to harm us," Lizby said. In her effort to talk quietly, her words came out in a venomous hiss.

Mathias glowered. "How can you be so naive? And don't call them soldiers. They're Sovereignty mercs. They're not exactly known for their selflessness."

Lizby paused before responding. *It's been such a stressful day. I just don't feel like arguing.* "Thanks for your advice, but I would probably stay anyway in case Sabos or Carmenta came by this place," she said, softer this time.

"Whatever." Mathias snapped, turning away from her.

What is with this guy? So intense. Her face flushed with annoyance.

"Mathias, chill out; I just got here. I need to—"

Mathias was shaking his head fervently. "Time is not a luxury that—"

"I just meant that there is no reason to—"

"Do what you think best," Mathias mood suddenly shifted toward indifference and his eyes stared vacantly. "But time will reveal everyone's truest, deepest *colors*," he exaggerated this last word as he looked up toward the ceiling. The light reached just far enough to etch the profile of massive stalagmites. Mathias' words hung in the air cryptically.

Lizby felt like she had emotional whiplash from Mathias' initially cordial advice followed by his terse rebuke. *Well, I'm uncomfortable already. Maybe the rest of the miners are sane,* she hoped. She turned away and scanned the room. Although the floor had been smoothed out, the ceiling had either originally been part of a cave pocket or had since formed stalagmites due to groundwater leakage and lack of maintenance. A pair of mercs walked away from the others with a lantern. As they neared the wall, they lit an exit that was on the opposite side of the room where Lizby had entered. A thick set of double doors was labeled "Tunnels TN–TZ". The mercs exited with a rusty squeak, and a minute later a different pair of mercs returned.

Conscious to avoid Mathias' gaze, Lizby glanced at the other miners. They seemed bored and listless. Although her arrival had sparked their interest briefly, she was now just another survivor waiting for rescue. If anyone was deeply unnerved by the day's events, they weren't showing it. It was possible that they had been sheltered away from the carnage in the deep tunnels, and so never felt overly threatened during the mine collapse around the Pit. They talked quietly, already formed into pairs or trios. She'd get to know them in a little bit, but for now, she just wanted to rest and allow her brain to make sense of things. For perhaps the first time since the alarm first announced the battle at their doorstep, Lizby's heartbeat slowed to a state of rest, and she allowed her guard to drop. But she was far from relaxed. She thought of Sabos and Carmenta, and wondered how she was going to be able to sit still here in the hope that they somehow were on their way to the chamber. Her alertness gave way to anxiety as her concern for them twisted insider her ever stronger.

Chapter 21

After hours of limping through the darkness, Gerund was still unsure of the vastness of his rubble enclosure. He navigated a labyrinth of collapsed structures, colliding with stray beams and mining equipment. At times, obstructions hung from above and he had to crawl underneath, scraping his palms and knees on bits of loose rock and metal where wreckage had blocked off the rest of the mine. He rationed his remaining water but his thirst tormented him relentlessly.

Gerund's discipline had been his sustaining force during his years with the Coalition, and even as it threatened to erode, his fearless condition helped him stoically focus on the facts of his survival. Gerund no longer thought of his mission, nor of the larger war that had consumed his life the past few years. He didn't care about clone legislation, clone rights, and associated economic ramifications. He wasn't concerned about taking down the governments of the Sovereignty. He just wanted out of this purgatory. In his trudge through the wreckage, Gerund had lost all sense of how far he had traveled. He speculated that he had plodded into the next day. He was exhausted.

Suddenly, Gerund stumbled over something heavy. He recovered before completely falling. *That wasn't wreckage. That was something...meaty.* Imagining the worst, Gerund knelt and tentatively reached out. Thick fabric, and then the distinct, empty feeling of a cold corpse. From this first frigid touch, Gerund knew that the person had been dead for hours. He reluctantly felt down the limb. *A leg*. The leg was of medium girth and was bent at an unnatural angle—a bone was badly broken. If this person hadn't died right at the collapse, they would have been completely immobile. He felt around the midsection and determined that the body belonged to a woman. Reaching a little further, Gerund discovered that she lay face down with a heavy beam crushing her lower back. He hoped it had been a quick death. *Are you from my Coalition battalion? Do I know you?*

Gingerly, he felt along the woman's features to see if he could form a mental image that resembled any of his comrades. The cold skin, taut and unrevealing under Gerund's worn hands, failed to give any clues to the woman's identity. The structure of her jaw, nose, and bony shoulders suggested a gaunt appearance, but this didn't jog Gerund's memory. She didn't have any noteworthy objects in her pockets or on her belt, and the generic design of the jumpsuit uniform could have belonged to any number of support roles from either army. Something jangled from her neck. *Wait, is that a dog tag?* Gerund paused. Deeply ingrained procedure dictated that he should have left the tags on the body. But he was more than curious to find out who the deceased woman was, should he find a light source later. *If I have the vision to see it, that is.* He pulled the dog tags over her head and stuffed them into his pocket. However, he felt a pang of guilt as he stood. *Come on, put it back.* The woman deserved to be identified. He might not make it out alive to tell the tale himself. He carefully wrapped the dog tags back around her neck and straightened her hair.

Wishing more than anything for a second of sight, Gerund drifted away without knowing if this woman was someone he knew.

Alternatively, she could have been one of the enemy. She was so serenely still; so non-threatening in death. So often his unit sought to crush their Sovereignty adversaries. It was hard to be certain in the mayhem of battle, but Gerund suspected he had contributed to the deaths of several Sovereignty opponents in earlier campaigns. The killing had seemed almost abstract then. *Always at a distance, too. And I've never had to confront the aftermath.* After literally stumbling across a pathetic body that might belong to the Sovereignty, the thought of the enemy's losses today brought no sense of progress—only a shared sense of loss. He realized that the Sovereignty troops were in the same situation as the Coalition survivors; most probably just wanted to survive this disaster and one day return to their families.

His shoulder brushed hard stone. *What the?!* He reached out and discovered a wall of stone. He stretched to his full length and found that the wall extended beyond his reach. He took a step in the opposite direction until he found another wall no more than 3 meters away. *This must be a tunnel—perhaps some good fortune at last...*Gerund slumped against the wall, wondering what he should do. At the very least, this was new territory with the possibility for some sort of relief and perhaps even the hope of escape. On the other hand, the tunnel brought new potential dangers, not the least of which was getting lost inside and too weak to find his way back out, away from the main Pit and the most likely location of any rescue attempt.

He decided to press onward, tracing the side of the tunnel with his hand. But after only a few minutes, the tunnel path remained the same. *How long does this tunnel go on?* For all he knew, it could carve several kilometers into the stone. Gerund felt his strength drain.

Finally, Gerund had to stop—he needed to rest his leg and sleep. He collapsed against the wall and was soon unconscious.

His sleep was fitful. He languished in a semi-conscious state with half his mind trying to surrender to much-needed rest and the other half shadowed by the stress of the battle and mine collapse.

After what seemed an eternity, Gerund clawed out of his sleepy delirium. He willed himself to stand, but was still dreadfully tired and even more clueless as to time's passage. His throat was parched and he reached for his canteen. In his powerful thirst he sucked in more than he intended. Gerund capped the canteen and shook it in frustration—there were only a few sips left. He touched the wound on his brow; it was now crusted over with dried blood. His leg felt more stable now but was deeply sore. He continued along the tunnel.

He traveled perhaps 50 meters, encountering nothing but heavy dust, but soon felt the terrain change. Where before the stone floor was smooth—almost polished—now it was scored with long grooves that were carved parallel with the tunnel. The slope steadily descended into a lower area of the mine.

Gerund wondered if any of the Coalition troops had made it this deep into the mine. *I'll risk the enemy hearing me—I've got to try to find somebody.* But Gerund suppressed the urge to shout out, as he had for the past day. The prospect of coming across a foe seemed just as likely as stumbling by a friendly survivor. This new passage didn't change that calculation.

He pressed on and gave in to outrageous fantasies. He envisioned deep fountains with cool, trickling pools; water so plentiful that he could fully submerge in it. He imagined refreshing iced drinks with hints of berries and other fruits. Almost immediately he regretted this indulgence of thought. His mouth parched at the thought of water flowing into it and he forced himself to abstain from the remainder of his canteen. But Gerund had little doubt that biology would trump willpower and he would deplete it within the next day.

What happened to everyone? There must be more survivors. There were perhaps hundreds of personnel within the Pit's perimeter, and an unknown number that had actually entered the mine. Yet Gerund had not found anyone alive in the past day except for the unknown man he had tangled with. As far as the rest of the universe was concerned, he was dead and buried. And as far as he knew, nearly all the people in his new unit were dead in the wreckage above, all of them far from home. This thought permeated his chest with a piercing ache.

Gerund yearned for the faintest glimpse of light. As he trudged on, a faint thud interrupted Gerund's thoughts. His ears perked up. *Did I just imagine that?* he considered. Again he heard the distant sound. *I'm really hearing that... Maybe it's just the wreckage settling and creaking out there in the Pit.* Gerund sat completely still, careful to not disturb any rock debris. He held his breath so he could listen in complete stillness, and heard the thud again. This time he was able to discern the direction it came from. Charged with alert energy, Gerund scurried down the decline while feeling along the uneven mine tunnel wall with his right arm. He didn't hear the sound, but soon his hand floated across an opening. He nearly stumbled in surprise.

Gerund walked through a stone doorway and immediately noticed a change in his footing—the floor was covered with smooth tile. He discovered that the ceiling was low enough that he could raise his arms halfway up before touching it. He stayed right, tracing the wall with his hand. He encountered a corner after only 10 meters in. He traced the next wall before banging his knee against a metal panel. He patted down the object. It felt like a heavy metal cabinet. He felt in front and found several drawers—all locked. Trays filled with a metallic-smelling liquid covered the top of the chest-high cabinets. Gerund felt along the wall and found a vertically tiled surface and piping. His hand followed the piping up to what felt like a showerhead. *What?* A mere meter further down the wall, and he felt another faucet and a handle. His confusion was short-lived as the thought clicked: a pair of emergency showers. He fantasized about taking a warm shower to remove his funk, almost forgetting his more obvious need of his thirst. He followed the pipe up until it ended in a cylindrical storage tank mounted high on the wall. A quick knock confirmed his dread. Empty. *What kind of operation is this—no water for the emergency shower? Maybe this isn't an active tunnel...*he reasoned.

On the next wall, he found a workstation. There were various odd-feeling tools adorning the entire height of the wall above a metal desk and a rickety, dusty wooden stool. On the desk, there were small bits of rocks in several bins. As best as he could speculate by touch alone, the tools may have been intended for extracting smaller samples from ore. He made a few passes across the center of the room, only to determine that the middle space was empty.

"Well, this sucked," he said aloud. He had at least hoped for some supplies. The sound he had heard was just another dead end in his journey.

His frustration was short lived—he heard the sound again, this time higher-pitched, and echoing from the far wall. Gerund's mouth quivered as he resisted the impulse to call out. He had so far maintained the discipline to keep quiet in the many hours before. Whoever making the sound could have been an ally or even a miner. However, it could just as likely been the Sovereignty—perhaps a squad executing wounded Coalition soldiers throughout the bowels of the mine. As the war had intensified in the past year, reports of executions on the front line became more frequent. Commanders from both sides often turned a blind eye to such brutality, or even tacitly encouraged such violence. Perhaps the enemy had hired a heartless group of mercenaries to have some hunting practice with their blind targets down in the mine.

The pings continued frequently over the next minute, often only a second between. Gerund was not deterred enough by the plausible dangers that could have been causing the sound—the desperation of his situation overcame his remaining caution. *I have no food, almost no water—I need to find someone.* Gerund approached the far wall, which was lined of cabinets. Another series of the ping, and he knelt down to track it. *This doesn't make sense,* he thought, frustrated. He dipped his head lower, and the echo led him to an open space where the lowest drawers of the cabinet should have been. His excitement spiked; overcoming his weary spirit. He felt a large gap in the floor—it was a way out.

Chapter 22

Sabos and Carmenta pressed on through the sparse tunnel. They came upon three derelict drill rigs with large numbers painted on the side; most likely maintenance reference numbers for each rig's malfunction.

"Is this not an active tunnel?" Sabos asked. "Are we going to reach something more than a dead end?"

"Parts of this tunnel are active, but some branches are dead ends because the ore veins went dry almost immediately. If we keep going, I hope we'll come across a main branch that will take us back to the Pit. That's our best chance for finding Lizby."

"If there's anything left of the Pit..." Sabos said in frustration.

"How are we going to get to the surface if the Pit is inaccessible?"

"I don't know, Sabos. I guess we'll just have to find ways to survive for a while," Carmenta sighed in exasperation.

"I know, I know; you don't have the answers. I just want to be sure that we're sharing the same gameplan. Which as I understand it is to keep walking and hope for the best."

"Right," Carmenta agreed halfheartedly. "Hopefully along the way we'll find someone who knows some details and can help."

Or kill us, Sabos thought.

They passed through a widened section of the tunnel that was partially filled with unprocessed ore and had to walk gingerly through the chunks that littered their path. Sabos was startled by a sudden whoosh of fluttering bodies and high-pitched, piercing squeaks. Strong, velvety wings beat against his face. He recoiled and ran away in a panic. Carmenta was equally startled and chased after him. Sabos's flashlight swung wildly as he charged around a narrow bend in the passage.

"Sabos! It's just the bats!" Carmenta yelled just as he started to process this information himself. "Wait!"

However, before he was able to stop, he heard Carmenta gasp. He swung the flashlight around just in time to see her stumble below a jutting rock in the tunnel wall and collapse with a dazed expression on her face.

"Carmenta!" His heart sank as he rushed to her side.

Chapter 23

Marina rested by Temeru's body, at first to recuperate after her near-drowning, but then it felt somehow inappropriate to leave her rescuer so soon after he had bled to death. She searched his body, taking the light rod, of course, but also found a half-filled lighter. She sat with his body and contemplated what was ahead of her. Would she find miners recovering from the disaster, or would she be entering a warzone as the miners had described, where both the Coalition and Sovereignty had reason to shoot her should her identity become known? While she wished she could stay by the quiet lapping of the coolant pool, she climbed up the embankment and left the reservoir through the sole exit.

Marina wandered the snaking passageway until it branched off. She made no attempt to keep track of which paths she took in the maze of turns that followed. Her forearm and thigh wounds from the crustaceans ached but she hoped the cuts would be okay since they weren't very deep, provided they didn't become infected.

Having escaped death twice in the past 24 hours, each breath entering her lungs was like a rebirth. *I'll never take life for granted again, I swear. I'm going to reconnect with my family. I'm going to do all the things I've wanted to try, not what I'm expected to do.* Her renewed vitality was tempered by the horror of the day. She put one foot in front of the other as if the distance covered could somehow separate her from the recent traumatic experiences. However, Titus' weakening words,

Octavia's terrorized eyes, and Temeru's ghastly blood kept cycling through her thoughts.

The light rod gradually dimmed and now flickered sporadically. Her feet sloshed uncomfortably in her soggy boots. *Just my luck*, Marina thought, recalling her trek through the moonlight pools during her escape from her Coalition base. *Wet feet two days in a row.* She had only the vaguest sense of her location within the mine complex. She strived to travel in the same direction but wasn't even sure if she was heading slightly downhill or slightly uphill toward the surface. She wondered if the surface was even accessible beyond the main lifts. She couldn't recall enough details about the mine layout from her rushed conversations with Carmenta. And there had been no time to sightsee on the way in.

Carmenta...I need to see this through for her. I owe her at least that much for sticking her neck out for me. A day ago Marina had imagined her future, far away from here, perhaps playing in concert hall or even starting a family. She had been so close to sustained purpose and peace. But it had all fallen away so quickly. *What a fool I've been*, she lamented. Now that she had been stripped of her plans, she struggled to imagine what form her future could take. She was estranged from most of her family; reconciling with them was the immediate goal once she got out of this mess—she had promised herself that much in the underwater cavern. But beyond that, she wasn't sure. She wasn't religious, either. She didn't yearn for a conversion or a cause if she happened to get out alive. For now, seeing this debacle to the end solely because her family deserved some answers would have to be sufficient.

Marina paused at yet another fork in her path. The light rod flickered rapidly and she lightly shook it. It made a crinkling sound and held steady, albeit even dimmer than before. She took the fork that she could only hope was closer to the Pit.

Marina recalled when she had gotten lost in the woods at age ten. She had taken a rare trip with her parents, back when they were still maintaining a semblance of a happy family. It wasn't quite a vacation in her mind; merely a day trip to the overcrowded forest preserve with a train ride just long enough to convince her childlike naivety that there must have been a great destination at the end of the line to justify sitting in the rickety train car so long.

She had wandered off to complete her checklist of local animals, shrugging off her parents' warnings of lost children who had died of exposure and dehydration as part of their overprotective nature. She was ten at the time after all; she *knew* what she was doing. Marina remembered the horrid feeling as she realized she had successfully ducked her parents but was completely lost. She had cried out until she was hoarse and then tried to climb a tree to get a better vantage point. She decided to head straight in one direction in hopes of finding a road or someone to help. After half a day of hiking alone through the rough terrain both her young legs and mind were ready to give up as the sun began to set.

As the tears of defeat had welled up in her, a woman's voice called out to her from the bluff behind her. This friendly rock climber quickly reassured that she was safe and would help Marina find her family. Before they set out to the nearest trail, the woman emphasized with her plight as a lost child who had overestimated her independence, as if anticipating the embarrassment and doubt she might have felt in the wake of the ordeal. She had not only provided safety to Marina, she made her *feel* safe and left her dignity intact. When finally reunited with her parents, they had been too relieved to question her earlier foolishness.

Marina smiled at the bittersweet memories from that trip, and forged ahead through the bare tunnel. She may have lost her way in life, but if she could make it through this ordeal, she knew she could find it again.

"Hey!"

The shout from behind made her jump. Too late, she saw the aura of another light bleeding into her path. She turned around to face two men in camouflage uniforms with their rifles equipped and raised to her midsection.

"Hold it! Show me your hands!" It was hard to see their features behind the light. She managed to glimpse their official Coalition insignia. They weren't mercs, at least.

Marina slowly complied. "Hello." She tried not to show her fear.

"Civilian?" One of them asked the other.

"She has to be. Looks like what the miners wear."

"Please, I'm not part of any of this," Marina exclaimed.

"What?"

"I'm a miner; I don't know what's going on with the fighting."

The men grunted but lowered their weapons. They seemed almost disappointed that she wasn't an adversary. One slung his rifle back over his shoulder while the other peered warily beyond Marina.

"Are you alone? What are you doing?"

"I, uh, dig in a different area. I escaped from the powerplant and now I'm lost." She figured it was prudent to provide the soldiers with at least some of the truth.

The light swept up and down her mining uniform.

"We're with the Coalition. We saw your light at the last intersection and followed it. What was in the direction you came from? And why are you wet?"

"There were a lot of different paths to take. But I lost track. I didn't see much besides some rock piles and some tools here and there." The men stared at her expectantly. "Oh, and I had to swim under the power plant cooling pool. That's why I'm soaked."

The men whispered back and forth beyond her earshot.

"Can you gentlemen tell me what is in the direction you came from?"

"Gentlemen?!" one of them scoffed.

The other jerked a thumb backward, "That turn last back there? We came from the right. The rest of our group is gathered there. Our commander asked us to recon in this direction."

"Oh." Marina wondered if there was any chance she could pass through without being discovered. The stakes were too high; if they detained her, they would inevitably come across the Sovereignty mark on her neck.

"Why don't you follow us up there? That will get you closer to the upper levels of the mine, if that's where you need to go. It's a bit a chaotic now, honestly. There is no contact with the rest of the task force."

"Thank you, but I think I'll be fine on my own."

"Huh? Really?" one said incredulously. He then whispered into his partner's ear, eyeing her suspiciously.

"Yes, good idea," he said, and pointed the flashlight at Marina. "Can you show us the base of your neck, please? It's just procedure." He chuckled nervously. "I really doubt you're a spy."

I'm not! But how can I refuse?! Marina felt her face flush and her ears get hot with distress. The tattoo would unveil her. Maybe they would treat her more favorably as a deserter than if they thought she was a spy. But she didn't know if she could convince them, and she didn't want to find out.

"Oh, okay...but why do you want to see my neck?" She made no movement to adjust her uniform's collar.

Her hesitation triggered the already wary soldier, and his comrade suddenly took a grimmer interest in their civilian guest. "Just a precaution. So we can tell our commander we were thorough." The men stepped closer. *What can I do?*

"Of course," Marina agreed, slowly reaching for her collar to pull it down. Then her face fell. There was no way to explain herself to these men. Who knew what they would do? *Their orders might be to shoot on sight. Hell, they might not even need orders to do that. No one would even know what happened down here.* She gathered a deep breath. "It's not what you think; it's never so simple."

The men cocked their heads in perplexed expressions, and then she darted around the bend in the tunnel.

"Wait! Stop!" they shouted after her.

Of course, there was no turning back. She ran as fast as her depleted energy would allow. Her light revealed only two meters in front of her path, and her brain only had a moment to process before she stepped into what had just been dense darkness a split second before. Marina looked back as the pair of shadows loomed over her. *I'm not going to be taken alive*, she asserted. *But do I even have control of that?*

"Last chance! Stop!"

"She must be Sovereignty; a clone-killer!"

She found one last gear as she imagined the bullets tearing toward her. She held her breath for the gunshots, but they didn't come. Instead, the ground vanished beneath her and she plummeted into the darkness.

Chapter 24

Sabos knelt by Carmenta and checked her head. She was unconscious and her scalp was wet with blood. For a dazed moment, Sabos stared at the wound, all his sister's possible complications flooding his thoughts. He snapped out of it and used his jacket to apply pressure to the wound, which looked nasty but upon closer examination didn't seem to be bleeding much.

"Carmenta?! Wake up. I'm here," he said as he inclined her head slightly. "Come on sis, you need to wake up so I know you're going to be all right."

For several horrific minutes, Sabos got no response from her. If she couldn't be moved, what could he do in this mine tunnel, totally alone? The feeling of helplessness was debilitating.

Finally, to his relief, her eyes fluttered and she stirred onto her side with a moan. He maintained pressure on her wound even as she tried to brush his arm away. *Thank the gods—I thought I had lost her.*

"Carmenta, it's okay. Hey—stop. I'm just trying to stop the bleeding."

"What?"

"You hit your head on the wall somehow. Take it easy."

"The flashlight—get it out of my face," she slurred.

"Of course, sorry." Sabos gave her space as she managed to sit up and apply pressure on her wound herself, but then she became unbalanced and nearly fell back down. “Woah, easy. You were out for just a few minutes. We were running from the bats.”

“Bats...oh yes,” she said, with some clarity returning in her voice. “Actually, you were running from them and I was trying to keep up with you.”

“Whatever. They were freakish,” Sabos said, allowing himself a little smile. “How do you feel?”

“My head throbs but I don’t think it’s too deep of a cut,” Carmenta tenderly felt her scalp. “I just need to rest here for a while.”

“Of course. I don’t think waiting for a bit is going to change our situation. We won’t get going until you are ready.”

Carmenta didn’t respond and Sabos wondered if she was going to lose consciousness again. Instead, she sighed deeply. *Something else besides the disaster has been troubling her*, he realized.

“Sabos, I need to tell you something.”

He was both relieved and worried. “What’s been troubling you?”

“You...I need you to understand that this wasn’t something I planned. I—I just wanted to help out, and she didn’t really give me much choice anyway.”

“What are you talking about? Who didn’t?”

Carmenta sat up fully. “Our cousin Marina. She’s here.”

“Marina?!” Sabos was shocked at the mention of their cousin. “Marina is fighting here with the Sovereignty? Was she part of the battle?”

"I mean she's here; down in the mine. She left her base—she deserted, and I brought her into the mine to hide as part of the workforce. I didn't—"

"What?! She's a deserter now?!" Sabos pulled at this hair anxiously. "And you helped her?

Carmenta nodded solemnly. "People saw her go into my apartment, so I didn't think it was safe to leave her there, in case the Sovereignty tried to track her down in Haast. She had a forged ID that could pass her off as a miner. She just placed it in one of my spare OreLife badges and got access to the mine with no problem. Sabos, we had no idea that the battle would come right over the mine."

"You were seen with her! Do you have any—"

Of course; I know it's a big deal, Sabos," Carmenta snarled even as she sucked in breath. "She contacted me on the net. She mentioned all the stress, and then later we talked through a secure channel, and she explained what she planned to do. I wasn't going to ignore her. She was hellbent on doing it, and so I decided to do my part to make sure she didn't get killed. We are—were—outside of the Sovereignty authority at the mine, so I thought she would be safe here until things cooled down."

"Did you try to talk her out of it? Why did she do it? Shit, this is ridiculous. Is she pro-clone now?"

"Of course I tried talking her down. But her mind was set, like I said. I don't think it has anything to do about the cloning issue. I think she's just...done. With all of it. The whole war, and apparently the oath and loyalty thing. Would that really surprise you, knowing her from growing up?"

I guess not. Sabos thought back to the years of their youth when their family lived in the same apartment building as Marina and her parents. People could transform from childhood, but it didn't shock him that Marina would want to quit on the Sovereignty. Sabos remembered her as a child rarely stuck with one activity for too long. She was a reclusive kid who wasn't reliable at following structure. In truth, he was surprised that she had the fortitude to have lasted two years in the front lines of the military. With no end to the war in sight, she must have set her mind on a change. But wanting to quit and pulling it off were two entirely different things.

"I can't believe this. Where is she now?"

"I don't know. I had her pretending to do paperwork this morning in an area where no one would bother her, over by the B facilities area. Before I could go back and check on her, the fighting started."

"So she's on the opposite side of the mine from us. Little chance we'll come across her. How did she get away in the first place? And why is she taking the chance now?!"

"She tried to slip away two nights ago, but she got spotted along with another soldier she was with; he was killed. She ran away before they could shoot her too," Sabos had never felt so flabbergasted. "As for the why, I'm not really sure there is a singular reason that pushed her over the edge to do this. I guess she figured that since she got deployed here so close to us, that this would be a good opportunity to slip away. She did tell me that. But you knew Marina back then. Once she's turned against something, she tends to ignore the consequences."

"Holy shit. She could get killed, Carmenta. As in executed on the spot, if the Sovereignty finds her. I'm sure her photograph has been circulated amongst their entire battalion. The Coalition won't be overly friendly, either."

"Yeah, but with the battle going on and then the mine collapse, I don't think she's much of a Sovereignty priority right now."

"That won't matter if they stumble across her—they'll recognize her. Assuming she survived the mine collapse in the first place."

They both were quiet for a bit, trying to calm down. But Sabos still breathed heavily. He again thought about their childhood. He had never been particularly close with Marina, and didn't recall that Carmenta had been either. But Marina was a Sasquire too, and that meant a lot of shared experiences, at least from their early years. They had come from the same impoverished city and been forged through the same fire of scarcity, fear, and tragedy. Marina and her parents had moved offworld when she had been a teenager, and he had scarce contact with her since. Although Sabos hadn't spoken to his cousin in years, the family bond still resonated deeply.

"Carmenta, when were you going to tell me all this?" he demanded.

"I was hoping I didn't have to, at least until our circumstances changed. With all we have to worry about right now, with Lizby unaccounted for...it didn't seem fair to burden you with this too."

"So what changed now?"

"I don't know what to expect around the next turn in this tunnel. I wouldn't want anything to happen and that...that we would die with such a secret between us. And who knows, we may come across Marina, and whether she's safe or, uh, not safe, I didn't want to surprise you in that way," Carmenta seemed to doubt her words even as she said them. "I guess you could also chalk it up to the bump in my head."

"OK—anything else to disclose while we're on the subject of secrets we'd rather not take to our graves?"

"No. You?"

"No. What you see is what you get with me," Sabos said tersely.

Carmenta raised an eyebrow that begged to differ, but she didn't press the subject. "So, what now? We should keep going in the same direction, but we're starting to transition to an area of the mine where I'm clueless."

"Right. We should keep going in this direction. Maybe we'll see some signs and be able to make sense of them."

Carmenta got to her feet again, but she was unstable and nearly fell.

"That's it, we need to rest. Just sit down." Sabos declared.

"I can keep going, I just need—"

"Nonsense. We are going to need to sleep at some point anyway—might as well be now. You're still shaken up, and we're both exhausted."

Carmenta conceded with a sigh. They sat down and leaned against the tunnel wall, turned the flashlight off, and drifted to sleep.

Chapter 25

The opening was perhaps half a meter tall and little wider than that. As Gerund got closer, he felt slightly warmer air wafting through. He lowered a leg into the opening and then nearly had to lower his whole body into the gap until he found footing below.

The trench he entered was barely shoulder width but much deeper; over 2 meters. He traced the wall and shuffled forward. Gerund no longer heard the sound that had drawn him in. He moved with renewed urgency to find its source before it moved on. Bits of gravel and an incredibly thick layer of dust covered the trench. The stale air and tight dimensions of the passage reminded him of a crypt. He partly expected to stumble upon some skeletal remains—they would have been fitting. He reached a 90-degree corner and followed the turn left. Nearly jogging now, he quickly covered ten steps before the floor disappeared beneath him.

He contacted stone almost immediately but continued to descend. *What the hell is happening?* He fell down a narrow vertical shaft with the stone squeezing him on all sides. He tried to stop his descent by spreading his arms and legs, but the stone was too smooth and his efforts only bounced him from one side of the shaft to the other. *If this is a fatal drop, I hope it is at least quick,* he morbidly reasoned. At last, after plummeting 20 meters, he broke through into open air and a moment later landed roughly. He sore leg throbbed with the impact, but the drop had been short and he didn't feel like he had injured anything.

The floor was smoothed concrete and the ceiling was barely a full arm length above his head. The air was stagnant and smothering. Even the darkness seemed especially all-encompassing. As Gerund caught his breath, with his ears finely attuned from hours of stark silence, he thought he could discern breathing somewhere to his right. *Who—or what—could be down here?* Gerund considered his options, but before he could formulate the best way to confront this entity, he heard footsteps. Faint, but close—coming in his direction. Gerund quieted his breath and unsheathed his knife. The experience of his previous assailant was still fresh and strongly preferred to avoid another close-quarters, potentially fatal encounter. *All right, what should I do differently?* he thought, oddly calm. He held the knife at his side as the stranger's steps sounded from mere meters away. Then the footsteps grew more distant, and Gerund abandoned his indecision. *He or she can't see me either.* "Hello?" he ventured.

The footsteps stopped as the other sharply inhaled. Seconds passed, and the tension hung in the air as the stranger remained silent. Gerund knew that if this person didn't share his Coalition allegiance, then the tension would only escalate. "Hello?" he repeated, this time more slowly, trying to project as much calm into his voice as possible.

"Wh-who is it?" The man's voice was hoarse.

"Gerund." The use of his first name made him feel exposed, as if it removed some of his anonymity.

"Which side are you on?"

Gerund hesitated. *If he doesn't like the answer, I need to be ready.*

"Which army? Tell me! What is there to think about?!" The voice became more aggressive with each word.

Gerund took a few steps back before he explained. "Corporal Gerund Williams. The Central Coalition, 84th unit." No response. As the silence lingered, Gerund continued retreating and brought up his knife defensively. *Come on.* "And what about you?" This last word dripped with suspicion.

"When did your regiment get here?" the man asked suspiciously.

"We came here two weeks ago," Gerund replied impatiently. "Tell me who you are," he demanded.

"Ralteer Grant, Lance Corporal. 21st unit." Gerund heard him step closer and imagined the deadly end of a pistol through the darkness. "Gerund, how do I know you're not posing as someone you're not?"

"I guess you don't know, Corporal. But be assured that my top priority is to survive. Coalition or not, I wish you no harm, but I'll defend myself." Gerund prepared himself for an attack by placing his feet in a wide stance and leaning forward slightly. "I wouldn't risk getting into a scrap with my people by pretending to be someone I'm not. And you know what? I should be asking the questions here, since I was the first to go out on a limb and identify myself."

"That's why I kept my gun with me; so I could ask the questions with whoever I came across." Ralteer noisily cocked the weapon.

Gerund palmed his knife. "Tell me things that only a Coalition soldier would know."

"Well, let's see...The power went out during General Messine's presentation during the last camp-wide briefing. We ran out of all meat rations two days ago. Same with the mango daiquiris from the so-called lounge." Ralteer spoke with no hesitation. Gerund imagined a smug smile on the other's face. "Captain Hark always smells like garlic. The base shitters have orange soap. Three soldiers were injured the night before the battle. Satisfied?"

Gerund hadn't heard about this last bit of information. Ralteer could not have known all of this if he was from the other team. "OK, OK. I get it. You've got the details." He sheathed his knife.

"Wait a minute, *Corporal.*" The smugness was gone from Ralteer's voice, replaced with cutting malice. "The thing is, I told you five truths and one lie. You should know which, if you are truly from our camp."

What? Gerund's mind raced. *Oh, I see.* "Well, I hadn't heard about three soldiers being injured."

"That one is true." Ralteer said. "They were out on patrol and got caught in a rockslide in a ravine. But not exactly widespread knowledge, I must admit, so I'll give you a pass. Rethink your answer."

Gerund reconsidered each of Ralteer's statements. Then he had it. "The soap...it's not orange. Definitely blue. It didn't register the first time."

"You got it! Had me worried for a bit." Ralteer was louder as he drew even closer. "So where the hell did you come from?" he asked in wonderment.

Gerund recapped his journey from the Pit.

"You didn't find any supplies along the way that would be useful?"

"Nothing."

"Come on, Gerund—you sound like you could be a resourceful man. Tell me that you in fact have food and water hidden on you," Ralteer asked with desperate eagerness.

"No, I have maybe a few swallows of water left. No food. Beyond that, just the clothes on my back." *And a knife, too.*

"Not much of a savior, are ya?"

"I guess not." *What were you expecting?*

Ralteer cursed. "And you haven't seen any trace of light? Back from where you came?"

"No, in all this time, I haven't seen a trace."

Ralteer grunted, and both were silent for a while. "Hey, when did you join up?"

"I enlisted a full 12 years ago, right when I was 18."

"Wow, a career soldier, huh?" Gerund thought he detected a scoffing critique in Ralteer's voice. "I enlisted as soon as the war started two years ago. Why did you join when you were just a kid?"

Gerund didn't want to reveal all the intricacies of his past to Ralteer. He doubted that this faceless voice in the dark would understand half his story, at least at this point. The basic outline would have to suffice. "I was kind of ushered into the military. It just fit: all my interests, schooling, the summer apprenticeships...they all pointed to a career in the military. So I joined right after my eighteenth birthday, before it was part of the Coalition. It felt like destiny at the time, and the army has provided me with a lot of purpose ever since."

"I guess so, but it's so much different now that when you joined," Ralteer said. "When the war broke out, I admit I didn't have a lot going on. Just a dead-end job. But beating down the Sovereignty was something I could definitely get behind. The Sovereignty don't really care about what happens to the clones. They're just concerned about the economics—and they're so wrong about that, too. I've gotta tell ya, I love the way things are trending. And when we finally win, I expect progress to really take off."

"What do you mean?" Gerund asked, cringing for the inevitable impassioned response.

"Real progress, man. I'm talking way beyond all this clone-choice bullshit. I mean controlling our destiny as a society. Only the strong surviving and thriving—because that's who will be left: the strong, the smartest, the most resilient. Clone genetics is the future, and there is no turning back. And there's not a damn reason to resist the future. That's why I joined with the Coalition."

This guy is a true believer. A complete whacko. I can't bullshit him; I've got to let him down easy.

Ralteer was impatient in waiting for his response. "Do you disagree? Come on—you've been in this thing longer than I have. I don't understand why anyone takes a moderate position against the Sovereignty; I hope you don't. It's winner-takes-all."

"Hold on. I'll fulfill my duty with the Coalition to see this war through. I've made a commitment and I follow orders. But the chess games, the political scheming behind the scenes, the idea that the

Sovereignty is completely wrong and everything the Coalition does is justified—nah, I can't get behind that."

"Hmmph. There's a reason after all your years in that you still are assigned to the front line and not to some cushy recruiter post, you know." *A complete asshole.*

"Because I prefer it that way?" Gerund replied snarkily.

Ralteer didn't have a retort to that. Neither spoke for a bit, and then Ralteer closed the silence. "Whatever. I brought this up, let's just forget about it."

"Amen to that."

"What do you know about what happened, Gerund? Where were you during the battle?"

And so it went back and forth, with the men discovering that they had been enduring under similar hardship. Gerund described his fortunate tumble down the mine lift and then his subsequent confusion and exploration. Ralteer claimed he had been escorting field medics during the battle. One of the short-handed commanders had grabbed him and taken him down one of the equipment lifts, and they had passed through a short tunnel before arriving in this chamber, apparently to scout out the location of any subterranean Sovereignty units. But no one had been inside, nor was there much of anything beyond stacks of unprocessed ore along some of the walls. Ralteer explained that before they could head back to the Pit, they heard the clash of gunfire before the lights went out. Then, the top of the chamber caved in, burying the tunnel entrance, half the chamber, and the other three men in Ralteer's squad.

Gerund found this account plausible but wondered if Ralteer was avoiding some details. Why did they really come inside the mine, and why this chamber in particular? Perhaps they were lying low, preserving their own sins and avoiding the carnage of the main battle...Gerund figured such questions didn't matter much in their present circumstances.

As a silver lining, Ralteer said he had managed to uncover two of his comrades' bodies to collect their flasks of water—nearly a liter in total.

"Gerund, I'm willing to give you exactly half my water, seeing how we are both in the same boat here. But not another drop after that. Be sure to make it last, because that's it," Ralteer warned. "Here, stick your arm out." Ralteer found his hand in the darkness and pressed one of the flasks into it.

"I'll ration it carefully. And thank you," Gerund said sincerely. "Really, that's honorable of you to offer from what you had claim over."

"Nothing honorable about it. I knew it would be hard to hold out on you; I didn't think I could hide the water. It's just easier to give you half now."

Yikes; you just squashed my gratitude. "Well, I intend to be worth your investment."

"Let's hope," Ralteer said dryly.

Gerund thought back to the recurring thud he had heard. "Hey, there was a thud, a banging sound I heard earlier, and it drew me toward you. It was you, right? What was that?"

"Ohhh, right. That was a waste of my time. There is a wide metal grate in the floor I was trying to open. I thought it might lead somewhere."

"Yeah? It must. Maybe we can access a new area and find other Coalition troops, get some help."

"I was striking at it for probably a half hour straight with an iron bar when you came. But it was pointless."

"How large is it? Where do you think it leads?"

"It's plenty big enough for a man to fit through, but I have no clue where it leads, if anywhere at all."

"How is the grate constructed? Maybe we could twist off the slats if they are thin enough. Or pry off the grate completely. This could very well be our way out!"

"Look, Gerund; I have no new hope for you. I don't see it happening. I used all my might on that thing and I doubt it goes anywhere anyway." Ralteer said.

We don't have an alternative. "Well...maybe. But no harm in me trying, right?"

"Honestly, it would probably just rob me of some peace at this point. Believe me, your ears would be ringing, too." After his initial surprise and subsequent interest in encountering a fellow survivor, Ralteer's tone had mellowed. He had retreated into a somber, contradictory mood. The swing in his personality was unsettling.

"So other than the hole I dropped down, you're positive there is no other way out?"

"Yeah, I'm positive." Ralteer sounded annoyed. This in turn annoyed Gerund.

"So...your plan is to just sit tight and eventually die of dehydration?"

"Look, you came to me. Don't act like I'm spoiling your party. And yes, that sounds as good a plan as any at this point. At least I'll get some rest."

An uncomfortable silence ensued. *I can't abide useless people.* While Gerund did not fear his own demise, nor the suffering that he would endure before his death, being stuck with this man until the end curdled his blood. "Just show me where this grate is. Please," Gerund finally said.

Muttering under his breath, Ralteer led Gerund to a corner of the chamber where they quickly found the grate, which lay slightly inset into the chamber's floor. It was certainly large enough for a person to pass through; about one meter wide and one meter long. It had a grid pattern spaced large enough to pass a fist through. Gerund did not feel any screws or other fasteners fixing it in place. He pressed his face to the grid and shouted into the space. The echo was cavernous—certainly man-sized dimensions lay beyond.

"It sounds deep. We could fit into whatever crawlspace is beneath."

"Yeah, I know. I already tried the echo." Metal scraped against stone. "This here is the best tool I could find. It's part of the wreckage that piled in. Made of a very durable metal," Ralteer explained as he felt for Gerund's arm and handed him a half-meter long rod. "It's quite dense, but I don't think I ever put so much as a dent on those bars."

"Too bad OreLife didn't leave anything else behind we could use. Did you find any of the other soldiers' weapons? Maybe a high-caliber rifle—a grenade, even?"

"No, I didn't, and I wouldn't waste any bullets on this even if I had. That's crazy," Ralteer rasped out. "Believe me, this is a dead end. I already wasted so much energy and barely left a mark. I say we try to crawl up the way you had come from and hope for the best as we backtrack to the Pit."

"Not happening. It was a vertical drop. Maybe 20 meters, maybe more. The stone was smooth. I don't think we're going to be able to scale it. We couldn't even get enough height to enter, anyway."

"It's a better chance."

"I disagree. Do you think the rock or maybe cement surrounding the metal might be brittle enough that maybe we could create an opening that way?" Gerund suggested.

"Goddammit Gerund, the rock is super-dense. There's no way we're getting through it."

"I'm going to have a go at it before I completely give up, even if I end up a fool." Gerund said resolutely.

"Hey, listen. I'm not giving up, but I'm not being an idiot either. I realized today that this might be the beginning of the end, that's all."

Gerund tried not to get flustered. Ralteer's despair threatened to drain him of his recent invigoration. "Even so, I'll give it a try, even it is means dying as an idiot."

Ralteer sighed before slipping away to an opposite corner of the cavern. “Knock yourself out. But I’m not going to lift another finger with that thing.”

“Fine by me.” Gerund hefted the bar and got to work.

Chapter 26

Marina woke to stark, smothering darkness. She grasped for the light rod. Instead, she felt the rough edge of a stone slab and thick, grimy dust beneath her palms. *What the hell...oh, wait.* Right then, she recalled her accidental leap into the collapsed tunnel. She remembered the horrible sensation of falling to her death, anticipating in a spike of vivid terror how all her bones would snap and her organs would splatter at the bottom of a dormant mine shaft, never to be found.

Instead, she had fallen down an incline formed by the collapsed tunnel floor. She had slid on the smooth stone with her limbs splayed out in futility. The sharp slope was close to vertical and she had rapidly picked up speed. Finally, after perhaps 50 meters, the slab had ended and she found herself in another terrifying moment of free-fall before she collided with a thud several meters below. Her horizontal momentum kept her tumbling before she came to a rest on her side. This rough landing had knocked the wind out of her. Marina had been semiconscious when she saw the soldiers' lights far above. She prayed they couldn't see her. It wasn't long before both the lights and voices disappeared. *They must have decided I was not worth the trouble. Maybe they spotted me down here and decided I wasn't even worth a bullet.* She had laid still afterwards, groggily fading in and out of consciousness.

Marina wasn't sure how much time had elapsed. She slowly got to her hands and feet. She was sore yet felt intact. *But I'm blind without the light rod*, she thought. *Probably couldn't even find my way out even when I had light. Now what?!* For a grave moment, she considered if surrender would have been a better option.

Marina crawled around in a widening circle and was rewarded with a clink as her knee bumped into a cylinder—her light rod. *Please, just a little more battery power.* Frantically, she tried it. Nothing. She shook the rod and toggled the switch back and forth to no avail. *I'm screwed*, she lamented. She suppressed her breathing and listened. Silence. However, she detected a cocktail of unpleasant smells; a taste of smoke, an ancient staleness, and a strong oil odor.

She tried to climb up the way she had come to see if that was an option, just in case she misremembered how steep the angle was. *No way.* It was a sharp drop from the broken slab and she couldn't reach anything even when she jumped. *The bad luck continues.*

Marina was alive and the others weren't; *I owe it to them to survive.* The space before her was immense and hostile in the shape of her imagination. She crouched down and began to feel along the dusty mine floor.

Chapter 27

Sabos woke first. He was still exhausted, but his limbs no longer felt so heavy. He flicked on the light rod and Carmenta stirred and mumbled for him to turn it off. He implored her to get up; it was time to go. Who knew how many hours had passed? *We shouldn't have slept so long. We need to keep searching for Lizby.* Surely Carmenta would be more stable now after resting from her tumble.

Indeed, Carmenta seemed recovered as they rose with creaking limbs and pressed on. They found no clarity from their surroundings—the tunnel was just as monotonous and featureless as ever, and there were no signs or labels on any of the five intersections they passed. They were no longer navigating from even the shadow of memory—they pressed on blindly.

The ground began to slope noticeably downward, and after a few more minutes, Carmenta exhaled loudly and wiped sweat from her brow. Sabos noted the increased heat too; he had suspected that the air had become gradually warmer, but here it was evident. He knew some of the tunnels that branched off the Pit descended several kilometers. Some used vertical shafts. Some descended gradually, like this one, as earlier generations of miners followed the veins of ore like the expanding distributaries of a river. He wasn't aware of how far this tunnel branch descended, but for a tunnel that didn't incorporate a single vertical shaft, the descent was impressive.

"It's stifling in here. Are you as thirsty as I am?" Carmenta asked.

“I’d rather not think about it, to be honest.”

“Well, soon you won’t have an option. I just want to know that I’m not—”

“Shhh! Turn off the flashlight,” he hushed.

“What?”

“Turn it OFF!!"

Carmenta tried to comply as Sabos grabbed her arm. Instead, the flashlight clattered loudly to the stone floor. Carmenta tried to collect it but instead kicked it further down the tunnel.

“Shit,” Sabos hissed.

The flashlight, still on, finally came to a stop and showed nothing but the same stone walls around the slow turn of the tunnel. Nothing, except a flutter of light at the edge of tunnel’s horizon.

Sabos scrambled forward and turned off the flashlight. They pressed themselves against the same side of the tunnel wall. The light fluttered once more and then became steady, illuminating the rock floor mere meters ahead of them.

A wall of boots—they weren’t alone.

Chapter 28

Time trickled by in the equipment storage chamber. Lizby closely observed both the miners and mercs. Most of the thirteen miners seemed to mirror her anxious boredom. A few were somehow calm and optimistic—one was relaxed enough to take a nap on a bench. In contrast, some miners were visibly upset, writhing their hands and pacing amongst the lockers.

She had met most of the thirteen miners in the prior hours. The conversations were mostly the same: they would talk about their backgrounds; and speculate on the day's radical events, the mercs' motives, and what might happen next. Mathias still ignored her—she had never met someone so vindictive—but she was glad that she had made connections with the other miners, if only to distract her slightly from her worry for Sabos.

The mercs had been anxious for hours. They had buzzed around the cavern in activity and increased patrols out both ends of the complex. Lizby had heard heated discussions in the break room from which their shouting escaped without any discernible words. Every hour, the mercs had spoken into a radio, but never received a reply. The mercs had rotated the responsibilities of escorting the miners to the restrooms or to get water. Lizby took note of each merc's behavior whenever they interacted with the miners. Most had been cordial, but some were much more abrasive in personality; they were derisive to the miners' needs and treating every request as a personal inconvenience.

Deep into the evening, Captain Halion asked for a few volunteers to help prepare a meal in the kitchen. One of the miners looked to his wristwatch and noted that the time was 9 PM, and Lizby wondered if the mercs let time slip away from them or if delayed meals were to be expected. Several of the miners prepared a room-temperature oatmeal dish, which they served to the mercs first before the miners were allowed to file into the break room to retrieve their portion and then return to the locker area to eat. The meal was unappealing but it sated her rising hunger, which had become very insistent while she had been sitting still.

When it was time for sleep, a pair of mercs exited each end of the tunnel to serve as sentries. A lantern was placed at the restroom but the rest were turned off to conserve the batteries. Captain Halion set a motion sensor at the entrance of the break room. *That seems...very paranoid*, she thought. The stone floor was uncomfortable, and the miners wadded up jackets or anything remotely soft to use as pillows. Lizby had nothing and did her best to get comfortable against a row of the lockers. *Come back to me, Sabos. Soon.* Mercs and miners alike were exhausted, and eventually all but the lookouts settled down for the night, and despite the uncomfortable sleeping arrangements, Lizby succumbed to her fatigue.

Chapter 29

Gerund set to work with renewed vigor. His first strikes against the floor grate gave him a feel for the bar. With repetition, he soon found a rhythm as each blow vibrated up into his elbow and shimmered along his nerve endings up into his shoulder. His hands grew numb from the impacts, even after one hand would relieve the other. As the minutes dissolved into a timeless trance, his arm became one with the bar. He was consumed by an industrious mindset.

After finding the metal unrelenting, he began to chip away at the rock it was embedded in. He managed to dislodge several small chunks but had no idea how deep he would have to go if he were to pry the entire grate from the stone floor. At least an hour passed and Gerund continued his toil with a surrender to the task. The ability to focus on a possible solution, even if a longshot, was liberating.

He moderated his effort just enough to maintain a sustainable pace. He was grateful for his years of rigorous conditioning in the Coalition. When he had first entered the service at age eighteen, he had been eager and energetic, but undisciplined over his body. After twelve years, he moved with a composed and efficient grace and routinely outlasted men even a decade younger on Coalition training hikes. He wasn't the strongest or the fastest, but his endurance had been honed to an art. He knew his body intimately—both its abilities and limits.

Occasionally, Ralteer would remind him of the futility; the wasted effort, and would beckon him to come join him by the wall. He didn't even bother to check on the progress. Gerund doubted that Ralteer could be relied upon if circumstances escalated to another level of desperation. At one point, Gerund told him to go as far away as possible if he wasn't going to help, though in truth he didn't want interference at this point, even if it was well-intentioned. Ralteer stayed put and continued to grumble, insisting they need to try to go back through the existing hole in the ceiling, but Gerund ignored him.

The chips became larger, suggesting that the stone was more brittle underneath, and Gerund became confident that he could break through. It was just a matter of time. which he had in abundance, as long as his strength didn't fail him. In his relentless fervor, he knew there was nothing more to fear, and no significant disadvantage if his effort ended up being wasted. *I've got nothing to lose, and maybe nothing to gain, but who knows? This passage could lead somewhere helpful.*

Gerund's determined focus kept his body at the task at hand, but his thoughts inevitably slipped into the past. His childhood and the formative years of his youth had been spent in foster homes and eventually as a ward of the state until he joined the military. Supposedly the woman who gave birth to him was a surrogate, taking part in a government fertility program but having no interest in raising him. He had been transferred to state custody mere days after birth. He had never known who his donor parents were. Gerund had some stabilizing influences, namely caring mentors and teachers, who kept him focused and succeeding at school and with friends. On the surface, he had been a model product of the foster system. But he had never truly comfortable; he was painfully aware even at as a young child that he had no true family. He had transitioned to six different homes throughout the years; some wretched, some loving; none of them truly a home. By the time he entered high school he was a stoic, independent boy who already had his sights set on the military and a purposeful future far away. With his background, it had felt so natural to fully immerse himself in the military and become a career soldier. He had excelled early, and the validation he received from his trainers and the comradery he shared with his unit became integral parts of his identity.

Gerund didn't know where he would reside once he retired from the army. Setting down roots hadn't been much of an option during the past 12 years, and he had never found traction toward finding a woman and starting a family. Whenever he went on leave, he felt disconnected from the civilian cultures. Few friendships had survived throughout his nomadic career. Romantic relationships had been complicated and usually doomed from the start, and most recently tinged with tragedy.

He had dated a journalist for a year when he was twenty-four. She wasn't the first or the last serious pursuit. But 3 years ago, when he was twenty-eight, he had learned while on a deployment that she had died unexpectedly. During a remote assignment, she caught a hard-to-diagnose virus that ravaged her respiratory system in just over twenty-four hours. News of her death had shaken Gerund harder than expected. It had definitely been over between them, but their connection had been genuine. This awful event had slammed life into painful perspective, and for perhaps the first time, Gerund struggled with finding fulfillment in the service. He mourned her loss even as he went through the motions of his duties with stoic composure. The wound had gradually healed somewhat in the years after. He stayed busy as his military career continued to succeed, but the loss of his former girlfriend remained profound even to this moment. The service continued to be important to him, but as he got older the end of his career and life itself felt imminent. He needed something more.

Assuming he escaped the mine alive, Gerund didn't know what the future held for him. He had expected to remain with the Coalition for years before eventually transitioning to a career in the civilian sector. But after his near-death experiences and the wild course of the war, that path was in doubt. With his clinical lack of fear, he questioned if he had the healthy dose of self-preservation required to stay alive on the front lines. He has seen far too many men and women lose all caution and then their lives shortly after.

Gerund stopped to check the grate for progress. His hands were numb. The rock was ragged, and the grate was slightly loose. He jarred it with a few swift kicks, feeling it rattle slightly, and tried to pry it out with all his will. It stayed in place, but Gerund knew his progress was accelerating. He was headed down the home stretch. He continued his assault with the bar. The rock was crumbling along the sides of the grate and weakening at the corners. He decided against sharing his progress with Ralteer and continued to work. *He's going to feel foolish when I get this open after he's been sulking in a corner the whole time.* Gerund pried at the grate once more and felt the whole piece shift along with some of the surrounding rock. His excitement spiked. *What could be down there?!* He prayed that it wasn't a dead end.

Chapter 30

Another swift kick from Gerund twisted the grate half out of the hole, and then another strike dislodged it completely from the stone. He yanked the metal free and announced his task complete with an excited yelp and a clatter as he threw the grate against the wall in triumph.

Ralteer rose from his lethargy. "Did you get it open, Gerund?!" he said as his voice drew closer. "Lead me with your voice; I don't want to fall in!"

"Just a minute!" Gerund cautioned. Blood flowed into his tired muscles as his heart circulated renewed adrenaline. "I'm checking it out now." Gerund tried to steady his breathing. He laid on his chest and extended his arm as far as he could into the center of the gap and felt nothing. *It's deep; good sign.*

"Well, does it go anywhere? Gerund?" Ralteer rasped excitedly.

After hours of Ralteer's complaining and discouragement, his sudden enthusiasm was beyond annoying. He reminded Gerund of the bad apples he had endured in some of his past units; those who would poison the morale of entire squads with their useless pessimism and crippling doubt. Gerund's face flushed with anger. "You son of a bitch; you said this wouldn't work. You sat on your ass and complained the whole time I worked."

"Hey, I—" Ralteer began in a growl, before uncharacteristically chuckling. "OK, OK! You got me, Gerund. I was an asshole. But you must admit, it was a longshot. So which direction does it lead? Are you in there?"

Gerund realized that a formal apology would not be forthcoming, so he decided to drop his indignation. "Not yet. It goes straight down—it's deep. We should have plenty of room to move."

Ralteer was at Gerund's side, focused on the glimmer of hope. "We got nothing to lose. I'll go in."

"Hold on, let me see how far this goes down. I need something to drop down there."

Ralteer tapped Gerund with a small rock. Gerund dropped it down from the center of the chasm and listened for the plunk. It was almost immediate. "Did you hear that? It's not too far down that we can't jump in safely."

"Let me try." Ralteer dropped other pieces of loose rock. "It can't be more than a few meters. I heard a bit of an echo—there's space down there."

The two were silent as they processed this information. "I knew what I was doing. There's always a way out," Gerund said. His tone carried relief but also some resentment, as Gerund felt like his *I-told-you-so* moment was not being properly acknowledged by Ralteer. Hours of the other man's nagging had soured any notion of comradery. But it was time to move forward. He just wished he could rely on the man at his back.

They both took a quick drink from their water flasks. Gerund still felt parched when he sealed the cap. He tensed with pain from sore muscles in his leg and shoulders as he lowered himself into the opening.

After he lowered the whole length of his body, he found footing and let go of the opening to come down in a crouch. Gerund was surprised to feel that the crawlspace was cylindrical—perhaps two and a half meters in diameter. The tunnel was uncomfortable to stand in because of the curved bottom.

Ralteer joined him when he gave the all-clear. "Wow, quite roomy, isn't it? I was worried it was only going to be a narrow air duct or drainage ditch or something. Uh, which way?"

Gerund walked a few strides before hitting a flat wall. "Well, it's a dead end here. The vent was the end of the line. Well, that makes it simple; the other direction it is."

Gerund and Ralteer proceeded cautiously along the roughly carved passage. Whatever had bored it out had left finger-width ridges that ringed the entire circumference of the passage, not unlike the thread of a giant screw. The tunnel rose on a slight incline. They started out cautiously, but soon Ralteer called for a faster pace, so he took point and shuffled onward by sliding his feet along the floor, no doubt imagining obstructions and bottomless pits in the tunnel floor. After a tense 100 meters the tunnel floor became smooth and leveled off. The walls quickly widened and suddenly they found themselves in an open space.

The floor was smooth concrete and the ceiling was barely taller than Gerund. The pair split in opposite directions to explore the boundaries of the room. As Gerund traced the perimeter, he felt nothing along the wall but grimy, mossy stone. Based on the curve of the wall, Gerund estimated that the space's area was about the same as a standard residence. He was surprised to discover a 3-meter gap in the wall representing the beginning of a hallway. He could reach the ceiling when he raised his arm. He took a few steps in, but there was no way to tell how far it might go, so Gerund decided to table its exploration. He relayed this information to Ralteer, who agreed it was a great sign, and they continued to explore the chamber.

After he had circled what he estimated was half the room, Gerund glanced behind and was taken aback. Instead of stark darkness, there was a dim, cool-blue aura. *Light?! From what?* He walked toward it eagerly before colliding into a large object, almost as tall as him. Metal paneling along the bottom that clanged loudly as he kicked it. Confusing knobs, sockets, and mesh paneling along chest height. He quickly surmised that the room was dominated by this massive piece of machinery in the center. Several small pipes encircled the rectangular machine. Gerund had to walk to the other side before he found the small point of light. The blue light came from a control panel on the side of the machine. There were gauges for pressure and temperature and a number of other indicators. The terminology was over his head, but Gerund pieced enough together of the gauges and labels to guess that the machine was some sort of air scrubber.

“Ralteer! Come here! We have light!" Gerund realized he was about to not only see for the first time in days, but that he would also see the face of a man he didn’t entirely trust. “Watch out, there's a large machine in the way. I think it’s an air scrubber based what I can read on this control panel.”

Ralteer jogged toward Gerund's voice and the light. “Holy shit! I see it. Do you think this part of the mine has some power?”

“No, the machine is definitely off. I just tried the power switch. I’m guessing this light is powered by a small battery built into the panel." The tiny diode illuminated barely a meter in any direction. The pair first examined their hands as if they forgot what they looked like, then studied each other’s haggard faces. The faces of both men resembled their voices; tired, hungry, strained; perhaps once vigorous but now surviving on willpower alone. Ralteer’s eyes shone brightly in the blue tint, but the rest of his face sagged as if paralyzed in a grim expression.

“You know I need to see you neck.” Ralteer said flatly. It was time to check for the Sovereignty mark.

Gerund nodded. “OK, let’s get to it.” He paused, wondering how his next suggestion would be received, and decided to just say it. “If one of us is not as we seem, we should just part ways, no fight needed." He doubted it would work out that way, but it seemed like a reasonable suggestion.

Ralteer took a few breaths to reply. “Agreed. But no need.”

When Ralteer didn’t make a move, Gerund pulled back his jacket collar and offered his bare neck to the diode, leaning close so that the light reached the skin where the Sovereignty tattooed all of its personnel. He knew he was incredibly vulnerable if Ralteer had concealed his identity, but he was content with the risk.

“Cool." Once Gerund was out of the way, Ralteer folded back the collar of his own uniform and bent over. No mark.

Gerund breathed a sigh of relief. “Glad we can put that to rest.”

"Me too. Honestly, if I was one of those clone-killers, I would have murdered your Coalition ass when we first met. Would have shot you right in the face."

"Uh-huh," Gerund mumbled, troubled by Ralteer's cold calculation and not the least bit amused. He at least took solace in the small comfort of their oasis of illumination. Too bad they couldn't take it with them, he thought.

"Hey, you shouted something about a hallway when we were first circling the room. Let's check it out."

Gerund reluctantly left the light and led Ralteer along the wall to the entrance. They entered the 3-meter wide hallway abreast. After the brief respite in the light, the darkness was suffocating. The smooth stone soon deteriorated into an uneven, pebble-strewn surface. They walked at a brisk pace despite their weariness. The air was cooler here, yet still powerfully stale. They each traced the hallway walls with a hand. As before, the walls were covered with a moss-like film. It made their hands smell bitter, like rotting tree leaves. Both men were all business and offered no commentary. Part of Gerund was curious to reach out and ask more about Ralteer's past, but he sensed even in the dark that the man was not in the talking mood.

Gerund continued to marvel at the expansiveness of the mine as their walk stretched on for minutes. He wondered where they were in relation to the Pit. *What purpose could OreLife have for all these empty chambers and tunnels? It must have cost them a fortune to dig this far.* The hallway represented their only hope, and as the length increased, so did Gerund's confidence that it led somewhere significant. Incredibly, they walked the straight tunnel for at least 10 minutes—it must have been over a kilometer—before the hallway finally opened up. By then, their hands were numb and grimy from passing over the moist, velvety stone. Unlike the hallway, the new chamber's ceiling was higher than they could reach, even when they jumped.

"Hey, do you smell this? Fruity." Ralteer sniffed loudly. Gerund inhaled deeply but didn't notice anything beyond the stale odor. But he followed Ralteer's footsteps and caught a whiff; it indeed smelled like fruit. *A good sign—maybe we're close to a stockroom or a breakroom.* He started to imagine the edible possibilities.

Their hunger drew them to the wall on the left side of the room. Traveling along its side, they discovered a storage area with items distributed in knee-high stacks in a corner of the room. *Yes, yes—this is good.* Gerund followed his nose and his outstretched hands came into contact with the source of the fruity smell—a large carton, already opened, containing what felt like dried fruit. *Yes, definitely food.* Raisins, perhaps? A close sniff confirmed this. Without any visual confirmation, Gerund could only hope that they were safe to eat. The container had rested upon several other boxes, which had a similar feel except these were still tightly shrink-wrapped. Gerund counted ten boxes resting upon a plastic pallet. They scooped these up between the two of them and eagerly checked out the other stacks. Their rising excitement was quelled a bit when a quick investigation revealed that the other pallets contained disappointing items: bleach-scented spray bottles and bulk toilet paper; three full pallets of each. These supplies were tightly shrink-wrapped around each side. *Why store these things here?* Still holding the boxes of raisins, they walked the remaining circumference of the room. Along one part, roughly opposite to where they had entered, they found another hallway.

Gerund took a few steps in, and realized they could be committing to another long hike. "Hold on. We don't know how long this passage could be. It could be a few meters or a few hundred. I say we refuel a bit and rest before we explore any further. Right?"

"I guess so. My stomach is not going to argue."

They collapsed against the nearest wall. Gerund was content to pause further exploration—his body craved nourishment. The raisins were perfectly edible; not abandoned for years like he had worried might be the case. They had a long, drawn-out feast from the open carton, first cramming handfuls into their mouths and, after their raw hunger was somewhat sated, enjoying each raisin one at a time. Gerund didn't particularly like raisins, but on this day they were delectable. They rested against the wall for an hour and experienced a less-than-gnawing hunger for the first time in days. They reclined to help their bodies adjust to the sudden digestion.

"What the hell?" A woman's voice startled them from across the room.

Chapter 31

Sabos and Carmenta were crippled by indecision, looking at each other to determine if they should run or see who was coming around the curve of the tunnel. In the end, indecision prevailed and they were confronted by a group of five soldiers with weapons drawn.

"Hands up!" someone barked.

Sabos cooperated and stood stock still, resisting the urge to look back and see if his sister did too. The soldiers seemed to calm slightly, and a pair moved forward. The lead man wore a black-visored helmet that encapsulated his entire head. The broad visor consisted of black opaque plastic and the sides of the helmet was studded with small, circular sensors. The helmet undoubtedly gave him a superior advantage in the dark. All the soldiers wore dark uniforms and carried assault rifles and a variety of equipment strapped to their waists. Sabos couldn't tell if the soldiers belonged to the Coalition or the Sovereignty; he saw no insignia.

"Keep your hands up!" the masked soldier commanded as he motioned for Sabos to spread his legs. He tried to contain his shaking as he was roughly frisked all over. He could hear Carmenta's anxious breathing as the other soldier searched her. With a closer view, Sabos saw the uniform in detail. It consisted of dark, snugly-fitting fabric and featured various insignia—including a fierce badger that must have been the group's logo. The sleek uniform implied a focus on aesthetics at least as much as functionality. Sabos was certain they were mercenaries. There were all types of mercenaries participating in the war, of course, but the presence of mercs in general was not a good thing, in Sabos's view. Their motives were often far different than the enlisted men, and both the Coalition and Sovereignty governments often subcontracted them for missions that blurred the lines of war. He had heard all sorts of horrible things when the battle lines intersected with civilian life: tales of plundered property, rape, and murdered civilians and POWs. These reports overshadowed the conduct of those soldiers who had conducted themselves honorably. Even the most moderate of personalities were compelled to pick a side in the wake of such carnage. Sometimes these crimes were brazenly committed—even with cameras rolling. And now that they were all underground, hidden from the world, Sabos felt particularly vulnerable. Being held at gunpoint by this group reinforced his suspicious attitude.

"They're clean," the Mask said, but kept his handgun drawn and raised to Sabos's chest. "Both of you, come here." He led them forward and directed them to stand against the tunnel wall. Carmenta joined Sabos and both kept their arms up.

"We just work here—in the mine. We're miners," Carmenta rambled. "You don't need—"

The Mask held his other hand up in a stop gesture. "Your names?"

Sabos had calmed down just enough to speak clearly. "Sabos Sasquire and Carmenta Sasquire. We're registered with OreLife, you can—"

"I don't need elaboration," the Mask said coldly.

Who is this asshole hiding behind a mask? Sabos wondered. *This is our turf.*

"Wait, same last names?" another soldier piped in.

"Yes, this is my brother," Carmenta explained. "Look at us; we're clearly related." She turned her head so each side could be compared to Sabos. The soldiers either didn't notice or weren't impressed by the physical resemblance.

"We're looking for my wife. Her name is Lizby Sasquire," he said, figuring it was worth a shot. "We're not exactly sure where she was working this morning. Have you seen her?" He gave the group a detailed description of Lizby, but almost immediately the soldiers started to shake their heads.

"Sorry, no—we've seen no one like that," the Mask said. Sabos expected as much, but it was still disheartening. "But we'll keep our ears open and ask the rest of our unit if they have seen your wife as soon as we can make contact with them."

"I greatly appreciated that," Sabos said, though he felt no better.

"Where did you come from?" the Mask asked.

Carmenta pointed. "We came down this tunnel, walking for a couple hours; we took several turns along the way. The exit to the Pit collapsed." She now looked more annoyed than afraid. "Can we put our arms down now? It's exhausting."

The Mask must have been in command because the rest of the soldiers looked to him. He nodded reluctantly. "You may," He holstered his handgun and the other soldiers lowered their rifles. "We're being cautious. Not everyone down here is who they say."

"That's no reason to be so rude to us. This is our mine," Carmenta scolded as she picked up her flashlight. Sabos couldn't believe her defiance, but she continued. "There's more miners in the other tunnels, I'm sure. Somebody is going to get accidentally shot—if you haven't killed anyone already. Who are you guys, exactly?"

"We work for the Sovereignty. The Coalition has infiltrated this mine and we're here to drive them out and help secure it," the Mask said with a rehearsed tone. Sabos didn't buy it.

"Wait," one of the soldiers interjected. "Are we just going to take their word that the other direction is blocked off?"

"Be our guest and check it out yourself. But it's several klicks away," Carmenta said.

"No need," the Mask agreed.

"Can we go now? Carmenta crossed her arms in a display of impatience. "Is there anyone else further along who is going to bother us?"

"No."

"No, what?"

"No—you can't go. You need to find a safe location so we are free to conduct our operations," the Mask said. He held up a hand to stifle Carmenta's protest. "If we can rendezvous with the rest of our squad on the other side of the mine, you'll be safe and have access to supplies there."

Why would they want to babysit a couple of civilians like us? Just let us go. Sabos looked to his sister, trying to gauge her thoughts on this proposition, but she wouldn't meet his eyes.

"Wait, you need us to help you navigate through the mine, don't you?" Carmenta said with smug realization.

The mercs glanced at each other, but it was hard to see what their faces conveyed in the dim light. "It would be in the best interest of all," the Mask said finally.

"We can certainly try to point you in the right direction," Sabos said. "But Carmenta and I need to concentrate on finding Lizby." He did not want to stay a moment longer than necessary with these foreign mercenaries.

"It's not safe for you to be continuing on your own; you need come with us," the Mask said gruffly. "It's not a choice." Sabos's palms seeped with fresh sweat. *This isn't going our way.*

Carmenta clasped her hands in front of herself in a placating gesture. "Thanks for your consideration but we need to be on our own way," she asserted. She tugged Sabos's arm and came off the wall. "We'll be careful, don't worry."

The Mask hastily drew his handgun and the soldiers bristled with hostility. "I'm tired of this shit, and I don't have time for it. I tried to be diplomatic. What you fools don't seem to get is that this is a warzone with the equivalent of martial law. You need to do what I command. You're coming with us." The other four soldiers surrounded them. "Bind them. I'm not playing nice anymore."

"You weren't before." Carmenta glared as the soldiers they took her arms.

"Carmenta, shut up," Sabos hissed as his arms were rough yanked behind his back.

They handcuffed their hands behind them and hustled them down the tunnel the way the soldiers had come. Sabos and Carmenta were kept in the middle. One of the soldiers took their flashlight but at least had the courtesy to shine it in front of their feet.

"There is a four-way intersection farther down this tunnel," the Mask said. "It's labeled but we don't know what the signs mean. We are trying to meet the rest of our squad in a large equipment area; they said it was accessible from a tunnel labeled RA. Do you know how to get there?"

"I know about the area they're in, and how to get there from the Pit—but not to get there from this tunnel," Sabos sighed. "I just know that it's not close; probably several kilometers away. What did the sign say?"

"I know RA wasn't one of them. I remember a MB, MD, and a GS, maybe? And two arrows corresponding to each direction of the intersection."

"Not ringing a bell, sorry."

One of the soldiers nudged Carmenta and she almost fell over on top of Sabos. "How about you?"

"Hey!" She glared at the soldier. "I know even less. Sabos is a mechanic—he sees much more of the mine than I do."

The Mask cursed. "Well, you can at least get us going in the right direction, I'm sure. Let's take it one intersection at a time."

Sabos knew the mercs' choice to handcuff them did not bode well for their future treatment. He looked over at his sister but she once again appeared more irritated than scared. This was not the time to challenge, and he worried that she would burst any moment and say something that would at the very least get them smacked. *And maybe much worse...*

Most upsetting of all was his inability to search for Lizby. He doubted that the soldiers were truly sympathetic to his plight beyond the brief lip service they had received earlier, and he agonized over the thought of being held for hours or even days while his wife wandered the mine alone, increasingly terrified and weaker each hour. Carmenta seemed to pick up on his anguish and gave him an empathetic head tilt and pursed her lips. *We gotta get out of this, sis,* he thought. *Wait for the opportunity.*

Chapter 32

Ralteer and Gerund quietly rose to their feet. "I don't believe this," the woman growled, a mix of bewilderment and frustration. "What did this?" she said, much quieter. "Rats? Bats? Maybe those damn giant bugs..."

Gerund reached over and cupped his hand over Ralteer's ear. "We should answer her. Find out who she is," he whispered faintly.

"Why? We have her stash of raisins, it appears. More for us. Why risk it?"

Gerund struggled to keep his voice from rising. *How did I get stuck with the biggest asshole in the mine?* "Well, maybe she has more things. Like water—or ideas on how to get to the surface."

"Gerund, she could be anyone. She could be Sovereignty—"

"It's worth the risk." Gerund broke away from Ralteer, not willing to discuss the choice in this instance any further.

Gerund crossed the room toward the voice. His footsteps echoed lightly off the concrete floor but was masked by the woman's rummaging in the storage area. He stopped at what he guessed was halfway across the room.

"Hello?" Gerund ventured.

She drew her breathe sharply and didn't answer.

Gerund tried again. "Hello?"

"Hey—who's there?!"

"I'm Gerund."

"Where did you come from?!"

"I walked down the long hallway—from a totally different area of the mine."

"Oh...did you take the raisins?" she asked, upset.

"Yeah, we did." Ralteer broke in defensively as he stepped alongside Gerund. "Where did you come from?"

The woman stood her ground. "Who am I talking to now? Who's *we?* Who are you guys?"

An uneasy silence lingered for several breaths.

Gerund didn't have time to plan the conversation. He grappled with how much to reveal. But he had to respond; her suspicion was palpable, building with each second he didn't answer. *She could be armed...* Gerund chose his words carefully while maintaining a calm tone. "Again, my name is Gerund, and this is Ralteer. It's just the two of us. We just came in through that really long hallway. We were in another dead-end chamber but found a different way out after breaking down a grate in the floor." Gerund's fists tightened nervously. The next part was risky. "We're reporters—we were following the action on the surface, right up at the front line, and got caught up in all this mess. Lost all of our equipment in the collapse."

"Oh." The woman took a couple of steps back. "And who are you with?"

Gerund didn't hesitate this time. "We are non-affiliated war correspondents. We're working with an agency based on the east continent. Ralteer and I were shadowing a Coalition brigade when the fight broke out, and uh, were stuck below seeking cover when the ship collapsed on the mine."

"I'm a miner," she said.

"What's your role?" Ralteer asked.

"I-I don't have role yet—I just started this week. They're training me in quality control."

Ralteer remained suspicious. "Who were you with? Is there anybody else here? And we didn't get your name, so why don't—"

"I—hey, I'm a little overwhelmed right now," she said, flustered. "Give me a minute."

Is she okay? Gerund wondered. *Is she going to be able to help us out or is she going to be deadweight? She could be injured, or too damaged...*

"That's ok. No rush." Gerund said instead, infusing his voice with patient understanding.

"But really, there is." Ralteer added. "Name?"

"Marina. Since I started—"

"First or last?"

"First—what does it matter?" Marina sighed deeply. "It has been just me in here. I got separated from the other miners during the confusion, and was walking down a tunnel, searching for other survivors, when I fell down a gap where the tunnel had collapsed. There's a large chamber that connects to this room through a short hallway. That's where I slid down from the higher lever. There are piles of massive stone slabs covering half the room." Marina sounded forlorn. "If there was another entrance to this area, I think the collapse buried it under the stone."

"So there is no way out?" Ralteer was distraught.

Gerund was also perturbed. But it made sense. Marina had been here hours longer than they had, and if there was a simple way out, why would she still be here? One entry. No exit. It was a sobering realization. Surely they had missed something; maybe Marina hadn't explored this last remaining chamber thoroughly. But he doubted it. They at least had plenty of nourishment to search, but it was a petty consolation.

"Umm...well, no way out that I could find. There were a couple of sheer drops when I was sliding down. It must have been a 50-meter tumble—nearly vertical. No way we could climb back up, even if we could reach the edge."

Gerund's spirits sank. Ralteer cursed loudly.

Marina clapped her hands to command their attention. "But listen; high above in the other room is a huge air duct opening. We could easily fit inside, if only we could reach it. It's above this large boxy machine that looked like it controls utilities or something. And the air duct doesn't go into this room; it goes someplace else. At least I didn't see any vents leading here." Marina said.

"Wait, how do you know all of that? How do you know what things look like?" Ralteer demanded.

"Easy. There was fire from the crash that burned for a while, and I saw the vent about 10 meters high on one side of the room. I could see it along the ceiling; it exited into the wall. So it definitely leads somewhere."

"What was on fire? The pallets?"

"Right. They were burning when I dropped in."

"Huh? How?"

"Not sure how. Maybe there was some equipment that was affected by the collapse and ignited. I was considering a plan, actually...I think it may be possible that the packages and pallets could be stacked on top of the machine so that we could reach the air duct.

"Is there was enough material to reach so high?" Gerund asked.

"Yes, there are mounds of loose pallets in the next room. More than enough, I expect."

"I like this plan. What do we have to lose?" Gerund said.

They waited for Ralteer's response, and he finally agreed. "Can't hurt."

"OK, we can do this," Marina encouraged. "Follow me—the other room is this way."

Gerund and Ralteer shadowed her footsteps closely. *I guess we're trusting her. Let's hope she is who she claims and is not leading us into a trap.*

"So in this room there are just some pallets and the machine you mentioned?" Ralteer asked.

"Right. I have no idea what OreLife use this part of the mine for," she said as they slowly walked forward. "Both chambers are spacious. I haven't discovered any mining equipment."

"Well, this mine is ancient, right? This area could have been dug before OreLife took over," Gerund offered.

"Maybe. Watch yourself. We are at the wall, and the passageway is just to our left," Marina's voice changed as they walked into a narrow arched hallway. They quickly emerged into the adjoining chamber. She led them through a tangle of the wooden pallets to the aforementioned machine.

"OK, but how are we supposed to do this?" Ralteer said doubtfully. "We can't see the supplies. How will we tell if we are even working in the general vicinity of the air duct?"

"Look, it's not the best idea," Marina said. "But it's better than staying trapped in this dead end and waiting for the chance that some miners or the Coalition will rappel down that hole and find us first. Or waiting to starve and be unearthed by some archeologist one hundred years from now."

"I've got an idea about figuring out where the opening of the duct is." Gerund bent to gather pebbles and began to toss them up. Marina joined him. At first the pings were confusing. Gerund heard thuds from both metal and stone surfaces. Gradually, it became easier to visualize the ceiling: with each metallic ping, he conjured a better mental picture of where the air duct was. The opening seemed to be above the exact center of the machine, which was where Marina had thought it was. Afterwards, Ralteer and Marina threw pebbles, too, and soon all three agreed that the top of the machine would be sturdy enough and therefore a good foundation to attempt a platform that they could scale to reach the vent opening.

"We should try to find some of the widest material to put at the bottom," Marina said.

"Is there enough material to build a stack that high?" Ralteer asked. "This just sounds a little nuts."

"It's not going to be a pretty creation, especially when you consider that the three builders are still getting used to moving around in the dark," she admitted. "But I honestly believe it can work. And besides, what else are you going to do?"

Gerund thought Ralteer was going to try to drag them through doubt again, but he was silent.

"You already ate one of my boxes of raisins. Please tell me you have brought something in return." Marina sounded like she already knew the answer.

Gerund shook his head even though she couldn't see. "Uh, sorry Marina, but no."

"OK." Her disappointment was evident. "How about water?"

"We drank some in the hallway, and we're down to maybe half a liter between our two flasks."

"That's not going to last long..."

"I'm really sorry, Marina. I hate to burden you like this."

Ralteer cleared his throat to assert himself. "Don't apologize Gerund, and don't let her make you feel like that—we're not going down that path. We've had a tough journey—"

"Same here, by the way," she interrupted. "That doesn't give you a pass on rudeness."

"Listen—I know you're going to claim first come, first serve, but I'm not going to beg for those raisins and for whatever water you have. We're all partners in this now. Equal shares."

Gerund was aghast at Ralteer's sudden assertion over Marina's supplies—he had no regard for diplomacy. He hoped Marina wouldn't spook and get overly defensive. Gerund chose to mitigate the soaring tensions. "Please, Marina; we are not going to take anything from you. I want to be transparent about this. We will appreciate any food and water you can part with, because it will help us with this plan, and honestly none of us has a lot of time if this tower doesn't work, correct? So we may as well put all our energy into it. But I'd like for you to feel comfortable working with us, because we're not here to steal." Gerund wasn't sure if he believed this himself, and even less certain that Marina bought it.

She paused to consider this. "Thanks for saying that. It's just really hard to get a read on people in the dark, you know? I intended that we would have equal amounts, of course. But we've got to be disciplined about it." She sounded much more at ease.

Ralteer scoffed under his breath. "What about water? You didn't deny having some."

"Yes, to confirm, I do have water. Enough for a matter of days, I expect."

That's such a relief. That's going to give us a lot more options as long as we can somehow get out of this part of the mine. "Thanks, Marina. I think—"

"How much water?" Ralteer asked. *This guy is always pushing things*, Gerund thought.

"Well, with you guys here now, just a matter of days. Three, tops."

"Huh? Show me." Ralteer demanded.

"No, I don't think so." Marina said firmly. "I'll bring us some water later. There is a lot of this packing stuff laying around that I know how to avoid. I have a good mental picture at this point." *A weak excuse,* Gerund thought. But he didn't blame her for holding out on them.

"Whatever," Ralteer pouted. "How much water do you got?"

Marina sighed. "I don't know, maybe 3 liters. Probably only good for a handful of days, like I said. Especially if we're exerting ourselves."

"More than we had before, so I accept," Ralteer said with a reluctant sigh. *As if there was another choice.*

"Where did you find it?" Gerund asked. "And do you have any other food than the raisins we found?"

"I had found some containers near the supply area not long after I dropped in. Left by some workers. And yes, there is a box of crackers, but it won't last the three of us long. Again, especially with the water, we've got to be disciplined. What's left is sacred." Marina said.

"Right," Gerund said. "We need to refuel at the same time, so we can ensure equal amounts, don't you think?"

"Definitely," Marina agreed. "We can refresh after we make our first push in getting this tower put together, so let's get to it."

Gerund knew it was important to be diplomatic on the topic of sharing her remaining supplies. But if they had a repeat of the previous day's gnawing hunger, and Marina denied them access to the food, then his cooperative attitude would come to a rude end.

"Wait—I'll be right back," Marina said. She hurried off across the chamber and soon returned, accompanied by a *swoosh*. She handed a plastic bottle to Gerund and another to Ralteer. Both containers had been rationed with only a few swigs of Marina's water supply. Gerund accepted graciously. Ralteer didn't say anything, no doubt resenting the fact that Marina had yet to reveal her larger stash to them.

Chapter 33

Lizby woke to shouting. The lanterns came on as both miner and merc were roused to their feet. Lizby knelt behind one of the benches in the locker alcove and looked all around the chamber for the source of the commotion. The mercs scurried across both directions.

"Portals is dead!" Someone screamed. "He's been stabbed in the break room!"

"Where are the other sentries?!" another merc yelled.

Captain Halion walked through the center of the lantern light and commanded the two closest mercs to surround Lizby and the other miners, which they immediately did with weapons drawn, as Halion pivoted in the direction of the break room. The mercs offered no explanation for their hostility, and by the look of her companions' faces, Lizby guessed the miners were too terrified to ask for one. A few meekly raised their hands in submission, but most stood rigidly still with their arms at their side, including Lizby.

"W-what's going on? What happened?" one miner finally asked.

The guards looked at each other, and one shrugged. "We're looking into it," he said in a tone that was equally placating and authoritative. "Just stay still for now."

"And keep your hands where we can see them," the other merc ordered. It was June—one of the first soldiers Lizby had encountered when she had found the equipment area after stumbling out of the tunnel.

For several tense minutes they stood rigidly at gunpoint. The mercs listened to what was being said over at the break room building as they held their guns raised at the center of the miners' group. Lizby was just out of range from understanding the frantic voices from the break room. The miners whispered back and forth but their speculation offered no new information.

Lizby made eye contact with June, who kept shifting her stance uncomfortably. The woman looked just as upset as Lizby felt. Lizby held June's stare for several uncomfortable seconds before the merc looked away. Lizby wondered if June could empathize with her position.

"He's not dead. Portals is still alive!" someone shouted.

"What?! How?" another answered.

"I don't know, but just barely."

June's expression brightened and the miners looked at each other in confusion. To Lizby's horror, the rest of the mercs emerged from the break room building carrying a bloodied body. Captain Halion followed, carrying a hefty comm device. His composed demeanor from the previous day was gone, replaced by an expression of contorted rage.

The mercs carefully lowered Portals in the center of the lanterns. Halion grabbed a nearby merc. "Go help him! Do what you can!"

The man, perhaps the squad's medic, knelt and took a long look at Portals and just shook his head. Portals lay motionless—a blade with an antique, decorative handle was sticking out of the top of his head. Blood had trickled down his body, but it seemed to have stopped some time ago. The medic again shook his head. "He's still breathing, but there's no way to tell if he will ever have conscious brain function again.

If by some miracle he does pull through in the short term, I don't have the supplies I need to help him down here."

Captain Halion's face was red. "Just keep him alive. Don't let anyone touch that knife."

"Of course. The blade needs to stay in place."

Another merc jogged from the break room and took Halion aside and they whispered back and forth. When they were done, Halion paced back and forth, fuming, before stomping over to the miners.

"Listen carefully. Twelve of you are with me and one of you is against us all." He paused, taking in the miners' perplexed expressions. "That's right, there's a murderous son-of-a-bitch in our midst. Stabbed one of my men. A good soldier. But he—or she—is not getting away with it. You need to help me find out who this bastard is." Halion eyes bulged with fury. The other mercs closely observed the miners' expressions as they squirmed under the weight of this news. Halion dialed back his rage. "Portals was stabbed in the break room. Someone used the LARC device to make a call to an unknown frequency. The entrances to this area were under guard all night, so we know this was done from someone inside who was trying to reveal this location to the enemy."

Oh my god. What kind of witch trial is about to start? Lizby glanced at her fellow miners. They all looked rattled, of course. She couldn't imagine any of them as stealthy killers, and she wondered how Halion could know with certainty that he didn't have a spy within his own ranks.

Halion resumed pacing in front of them. "I think this *spy* is a new plant. I doubt any of you know this individual from before. So I need to find out who can vouch for whom."

Lizby glanced at Mathias but his eyes were focused on the mercs. She was fortunate that he had remembered her, otherwise she would have a lot of explaining to do since none of other miners recognized her.

Halion motioned June and the other merc on guard to get closer and stay. He then called on the miner on the far left to step forward. The man took a few shaking steps as all eyes fell on him. When Halion demanded to know who knew him, four hands shot up. Each of the four miners recounted the details of how they knew the man, and for how long. Satisfied that their accounts constructed a consistent history, Halion told the relieved man to step back and moved on the next miner. Several of the miners had also worked with this next man and Halion cleared him as well. And so it went down the line, with each miner having several others to vouch for him or her. Lizby wondered if a small group of spies could have infiltrated the group, but there was enough overlap in the connections between the miners to make this idea implausible. The attack on Portals had surely been a solo job.

Finally, Halion came to Lizby. She stepped forward and looked to Mathias, but he avoided her gaze. When Halion asked who knew her, there was shocking silence. *Wait, he knows me! Why is he being like this? He just vouched for several other miners!*

Halion looked surprised. "Wait, no one? Is there anybody that knows Lizby from before?"

"I've worked in this mine for years, but mostly in a different section. But he knows who I am!" Lizby explained, pointing at Mathias.

Mathias perked up, shaking his head. "Sorry, I don't recognize you. What's your full name?"

"What?! Yesterday, remember? We talked for a while—you know me from the control hub room. Lizby Sasquire!"

Mathias looked to Halion, and shrugged meekly. "I don't understand what she's talking about. I certainly don't know her."

Lizby was aghast. She shook her head and balled her fists, but somehow held her tongue before another outburst. Clearly, Mathias was trying to condemn her with his denial. But why? Because of their little spat from yesterday? In such a deadly serious situation, the idea struck Lizby as ludicrous.

Halion looked at Lizby more closely. By his expression, he also thought the idea of her as a killer seemed far-fetched. "Hold on," he said, turning to Mathias. "What's your name?"

"Mathias Burdeen."

"Who knows this man?" Captain Halion asked the other miners.

Five miners raised hands. Lizby listened in growing trepidation as each testified to having known Mathias for months and in some cases years. One by one, Halion cleared the last few miners upon determining that others could vouch for them too. Only Lizby had raised suspicion.

Suddenly, Mathias' eyes widened. "Wait, what's that on her leg? Look! Just above her left boot."

Lizby looked down, and was perplexed to see a dark stain on her pants, and then horrified to see that it looked like dried blood. "Wait, that wasn't there—I don't know—"

"That's—that's blood," June sputtered, her eyes wide in surprise.

Halion ordered June to grab Lizby. Lizby's protest caught in her throat as she was led away from the other miners. "Try explaining that away. Looks like you were sloppy."

"Maybe I cut myself during the collapse. I just don't remember. Why do you assume its Portals' blood?" Lizby tried.

"Captain, she's lying." June said. "I wouldn't have noticed the blood when I first encountered her in the entry tunnel. Portals would have too. But we searched her and cleared her. As did you. This blood is fresh."

"And no one knows who you are, Lizby. The rest of the miners have been here all season, some for many years—"

"I have too! Mathias is lying! You need to find out why. This doesn't—" Halion held up his hand to stop her and June roughly squeezed her arm.

"Portals has been stabbed by someone in this room, and the circumstances of you showing up here alone after the others, and the bloody smudge make you stand out."

"Seriously—I stand out as a spy and a killer?" Lizby hollered.

"Technically Private Portals is not dead yet," the medic piped in. He had applied bandages around the wound and found a mat to lay his motionless patient.

"Look at me, listen to me, and ask me anything," Lizby pleaded. "Do I seem like the type to do this?"

"The Coalition doesn't have a 'type'. Hell, the fact that you don't look the part would actually make you an ideal candidate to make such a bold move as coming into our midst." Halion started pacing again. "Women are well represented in their ranks, even in espionage. Just like it is with the Sovereignty. Y'all are just as capable as men, right? So don't insult my intelligence," Halion motioned for one of his soldiers to check Lizby for weapons. "In fact, I had an old squadmate who happened upon a brothel a few months back. He met a woman who was a whore in more ways than one, and that Coalition bitch shot him right in the face just so she could hack into his datapad. So I won't be dissuaded by a pretty face."

He's unhinged. Why is he so quickly turning against me?

"Look, I'm sincerely sorry about your friend, and that this has happened to Portals, but can't you see that this is—"

"Shut up." June twisted Lizby's arm behind her back, stifling her response into a yelp.

Upon finding no weapons on Lizby, the mercs led her toward the break room. She looked desperately to June, but whatever tenuous connection they had from before was gone, replaced by angry suspicion in the woman's eyes.

"Mathias, please." She didn't know what else to say. But Mathias only stared coldly as she was taken away.

Chapter 34

Gerund, Ralteer, and Marina were slow to rise several hours after they had collapsed in exhaustion. Gerund and Ralteer leaned against a wall after they discovered the other was awake. Careful not to deny Marina rest if she was indeed still sleeping, they kept their conversation to whispers. Marina appeared from the adjoining chamber soon after. They speculated on how long they had slept. Based on their discomfort on the stone floor and continued exhaustion, they didn't think it had been long—but it was impossible to know how many hours had passed. The trio began pulling sturdy boxes and pallets from the storage area and sorting them together for use in the platform to reach the air duct. After gathering the largest and densest of these, they hauled them on top of the large machine that dominated the middle of the room. Marina remembered that the air duct was just off center from the middle of the wall and that it extended several feet into the room; just enough, she theorized, for them to be able to reach out and pry open the vent once the platform was built high enough.

The work was tedious and dangerous in the dark. The amount of material to sort through was overwhelming, and the pace of their work slowed after just a few meters of the tower had been built. The three survivors regularly bumped into each other as they carried the supplies. Occasionally, someone would falter while climbing up and on the boxy machine and fall to the unyielding stone floor. They talked minimally; just enough to keep the task going. They stopped once for water, and once again Gerund and Ralteer stayed behind to drink from their small supplies while Marina disappeared to drink from her main stash where she had claimed to have 3 liters. Despite tired muscles and the uncertainty facing them, the trio continued undaunted.

Chapter 35

Carmenta, Sabos, and the mercenaries trudged on despite their hunger and lack of sleep. Some mercs had tried to keep the mood jovial with casual conversation amongst themselves, but after several more hours of fruitless walking, the talking became sporadic and the overall mood turned dour. Carmenta and Sabos talked minimally—just a little encouragement, offered both ways.

Their relentless march reminded Sabos of a time he'd prefer to forget but would always remember: their plight as refugees on their homeworld. He had been sixteen and Carmenta had been eighteen that summer. Marina and her parents had been fortunate to have already migrated off-planet two years prior. When a solar flare storm had hit their homeworld, the entire biosphere collapsed under the devastating hit. First. the ultraviolet radiation from the solar flares directly killed only a few thousand people who couldn't find shelter fast enough during that first day of the storm. Sabos had seen many unfortunate souls who had been caught outside; their exposed skin horribly blistered, and many blinded. Few survived who were outside for more than a half hour of the intense radiation, and those who did prayed for death, so grotesque were their burns.

But the solar storm didn't relent until sunset, and returned with full fury the second day, and the day after. By the time the all-clear was given a week later and people finally emerged from their homes, they discovered mass extinctions of both plant and animal species, destroyed crops, damaged infrastructure, and panic in the streets. Famine hit almost instantly and millions died in subsequent months. Many survivors headed for the poles, where the solar storm had not so drastically scourged the land. But travel became treacherous, especially over so long a distance, and few were able to successfully migrate and find refuge. It was a bleak time that Sabos only remembered in bits; mostly the screaming outside their little apartment, the bursts of gunfire that would wake him night after night, and haunting impressions of his ever-weakening mother and father.

Sabos and Carmenta had lost nearly everything. Their homes, their possessions, most of their extended family, and ultimately their parents to starvation. They had emerged from their shattered city with just each other, and marched for weeks toward the poles before finding refuge. Sabos recalled the seemingly endless march with Carmenta, as their fellow travelers dwindled each day, picked off by robbers, rapists, and even a few unhinged cannibals. Sometimes the only thing that saved them from the assailants was the fact that they were surrounded by more vulnerable refugees. Bodies missing limbs or parts of their torso became a disturbingly common sight as the famine wore on. His sister got him through the living hell by urging him on when he was ready to relinquish all hope. Carmenta had developed a hardened edge that persisted to this day; a cynicism and weariness that followed her like a ghost. Part of her had perished on that journey, and Sabos didn't think it would ever be revived.

But Sabos was also quick to remember the incredible turnaround in his life. During their trek toward the pole, they had survived on whatever they could scavenge from the countryside, and had managed to reach a camp established by an offworld aid agency. They found sanctuary there as they spent months recuperating. Their health recovered and they migrated offworld and found jobs, and he had married the love of his life. If they could overcome the loss of their parents and the end of their homeworld as they knew it, they would overcome this mine disaster, too. Their current predicament paled in comparison, he told himself.

Sabos kept fantasizing that they would encounter Lizby around the next bend in the tunnel. She would leap into his arms, smiling and unscathed. Then the mercs would let them go, and then they would encounter an OreLife crew and be rescued to the surface. However, his hopeful fantasies faltered almost as soon as they began. There were no signs of miner activity: they met nothing besides dead-end alcoves and discarded ore piles. There were dozens of kilometers of tunnels, spread out through hundreds of branches. The chances of stumbling across Lizby seemed increasingly remote the farther they walked from the Pit.

He also dreaded that they might somehow encounter Marina. He would have to disavow her, of course, and he could only hope Carmenta would be able to do the same. Sabos wished their cousin the best, but prayed she stayed far away. They couldn't afford another complication, and if these Sovereignty mercs found out Marina was a deserter, they would either keep her as a bounty or kill her on the spot. And if Marina spilled the beans on him and Carmenta, then they could meet an unsavory end, too, for Carmenta's role in the desertion.

As their walk had stretched on, the convoy had loosened up, and the mercs finally allowed Sabos and Carmenta space. It was hard to see anyone's face since all the flashlights pointed at the path ahead. The Mask asked for Sabos's assessment at each intersection they crossed, but Sabos kept them along the main path and warned that they still might have hours in the labyrinth ahead before they neared their destination.

"Barker, go ahead and try to reach Halion again," the Mask commanded.

"Yes, sir." The group stopped as Barker lowered a large, boxy device from her shoulder sling. Sabos thought it looked very similar to the specialized communicators the miners used to penetrate hundreds of meters of rock—perhaps even the same manufacturer. Barker held a button down, which lit of panel of diodes as the powerful radio hummed. They heard choppy static as Barker transmitted from the frequency.

Barker adjusted a dial that only made the static increase in volume. "I think it's detecting another LARC radio. Hopefully Halion's group. We must finally be close enough. But we can't keep it on continuously; we'll have to keep checking back often. The outgoing signal has to be so strong and the battery will drain too fast if we just leave it on."

"So why can't it get a clear channel?" the Mask asked.

"My guess is that our device is a little more powerful with its outgoing signal than theirs. They both need to cross a certain threshold before a complete connection can be established through all that stone. We just need to get closer to them."

Satisfied with Barker's explanation, the Mask ordered the group forward, and they moved with increased energy. The mercs tested the radio every few minutes after, getting the same detection signal but no response.

Chapter 36

Lizby sat at a table in the break room. Captain Halion and June stood over her. They had asked for her story again and she once more explained how she came to work at the mine, her tasks as a miner, and what had happened to her when the mine had collapsed. She had thought that she could win them over with her sincerity, but she could see their suspicions festering as she explained. Halion focused on the conclusion that either she or Mathias was lying. This, combined with the fact that she was the only one that none of the miners claimed to know, made it clear that the interrogation was headed down an unpleasant path.

"I didn't do this. I—" Lizby insisted.

"Shut up!" Halion snarled. He leaned out the door and whispered to a soldier posted outside and then waltzed back to the center of the room with his arms behind his back.

Lizby sat rigidly with her hands flat on top of the table. She sweated anxiously, expressing equal parts irritation and vulnerability with her red-rimmed, tired eyes and sullen posture. June leaned against a row of the kitchen cabinets with her arms crossed. The small break room was brightly lit by three lanterns; two on the countertop by the dingy kitchen area, and another on a nearby table which glared into Lizby's face. "L-look," she stammered. "I have a husband and a sister-in-law, right here in the mine. Plus a lot of other people I know, if you were to just search in the right area and—"

"Enough," June said. After so warmly welcoming Lizby when she had first arrived, the merc had turned against Lizby completely. "Let us ask our questions."

Lizby sighed and threw her hands up but said no more. *I can't believe I'm dealing with this—I need to find Sabos.* Lizby was not practiced in defending herself. She had stayed out of trouble as a youth and had never been interrogated by the police or any other authority. Her skin crawled and her muscles twitched under their interrogation.

"The miner named Mathias; how do you claim he knew you?" Halion asked.

"Yesterday I had talked with Mathias, and right away he said that he had seen me in the control room hub many times before. I don't know him, but he knew about me. And since he's lying—either then or now—he's the one you should be grilling."

"It's just your word against his. But people know who he is. And they have nothing but nice things to say about him," June said with a smirk.

"And the blood? And I suppose the real attacker set you up?" Halion sneered.

"Yes!" Lizby had been racing through plausible scenarios of how the suspect could have pulled off the stabbing. "When I slept. It was dark. Someone must have come over, and brushed the knife or a cloth or something against my pants. Probably Mathias—but it could be anyone. If...if you were to test the blood, and see if there is a print or something in it, you would—"

"Please. I think you are under the impression that there is going to be a trial. You're not going to be able to weasel your way out of this. This mine is under martial law."

"If I did it, then how did I stab Portals like that? I saw the blade—it was sticking out of the *top* of his skull. Portals is at least a head taller than me. How could I have done that?! Think, Captain, think!"

June and Halion exchanged looks, and Lizby thought she saw a shadow of doubt in each face. Halion shook his head. "He could have been sitting. He—"

"I thought he was guarding this break room. He would have seen the attacker and stood. I'm too short to stab him in the head. Your men didn't find him in a chair, correct?"

Halion's face grew red. "Doesn't matter. You could have got it done—girl power, right? You can't lawyer your way free, Lizby. This isn't a court."

Lizby's protests hung in her throat, so great was her frustration.

Another merc walked in and handed the bulky communication LARC to Halion, whispered into his ear, and then exited without ever looking at Lizby.

Halion examined the device for a tense minute, turning it over in his hands and scrolling down a small digital screen, and then set it down on a counter. He sat directly across from Lizby. As a large man decked out in gear, he looked absurd in the rickety folding chair. "This frequency...it's not something Badger squad would ever use. And the call log indicates a 39 second connection was established with another LARC last night." He paused, letting this information sink in. "Who'd ya call, Lizby?" he asked, almost casually. "Who is coming?"

Lizby shrugged her shoulders helplessly. "I didn't! I don't know!" *Think Lizby—you need them to believe you—right now.*

Halion seemed to have complete autonomy down in the mine with his Badger unit. It was doubtful he could have maintained communications with the surface and his Sovereignty superiors at any point since the collapse. Nonetheless, he seemed comfortable making even life-changing decisions. Lizby didn't know a lot about the war, but it was commonly known that both the Sovereignty and Coalition increasingly relied on loosely-affiliated mercenary groups to carry out their missions. It was quite possible that the Sovereignty gave Halion a wide berth to accomplish his unit's objectives. The thought that the mercs could do as they please with Lizby and the other miners without the higher-ups ever even knowing was deeply unsettling. They were a kilometer underground, after all. No one would know what Badger squad did to her or the other miners.

Halion leaned forward in the chair. His face was a mere arm length from hers. He stared unblinkingly. "Just tell us right now, and I give you my word that you will make it out of this alive. We'll process you as a combatant. You'll do some time after this, of course, but at least you'll be breathing." He said this as if he was conceding the bargain of the century. "Think of the long-term, Lizby. I'll say this in front of everyone out there so you can trust me to follow through."

"Captain, I can't help you. I was sound asleep last night. I woke up when everyone else did."

Halion and June shared a weary glance, then stared back at Lizby. She could practically feel their malice on her skin.

“Look at her palms, sir. Why are you sweating so heavily?" June asked slyly. “The truth should be liberating; instead you look weighed down by a mountain of lies.”

“Huh? Of course I’m sweating. Of course I’m nervous! I’ve been accused of stabbing a guy in the head and then using a radio thing to, I don’t know, send a spy message or something,” Lizby’s voice gradually rose and she felt herself beginning a tirade, but then she caught hold of her words. “I have nothing to hide. Just think this through, the facts will—”

“The facts don’t look good for you, Lizby,” Halion said grimly. He looked to June. “We need to dig into another layer here. We need to know what sort of message was sent and we can’t wait.”

“Hold on!" Lizby said, feeling any sense of control over this situation evaporating. “Portals is still alive. What if he wakes up? He may be able to clear me.”

Halion waved his hand dismissively. “Doubtful that he wakes up, and doubtful that he got a clear look at his attacker. And you know that. You’re really grasping at straws now.”

Halion proceeded to ask Lizby questions about her background again, this time from different angles, hoping to catch her in a contradiction or outright lie. But even after she gave the same detailed answers, Halion was undeterred. “I’m going to give you one last chance, before June and I have to get a little more...direct in our methods,” Halion warned. Lizby didn’t respond.

The merc from outside stepped into the room with an urgent stride. "Captain?"

"Yes?"

"Private Portals tried to wake up. He—"

"Shit, soldier. Can you not say such information out loud in front of the prisoner?"

"Oh. Sorry sir. I didn't realize..."

The medic came into the room too. "Sir!"

Halion twirled his hand impatiently. "Go on—cat's out of the bag. What's going on with Portals?"

"It's safe to say the Private has significant brain activity," the medic said excitedly. "He woke up and tried to remove the knife from his skull. He was mumbling but I couldn't figure out what he was saying."

"Why didn't you send someone to get me right away? I need to talk to him."

"I restrained his arm just long enough to give him a sedative. He needs to be stabilized right now. He can't be moving around—at all. If he rips that knife out the wrong way, it's all over for him."

"Go take care of him. And prepare to try to wake him soon, just long enough to answer a handful of questions. I'll be right there."

The medic hurried off. Halion and June watched Lizby for a reaction. She figured there was a chance that Portal's return to consciousness could bode well for her, although she didn't have confidence that he would be able to conclusively clear her while he was still so critically wounded. And if Portals didn't wake up again, she saw no good end to her predicament.

"Looks like we're about to get some answers, Lizby. Bet you didn't expect him to survive a knife to the head, did you?"

Lizby said nothing. She thought of her loved ones, and wondered if she would live long enough to see them again.

Throughout the day, Lizby pieced together what was happening with Private Portals. She overheard conversations from the mercs who took turns guarding her and the ones passing through the break room to get a snack. It wasn't going well. Portals' vital readings were sporadic and as the medic tried to ease him into consciousness his movements were unpredictable and spastic. She could hear the mercs' conversation grow heated as the medic tried for hours to stabilize Portals. Apparently, at one point the knife was removed in hopes that it would improve his condition. Instead, Portals declined swiftly and was soon dead. Lizby's heart sank at the news. He had never fully regained consciousness and so was unable to reveal his attacker's identity.

A pair of soldiers sat with Lizby in the break room after the news of Portals' demise. One had his sidearm on a table in front of him. Both seemed more bored than on edge with the situation. Lizby wasn't sure what else she could do. She tried to mentally prepare herself for what might happen next, but she could find no peace. It wasn't long before Halion walked in, once again with June trailing.

"Portals died. I need answers," Halion said tersely. "Get up."

"What? Where?" Lizby said, making no move to stand up from the chair.

"Silence, bitch." June grabbed her arm and violently yanked her to her feet. "We were civilized, and you refused to give us anything. You've lost your opportunity."

"Huh?" Lizby was led out of the break room with June holding one arm and one of the soldiers grasping the other.

They walked around the break room building toward of the back of the chamber. Lizby craned her neck to see if any of the miners or other mercenaries were watching. The mercs stood in the ring of lanterns and regarded her coolly, but there was no sign of the other miners—they must have still been confined to the locker alcove. Lizby wondered how the remaining mercs could stand by idly and watch this happen. Did not one of them have a strong conscious? She searched each of the soldiers' eyes for help, but they either looked away or glared at her. They didn't have to disobey orders in order to stop this—but rather step in and counsel restraint or patience in their plans for her. But after having experienced Badger Squad's true colors in the past 24 hours, she wasn't surprised by the frigid response she now received from the onlookers. *They're not honorable. And they are probably dirty in all manner of ways.* But it was Lizby's nature to always look for the best in people, and even given the mercs' suspicions about her, their collective hostility was no less disappointing. *Not one of them will stand up to this.* June jerked her head around to face forward. Halion led them to a line of equipment along the back wall. He set his lantern down in front of a large cylindrical drum beside a pile of irregular rock chunks. It was suspended at 45 degrees and ended in a large crank at its base.

"Just tell us who you contacted. Where are they?" Halion tried.

"There's nothing to tell."

He opened the hinged lid of the drum with a menacing squeak. "Load her in."

"Captain, wait!" Lizby struggled with her captors as they dragged her forward. "I didn't *do* this! I'm a...I'm a clueless civilian and you're making a huge mistake here!"

But Halion ignored her, and as the mercs brought her forward, she could see what they intended. The cylinder was filled with jagged rock fragments and was just long and wide enough for a person to bounce around like a meaty ball. They would spin her relentlessly within the drum, and she would become cut, bruised, and unbearably disoriented in the claustrophobic space. It was a crude and opportunistic method, but surely effective at breaking down the will of a prisoner. She thought it was odd that in an era of rapidly advancing technology, the simplest things were often the most effective. But she refused to show them any more fear. *Fuck them*, she declared. She thought of Sabos and Carmenta and their past; all the hardship they had been through as refugees. *They went through so much tragedy. And remained strong. I can, too.* The thought of their endurance sustained her composure, even as the mercs tipped her forward to enter the cylinder headfirst.

"Captain Halion!" someone shouted. The sound echoed in the container, ringing Lizby's ears as if she were in a candy tin. June and the other soldier paused with Lizby's waist precariously balanced on the edge of the container. She felt so exposed—humiliated on top of her fear and anger. "We've got contact from the Lieutenant and his crew. They're close."

June and the other soldier shrugged at this news and pushed the rest of Lizby into the cylinder. She slid headfirst to the bottom and only partially shielded her face with a forearm. Inside, the heavy dust prompted her to cough. They shoved her feet inside and she curled herself in a protective position, expecting but still not prepared for the worst.

"Are they still on the line? I'm coming!" Halion said, beginning to run off. Lizby could only see the torsos of her captors through the tapered opening.

"Sir, I must tell you: they have some miners with them, and the miners said they know that woman." June stopped just short of slamming the lid on her.

"The prisoner?"

"Yes, sir."

Halion motioned for June to stop, and the lid clanged fully open to hang from its squeaky hinge. *Thank god. This was about to get ugly.* Lizby's spirits soared. Who were the miners that had vouched for her? Sabos and Carmenta?

"Did you confirm with the Lieutenant that we have Lizby Sasquire?" Halion asked anxiously.

"Yes, sir."

"Shit," Halion said under his breath. He approached the container and peered at Lizby. She glowered back at him from her absurd position—folded up like a hamster in a ball.

"Captain, I'm telling you, Mathias set me up. He lied about not recognizing me. He may be an OreLife employee, but he's something else too—he could be a Coalition agent. You need to investigate him."

Halion seemed to be debating internally, and finally relented. "Get her out. Now!"

June and the other merc helped pull her out by the shoulders when she had crawled to the front of the bin, no longer rough but not exactly gentle, either. She stood defiantly and brushed the thick dust off her clothing and off her hair and eyebrows. She looked from face to face, and kept returning to Halion. But no one would meet her gaze. She wondered what the captain would have done if the other crew had not been informed of her presence. How far would they have taken their torment? And what about afterwards, when she still had nothing to tell them? Would Halion have disposed of her in one of the tunnels?

"I'll finish the call," Halion barked, still unable to make further eye contact with Lizby. "In the meantime, clean her up. But that's it—I'm not ready to clear her, yet, so keep her here. And stay on high alert. There is still a killer out there. You!" He pointed at the messenger. "Grab another man and detain this Mathias guy, he must have lied to us—do you know the one? OK, do it now."

"Wait!" Lizby called as Halion started to walk off with the messenger. "Who were the miners? Were they Sabos and Carmenta? Just tell me that."

Halion turned to the messenger and nodded for him to answer. "I don't know," the man said. "We'll find out, if the line is still holding open."

"I'm coming," Lizby tried.

Halion finally regarded her. "Don't push your luck, Lizby. I'll have a talk with you soon. Just sit your ass down in the meantime. I haven't made contact with the rest of my crew in days." Halion rushed off.

Lizby's fortunes seemed to have drastically changed for the better. June starting dusting off the remaining grit from her prisoner's clothing, but June's eyes were downcast, her face red, and lips tight in an expression that was equal parts frustration, shame, and anger. What a rollercoaster of emotions for these men and women, she realized. They had first greeted her warmly, offering protection, then turned their venom on her when she fell under suspicion. And now they had to view her differently in the face of the new evidence. But there would be no going back to cordial relations. Not with her, and probably not with the other miners.

After a few more half-hearted swipes, June finished dusting Lizby's clothing and backed off. The merc's face was still a bit red. When her eyes finally met Lizby's, June blinked anxiously, and it was clear that she was struggling to rethink the suspicions she had clung to during the past day.

Lizby was still rattled, but she allowed herself a nervous grin. There was a great chance the miners on their way were Sabos and Carmenta, and she would have her family with her once again.

Chapter 37

"Barker, go ahead and try to reach Halion again," the Mask commanded.

At last, the radio registered something other than static when the Lieutenant activated the correct frequency. The Mask immediately halted the group. "What's going on? Do we have contact?"

Barker held a fist up for silence. "Captain Halion? Hello? This is Lieutenant Barker. We encountered some dead ends but we intercepted some civilians. We think they can assist us with directions to your location." Barker listened to the other end for a few seconds. "No sir, we do not. They didn't raise any red flags. Their names? Uh—" Barker looked at the Mask to aid in her memory, and he reminded her of their names. "Sabos Sasquire and Carmenta Sasquire—a man and a woman. They claim to be siblings."

Barker was silent for almost an entire minute. The Mask spread his arms in an impatient gesture and Barker held up her index finger as she listened intently. Finally, she looked at the rest of them to relay the message. "Captain Halion says that we are to proceed and make haste." She looked at Sabos and Carmenta. "He says that you two will assist us in finding the equipment area that connects to tunnel RA and in return will receive security from us. He, uh, says your wife Lizby is there, safe and sound."

"What?! Can I talk to her?!" Sabos stepped forward in jubilation, but almost fell because of the handcuffs.

Barker held him back with a palm and then turned her back on him to listen. "OK...yes, sir. Do you wish to speak to—OK, understood. Over and out." Barker toggled a switch and closed the channel.

"Wait, can Lizby come to the radio? Couldn't we talk just for a little bit?" Carmenta asked.

The Mask shook his head. "We shouldn't have stayed on the line as long as we did. There's a risk of interception—it's for critical messages only. You got the information you needed. Barker said your wife is safe, and now she knows you two are alive also. Congratulations," he said sarcastically, passing them as he went to take the lead. "Good news for both of us; now you have incentive to help us regroup as fast as possible. Get in line," he snarled with such venom that it nearly sucked all the newly born enthusiasm from them.

With the conversation over, the group again formed up and continued along the tunnel. Sabos looked at Carmenta and she shared his relief. He was still wary of this group of mercenaries, but surely they were telling the truth about Lizby. How else could they have her name? Although having confirmation that she was alive and presumably unhurt was wonderful, he would not be himself until he reached her. There were many questions he wanted to ask the mercenaries on the other side of the transmission. He also hoped that the Mask would cool down enough to remove their restraints soon. Sabos decided not to press his luck with his questions and would wait for the opportune time to begin a dialogue again. He could only hope Carmenta would do the same. *Hold on Lizby. Just a little while longer,* he hoped.

Carmenta and Sabos led the five mercenaries throughout the night with few rest stops. They trudged on through all the turns and slopes as Sabos led the way on vague memories. He continued to make it clear to the mercs, as he had from the start, that though he thought they were headed in the general direction of their destination, his experience in these particular tunnels was minimal and he wasn't sure what they might encounter.

The mercs periodically tried to make contact through their LARC radio, but either no one was listening, or the stone was too thick despite the specialized capabilities of the device—designed to penetrate hundreds of meters of stone. They didn't even detect the other LARC's outgoing signal. The uncertainty was disheartening. Barker theorized that they had signal before because the pulse was able to cut through the mostly hollow pit, but now that they've gone deeper into the tunnels, a quasi-direct signal was no longer possible until they got much closer to their destination.

Some of the soldiers grumbled during their relentless pace but the Mask insisted they press on. He finally reversed his decision and removed the handcuffs from Sabos and Carmenta, his only explanation was grumbling that they could move faster without the restraints. As they continued through labeled intersections, Sabos felt reassured that they were headed in the right general direction. But when he directed them to a dead end shortly after their path forked, the uneasy tension nearly boiled over.

"What. The. Hell," the leading soldier snarled as he shone his flashlight at a drill rig and the wall of recently cut rock. "This chump has led us this far into the mine and now we're lost? Do you have *any* idea what you're doing?"

Carmenta looked nervously at Sabos. He shared her unease. *We need to remain useful to them*, he thought. "Look, let's just turn around and try the other option. It's not like—"

"This is insanity," another merc broke in. "This idiot doesn't know where he's leading us; he's probably never even been in this tunnel. He—"

"I never said I did," Sabos said indignantly. "But I do know the general layout of this mine, and the approximate location of the sector we're heading toward. I'm pretty sure we'll be on track if we just go back to the last intersection and take the other branch."

"We don't have time for you to be *pretty sure*," Barker said. "We've been out of contact with our group all night. We are low on water and food. We'll drop from exhaustion before long."

Carmenta crossed her arms defiantly. "Well, feel free to part ways with us. We'll certainly take our chances alone."

The Mask held up his hand to silence everyone. "Enough." His helmet tilted toward the soldiers. "I expect more from all of you—you are professionals. Compose yourselves." He turned toward Sabos. "Where do you think our destination is? Don't bullshit me."

Sabos chose his words carefully. "I knew we needed to walk to the other side of the mine; almost the whole length of the tunnel network. Going through the Pit wasn't possible from where Carmenta and I started from, and I doubt we would have any luck trying to cross through the center of the Pit at any other point. So yes, we are taking the long way, but I think we are in the right cardinal direction to where the rest of your people are." *And where Lizby is, of course.*

The Mask nodded and Sabos looked at the other mercs, who looked impatient but at least held their tongues for the moment. Sabos chose to elaborate, hoping it would reassure the group. "We've been going through the outermost perimeter tunnels that circle the mine for kilometers. Some of them slope up and down a good distance, kilometers even, and that adds a lot of distance to our trek. But we're in the right quadrant and now we just got to get to the right level to find this equipment area." Sabos pointed toward the tunnel wall at a slight upward angle. "If we go back and take the alternate branch, I think it will curve in that direction, which is about where I expect our destination to be. My guess is that it is several klicks away but nearly a kilometer above us, which means we're going to have a pretty nasty slope to overcome."

The Mask seemed satisfied with Sabos's assessment. "Then let's keep going." Some of the mercs continued to grumble doubtfully, but the group quickly mobilized and continued on their way. The mercs' brisk pace gave Carmenta and Sabos enough space to briefly escape earshot from the others. She nudged him, and he tilted his head to hear while still facing forward. "Sabos, I still don't like this. We're not out of danger," she said softly.

"What do you mean? I know it's not ideal to remain with these mercs, but we're going to reunite with Lizby once we reach the merc outpost. Then we should be able to stay put to wait this out."

"I really don't like this group, and not only because they've been so harsh with us. They seem to be autonomous from the Sovereignty—they would wash their hands of civilians like us if it suited them."

"And then they would cover it up, and hope word of our demise never got back to the Sovereignty command?" Sabos asked skeptically. "Why risk that?"

"I've heard of such things—so have you. And it's not just that. The Coalition is still out there. We don't want to get caught in any crossfire. They could be just around the next bend in the tunnel."

"Carmenta, I don't disagree. But I don't think we have an alternative right now. Wandering the tunnels alone will probably be even less safe, which is what these guys told us from the start."

The caravan tightened up, and Carmenta was compelled to whisper in an even fainter tone. "I think we should take our chances, as soon as we catch up with Lizby, and maybe even before. We need to get away from the mercs, I'm telling you."

"We'll talk later," Sabos said, casting a wary look towards Carmenta. She nodded—there were too many ears close by.

Chapter 38

Gerund, Ralteer, and Marina toiled ceaselessly, for what they figured was closing in on 24 hours, steadily constructing the tower high above their heads. While in the first few hours in the dark their work had been tedious and clumsy, with the trio often colliding due to poor communication, now they moved with silent and machine-like order. But even well-run machines eventually fatigue, and they began to slow down and lose their precision. And as they built higher, a fall from the top of the tower could prove debilitating.

Finally, when Ralteer groaned that it was time to pause their tower-building and sleep, Gerund and Marina agreed. They had stacked almost 5 meters of wooden pallets and other packaging materials on top of the sturdy rectangular machine, which itself stood over a meter off the ground.

As the tower had risen toward where Marina had said the large air duct ended in an open vent, they continued to throw pebbles to approximate the proximity and position of the opening. They were close—just after the pebbles left their hands, they clanged against the metal. A meter or two more and they would be able to stand on top and grab the edge of the vent. Still, the tower had become unstable as they built, and in order to finish the job, they would need some more careful planning. The trio also agreed that this would require more time and energy than they could summon right now. The next day would be decisive; they would gather their dwindling strength, complete the tower, and see where the vent took them.

They each ate the crackers from Marina's supplies and drank a few gulps of water. They were tired and allowed themselves to succumb to their weariness, laying down on flattened cardboard boxes, which barely softened the unrelenting stone floor. Marina dragged her boxes further along the wall until she was almost out of earshot. Gerund gave himself some distance away from Ralteer's chosen spot, too.

"If we can each get several hours of sleep, I think we'll be rested enough to get things done when we wake up." Gerund said. Both Ralteer and Marina mumbled affirmative replies, and Gerund quickly succumbed to long-delayed sleep.

Chapter 39

Sabos, Carmenta, and the Sovereignty mercs had traveled far with no further contact from Captain Halion's group. The long radio silence began to cast doubt, once again, if they were traveling in the correct direction. But just as the mercs' declining morale threatened to sour, the group was surprised by the crackle of the radio, which had been left open on speaker-mode on Halion's last frequency. At first, the transmission was frustratingly choppy, picking up only bits and pieces of a man's voice. The Mask frantically toggled the microphone, telling the man to hold on. He jogged forward, and seconds later they finally cut through the static and a clear voice returned the Mask's greeting.

"Can you hear me? This is Halion."

The Mask identified himself and continued to walk the tunnel. "I hear you now," he said. "We must be close. I can hear the static dissipate as I walk on."

"Shouldn't talk long, Unsecured. What tunnel are you in?"

We are in tunnel F, uh—" The Mask looked to Sabos to answer.

"Tunnel FV. Is Lizby there?" Sabos tried leaning over the mercs between him and the radio,

The Mask ignored him and shoved him back with his free arm. "Hear that? Tunnel FV."

"We scouted out a tunnel FV—you're almost here," Halion said excitedly. "Just keep going to you reach fork that splits into FW, and take FW."

“FW. Got it. We’ll check in every 10 minutes.”

“Oh, you’re close. You might get here before then. If not, we got to keep the calls brief.”

“Will see you soon, Captain.”

“Make haste.”

The Mask ended the transmission, but kept the frequency open. *Hold tight, Lizby,* Sabos rejoiced. *We’ll be together soon!*

They had to be so close to the merc outpost. The thought of seeing his wife again energized Sabos’ previous sluggish mind and tired body. *Stay sharp,* he implored. *Almost there.*

The rustling began subtly. Carmenta heard it before the lead pair of mercs responded. It was a fast chorus of scratches against the stone that seemed to be coming from all around them—the sound reminded her of fallen leaves being tossed along pavement by the wind.

“What is that?” she whispered into Sabos’s ear. “Do you hear?”

“No, what?” Sabos arched his eyebrows.

“It’s like a...*crinkling* sound. I hear it everywhere.”

Sabos listened carefully and heard the noise she spoke of. He looked ahead, but all he could see was the silhouettes of the soldiers in front of them.

The lead mercs stopped when they heard it too. They scanned the floor and arched tunnel walls with their flashlights, and then stopped at the ceiling with a shared gasp. Carmenta saw why—the ceiling was crawling with the leading edge of a bug storm. The cluster of giant insects moved quickly along their many legs and covered the ceiling with their long bodies—each the length of a human foot. They resembled ancient ocean crustaceans, with segmented scales along their oval, upward-curving bodies. The dark brown bugs had two dozen legs, dark deep-set eyes, and short antennae that twitched rapidly ahead of them. The remaining three mercs behind them stopped and looked at the ceiling also, cursing as they observed the scope of the swarm. Two of the men squirmed in disgust and brought their arms in front of them defensively. Carmenta shuddered when she imagined the bugs crawling across her forearms falling on her head. She considered herself to be fairly comfortable in encountering wildlife, including insects. But the sheer size of these creatures, in such great numbers, coming right at them...She felt panic build in her chest as her heart thumped powerfully. She wanted to dig her heels in, but the mercs behind pushed her and Sabos forward.

"It's just a bunch of oversized bugs," Lieutenant Barker said. "Badger Squad has seen worse."

"Fuck it," the Mask said. "Keep going."

The group walked forward, albeit slower, with flashlights pointed upwards. Since the mercs were foreign, Carmenta could understand their dismissive attitude towards the insects. Perhaps they didn't realize the potential size of this swarm and the danger caused when the bugs funneled themselves into the constrained tunnel. Normally the lights, noise, and movement of the mining operation kept the bugs at bay. OreLife actively deterred them when they were spotted near the Pit surface, too.

"This is a bad idea. This could be a huge group," Carmenta cautioned. "We should go back and wait at an intersection."

"Absolutely not!" the Mask barked. "We're almost there—not one step back."

"Where are they coming from?" one of the mercs asked with a mix of trepidation and amazement.

"Just leave them alone and they will leave you alone," Barker added, her neck craned upwards as she walked in front of the siblings.

Hey, Carmenta thought. *I'm the one who has lived on Sarabek most of her adult life. I know what I'm talking about.* "I'm serious, this could be dangerous. People have been killed."

"Huh? Are they poisonous?" the Mask asked.

"No, but—"

"We can handle the bugs, all right? Just shut up."

Arrogant prick. Carmenta glared. Part of her wished that the swarm became a threat, so she could prove the mercs wrong.

As Carmenta, Sabos, and the five mercs continued, the bug swarm thickened, almost covering each side of the tunnel. The fluttering stampede of countless feet became loud. The bugs crawled in the opposite direction almost as fast as they walked. *This is a huge swarm. We're probably too late to turn back, though,* Carmenta worried.

If the bugs were agitated by the group's intrusion into the heart of their swarm, they didn't indicate it. Though the fact that they concentrated near on the top of the tunnel suggested that the bugs were avoiding them. Carmenta thought back to her encounters with the bugs on the surface. Near the end of the breeding season, the swarms dispersed and bugs could be found throughout the community. They were very territorial in this stage and intruded into neighborhoods, homes, and businesses. Carmenta recalled Lizby's account of squashing countless bugs after they had interrupted her outside play as a child. Lizby told her about vivid memories of the colorful stains their guts had left on her sneakers. Fortunately, the creatures were not dangerous in small numbers. They would bend at their midsection and raise the front third of their legs, but couldn't do much else if that failed to intimidate their adversaries. During the breeding season Carmenta had to contend with bugs on her way to work and—worst of all—those that found their way into her apartment to harass her.

The swarm became thicker and less orderly as they funneled down the tunnel's arched walls onto the floor. The leading bugs scattered around Carmenta's feet and she was forced to squash several as she waded forward anxiously. Their crunching bodies felt awful under the soles of her boots.

"Just keep moving!" The Mask shouted as the group's pace slowed. "It's just a bunch of insects!" But they continued to step hesitantly through a sea of bugs that now carpeted the tunnel floor. With a curse, the Mask pushed his way past Sabos, Carmenta, and then Barker to take the lead. He tromped through the bugs, noisily crushing their exoskeletons against the stone. The bugs made no effort to get out of the way but instead reared up on their back legs. Individually, they were no match for the mercs' military-grade boots, but collectively their bodies formed a thick morass of segmented exoskeleton and writhing, feathery legs. It become hard for the members of the caravan to raise their legs.

No no no...This is bad, Carmenta thought. *The swarm is going to turn on us.* She looked over at Sabos and saw the same concern in his eyes. Like most invertebrates, the bugs had ways of communicating that defied human comprehension and had a sort of collective awareness and will. It was this shared purpose that kept the swarms moving in orderly patterns across the plains to pursue the greater good of the species. Now, the critters sensed a common threat in the form of the boots plowing through their midst. The disruption sent ripples through the tunnel as the bugs flexed their abdomens, subtly reflecting the flashlight's glare down the tunnel until it flickered out of sight.

"They're bunching up!" Lieutenant Barker exclaimed.

"What are they capable of?" The Mask demanded as he grabbed Sabos's arm. "Are they venomous?!"

"No! Carmenta was trying to explain that," Sabos said. "This space is too confined, and we're agitating them stomping through like this."

"I say we waste them," one of the mercs said.

"No, that's not going to work," Carmenta replied.

"Keep your balance. Just keep moving!" The Mask commanded. But he himself was slowing down, knee deep in the bug storm. He swatted the bugs that crawled up his thighs and halted with the effort. The rest of the group bunched up behind him, similarly swatting and smashing the bugs that impeded them.

"Boss, there's no end to them," Barker said as she frantically pulled off bugs that were now on her torso. "We might have to start wasting them. Just got to be careful about friendly fire."

The Mask swiped at some bugs that were dropping from the curved ceiling. He pointed his flashlight straight down the tunnel and the swarm only looked denser. “Shit,” he growled and motioned for Carmenta and Sabos to stand to one side, which they did with difficulty as they waded through the fist-sized creatures. “All right, Badgers. We’re going to have to make a lot of noise and possibly alert our enemies. But I don't see an alternative. Aim low.”

Without hesitation, the mercenaries started firing into the mass ahead. The sound of the concentrated gunfire was deafening in the enclosed space. The floor exploded in a display of bug guts and flailing legs as the automatic fire and shotgun blasts ripped through the bug storm. The scene was both grotesque and visually mesmerizing. But the bugs flowed on relentlessly, undaunted by their dismembered comrades. They no longer passed the group but rather bunched up at their feet and hung down from the ceiling like living stalagmites. The group backed away slowly as they continued to fire, but the bugs were just as thick behind them.

Carmenta knew how vast the bug storms could be at the surface. If this swarm had managed to stay together as it crawled down through the tunnels, then she feared it could stretch for a kilometer or more.

One of the mercs broke rank as he tore bugs off the entirety of his body. He had holstered his weapon and was swatting the bugs frantically, but news ones replenished those tossed aside. He crossed dangerously into the other mercs’ line of fire, and was fortunate that they were composed enough to hold fire as he bounced to the other side of the tunnel.

The mercs' flashlights swung erratically in a dizzying display that briefly illuminated the masses of flailing insects to the background of deafening gunfire. Carmenta longed for a flashlight of her own to reorient herself, and deeply resented that the mercs had taken hers when they had first met. She looked for her brother through the chaotic lighting. Like her, Sabos was pressed against the wall to stay out of the merc's line of fire. As he continually swiped bugs off his waist, their eyes met in the low light and they shared a moment of trepidation. As children, Sabos had been far more squeamish than her when it came to insects and other invertebrates. Not quite phobic, but she had definitely been able to torment him with worms, snails, and moths by pressing them to her little brother's disgusted face. With the largest insect on the planet in a huge swarm around them, Carmenta wondered how long Sabos could keep his sanity. She was barely keeping grips on her own.

Sabos was yelling something, but the racket of gunfire drowned out his voice entirely. Carmenta tried to motion that they should try to step back along the tunnel wall, but the flashlight beam had moved away from them.

With a brilliant flash and sudden pulse of heat, the tunnel behind them exploded in flame.

"Hey!" the rear soldier shouted as he leaped forward in panicked bewilderment. "Grenade!"

The incendiary grenade continued to burst with light, and in the immediate vicinity, flames spread among the bugs, who retreated into the swarm even as they burned. The stench of burning chitin and sizzling fluids was overwhelming.

"No more grenades!" the Mask ordered in a lull in the gunfire. "Who did that?"

No one answered, and soon the bullets continued in full force. But the futility was becoming apparent. The bugs filled a large part of the tunnel's diameter. The fire spread among the part of swarm that had passed them, cutting off any notion of retreat even a few steps back.

The heat from the incendiary grenade continued to expand. In response, the bugs no longer flowed in their direction but instead attempted to scatter. However, with nowhere to go, their diffusion just served to fill the tunnel more. The heat prompted the bugs on the ceiling and walls to jump off onto the mass below, further exasperating the congestion.

By now, the tunnel was fully bathed in light. Carmenta saw the mercs drop all premise of discipline and stop firing. The Mask was gesturing frantically, and she heard muffled shouting behind his opaque visor, but either the other mercs didn't hear or they didn't care. Each soldier was on his own. The pair closest to the flames tried to trudge through the pile of burning insects, but were repelled by the heat, hopping and yelping in pain. Lieutenant Barker fought her way through the swarm, practically swimming over to Carmenta and Sabos.

"They're going to bury us!" she yelled. "When they do, try not to hyperventilate!" Carmenta thought she was the only one who heard this. The Mask shouted something but once again it was unintelligible. Bugs clung to the sensors of his mask—he looked otherworldly against the backdrop of flame. Carmenta reached over to grasp Sabos's hand, but he was no longer on the wall. Horrified, she looked through the blur of insects to find her brother flailing on his back, slipping deeper into the swarm as his body shifted through the layers of tightly packed insect shells.

"Sabos! Get up!" She lurched forward, grasping for his arm. But a mass of bugs hit her like an ocean wave and she stumbled backwards. Barker was tossed across her and both fell as the swarm drowned out the light.

Carmenta tried to push Barker off in vain. The heat from the grenade was still overwhelming but its light was being smothered by the swelling mass of insects. Dozens of spindly legs covered her face, tickling at her eyes, nose, and mouth. She struggled for breath while trying to keep the insects out of her airway.

"Sabos!" she tried again. But she couldn't see her brother, or anyone else. Carmenta felt suffocating pressure on her chest as the swarm enveloped her. *We can't go out like this. Not by bugs; not after everything we've been through,* she lamented.

Barker's knee jerked up and knocked her on the side of her head. She saw stars. The movement of bugs across her body felt almost liquid now. Her limbs were heavy, and her breath came in short rasps. The bugs seemed to have sucked the oxygen out of the tunnel. She knew death was imminent, and regretted that she didn't have time to ponder what was next. As the last glimpse of light disappeared, snuffed out by the swarm, Carmenta blacked out.

Part Three: Rebirth

Chapter 40

Captain Halion's promise to talk with Lizby, presumably to make some sort of amends, was quickly discarded. After he had finished the call with the other mercenaries, he ordered June to return Lizby to the group while he huddled up to talk with a few men from his squad. Lizby didn't care to talk to the commander anyway.

Mathias, her accuser, was flanked by two mercs, being led away from the miners. He tried to act unperturbed at her sudden reappearance, but Lizby noticed that his eyes moved quickly between her, the other miners, and then to his interrogators. She wondered again why he had framed her. She knew it drew attention away from himself, but why kill Portals in the first place? It was a risky move, even for a spy. *Why me? I'm not part of the Sovereignty.* She couldn't help but take it personally.

Lizby reached the miners, and as she sat down on a bench, they leaned forward expectantly. Their surge of interest was almost immediately exhausting, and she deflected all their questions, insisting that it was a ridiculous misunderstanding and that she didn't want to talk about it right now. She was too stressed to relive her past day of interrogation and torment. After the miners finally left her alone, Lizby sat and waited. She became anxious as an hour passed since the mercs had made contact. *Where are they—are they lost again?* she wondered. Her doubts began to cloud her thoughts.

Badger squad appeared confused. With Lizby less of a suspect, albeit not completely vindicated, from Halion's suspicions, the group had to reconsider how Portals had been stabbed in the middle of the night. Portals' body remained in the middle of the room within the ring of the lanterns. Someone had draped a tarp over him, which dulled the jarring sight of the corpse only slightly. Mathias had been taken through one of the hallway doors, out of earshot. But his guilt in Portals' murder was unclear, and so the mercs warily watched each other's movements while keeping the miners tightly contained in the locker alcove.

To make matters tenser, the Badgers had withheld the evening's rations, too. Halion didn't bother explaining, and finally after persistent questioning one of the mercs tersely snapped that they needed to conserve what was left. Water was more plentiful, but carefully regulated, with the mercs pouring a small amount for each miner when requested. Lizby noticed that there was no such rationing for the mercs, who drank the water whenever it suited them and made no attempt to hide their consumption from the miners. She suspected that they were dipping into the food rations with little oversight, too; because they were always circulating into the break room and she thought she saw some of them emerge chewing minutes later. The other miners were well aware of this also and their grumbling was persistent and bitter. If Halion didn't grant the miners rations or more open movement soon, the civilians' morale was bound to take a more rebellious turn.

Several possibilities danced through Lizby's mind about what was happening with Sabos and Carmenta and their delayed arrival. Few were good. The other miners undoubtedly noticed her intense worry and one of them chose to try to reassure with a knowing look. Lizby smiled slightly back, politely, and then remained transfixed on the entry hallway, awaiting the emergence of her sister-in-law and husband.

Chapter 41

Carmenta was buried alive.

At least that was the overwhelming sensation when she woke. Struggling for breath, her memory of recent events flooded back. With a troubled cry she burst through the bugs—half of them dead—that still smothered her with their weight.

The light was fading. The incendiary grenade had finally fizzled out, but piles of bugs stilled burned. A carpet of living bugs remained, but most of the swarm had dissipated down the tunnel. Carmenta frantically searched for her brother. She pushed passed Lieutenant Barker, who was trying to find her balance. She saw a protruding boot and pulled, and the limpness felt horrible. *Sabos!! Move!!*

As she stood over him, she knew for certain he was gone. *No. Come on, brother. You're needed.* But his bloodshot eyes were lifeless, and his mouth agape. It was clear that the mass of the bug storm had smothered him. Carmenta didn't understand how she was fortunate enough to escape the same fate. She had lost consciousness herself, after all.

She felt Sabos's face to confirm that he was really gone. His flesh was still warm but had already lost the vitality of life. His jacket was wadded halfway up his torso, and bugs continued to crawl over him in disrespect.

Carmenta released a primal scream as she bent down to sweep the insects off. Her brother had died mere meters from her, and they didn't get a chance to say anything to each other in his final minutes.

She thought again on the aftermath of the solar flare storm that had ravaged their home planet. During their desperate retreat as refugees, in which they left their home city and all they loved behind, Sabos had been the sole reason she had pressed on during the all-encompassing famine. She had wanted to lay down and fade away after their parents had passed within 2 days of each other. First their mother had died from dehydration, and then their father had also succumbed to weakness, though his pulse had been negligible for at least 5 days. Carmenta would have stayed in their neighborhood to die if it had not been for Sabos. But her 16-year-old brother had refused to give up, and she carried on for his sake. In a way, he had carried her through the present; a trusted foundation in an otherwise tumultuous life. But no longer.

She looked around through watery eyes. Barker was now leaning against the tunnel wall, breathing heavily. Further down, close to where the grenade had ignited, the Mask wiped frantically at his helmet. The visor was hopelessly stained by bug blood and guts. Carmenta saw bodies of two of the other mercs, but didn't see the fifth.

She lifted Sabos under his shoulders and leaned him against the wall. His head rolled to one side, but the posture was somehow more dignified. Her thoughts flooded with memories of her brother, beginning with their bond from the past year, and then going all the way back to her earliest memory of him as a baby as he tried to waddle across their living room floor toward her. She thought of all their shared trials and triumphs in the years that followed their exodus as refugees; making a new life together as they moved to Sarabek, the culture shock, the hard work they both endured in the mine, her initial skepticism toward Lizby before eventually welcoming her into the fold, and their shared dreaming of a life on a more hospitable world. There would be no new memories. The realization took her breath away even as she sobbed.

What am I going to do now? How am I going to tell Lizby? The thought of poor Lizby made the already unbearable sorrow worse.

"What happened?" Barker shrieked, stumbling toward the Mask. "We lost the rest of our squad!"

"What do you mean 'lost'?" the Mask yelled, still struggling to see through the visor. He turned to look to either side.

"They're fucking dead! Suffocated! I almost died myself," Barker said, pausing to catch her breath. She gestured casually at Carmenta, as if finally noticing her. "Carmenta is alive. The other miner—Sobos—didn't make it."

"That's right! My brother's dead! And Sabos is his name. Not *Sobos*," she screeched, her voice breaking partway. "He wanted to go back; we both did. We shouldn't have even been in this situation."

The Mask removed his now useless helmet with a click and threw it at a stream of bugs. His face was haggard against the glow of the dozen little fires, with intense, deep-set eyes and thick stubble. Perhaps it was his weariness, but his appearance suggested a man in his forties. His face had a soft structure that looked more like a starving artist or writer than the warrior than Carmenta had pictured. "Fuck this mine. Fuck this planet. The money's not worth it," he snarled.

"None of us threw the grenade," Barker said. "I think we were followed."

"And someone decided to light up our predicament," the Mask hissed, nodding his agreement.

"Then we shouldn't linger," Barker implored.

Carmenta looked back at Sabos's slouched body. She couldn't leave him like this. Not so soon.

The Mask finally seemed to notice her and sensed her hesitation. "He's gone. Nothing but meat now. Leave him."

Carmenta felt her blood boil. "Fuck off, merc. I'll do what I want." She didn't care what came next.

The Mask's face reddened in the firelight, and he looked like he might snap, but then he shrugged. "Whatever. I don't need you. Stay here and die if you want."

Carmenta opened her mouth to retort but she saw shadows along the wall behind the Mask. The Coalition soldiers swept in quickly with weapons drawn. Carmenta counted at least four as she dropped to the ground.

"Too late," Barker gasped.

As the Mask turned around, unarmed, to face the commotion behind him, the soldiers opened fire. The Mask's head jerked back and he collapsed to the ground. Barker dove for her rifle, which protruded from a pile of bug bodies. She was illuminated by flashlights, and she tried to roll to the wall while clutching her weapon. The soldiers fired three bursts and Barker's torso sprayed blood all over the carpet of bugs as her roll came to a fatal stop.

Carmenta pressed her face to the ground with her hands intertwined behind her head and lay motionless. There was no escape, and it was her only play. She listened as the soldiers crunched through the carnage.

"Path clear. These other troops are already dead."

"Careful. Verify that."

Carmenta wondered how the soldiers would verify death. Was she about to be shot? Running was now out of the question, but she was too petrified by terror to move anyway. She listened as the soldiers rummaged through the tunnel, walking ever-closer. Her face remained pressed to the ground and she couldn't see a thing. No gunshots, but she couldn't rule out that the sounds she heard weren't knives diving into cadavers. It's probably what she would have done.

"Pick up their weapons. Looks like they had some good gear."

"Roger that."

"This stench—worst thing I've ever smelled."

"What do you expect, setting off a fire in the middle of that swarm?"

"We got two civilians in front. And I counted five mercs." Her blood chilled at her mention.

"Do you think anyone got away?"

"Doubtful. We came upon those two mercs and they looked like they were still recovering from the stampede."

"I think this one's dead."

Were they talking about Sabos?

"Just be sure," *Oh god...*

Carmenta imagined a dagger entering her neck, right through the vertebrae. The soldiers sounded like they were right above her. She could no longer remain motionless—but she couldn't move too suddenly, either. She flexed her fingers outward behind her head.

"This one's alive," a man said flatly. Carmenta tried to choke out an explanation but her voice was uncooperative.

"Who?" someone else asked.

"The other civilian." The voice was dispassionate. She opened her eyes and tilted her head slightly, but could only see a pair of boots.

"Wait," she managed to say. Finally finding her voice gave her strength, and she decided that if this was the end of her family line, then she would not meet it pleading for her life. "I'm an OreLife miner," she said, a bit louder. She raised her head, and with hands still behind her head, slowly rose into a crouch. "I have nothing to do with this fight. I...I just lost my brother and I'd like to be on my way." The reactions of the six men she could see ranged from indifference to suspicion to hostility.

One of the men pointed a threatening finger. "Hold on. We don't—"

Another man with more stripes cut him off. "We have some questions for you; that's all, miss. But you had best be truthful."

"I've got nothing to hide," Carmenta said, meeting the man's eyes unflinchingly.

The man held her gaze uncomfortably. "Good," he finally said. "What's your name?"

Damn, what if the Coalition had caught Marina? What if she gave up my name? But there was no time to think. “Carmenta Sasquire.”

The man didn’t seem interested in her name, though. “First of all, what are you doing with this group, Carmenta? Are you assisting them?” The question seemed inquisitive and not hostile. But she still held her hands up, and the Coalition soldiers still held their weapons at the ready. She knew her life remained precariously in the balance.

“Yes. But not by choice, and solely by showing them where we thought they wanted to go.” *Shit. And of course, they’re going to ask about that now.*

“How many of the mercs were there in this group?”

“Uh, five.”

“No one got away just now?”

“No, me and Sabos—my brother—were out in front when the bug storm hit,” Her voice cracked on the word *brother*. “No one got by us. I blacked out, but you said you counted five dead mercs. So all are dead.”

“There were no other mercs before? Did any break off from this group earlier?”

“No! This was it.”

“Where did they want to go?”

Carmenta thought of Lizby, and wondered how she could protect her sister-in-law. “They, uh—”

“Hold up, Carmenta. I see the wheels spinning behind your eyes. What are you fabricating?” His voice was full of menace. *This is it,* Carmenta thought. *This is where he decides if he can trust me or not.*

Carmenta had always had a quick tongue that had gotten her out of so many prickly situations, but her grief clouded her thinking, and she sighed in defeat. She had to tell them about the chamber where Lizby and the others waited.

"The mercenaries wanted to regroup with the rest of their battalion or squad or whatever," Carmenta said. "They had recently made contact, so we were expected."

"How many are waiting?"

"I have no idea."

"What else was said?!"

"I don't know. I wasn't on the call," Carmenta gestured in frustration at the LARC radio which lay on the ground by Barker. The soldiers bristled in annoyance. "Supposedly, we are really close," she added, hoping to convey her cooperation.

Someone in the back sighed. "We already know all this. She has nothing new." *How do they know all this already?*

"Yes, just leave her," another soldier added. "We need to hurry, especially if they are expecting someone else and are going to wonder why they haven't arrived."

The lead soldier waved them back and turned to face Carmenta again. "I'd rather not have to come back to find you if you're leaving something out."

Carmenta couldn't imagine a way to get to Lizby before this group. "Uh, just one thing. I know there are several civilians with the mercs. Not by choice; they were there before."

"We have no quarrel with the miners as long as they stay the hell out of the way." He made a motion above his head. "Let's roll out!"

Carmenta finally lowered her arms to her side as the soldiers shuffled past. "Commander," she called. He slowed, tilting his head. "I just lost my brother because you wanted these mercs dead. He had nothing to do with this stupid war and you don't seem to care."

The commander halted in clear agitation. "You idiots were hiding amongst combatants—this is a war zone. I've lost some of my own people, but there's been no time to mourn. So I feel nothing for your brother."

"No. This is a disaster zone in a mine full of civilians," she snarled. One of the men shook his head in caution. But Carmenta didn't care. She knelt by Sabos and cradled his head. "His death; this is on you."

The rage simmered on the commander's face before melting into a haunting hollowness. "I don't have time for you. Stay out of the way, and you might make it out alive."

The Coalition soldiers continued on their way.

Carmenta tried one last time. "The miners just want to get through this," Carmenta said in a soft voice, her eyes fresh with tears. "These are the people I work with. Protect them. Please."

But no one acknowledged her, and they quickly disappeared and she was left in the glow of crackling fire with Sabos. She knelt by her brother and wondered how she was going to find Lizby for him. With the soldiers on their way, Lizby was about to get caught in the middle of a nasty slugfest, and who knew what would happen in the aftermath. However, Carmenta spotted the antenna of the LARC radio near Barker's body. Whether because they were in a hurry, or because they had no need for it, the soldiers had left it behind. She considered how she might use the device. *What do I have to lose?*

Chapter 42

Marina had slipped away from Gerund and Ralteer after she heard a chorus of snoring from the pair. She navigated to the adjoining room, and quietly crept through the pallets, careful not to knock into any of them. Finally, she felt the pile of loose rock she was searching for. She took the LARC radio from its hiding place under a discarded tarp. She adjusted the volume to its minimal setting and clicked the device on. She rapidly dialed between the frequencies, keeping her ears peeled for any voices. She had done the same the previous night, thought she heard conversation, but then it had quickly dissipated into static.

The radio crackled and spat unpredictably, threatening to echo within earshot of her sleeping companions. A bead of sweat crept across her grimy brow. *I can't do this long. If they notice I'm gone, I can say I went to pee, but that's only going to cover a little time.* The prior day, before Gerund and Ralteer arrived, she had spent an hour at the dial, not quite sure what she had been waiting to hear and with no planned speech if she were to reach someone on the other end. Part of her itched to turn off the purring radio and creep silently back to her sleeping pad.

Suddenly, the static smoothed out. Marina had landed on someone else's transmitting frequency. Her pulse quickened. She decided to prompt the other LARC radio to get a response if anyone was around. She toggled the mic on and off three times and waited.

Marina heard the line open with a soft hum. She held her breath.

"Hello? Who's there?" a voice finally cracked. It sounded familiar; she couldn't believe her ears. *Could it be? Carmenta?!*

Chapter 43

No response. Carmenta's call on the LARC had been born of desperation. Anyone within range could have heard her. But she didn't care.

"Hello?" she said. "Anyone there?"

"Carmenta? It's me!"

"Marina?!"

"Yes." Marina was quiet—almost a whisper.

"Where are you?" Carmenta felt a small measure of relief at the sound of her cousin's voice.

"We may not be the only ones listening." Marina sounded worried.

"Of course," Carmenta agreed. *But then again, we don't have the luxury of a covert conversation.* "These radios are limited in how far they can transmit through this solid rock. I can't be that far from you."

"You think so?"

"I know it."

"Great. I'm trying to head upwards. Through an air vent. Where are you? Are you ok?"

"For the moment, but there's been—"

"Are you alone?"

"Yes. Are you?"

Marina paused. "There are two others. But they don't know. Listen, I might have to call you later. It might be a while—"

"Why? What's going on?"

"Shit," Marina hissed. Her breaths sounded panicked. The transmission clicked off.

Oh no… What had happened to her cousin? She examined the radio in the ever-dimming firelight, still fueled by the bodies of fallen insects.

Chapter 44

Like his nap from the first day, Gerund's sleep was fidgety and uncomfortable. His fatigued body kept him asleep, while his anxiety made his dreams foggy.

Hours during this fitful sleep, a pinpoint of green light caught hold of his groggy consciousness. Gerund woke but lay quietly in place, half opening his eyes. His ears ringed with the stark silence. He again noticed a green pinpoint of light hovering in the blackness in his peripheral vision. He held his breathing in check as he thought through the possibilities. As he tried to process this light—so miniscule that it was only discernible in an environment of absolute darkness—he quickly regained his full consciousness. He slowly turned his head. The light swung downward and disappeared. Gerund sprang to his feet and took off despite the aches and stiffness in his legs. His pursuit was apparently unexpected, as the light shook and gasped in surprise. After a few bounding leaps he quickly collided with the source. They both landed with a gasp. The other tried to scamper away, but Gerund grabbed an ankle. He leaped forward and placed his forearm forcefully against the other's spine. "Who is this?" he yelled.

The other relented under the pain. "Let go! It's me!" Gerund recognized Marina's voice and removed his arm. She shoved him away and got to her feet. "What's your problem?!"

Gerund got to his feet just as quickly. He brushed his hands down her sleeves and took the object that her right hand ended in. She tried to grab it back, but he twisted away.

"What the fuck is going on?" Ralteer snarled as he stirred. "It's way too early. I need to regain my strength."

Gerund felt the device, which fit comfortably into his hand. "I woke up and Marina is standing near us with some sort of gadget—I saw a green light," Gerund explained. "She tried to run off when she knew I was awake."

"No, I was just startled, that was all," Marina said.

"What is it?" Ralteer inquired suspiciously.

"It's probably nothing. Probably some type of survey tool the miners use. There's a small indicator light but I don't think the rest of it works."

"OK, let me see it." Ralteer said.

"Just a minute, I'm uh, feeling some of these buttons. Marina, how does this turn on?"

She caught him off guard and furiously snatched the device back. "Get your paws off my stuff! You two came into *my* chamber, remember? This is mine!" Marina said.

Ralteer lurched forward in the darkness. "Give it here—now!"

There was a crash against the wall. Marina had thrown the device, shattering it against the stone. "You assholes. You arrived here as strangers. I welcomed you, offered my food and water—which you devoured like hogs—and now you're treating me like garbage."

"What the hell are you hiding?" Gerund yelled. He wasn't buying her defiance. He moved closer to Marina while Ralteer shuffled toward where she had thrown the device. Ralteer crunched over some pieces before picking up the remains with a gasp of discovery.

"I've got nothing to hide—ask me anything." Marina said.

"OK, why did you break it?" Gerund snapped.

"Because you guys pissed me off, and there was nothing to see anyway. It was just something I found near the tunnel cave-in. Some sort of datapad, I think, by the feel of it. You're lucky I didn't throw it at you," she spat. "Anything else?"

Ralteer cleared his throat. "Yes. Why didn't you tell us you could see?"

Stunned silence for a few breaths. "What?" Gerund and Marina both exclaimed.

"This isn't a datapad, Gerund. Or some other useless gadget. This is a camera—probably the tough type the miners would use in the tunnels. I can feel the lens and everything else plain as day. She used it to spy on us," Ralteer accused.

"What?! No—I didn't even know it was a camera—I'm no good with gadgets. It never worked to begin with, or at least I didn't know how to turn it on."

"Bullshit," Gerund said.

"Gerund, come on. It's nothing," Marina insisted.

"Marina, I saw the green light. You had it pointed right at us. In the middle of our sleep. How does that make sense?"

"It's late and I'm exhausted. Honestly, I didn't even realize what I was doing. I just picked it up and was fidgeting with it."

Suddenly, Gerund heard a subtle whirring sound.

"It still works," Ralteer declared. The green light flashed into existence.

"What?!" Marina exclaimed.

"I'm looking at you both right now."

Silence. Then footsteps as Marina backed away.

"Gerund, I think she's one of them."

"What are you talking about? I'm just a miner."

"She's part of the Sovereignty!"

"Ludicrous!"

"Turn around and show us your neck, then," Ralteer demanded.

"What—why? No!" she protested.

"Until you show me otherwise, I'm assuming you have the tattoo. I'll shoot you if I have to, Marina."

Ralteer's threat shocked Gerund. His heart started racing. The war wasn't worth taking another life; not if it could be avoided. *This is getting out of control. Ralteer is unhinged, but I can't trust anything Marina claims.* Gerund looked over Ralteer's shoulder into the small viewscreen of the camera. Through the green tint of the camera's night vision filter, he saw an exhausted young woman in a tattered, discolored miner's trousers and jacket. Despite being upset, her eyes flashed with cool calculation. And despite having no light, she stared directly at them unflinchingly.

"I know you're not really journalists like you claimed." Sighing in defeat, Marina turned around and pulled her collar back. Ralteer and Gerund stepped forward to get a better look, but the tattoo was already unmistakable. She was branded with the Sovereignty mark and ID number.

Gerund finally lifted his gaze from Marina's Sovereignty tattoo. He positioned himself between her and the doorway leading to the adjoining chamber with the rest of the storage materials. He heard her rapid breathing.

"Shit, Gerund—she's a spy!" Ralteer gasped.

"No! You've got it wrong," Marina protested.

"Really? Why else would you be disguised in a miner's outfit?" Gerund demanded.

"I...I deserted. I had enough, and quit just before the battle."

"Bullshit. That doesn't add up," Gerund said. "What were you doing in the mine?"

"It's a long story, but I can—"

"And why were you watching us?" Ralteer demanded.

Marina noisily backed into the rough stone wall. "Look—I'm sorry! I didn't plan to deceive you. I used the camera because I didn't know if I could trust you guys."

The green light moved as Ralteer explored their surroundings.

"Well, clearly we shouldn't have trusted you," Gerund said.

"You two told me you were reporters—what about that?"

"That's because we couldn't figure out who you were, and if we were upfront about being Coalition soldiers, you could have cut our throats while we slept!" Ralteer countered in a raspy snarl.

"OK, I get it—I was lying to you both, and I understand why you're threatened by that. I'm sorry. But I just figured if we were working on a way out together it didn't matter," Marina said with a placating tone.

"Look, I just want to get out of here. If you had been in my situation, what would you have done?"

Ralteer noisily checked the ammo in his handgun and clicked the clip back into place.

"Gerund?" Marina called

Gerund leaned close to Ralteer. "Slow down. What are we thinking here?"

"We need to see if she's hiding anything else," Ralteer whispered in Gerund's ear. He angled the camera so Gerund could see more of the chamber. The ceiling was rougher than expected, with little stalagmites forming throughout. The floor was mostly barren, at least where they stood.

Gerund nodded. "I'll make sure she's doesn't wander off."

"OK, how about you guide her in front of me and we'll check out the storage area first?" Ralteer said.

Gerund peered through Ralteer's viewscreen once more. Marina's eyes furtively darted from side to side; uncertain about where to focus in the darkness. "Is there anything else you would like to inform us first, Marina?" Gerund asked. "We'll be in a far better mood if you tell us now instead of finding out by ourselves later."

Marina was caught off guard by this ultimatum. She opened her mouth, but held her tongue and lowered her gaze to the ground. "No," she finally said, shaking her head. "You already know where the rest of the food and water is." Marina no longer sounded defiant but instead defeated.

Gerund found Marina in the dark while Ralteer stood guard with both the camera and the gun. Gerund would have preferred if they could just use the threat of the gun and not come close to her, but it was pitch black and she needed to be guided on where to walk.

"You watch her while I pat her down," Gerund said.

"Right," Ralteer agreed. With a quick pat-down, Gerund determined that there were no weapons under Marina's mining uniform, and then spent some time turning her pockets inside-out. Marina's body language communicated her displeasure at this invasion of personal space, and Gerund found nothing else.

They slowly walked around the machine from which their tower was erected and into the adjoining chamber with the storage materials. Gerund guided Marina with a firm hand on her shoulder and stopped her against the wall as Ralteer instructed. Ralteer stepped further to the corner of the chamber that held the food and water supplies. A small pile of cardboard boxes marked the spot along the wall where Marina slept. Ralteer checked along the perimeter of the room, finding nothing but loose rock, and began moving through the boxes and supply pallets in the center. Since the three of them had dragged things out of this area almost every waking moment in order to build their tower, it seemed an unlikely permanent hiding place.

"I'm checking out the machine room!" Ralteer yelled and went back to the chamber dominated by the rectangular, boxy behemoth.

Marina shifted uncomfortably under Gerund's hand. Gerund took a step back in case she decided to swing back at him with an elbow.

"I kept the camera over there where I sleep," she said. "I didn't tell you about it, but I wasn't actually trying to hide it either."

Marina became even more unsettled when Gerund didn't respond.

"Hey, I know it's been a long war, Gerund, and things can't be undone, but I just want to be done with this fighting; to go home and move on. I don't care what happens with the Sovereignty. I really am a deserter. I was just trying to get away from the war."

"What do you really do? In the Sovereignty," Gerund asked coolly.

"I am—was— a communication specialist. Mostly I hauled a bunch of radios to the front line and then found cover," Marina explained. "What do you do in the Coalition?"

"I'm a soldier who executes missions. Just a frontline officer," Gerund said matter-of-factly. "Have you ever had to shoot at anyone?"

"No."

"Ever had to otherwise put someone down?"

Marina did not answer as quickly this time. "No.....no, I haven't. That would be a last resort, and I'm minimally trained for combat anyway."

"How did you make it this far through this disaster?"

"It wasn't easy. I saw some others die along the way. But none at my hand," Marina added quickly. She tried to turn around so she could face Gerund, but he forced her back around.

The minutes passed in silence except for the rhythmic pattern of the pair's alternating breaths. As Ralteer's search in the machine room dragged on, Marina sucked in more stale air with increasing noise.

"Ralteer is such an asshole. You must see it."

"You are in no position to complain."

She snorted at that. "He doesn't intend to shoot me, right? You wouldn't allow that, would you, Gerund?"

"No," Gerund said with more certainty than he felt.

"There's other options—I'll finish the tower by myself and you two can just, uh, rest."

"No."

"You guys could help, like before. Or just leave me behind once the tower is completed and we can go separate ways. I would—"

Finally, they heard Ralteer's footsteps and saw the green light as he used the camera to come alongside Gerund. "I didn't find anything," he snarled angrily.

"Let me have a look around."

"Why? I checked everything."

"Just to be sure. Why not?

"We really shouldn't separate now."

"She's got nowhere to run. And that didn't stop you from looking around just now."

A long pause in the darkness, and then finally a frustrated sigh. "Fine. I guess you're right. We're in no hurry anyway." He handed the camera to Gerund. "I'll keep a hold on her."

Ralteer roughly grabbed her wrist and held the gun in the other hand. *If Marina is truly dangerous, then Ralteer is way too close. This is such an amateur way to detain her.* But Gerund didn't see a lot of other options. Once he saw that Ralteer had her secure, he swung the camera around and scanned the chamber in greater detail. He walked slowly into the other room, leaving Ralteer with Marina.

After over a half hour of meticulously inspecting every surface and irregular of the large chamber's rough walls, he had found nothing but loose rock and small scraps of metal. He turned to the interior of the chamber and began inspecting the area around the pallets with more scrutiny. He saw the same meager food supplies as before, along with discarded packaging. He wondered if Marina had hidden something in some of the packaging, but the loose stuff he kicked was all empty, and the cleaning supplies on the undisturbed pallets were all still tightly shrink-wrapped. He doubted Marina would have risked them finding something in the food supply, but he checked anyway. Nothing.

Next, he lifted the loose white wrapping on the only pallet that was completely empty and spotted a bulky device. Kneeling closer, he realized he had seen this type technology before. It was a LARC—a sturdy military-issued radio with a variety of dials and diodes and streamlined for the singular function of communicating with similar devices. The kind with amplified, penetrating signal that could penetrate layers of rock.

"What the hell?" Gerund uttered. *This radio...did Marina hide this? Of course, she must have...*

He picked up the LARC to confront Marina with her continued deception. *Wait.* He paused as he fought against the impulse to trot back and show Ralteer. *I've got to control this. They're both going to flip out.* He needed to get to the truth and somehow not escalate the situation.

He crossed into the other chamber. "Check out what I found," he exclaimed. Marina stared suspiciously in his direction. Ralteer looked up as well, breaking his scowl that had been boring a hole into Marina.

"What?"

"I found a radio. Specially designed to pierce through rock. It was hidden; not far from her food and water."

"Put it down, let me inspect it. Here," Ralteer handed him the gun, roughly; dangerously. "If she makes any move, shoot her."

"I'm not going to make a move," Marina protested. "That's stupid; where would I go?"

"Shut up!" Ralteer snarled.

The situation was slipping away. Ralteer wasn't seeking a peaceful resolution; at least not at the moment. Marina needed to come clean, but Ralteer was not in a position to handle the truth. Gerund doubted that he was ready for it himself. *I've got to maintain possession of this gun in the meantime.*

Ralteer mumbled to himself as he more closely examined the LARC in darkness, before asking for the camera so he could see it too. Since Ralteer didn't have the gun, Gerund handed him the camera.

Finally agreeing with Gerund's identification of the device, Ralteer guided Gerund ten steps back, far away enough for their whispers to escape Marina's ears. "Check this out. I think this thing works," Ralteer rasped. He held a switch until the radio powered on with a strong thrum and a grid of LED displays and sensors. Ralteer paused a finger on the side to show Gerund a frequency bandwidth indicator and pressed a large button in the center of the radio. Static filled their ears.

"Is it all static?" Gerund asked. He reached for the dial, but a single click interrupted the static.

"Wait, leave it on this frequency!" Ralteer growled.

Gerund complied and they waited in silence. 10 seconds later, the static cleared. "Hello?" a woman's voice ventured forth. "Marina?...Talk to me, Mar."

"Quiet!!" Marina shrieked when she realized what was going on.

But Ralteer had already cut the signal before she had finished the word. He handed the radio to Gerund, who awkwardly tried to hold it against his body with his free arm. Suddenly, Ralteer grasped his wrist with one hand and pried the gun away with the other.

"Hey!" Gerund shouted. "What are you doing?! Trying to get one of us shot? The gun could have fired, asshole!"

"Well, it didn't," Ralteer snidely remarked. He held both the camera and gun on Marina. "You have some explaining to do, Marina." Gerund stood behind him, trying to look through the camera viewscreen over Ralteer's shoulder.

Marina shuddered.

Chapter 45

The transmission cut off abruptly. Carmenta toggled the radio microphone once more. "Marina?" Her cousin had tried to say something before the line died.

What happened to her? There's not even static from her frequency...

Carmenta found one of her former captor's flashlights in the glow of the meager remaining firelight. She picked up the bulky LARC and immediately started to backtrack the way her group had come, kicking aside a couple of surviving bugs that bumbled across her path. She remembered that there had been a major fork in their tunnel perhaps half a klick back; an intersection that had been labeled with signs and had looked like it had been well-maintained. If the soldiers that had just swept through and murdered the mercs were headed in Lizby's direction, then it was unlikely that Marina's prior call had also been in the same direction. Plus, there was little Carmenta could do for Lizby; the soldiers were probably already there. Surely they would spare sweet Lizby...*oh god, who am I kidding? If she's not killed outright, they might rape her. And then kill her.* Carmenta hated to think of these violent possibilities, but couldn't deny their plausibility. *Maybe I should hurry toward Lizby and do what I can.*

Still, she was conflicted. Marina could be just a few minutes away. She might be able to help her, and the two of them could then go and try to find Lizby, praying that she survived. She wanted to kneel by her brother's body and ask for his counsel. Her heart ached. *What would you have me do, Sabos? I don't know if I can help anyone in my current state.*

She felt paralyzed by the choice, and her feet felt heavy. *I've got to do something—now. Can't just stand here. Marina...Lizby...both are still in danger*. She decided to head toward what she thought was Marina's direction and see if she could again make contact with her cousin's radio by traveling a short distance. If not, she would turn right back around and hope for the best in the search for Lizby.

Chapter 46

Marina shifted her weight nervously. Despite the past two days of successfully enduring smothering darkness, suffering through claustrophobic isolation, and escaping imminent death, all while keeping her wits intact, she felt her remaining composure disintegrate in a matter of seconds. She had nowhere to direct her eyes in the dark besides the green camera light that had betrayed her earlier. Marina imagined the gun raised toward her and began to back away. Gerund and Ralteer were talking, but she didn't comprehend what they were saying. Her memory of the room's layout faltered, and she wasn't finding the wall where she expected it to be. The voices came closer. She backed into a stack of pallets and packaging waiting to go into the tower, noisily toppling the materials over. She stumbled several more meters and suddenly had her back against the wall.

"...and whoever she called could have known for the past day," Gerund was saying. "The signal couldn't reach the surface through all the stone, do you think?" He became louder. "Tell us Marina, who the hell was that?!"

"Don't even bother. I don't want to hear her lies," Ralteer snarled.

Oh god, what are they planning? Marina slid along the rough wall. Her ankle nearly buckled as she stepped on a rock. She picked up the hefty stone and clenched it in her fist.

"You know I can see you, right?" Ralteer sneered. Marina imagined that he had the gun raised at her face, all too eager to act on his grudge against her.

I know. Stay away. Marina mouthed the words, but no sound came out. She still gripped the rock. Her plans to escape the service and her attempts at concealment now felt foolish. Her dreams of the future—Carmenta's help and encouragement, too—seemed so far away and meaningless.

The day before, as the three worked together building the tower, she had been unsettled knowing that her deceit would have to end eventually; but she had told herself that it would happen on her terms. Now, her fate felt out of her control, at the mercy of their volatility.

Looking through the small camera viewscreen, Gerund watched Marina back into a corner of the cavern with a thud. He and Ralteer stopped just a few meters away. "OK, just wait a minute—all right? I'll tell you what you need to know," Marina said.

"You claim to be a communications specialist but are probably a spy. You are a liar and I bet you would kill us in our sleep as soon as you could get your buddies here to help you do the deed." Ralteer said.

"Gerund, can you at least hear me out here? I know, I lied," Marina conceded. "But I...I just wanted to get away. I don't have any Sovereignty people coming here. I don't want to cause you any harm," she insisted.

"We need to know exactly who you have been talking—" Ralteer yelled.

"Yes, all right! I can explain—"

"No more bullshit," Gerund said. "We need complete transparency, or this isn't going to end well for you."

He's not bluffing. "It's just been my cousin, all right? She's the only one I talked to. She's a civilian—an OreLife employee."

"Bullshit!" Ralteer challenged.

"She was my contact in the mine. I had left the Sovereignty and she was helping me. But I have no idea what happened to her after the mine collapse. I was listening to the radio channels and I just happened to hear her voice."

"Uh-huh. Quite the fucking coincidence," Ralteer observed.

"I got the impression that she's alone, but we talked only for a minute," Marina continued undaunted. "I thought that she was close, though."

"How did you suggest your *cousin* kill us?" Ralteer said.

"Ridiculous! I barely even talked to her, like I said. And it was a total accident that I reached her."

"OK, here's the deal, Marina—or whatever the hell your name really is," Ralteer said.

"It really is Marina," she snapped.

"Whatever. Listen, I grew up in a rough neighborhood. The kind of place where fools don't last long. So I have a very fine-tuned bullshit detector. I understand that continuing to lie feels like a natural defense, but believe me when I tell you that it will be better for you to be totally honest with me."

"I'm not lying. You're not as smart as you think you are."

Ralteer angrily exhaled, and Gerund could feel the man's fury building into a response. *I don't like where this is going.* Ralteer was turning the confrontation into a battle of stubborn wills.

"What do you know of what's happening on the surface?" Gerund felt that tensions had been running too hot for too long, but he also figured that if the interrogation lost speed then Marina might have more opportunity to carefully word her responses. The time to get any truth out of her was now.

"I really don't know. I didn't have any briefing from my unit," Marina said, perhaps with a hint of relief at this new line of questioning. "I mean, we all knew the mine was important, but we thought our forces had secured the region. There was no plan to enter the mine. At least there wasn't the night before, when I escaped from my base. So when you guys—the Coalition—showed up, we must have responded impulsively. I mean, that's why there was so much chaos down here, right?"

"Not very useful," Ralteer assessed. "My bullshit detector has had enough."

"I don't know what else to tell you. I think no matter what truth I told you, you wouldn't be willing to accept it."

"All right, enough," Gerund said, gesturing downwards to tell them both to relax, though neither could see him.

"Just keep in mind that I deceived you only because I thought it was my best chance to escape this whole travesty down in the mine, ok? This wasn't personal."

"Got it—now sit down," Ralteer said.

Sensing the situation settle down a bit, Gerund felt for the radio in the dark, and pressed the toggle switch. The static faded to nothing.

"Is it off?" Ralteer asked.

"Yes, it's off."

"Let me see." Ralteer approached with the camera. He tussled with the device, and then backed away, satisfied that it was inactive.

Gerund signed. "All right, we don't need to be judge and jury with Marina right now. Let's get this tower built so we can get the hell out." Gerund knew they couldn't keep a long-term captive, but neither could they just turn her loose here. At some point they would have to decide what to do with Marina, and it was not a crossroads he was eager to reach.

"I'm all for focusing on the tower, Gerund, but how do we do that with a spy in our midst? How are we supposed to watch her and still do the work?"

"Hey, I'll still help. I want out of here, too. That's all I've wanted."

"No way." Ralteer stepped closer to Gerund and whispered. "If we're not going to take her out, we need to at least immobilize her."

"I can still hear you!" Marina hissed. "Let me help. It will go so much quicker."'

"You would have to give us full cooperation," Gerund said.

"I will. Definitely."

"The tower-build would go much easier..." Gerund admitted.

"Yes, let's just get out of here," she prodded.

"We just have the camera, which means one of us has to keep her directly in sight at all times."

"That's not going to work," Ralteer said. "We don't have handcuffs or anything to keep her in check. She's a danger to us. We need to end this—"

"Hey, shut up. I've got a solution, ok?" Marina said forcefully.

"Yes?" Gerund asked expectantly.

"Promise me you'll let me help. And let me go once we get out of this room."

Ralteer cackled. "Absolutely not, no—" he began.

"Just help us out for now," Gerund implored. "What do you have?"

"I've got a lighter. I found it when I was first wandering the mine."

"Gerund, I thought you patted her down," Ralteer spat. "Evidently, you did a poor job of it."

"I did a quick pat-down in the dark. What does it matter now?"

"Who knows where she has that thing shoved."

Gerund ignored the crude response but wondered how he had missed the lighter, on top of the camera and the radio that Marina had hidden in the chamber.

"The lighter works," Marina insisted. "Half full. I was going to use it myself to ignite some of this debris before you two showed up."

Both Gerund and Ralteer were silent. Gerund considered Marina's story once more. She could have provided them light the whole time, but knew that meant risking the exposure of the Sovereignty mark tattooed on her neck. He didn't really trust her—he couldn't. He didn't trust Ralteer, either. But the only way was forward, or in this case, upward.

"All right, let's get this fire started then," Gerund said at last.

Chapter 47

Lizby kept her head down after the barrage had ended. She remained prone long after the last cry of anguish, long after the last lingering gunshot, and perhaps a full half hour after she heard the last footstep. She had heard intermittent voices since but couldn't judge how far away they were because she tightly protected her head with her arms. At last Lizby turned over and sat up, not knowing what form the carnage would take.

The lantern ring was still lit and Lizby could see most of the chamber. Five miners remained in the equipment alcove. Three of them huddled despondently on the benches. Two others were slumped against the wall; one was clearly dead, as evidenced by the hole in his skull and the blood splatter against the wall, and the other cradled a wounded arm. The four surviving miners barely acknowledged her as she rose into a crouch. Their faces conveyed a mixture of shock and confusion. Peering beyond the equipment alcove, Lizby could see the bodies of five dark-clad soldiers and their scattered equipment in the open main chamber. However, she couldn't determine their identities because the faces were either turned away from her or obscured in the dim lantern light.

Lizby faced the three miners on the benches and widened her arms in exasperation. “What happened?” she asked. “Where are the other mercenaries that were coming here? My husband was with them. Carmenta was with them too. Who did this?”

"The Coalition—who else?" one of the miners spat in frustration. "The Coalition; the Sovereignty; they're both beyond corrupt. They don't care about us down here. They don't care about any of the civilians they kill. We're just a collateral nuisance."

Lizby rose to her feet and peered carefully beyond the wall of the alcove. She saw a pair of bodies at both entrances to the chamber. "Where is everyone else? Where are the rest of the miners?"

"They ran." It was the wounded man this time. "We huddled down when the gunshots and screaming started, but some of the miners bolted for that door." He pointed to the entrance leading to the tunnel that Lizby had emerged from over a day prior. "Some of the others tried to run out later, too, when it was really ugly. I saw some of the Badger mercs retreat, also."

"And then the Coalition troops swept through and followed them. They left us alone."

Lizby raised an eyebrow at this last statement, looking at the dead and then at the wounded man, who caught her gaze. "We tried to dash to the exit during the firefight. Bad idea. I don't know which side shot us."

"What happened to Mathias?" She looked to each face, but no one answered. "The man's a killer. What happened to him?"

"We don't now," one of the miners finally answered. "Don't see his body. We think he got away...or was freed by the Coalition soldiers."
Great, all these dead people, and Mathias escaped justice?

Lizby sat on one of the benches across from the miners. Her eyes were hollow. "Sabos and Carmenta are out there."

"Who?"

"My husband and sister-in-law. They were supposed to be here. What happened to their group?" She looked to their faces in the long silence.

"I would, uh, speculate that they were ambushed before they got here," a miner said. "But maybe they left civilians behind like they've done with us," he added quickly.

Lizby held back tears. "No one else came through?"

"No. Just the Coalition soldiers. There were only five or six of them, but they got the drop on the mercs."

"I gotta go out and try to find my people," Lizby declared, surprising no one. She knew better than to ask for help, and doubted she would want it from these survivors, either. "What will the four of you do?" She eyed the wounded man, who looked pale.

"Dunno. Probably keep our head down here for a while."

"Oh." Lizby eyed the break room, and the man guessed her intent.

"You should check out the break room to see what's left. Take what you need to refuel in order to find your people."

Lizby nodded through grateful tears. "Thank you."

"But not too much," another miner added with a worried scowl. "Here, I'll go with you."

Inside the break room, they found some scattered trash and several large plastic jugs of water. There were also several kilograms of energy bars. Lizby had her fill of the water and filled a canteen and slung it over her shoulder. She packed as many of the energy bars as she could fit in her pockets, all the while hearing the miner sigh in frustration. *What's his deal? I'm not even taking a fifth of this.* But he allowed her to exit the break room with the supplies.

She grabbed one of the lanterns and walked over to the five bodies near one of the chamber's exits. She recognized some of the members of Badger squad, including Captain Halion. He lay on his back with arms spread wide. His half-open eyes stared at the cavernous ceiling. She felt nothing at the sight of the man who at first welcomed her and then threatened her.

Lizby realized her own numbness and this gave her pause. She hesitated. She realized that going off on her own was reckless and that staying with the miners here was a sensible alternative. The danger had passed and they had supplies to last them days. *But I've got nothing to lose,* Lizby told herself. *I've got to try to find them.*

She strode across the room. The miners were staring at her. She nodded grimly in their direction and continued.

"Wait..." one of them began, but she did not heed him. "Lizby, was it? Just hold on."

"What?" she asked wearily.

"You should stay here," he stammered. "You don't know what happened to your people."

"Exactly." Lizby didn't wait for him to elaborate. She strode toward the exit where the Coalition soldiers had stormed through instead of Sabos and Carmenta. Before slipping through the ajar door, she knelt by a pistol that had been discarded in the chaos. She hesitated once more. She wouldn't win any shootouts. She had only fired a gun a few times in her life out in the countryside, and hadn't been particularly good at it. The gun might just get her killed instead. But she wouldn't be taken prisoner again either—not without a fight. She flipped the safety of the pistol and stuffed it under her belt. *I'm coming, Sabos.*

Chapter 48

As soon as Marina handed over her previously concealed lighter, Gerund flicked it on, bathing their surroundings in the orange light. Similar to the glimpse Gerund had gotten in the blue light of the machine panel from over a day prior, Ralteer's face was tired and haggard. Ralteer remained tight-lipped and wary as Marina bent down to scoop up some discarded packaging at her feet.

"Here, get this trash burning," she suggested. "We don't want the lighter to run out of fuel. And then we can light some of the wooden pallets."

Within minutes, all four corners of the room had compact burn piles going, and for the first time Gerund was able to properly see the chamber. It was nearly as barren as he imagined it, with the center of the room dominated by their stacked tower. The flames bathed the rough walls in a dance of shadows and their light faded almost completely into the high ceiling, but lapped just enough illumination onto the air vent—their means of escape. To their relief, the vent was just as Marina had described it. It had a large, man-sized opening and the duct extended horizontally along the ceiling until exiting the room. However, their method of throwing pebbles at the air vent to hear its approximate location had been imprecise, to say the least. The tower stretched precariously upward, not quite straight, but maybe good enough. It ended several meters below the large open vent, not directly underneath but close enough that they could lean over to grasp the lip of the vent.

The smoke from the four fires quickly dissipated as it rose into the expansive ceiling. Gerund figured that as long as they worked quickly, the smoke buildup wouldn't be a problem.

Now that they could see, the tower's construction accelerated quickly. It had already stretched 6 meters high and they began to rapidly close the remaining gap of several meters. *This is going to work,* Gerund thought as he eyed the open maw of the vent. He made quick trips into the adjoining chamber to bring back the pallets, and Ralteer hoisted them up to Marina, who carefully centered them on top of the tower. Gerund felt the oddness of working with the woman that he and Ralteer had threatened only a short time before. As the lightest, Marina was able to hang on one side of the tower without tipping it despite no counterweight on the other side. If she had reservations about being so high, she did not voice them. At the tower's present height, the fall would cripple her.

Ralteer had stored the gun into the waistband of his trousers. He handed the building materials to Marina with stoic efficiency. His begrudging attitude toward her was palpable. They barely said a word to each other, and each preferred to discuss tower progress with Gerund.

The tower stretched ever higher, but their stock of usable packaging materials was dwindling. The top of the tower was narrowing as the remaining materials became smaller. They needed to raise the tower 2 meters to establish a sufficient foundation to pull themselves into the vent. By now, Gerund had to hand materials up to Ralteer a couple meters off the ground, who in turn had to climb up the tower halfway to pass the materials to Marina. The tower creaked and wobbled, and Gerund wondered if it would come crashing down. Would they give up at that point? Gerund considered the shaft he had fallen through, but he already knew there was no way any of them could scale it. Ralteer's tunnel was completely collapsed. And the sheer slope that Marina had skidded down was insurmountable. *We really need this tower to hold. I'd rather not think any more about what happens next if it doesn't.*

"Almost there," Marina announced. She carefully stood up at the top as soon as Ralteer was off the tower. She reached up and touched the lip of the vent with her fingertips. "Let's get this just a little bit higher; I think I could pull myself up with just a couple more pallets underneath me."

"Gerund goes in first. You stay in the middle. I'll keep guard in the back," Ralteer said gruffly.

"Whatever," Marina dismissed.

"Don't *whatever* me, bitch, I tell you—"

"Hey, enough!" Gerund shouted. *I can't believe this. The ego of this guy.* "Let's get this built and get the hell out of here, ok?"

"That's what *I* want," Marina growled, sneering down at Ralteer from her perch on the tower. *And Marina is not helping the situation either.*

Ralteer pulled on his waistband, not-so-subtly exposing the hilt of the pistol. Incredibly, he didn't say another word, but instead tossed a light plank of plywood up to Marina, who caught it with one hand as she steadied herself with the other arm. Her smirk was gone, but right before Ralteer turned away, she stuck her tongue out at him.

Ralteer returned hastily to Gerund, who extended the next piece of plywood to him. But Ralteer batted it onto the ground.

"What?" Gerund hissed.

"You know, I'd like you to back me up for once," Ralteer kept his voice low so Marina couldn't hear. "I'm tired of always having to be the bad guy."

Then stop being such an asshole, Gerund thought as he stared impatiently.

"Seriously," Ralteer continued. "She's our prisoner. She wasn't even wearing the right uniform. We'd be fully justified killing her on the spot. If she is willing to cooperate to save her own skin, I will accept that. But I won't accept this constant disrespect from her."

"It doesn't matter, Ralteer. Let's just get this tower built. I'm still keeping an eye on her, too. But you are being too paranoid."

Ralteer's face turned bright red, even in the converging orange glow from the four fire piles. "Really? I'm too paranoid about the Sovereignty? Have you forgotten what they've done to us? What they continue to do to us?" Ralteer looked over his shoulder as if Marina was scheming that very moment. She merely stared idly up at the shadowed ceiling.

"No, I haven't forgotten. I've been the service much longer than you." Gerund breathed slowly, feeling his need for vindication evaporate. With fear no longer part of his equation, it was easier to let go of his frustrations. He eyed the vent, eager to see if it would bring them one step closer to escape or if all their toil had been a fool's errand. "We can't fight the whole war down here. Let's all concentrate on surviving, and figure out the justice later." He said this last part louder, and Marina stared at him intently.

"Gerund, you take the last pieces up. You should be first," Ralteer said.

If Ralteer was willing to move on, then Gerund was quick to acquiesce. "All right. First we should spread out the supplies so we can each carry an equal load."

"Fine."

After an earlier break, there wasn't much food left, though there hadn't been much to begin with. Even more distressing, they had just over 1 liter of water remaining, carefully spread out into three plastic bottles. As Marina climbed back down to ground level, Gerund handed her a third of the food, tightly wrapped in shipping shrink wrap. She stashed the morsel into her front trouser pocket and she awkwardly stuffed one of the bottles of water into her back pocket. He and Ralteer did similar cumbersome configurations with their own portions of food and water.

"What about the radio?" Gerund asked.

"What about it? Too bulky; just leave it. We haven't heard anything since anyway."

They found just enough wood from the pallets and a wide plastic crate to raise the tower another meter. It had a foreboding lean to it and Gerund wondered if it would succumb to his weight or Ralteer's. Both men were substantially bigger than Marina, who had already tilted the structure precariously during her frequent up and down trips. Gerund climbed up one side of the tower as Marina clung on the opposite side three-quarters of the way up to act as a counterweight. He placed the thick plank of wood first and then the plastic crate at the very top. He shifted it firmly under his hands. Satisfied that it had enough traction, he carefully crept over the top, keeping his center of gravity as close as possible to the tower.

Gerund saw that both Marina and Ralteer held thin torches as they waited at the base of the tower. *Are they trying to climb with those?* "Hey, what are you doing?! Put those flames out—you're going to burn us down. And you're not going to be able to climb into the vent with those lit. We have the lighter, remember? We'll relight the wood once we get inside."

"Oh. Duh." Marina mumbled, and then blew out her torch. Ralteer followed suit, and the resulting smoke rose directly up to Gerund's nostrils, but he was able to bat it away. The climb was now a bit darker, but the fires in the corners of the chamber continued to blaze. Marina started to climb next. Gerund stayed put as she slowly scaled the wobbly structure.

"OK, you both are providing some stability near the base; just stay there as I enter the vent," Gerund said. He peered down, seeing Marina's dark-circled eyes looking up at him from 3 meters below. Ralteer was another 3 meters below her starting to climb, but on the opposite side of the tower.

"You got it," Marina acknowledged.

Gerund rose to his full height and reached toward the edge of the vent. He had to extend over the edge of the tower, shifting his balance in a vulnerable direction. If the air duct failed to support his weight, then he had a 10-meter fall onto an unforgiving stone floor. *No worries. No fear—literally. Just do it.* Gerund could easily place his entire outstretched forearm into the vent. Placing his weight against the edge, he stretched his other forearm into the duct and braced them against the sides. He felt thick, unyielding metal. The duct was solid, industrial construction. Leaning forward even farther, Gerund leveraged his body up and then pulled himself forward into the vent. His fatigued muscles shuddered in protest. There was complete, dusty darkness. The only light was the dull glow behind him. Once he was fully inside, he was able to squirm his body around so he faced the opening. Marina was already at the top of the tower. He braced his body against the sides and reached down to help her up.

Marina stretched and grasped the vent with one hand. "I've got it, give me room," she said. However, she was a few inches shorter and it made a difference. She struggled to get her elbows over the edge. Gerund grasped both arms firmly. She tensed in panic.

"Damnit, Gerund; don't touch me. You're going to make me fall!"

"Relax. Push with your legs and I'll pull you from up here."

Marina sighed, but there was no time to argue. She was in a precarious position. "OK. On the count of three."

She counted down and Gerund easily pulled her up to her torso into the vent. He retreated as she fully scrambled into the vent, then they both backed up to make room for Ralteer. Gerund used the lighter to reignite their torches, revealing the remaining dusty stretch of their duct, which turned horizontally out of sight perhaps 10 meters away. Not a dead end, but instead a possible way out. Marina's face softened with relief, and his own hope blossomed.

Ralteer didn't ask for help and Marina didn't offer it. Ralteer was able to easily pull himself inside, and soon their crawling caravan was underway.

Chapter 49

Lizby had been hiking for 10 minutes. The passage had been arduous and exhausting, with winding turns, steep inclines, ankle-straining drops, and rough terrain where neglect and leaking groundwater had allowed bumpy mineral deposits to form on the ground and ceiling, destined to become stalagmites and stalactites. She wondered how OreLife moved any of their mining equipment through this remote sector of the mine. Perhaps they gave up on operations in this area long ago. She was accustomed to well-lit tunnels, often traversing in a battery-powered minecart over level or gradually sloping ground. These tunnels felt more like a cave than a mine. Despite her years of working in the mine, this tunnel might as well have been on an alien world.

She detected no trace of the soldiers that had walked through the passage an hour earlier in route to kill Captain Halion and most of Badger Squad. There was no sign of Sabos, Carmenta, or their captors. But it was the only tunnel in this direction, and she had passed no intersections—they had to be ahead.

Before long, Lizby came across scattered clusters of giant bugs crawling on the tunnel floor and walls. At first, she saw only a dozen. They looked like the specimens she was familiar with. She smelled smoke, and soon the trail of bugs led to massive piles of dead or mortally wounded twitching insects.

What the—what happened here?!

Her heart sank as she saw the devastation. She had a terrible feeling about her husband, a horrible shadow of dread which she refused to fully acknowledge. Her torch illuminated a dead soldier, lying on top of the bugs. The woman's blood-stained torso and legs glistened in the firelight. There were several exit wounds across her back, and a pair of bugs had wedged themselves into the exposed flesh up to their thoraxes to feast. The smell of smoke was stronger as she drew closer. The fire had died out very recently. Breathlessly, she walked around the corpse, and spotted another body in the center of the carnage. This soldier wore an enclosed helmet, which had been blown open on one side, exposing a mess of plastic splinters and bloody skull fragments. Another clear sign of a gunfight. The bugs were piled in thick mounds, not unlike snow drifts, stretching across the width of the tunnel and requiring her to trudge through their bodies. *Maybe Sabos...maybe he was able to—*

And then she saw him. He lay on his back with one side of his torso tilted into a pile of the misshapen, curled bodies of the insects. One of Sabos's legs was bent awkwardly behind his back. His eyes stared vacantly at the side of the wall. One glance and she knew he was long gone. Unlike the soldiers, he had no obvious wounds; she knew enough from the tales of fatal bug storms to understand that he had somehow been overtaken by the swarm.

Lizby stood by his body, feeling oddly detached for a moment, and then the full realization of her husband's death flooded into her chest. She fell to her knees, and cried out like a cornered, wounded animal. She clasped his hand, but it was cold and grimy. She couldn't bring herself to embrace the corpse. This wasn't her husband; the love of her life. It was merely a mockery of the man.

She knelt for an hour, her shrieks eventually subsiding into bitter sobs as she remembered the 5 years she had spent with Sabos and grieved the decades that had been robbed from them. A limitless future snuffed out. In an honest moment, she didn't care if she survived the whole ordeal or not.

The raw shock left her quicker than expected. She was left with immense sadness, consumed by the sight of his body and the rolling tide of her memories of him, every one of them now tinged with pain. *I need to remember you as you were.* With this thought, she got to her feet at once. She couldn't fully dwell in her grief any more. She had to keep moving. She spotted the corpse of two other soldiers, partially buried in bug piles. No guns, and no other equipment. And no Carmenta.

The thought of her sister-in-law kept her head above water. *She's not here...She wasn't in the tunnel—she might have made it out alive!* Despite the veneer of hospitality she had always put forth toward Carmenta, at times the woman had been an annoying basket-case. Lizby used to see her as an inevitable burden brought on by her marriage to Sabos. And yet despite her deep initial reluctance, their bond had developed anyway through the years. There was no one left alive that Lizby wanted to see more right now. Not even her parents.

I need to find Carmenta. It's what Sabos wants for me. The sentiment rang true as she repeated it. Sabos had loved his sister deeply, and besides Lizby, Carmenta was the closest thing left of him. Finding Carmenta gave her purpose, and it would give her relief to share her grief.

She knelt by Sabos again. This time, her cries remained in her head, and her tears welled up but didn't leave her eyes. "Fuck," she managed. "I'm sorry this happened. I'm so sorry. But I'm going to make it out alive. And I'm going to find your sister and we're going to take care of each other from now on. For you." She kissed his forehead, rose steadily to her feet, and walked down the tunnel without a glance back.

Chapter 50

Gerund led the way through the air duct, with Marina at his heels, and Ralteer in the rear. Gerund and Marina each held their little torches. The duct was sufficiently wide but not particularly tall—it was a struggle to crawl through on hands and knees. Furthermore, the panels creaked and popped horribly with each movement. Gerund wondered if the duct would collapse under their collective weight, and what horrible injury would result from this height. They were at least 10 meters above the cavern floor. Marina's hands kept clipping his heels as they crawled. She was surely eager to get out of the vent, but likely avoiding Ralteer, too. *Can't blame her. He's such a nut.*

"I see a turn ahead, maybe 8 meters."

"Good. Keep going," Ralteer said.

Gerund should have been claustrophobic. The crawling portions of the obstacle course during basic training had always been the most difficult for him. But now he felt strangely at peace, even empowered, by his lack of fear. He was still getting used to his condition. Ralteer and Marina had raw nerves, and he didn't trust either, but at least they were all moving forward. It wasn't that he didn't care what happened—he just didn't fear what came next. And now that they were no longer trapped in darkness, he felt like he had control over his destiny.

A pair of large insects, one piggybacking the other in a mating position, veered to the side of the duct as Gerund approached. He had heard about the large fauna in the region, including this creature, but he had never seen one in person nor had ever seen a bug so gigantic in all his travels. They were each the size of his fist. Their combined weight and the smooth surface of the metal made it impossible for the conjoined insects to escape up the side.

"Watch out, there's some bugs in this vent."

"Gross. What are they doing down here? Let's pray that the rest of the swarm is not around the corner," Marina said. "I heard they can be a major nuisance on Sarabek. They call them bug storms. Can you believe that? A bug storm. Like a force of nature."

"They aren't poisonous, are they?" Gerund asked as he squeezed by the bugs, who continuing to writhe in their mating grasp.

"No, I don't think so—"

"Gerund, pay attention," Ralteer interrupted. "Don't let her take off whenever we reach the end of this thing," he warned.

"I won't," Marina hissed.

"I'm not talking to you," Ralteer snapped.

"I'm not going to run away," she insisted.

"I'll take care of front. Don't worry," Gerund said. The incessant mistrust between Ralteer and Marina would boil over soon, he knew.

The rounded corner was just a few meters away. The torch illuminated its features more distinctly now. The tunnel inclined slightly. Perhaps they would find an exit sooner than expected.

"Quiet!" Marina hissed. "Stop!"

"Huh?" Gerund stopped, and the creaking finally ceased behind him.

"Listen!"

It was a voice from below, echoing from the radio they had left behind. They must have accidently left it on. The voice was draped in static, but spoke an unmistakable name. *Ralteer.*

"Ralteer, you there?" the gruff voice repeated. It wasn't particularly loud, but it was distinct in the absolute silence. "Are you trying to call us? Your frequency is on. Shit has really hit the fan. If you can hear this, call me back ASAP. I can't hear anything if you've been talking. Over and out."

There was an insufferable pause after the signal clicked off. Gerund craned his neck to look behind. Marina's body was frozen in terror as she continued to look straight ahead. When he met her glassy eyes, it was clear that they shared the same realization. He then looked beyond her to Ralteer, who also looked to be in a state of shock, with his head drooped and shoulders slumped. Suddenly he bristled with anger, and when he looked up at Gerund, he grinned like a lunatic. *Oh, shit!* The corner was still several meters away.

"Liar!" Marina screamed. She twisted around to face Ralteer.

"Not one more move, both of you," Ralteer growled. "You must have always had a death wish, huh bitch?" Ralteer raised the pistol. Gerund realized that there were very few outcomes. Now that Ralteer was exposed, would he have enough incentive to keep them alive?

"Run Gerund!" Marina kicked straight back and the end of her boot connected with the gun. A perfect strike. The weapon flipped backward out of reach and Ralteer's hand twisted back in a gruesome angle.

Ralteer yelled in pain and surprise. "I'll kill you! You're both dead!"

But Marina kept kicking. She struck savagely at his face. Ralteer grasped at her ankles, but Marina braced herself against the tunnels walls to get more leverage and kicked even harder. There was a sickening *crack* after Marina connected with Ralteer's mouth repeatedly, and he howled and was driven backward.

"Go, go!" Gerund yelled. He scampered toward the corner, crunching one of the disturbed bugs under a knee. Marina thudded right behind him. As he reached the corner, Gerund glanced behind once more. Ralteer had put his torch down and found the loose pistol—he raised it in his other hand. He squinted through his non-swollen eye as he took aim.

"Marina, watch out!" However, Gerund knew it was a futile warning, they were both already prone; no way to further reduce their target area. They would not evade Ralteer's line of fire until they made the turn, and Ralteer couldn't have been more than a few body lengths behind them. It would be an easy few shots to stop them. Maybe a few more to finish the job.

The first shot rang out. Gerund imagined the bullet passing through Marina and then his body, but he felt nothing except clarity. No spike of adrenaline; no confusing fear. He continued to move as the next six shots burst out. He couldn't believe his luck as the first five missed him. When the last bullet finally tagged him in his calf as he snaked through the turn, he almost considered it a fair compromise. *A single bullet to the leg over certain death? I'll take it.* However, the spike of exquisite pain that followed dampened his feeling of fortune, as did Marina's yelp of agony right behind him. He turned to see her grimacing and pulled her through the rest of the corner. She had oozing nubs where her pinky and ring fingers had been. Blood already covered her wounded hand. Gerund was surprised that Ralteer had missed with his other shots, but he also knew from experience that bullets could take unexpected trajectories, even when the shooter had a seemingly easy shot like Ralteer had. Marina eyed her incomplete hand with disbelieving horror, but her legs kept churning, propelling her forward.

"Keep going," he urged. They were out of Ralteer's line of sight, but they could still be hit if he pierced the duct at the proper angle.

"Shit," Marina wheezed. "You got hit, too."

"Yeah, I got tagged in the calf. But I think it's survivable," Gerund said dispassionately, more confident in Marina's chances than his own. "We'll patch up once we get away from this psychopath."

They scampered down 10 meters of vent before taking a right. This section of the vent also inclined slightly. Ralteer could be heard banging through the vent in pursuit.

"Let me finish it," their assailant growled. "You're just going to bleed out. You're making this a much bigger mess than it needed to be."

"Screw you, Ralteer!" Marina called as they continued to crawl away.

Gerund's dwindling torch only showed a few meters in front of them. He couldn't move as fast as Marina with the torch in one hand and with his wounded leg. She pressed against him, urging him to speed up.

"Damn! I lost my water bottle," she hissed.

That gives us maybe one more day with my bottle split between us, Gerund calculated. Even after being shot, he hadn't registered fear or shock, and so his body hadn't released adrenaline. His mind hummed along smoothly even with the imminent threat right behind. He thought about how they could conserve their energy and hydration in order to survive longer than a day if they remained trapped in the mine. It had already been far more than 24 hours since the mine collapse, and Gerund realized he had needed far more than half a liter during that time.

"Is it by you? We're going to need the water," she moaned.

You might have dashed our chances Marina, assuming we even get out of this duct, he thought. "We'll figure it out later," he said instead.

"What's ahead?"

"Can barely see anything." Their voices echoed several times, suggesting multiple turns up ahead. The pops and thuds from Ralteer's pursuit in the bend behind them echoed menacingly.

Gerund knew that they desperately needed an exit. His calf wound bled steadily as he scrambled, and Marina's wound was certainly survivable but not if it continued to bleed unhindered. If they didn't find an opportunity to tend to their wounds fast, then Ralteer might not need to finish the job.

Chapter 51

The muted but unmistakable crack of gunfire echoed from further ahead. Perhaps six shots—all fired within 5 seconds. Carmenta cautiously walked along the wall of the gradually curving tunnel. *Was Marina involved in the shooting? Maybe this is another group of mercs...* Her torch had a very limited view of what lay ahead and she didn't have a weapon, but she was compelled to find out. Carmenta increased her pace to a trot despite her weak legs.

Following the brief radio contact with Marina, she had dealt with creeping doubt about why she was again sticking her neck out for her cousin. Marina was a relative from a different stage in her life, who she barely knew anymore and had imposed her plea for help after turning her back on her sworn commitments to the Sovereignty. Nevertheless, the gunfire had stirred a protective instinct in her. Inexplicably, Marina still felt like family. It was why Carmenta had agreed to help her in the first place 2 days ago.

She heard muffled voices; a man and a woman. The tunnel straightened out, revealing a widened stretch of the tunnel with a mine cart parked on one side and a long air vent running up high. Carmenta eyed the mine cart, a small 2-seater with a basket in back for light cargo, hoping it was operational. She ran as fast as she could while keeping a tight grip on her torch. She didn't see anyone as she approached.

"Hurry, kick it out," said a frantic voice which sounded like Marina. *At last. Who are you talking to?*

Light flickered from inside the vent. Suddenly the grate shuddered from a violent strike.

"Marina," she gasped. "It's me: Carmenta. What's happening?!"

"Carmenta!" Marina's voice was strained, possibly injured. "We need to get out right now!"

As if to answer, the grate popped free after a powerful kick. A uniformed trouser leg stuck out, followed by the rest of a man as he dropped down to the narrow space between the tunnel wall and the mine cart. He wore a Coalition uniform, stained with grease and blood. He held a small torch made from a scrap of wood in one hand and braced himself against the stone wall with the other. The man acknowledged Carmenta with a wary glance and turned back to the vent to help pull Marina out, who was emerging headfirst, dripping blood from one of her hands. It looked like she was being birthed from a grotesque industrial machine. Carmenta stared at Marina's hand in horror. Her ring and pinky finger were missing, right above the knuckles. Ragged flesh surrounded the bloody wound. She wondered if Marina had been hit during the recent gunfire, or if the injury had happened some other way. Marina's wrist was curled defensively against her side.

A deafening gunshot clanged through the vent. Marina's eyes widened. *Oh god, was she hit again?* Marina scrambled the rest of the way out of the vent just as another bullet ricocheted through. There were smears of blood on her mining clothes, but the rest of her body looked intact.

Carmenta half-embraced Marina as she helped her down to the tunnel floor. "What's going on? Who is this guy?"

"Gerund. He knows I'm Sovereignty." Marina nodded at the limping man as the three of them backed away from the open vent. "We're being chased by a lunatic soldier. Or spy. Or whatever the hell he really is. Where to?"

Carmenta needed more answers, but there was no time to discuss. She had no idea what lay ahead if she continued forward. She hated not knowing if there was a haven or an exit just around the next curve. But leaving Lizby behind was not an option; she was one of the few things in the mine that was truly worth saving. "Uh, back the way I came. Lizby is in that general direction."

"She is? What is she doing?" Marina asked.

"She was with some mercs. We need to find her. She might have been in some trouble."

"What about Sabos? Where is he?

Carmenta broke eye contact with Marina. "Sabos, uh, didn't make it," she managed quietly.

"No! What happened?" Marina gasped.

"We'll talk about it later. We need to go right now. We should take the mine cart."

Marina hopped onto the mine cart and fiddled with the small dashboard touchscreen. "How do I start this thing?!"

There was curse from inside the vent. Their pursuer was right there.

"Never mind—no time!" Carmenta shouted. Marina dove off the front seat of the mine cart and scrambled away from the vent. Carmenta began backtracking, leading the trio at a quick walk, which was as fast a pace as Gerund could maintain with his calf wound. After a minute, she stopped and spun around to face her two stragglers. They were too busy trying to stop their bleeding to keep up.

"C'mon! First we've gotta put some distance between us and whoever is chasing you."

They stumbled for another minute before Marina leaned against the wall. "OK, that's far enough. We need to bandage up." Marina said as she pressed her shaking red stumps into the folds of her shirt.

Carmenta started to protest. The assailant couldn't be far behind, and besides; what supplies did they have to patch themselves up with? But then saw how much Gerund had already bled from his calf wound and Marina from her hand. It was clear that neither of them could press on with their wounds still leaking. They had to act now.

Gerund removed his long sleeve uniform. Fortunately, he had an undershirt they could use, which he also took off. Despite their crisis, Carmenta observed a fit, slim torso that she wouldn't have minded ogling on a beach. She noticed a few deep longitudinal scars along one shoulder, along with more recent scrapes on his side. Somehow, the marks made him that much more appealing. His body had taken a beating but still held the hard, wary posture of a career soldier.

Gerund looked her way as he tore the thin undershirt in two. She quickly averted her gaze. He offered half of the fabric to Marina. He reached underneath his pant leg and used his half to tightly compress the wound. He cried out in pain as the bandage put pressure on the frayed, raw flesh surrounding the bullet entry. But he didn't relent; he tied the shirt snugly. Marina tried to wrap her stumped hand but couldn't get it tight. She cursed as soon as the fabric touched her tender fingers.

Cousin, we don't have time for this, Carmenta mentally scolded. She set her torch down and hurriedly wrapped the wound. Marina's eyes watered in pain, but she nodded her thanks as Carmenta tucked the end of the cloth under the final loop.

"All right, good enough," Marina gasped. The trio fled as fast as their weary bodies could carry them.

Chapter 52

Lizby sprinted down the tunnel, as if by running faster she could somehow leave behind her raw state of grief. She had to keep moving to find Carmenta. She knew if she slowed down, she would become immobilized by her sorrow—reduced to a weeping fetal position on the stone floor.

The food and water she had scavenged from the merc outpost jostled in her pockets. When the mercs had received the radio call yesterday, they had confirmed that Carmenta and Sabos had been together. There had been no other branches in the tunnel either before or after she had found Sabos. Therefore, she was confident she could find Carmenta if she continued this path. She just hoped she would find her alive.

Lizby didn't have to walk far. She saw the torchlight before she heard footsteps. She approached eagerly, only to be halted by a harsh *stop!* as she neared a rare 90-degree corner in the tunnel.

It was a man's voice. "Who's there?" he barked. She heard at least two other voices whisper.

"I just want to pass. I'm looking for someone." She leaned against the corner and gripped her weapon. *I'm in no mood to negotiate. I'll blow you away without regret.* She had fired a gun only a few times before, out in the badlands. It had been an interesting and ultimately humbling experience, as striking her targets had been more difficult than she had imagined. She had shot a different model of firearm too; the merc weapon seemed far more powerful. Nevertheless, she felt comfortable with the basic function of the weapon and confident of a deadly hit in the close quarters.

"Lizby? Lizby? It's Carmenta!" her sister-in-law said ecstatically. "We're coming around the corner."

Lizby put the gun away and smiled as Carmenta appeared. She hugged her deeply. There was a man in Coalition uniform with a blotchy red calf wound and a woman in a miner's uniform with a stained thick bandage around one hand.

"So glad you're safe," Lizby beamed. Carmenta's face was deeply lined by stress but she seemed physically unharmed.

"Me too. Are you okay?" Carmenta said with a twinge of reluctance.

Lizby shook her head. "I found him," she stated, her voice nearly faltering.

Carmenta nodded. Her sullen eyes showed that she understood. "Oh god. I'm so sorry. I was there—it all happened so quickly."

"It didn't even look like him," she said into Carmenta's ear as they embraced again. She withdrew and they shared eye contact and a moment of pain and understanding that assured Lizby that she wasn't alone in her suffering. Carmenta was already changed by Sabos's death, maybe not in the exact way as Lizby, but with similar weight. Lizby had lost her husband and Carmenta had lost her little brother. With this glance, Lizby knew there was a path to recovery even though her grief felt so profoundly raw. As beautiful as the moment was, it couldn't last; it was too intense and they both had to deal with the present reality. "But

I'm so relieved to have found you, sis," Lizby said as they broke away from each other.

"I'm sorry it took this long to find you." Carmenta nodded at the man and the woman behind her. "I had stumbled upon Marina on the radio and figured out she was close and needed help."

"Marina..." Lizby mumbled as she took a closer look at the woman over Carmenta's shoulder. She was familiar looking, but she didn't think she had ever met this miner. And then her memory clicked, recognizing the dark Sasquire features from a photograph of long ago. "Marina! What are you doing here? Wait, I thought you were serving in the Sovereignty, far away from here?"

"Not so far away, I'm afraid," Marina said. "And not doing the serving part anymore."

The man raised his eyebrows, incredulous. *Oh no*, Lizby realized. *I wasn't thinking. Maybe he didn't realize Marina was Sovereignty...*

However, the Coalition soldier remained calm. He already knew. "Hold on—you all know each other?" he said.

"Yes. This is Gerund, by the way," Marina said, introducing the Coalition soldier with a sweep of her arm and turning to face him. "Lizby is married to Carmenta's brother."

"Sabos," Lizby added, almost a whisper.

"Oh, I see," Gerund said, though still sounding a little perplexed. "Hey, we need to talk later. We got someone in pursuit—he could be here any second. He's the one who shot us. Lizby, is it? Give me your weapon," he commanded, eyeing the hilt sticking out of her waistband.

"Hold on," Lizby stalled and took a step back and looked to her sister-in-law for direction. "Carmenta?"

Carmenta didn't answer but instead deferred to Marina with a nod. "Lizby, he knows what he's doing," Marina said. "He could have killed me before but instead advocated on my behalf. Give him the gun; what he says is true."

Lizby shrugged and handed the gun with handle facing outward. Gerund swiftly grabbed it and motioned everyone behind him as he leaned against the wall of the corner turn.

"Who is this guy?" Lizby asked as she looked at Gerund in greater detail. His face gave away nothing; he was focused in the other direction.

"Quiet. And go back farther with those torches," Gerund ordered.

Lizby didn't completely trust him, but it didn't matter. He already had the gun and Carmenta and Marina were backing down the tunnel, so she joined them.

Gerund stayed in position about 10 meters ahead of the others. Lizby waited with the other two women in a crouch. She made awkward eye contact with Marina. She hadn't been at the wedding or any other family events, but Sabos's family was so spread out that few of them ever gathered anywhere. Many of the Sasquires had been dispersed as refugees, just like Carmenta and Sabos. In fact, Carmenta was only relative of Sabos she had met. If Lizby's memory served her correctly, she had never communicated with Marina, and she didn't think Sabos had kept in touch. Marina drew breath to whisper something, but then chose to remain silent. Questions could wait. Everyone was on edge as Gerund waited to spring the ambush.

A minute later, Gerund leaned out into the tunnel with the gun drawn. There was a hostile shout in the distance and then a violent exchange of gunfire: a quick double pop followed by a stream of seven shots from another weapon, interspersed with another double pop halfway through. Gerund remained steady, but his stance seemed odd, mostly likely because of his previously wounded leg. After the barrage of gunfire, Gerund leaned back behind the cover of the wall, then lowered himself before spinning back around the corner. He quickly fired four more shots with far less composure and then again sought cover.

"You're dead, you hear me?!" the irate assailant screeched. "You won't make it out of this mine alive!"

After 30 seconds, Gerund risked a glance down the tunnel. He shook his head and slumped against the wall in exhaustion.

"Ralteer ran off," Gerund reported as the three women walked up to him. Lizby thought the man was impossibly calm after being shot at and threatened.

"Are you okay?" Lizby asked.

"Yes. I surprised him. He fired in a panic."

Marina slid along the wall and approached. "Are you sure he fled? Did you get him at all?"

"I don't think so. He dove against the wall as soon as he saw me raising the gun—he wasn't expecting me to be armed."

Carmenta dropped her torch on the ground—it had been reduced to a blackened stake, nearly consumed by the fire. Now Lizby had the sole source of light with her lantern.

"I have a lighter as a backup, so no worries," Gerund said, showing Lizby the metal lighter.

The four of them huddled up and discussed their options. They each explained their paths through the mine in very broad terms. Lizby told them about coming from the overrun merc base and her memory of the mine layout when she had arrived there from the Pit. They all agreed that they should proceed with their current direction. Although Ralteer had run off in this same direction, they thought it was their best chance of finding a way to the surface or a better refuge than the open tunnel they currently crouched in.

They started their walk with Gerund leading the way with gun drawn. The three women walked a few steps behind. Lizby lit the group with her lantern, which continued to blaze brightly despite operating for most of the past day and a half.

Lizby tugged on Carmenta's arm and pulled her back to a slightly slower pace. "What's going on? Did you know Marina was here? You knew all along, didn't you?"

Carmenta nodded meekly.

"She's a deserter! Do you know how much trouble you could get our family in?!" The words came out harsher than she expected. Her grief made her intense, she knew. But she didn't care. Carmenta hesitated to answer as she searched Lizby's face. Marina overheard, but continued to stare down at the stone ground as she walked ahead of the pair, not wishing to be a part of the confrontation.

Carmenta nodded again. "It was supposed to be simple," she squeaked. "Let me explain."

"Please do," Lizby insisted.

Marina let Lizby and Carmenta have their space. She was the outsider in this family triangle. From the portions of the conversation she overheard, she knew Lizby wasn't pleased about being kept in the dark about her.

Marina couldn't blame the woman. A stab of guilt flared up in her gut. She had imposed her troubles on Carmenta, and it had effects well beyond her cousin. Fortunately, the spat between Carmenta and Lizby was short-lived. Carmenta's posture loosened, and Lizby's angry gestures melted into sighs. The argument, if it could even have been called that, was born out of frustration. No ill will; no grudge. The cousins embraced.

Marina couldn't help but envy their bond. *I have no one like that anymore. Maybe my parents, but I haven't seen them in years. Titus was the closest thing.* She had some other friends in her Sovereignty unit but she had severed those bonds when she had deserted. And she had been away from home for so long that she doubted many people there would even recognize her.

Carmenta and Lizby increased their pace and tightened formation with Marina and Gerund. Marina reminded herself that survival was the priority in her current circumstance, but she couldn't help but contemplate what she would do differently if she lived to see the end of this disaster.

After a 10-minute hike in which they shared some critical details about what they had seen regarding the mine collapse, they all agreed to rest briefly and take stock of their inventory. They weren't sure what region of the mine they were in or how long it would take to get back to the central Pit area, assuming the path wasn't blocked off. Marina herself had lost track of time and space. She was parched and hungry, but didn't want to bring up the topic of refueling since she didn't carry any of the supplies that served as their remaining lifeline. She had to be diplomatic. Gerund still carried a half liter of water and perhaps a kilogram of food; dried fruit and nuts from the chamber he had been stuck in with Marina. Carmenta had nothing. Lizby fortunately had a full liter of water and some food that she was able to scavenge before she left the merc outpost in search of Sabos. She had some crackers, granola, and an unfortunate bag of uncooked beans. Marina again regretted losing her food and water during their frantic scramble through the air duct.

Marina and Gerund were especially weak after bleeding from their gunshot wounds. A few gulps and nibbles weren't going to cut it. *Besides,* Marina thought, *sooner rather than later we're probably either going to find a way out or die down here. Why do so on an empty stomach?*

Carmenta and Lizby didn't seem to be as feeble but still favored eating when Gerund suggested that they all take a break. Or at least they didn't make a fuss when Gerund divided half of the food into four equal portions, which each survivor eagerly consumed without a crumb hitting the ground. When the pit stop was over, fully half of the water was also gone. It was time to go. By depleting their stocks, they had accelerated their urgent need to exit the mine while they still had the strength to travel. Also, they had essentially eliminated any strategy of waiting for a rescue, though Marina suspected that the possibility of rescue might have been gone already. Even if a crew did venture down into the mine, it meant bad news for either her or Gerund, depending on if the "saviors" were Coalition or Sovereignty. *I need to control my destiny,* Marina thought. *I can't count on others for my fate.*

The survivors pressed on with purpose. Soon, they returned to the vent, and all eyes eagerly fell on the parked mine cart that there hadn't been time to activate before when Ralteer had been in hot pursuit. The cart was one of hundreds in the mine, though Marina had seen most of them parked in the Pit, where they were now presumably buried. There was a cord that was attached to a cable that ran along the tunnel overhead, presumably to charge the cart's battery and any other mining equipment. The plug hung loosely above the cart; Marina hoped someone had remembered to charge it before the mine collapse. It was a two-seater with a shallow basket on the back for light cargo. The lightweight plastic and compact design of the vehicle suggested a sole purpose of shuttling employees. It certainly didn't look equipped to move ore or heavy equipment. The small cart looked like it would be better suited in a child's carnival ride rather than as part of an industrial mining operation.

Carmenta hopped on the driver's bench and examined the control panel. "I use this model all the time. No keys in the ignition but there is another switch in the battery compartment that activates the cart." She leaned forward over the hood and popped the panel off the battery and reached under the unit. The cart hummed to life and Marina joined Carmenta in front while Gerund eased into the empty cargo basket with Lizby. Carmenta carefully maneuvered the cart out of the alcove and they were rolling down the unfamiliar tunnel, easily twice as fast as their quickest walking pace. Carmenta toggled the cart's headlamps to low power and Lizby turned off her lantern to conserve battery. The vehicle produced minimal noise and moved along steadily; it must have had a strong charge left on the battery. The ceiling dropped to barely 2 meters. The riders nearly had to slouch in their seats as the ceiling sloped down at them. One side of the tunnel was smooth and the other had loose ore still clinging to rock shelves where the mining equipment had cut. Some abandoned tools and busted hydraulic hoses were left behind on the shelf. With such an expansive mine, OreLife had many unfinished projects at any given time. The mine had been expanded in several stages since ancient times and some tunnels had been left in various stages of development before OreLife had taken over management. Marina wondered if this might be one of the old tunnels. She was no miner, but the neglected tools looked exceedingly old to her.

For the first time since the mine collapse, Marina allowed herself to hope and to consider that there might be a chance at a real life afterwards. The faces of death still threatened to overwhelm her; Octavia, Jethro, Temeru, and of course Titus. But right now, she felt safe on the cart as they rolled through straight passages and gentle curves.

Although Marina trusted her companions not to harm her, she suspected that Gerund might have still hold hard feelings about her deception and the fact that she was a deserter. Gerund had so far been tolerant with her, especially when Ralteer had been ready to drop the proverbial axe, but maybe he did so out of pragmatism or some inherently honorable aspect of his personality. Either way, if the going again got tough, she didn't know how far Gerund would stick his neck out for her.

She thought Lizby had animosity toward her, too. It was hard to be certain: they had barely talked in the walk down the mine and during their pit stop. Lizby had just lost her husband of course, so Marina tried not to put too much weight into the cold vibe she was getting from the newly widowed miner. Carmenta was their common link, and at least she felt like she could trust her cousin with her life. *Hell, I already have, and she came through for me.*

Carmenta braked the cart to a sudden, squeaky stop. Marina nearly fell over the compact front end and she heard the pair in the back bounce around in the cargo basket. "What? What is it?" Marina asked when she was whipped back into her seat. She didn't see anything in the tunnel ahead.

Carmenta kept the headlamps on low. She jabbed her index finger to a narrow plank that lay a few meters in front of the cart. "See that? It's a piece of wood. *Burnt* wood."

Gerund nodded. "Ralteer's torch must have burned out and he tossed it. He's without light, unless he found something else to ignite before his torch went out. This also proves that he came this way."

"Do we really want to catch up with this jerk? He could see or hear us coming and then shoot us. Maybe we should wait a while," Carmenta suggested.

"We've already waited plenty. And we don't know what pace he's traveling at. He may have found a different tunnel up ahead. We can't wait on what he might or might not do," Marina countered. They had been stuck in the mine so long and overcome so many threats. She didn't want to wait another minute longer, no matter the risk.

Gerund nodded in agreement. "We should press on. Ralteer has an hour head start, so it's up to him on whether or not we're going to have another confrontation."

Carmenta accelerated the cart again. Marina glanced back. Gerund stared ahead attentively, with his gun held at his side. The rock shelf on one side of the tunnel carved deeper, leaving the stone above with much less support. They spotted a dozen long-tailed bats roosting in the crack, but the bats paid them no heed as they quietly passed. Marina wondered if they got hungry enough if they would consider the creatures as a meal option. They were quite large for bats and she imagined they could be roasted if they could get another fire going. *I don't think I'm to that point yet. You're safe for now, you flying rats.* The tunnel sloped upward more sharply and the mine cart slowed to barely a walking pace. It wasn't designed to haul four people uphill.

The cart's lights reflected on a large object at the edge of its range. The object was draped lengthwise across the tunnel floor. Even in the faint orange light, glistening wet blood was evident everywhere. *Is that...a person?* Marina realized in horror. Carmenta let the cart roll to a stop and engaged the brake. Gerund leaned forward with his pistol pointed at the still form. It was Ralteer. He lay with his side facing them. His Coalition uniform was drenched in blood and a leg was missing below the knee. He was motionless with eyes closed. *Looks dead,* Marina concluded. *Someone must have laid an explosive trap.* They all climbed off the cart with Gerund taking the lead position. Lizby activated the lantern and to their shock, Ralteer's eyes fluttered open.

"Watch out, he's alive," Gerund warned as they approached. "Where's his gun?"

"Over there, on the floor," Carmenta pointed to the side of the tunnel. It was well out of Ralteer's reach, and he didn't look like he was capable of even raising his arm.

Gerund looked around as Marina scooped up Ralteer's gun. Part of the stone behind Ralteer was blackened and littered with shrapnel and what he could only imagine were strips of Ralteer's missing leg. "Keep your eyes peeled. This was a bomb's work."

Ralteer managed to raise a shaking arm in protest as Gerund rifled through the breast pockets of his torn jacket. Gerund swatted it aside.

"F-fuck you," Ralteer murmured in feeble frustration. Gerund was amazed he was still conscious given the amount of blood that had sprayed over the floor he now squatted in. He had seen enough battlefield carnage to know that Ralteer's death was a certainty within minutes. If there had been a medic team on the scene immediately, then maybe he would have had a chance. Gerund felt a wad of paper and brought out several folded documents from the pockets. It was time to get some answers. Ralteer's window was closing. His eyes glared into the ceiling before again settling on Gerund, who met his enemy's gaze unflinchingly.

"What happened here?" Gerund asked in a calm tone. He tried to sound authoritative but also patient in order to coax Ralteer's cooperation. In Gerund's experience, the dying were eager to speak.

"Bomb," Ralteer rasped. "Well hidden. Pr-proximity sensor...most likely. Probably my own people," he grimaced.

Gerund nodded as he flipped through Ralteer's papers. There was the standard Coalition identification stating Ralteer's rank as Sergeant, commanding officer, and key information such as blood type. The Coalition ID seemed well-worn and legitimate from this quick glance. Behind it, there was a Sovereignty identification card from the intelligence division with supporting codes. The slyly smiling man in both ID's photos was the same. The situation became slightly clearer to Gerund. For whatever reason, Ralteer had been impersonating a Coalition soldier. He must have kept his Sovereignty ID in case he was confronted by unwitting soldiers and needed to show his true allegiance.

"You're a spy?" Gerund asked.

Ralteer sighed and his eyes drooped. Gerund thought he might have just breathed his last. But their eyes met again. "More or less. Not even supposed to be down here. Duty called, I guess."

"Ralteer, what were you trying to do? Why did you try to kill me and Marina?"

"Can't believe I missed. Kill shot, that is. Glad I at least nicked you both."

"Why did you turn on us? Who were you talking to?" Marina asked as she crouched beside Gerund.

"Oh, don't worry Marina. Plenty of us still down here. We'll find you."

"Huh?" Gerund searched Ralteer's Sovereignty I.D. for more clues, but it was basic with just the few lines of information he had already seen.

"You probably think you are not so bad, Gerund. But anyone who continues to fight for the Coalition is the scum of the universe," Ralteer's voice fell to an almost inaudible whisper and he paused. "What they do...it's unforgivable. Brainwashing captured cities, raping our women and children. We'll stop all of you."

"True believer, huh? I've heard the same propaganda, asshole. It's bullshit." Marina shook her bandaged hand in Ralteer's face, but he only smirked.

Time for answers, not outrage. "You were using me to get to more of my people?" Gerund asked in a neutral tone.

"Yep. I had people too. Tried to connect with them over radio," Ralteer wheezed for breath. "Figured they could help me get some answers out of ya. Unfortunately they called at the wrong time. Forced my hand."

What the hell? I'm just trying to survive, and this psychopath was still plotting to carry on this war of...attrition.

"I'm not Coalition. You found out I was Sovereignty. Why did you want to kill me?" Marina demanded.

"Still do. You're even w-worse. You're a *coward*," Ralteer gasped. "Gave up on your cause."

"Gladly. Anything else?" Marina growled. She was looking at Gerund. "I'm done with this asshole. He's nearly done himself."

Gerund shook his head but stayed crouched in front of Ralteer. "Care for a last sip of water?" He hoped that this token of kindness would show how absurd Ralteer's characterization of the enemy really was, plus it felt like the right thing to do. Gerund produced the water bottles with precious little water remaining.

"Forget him!" Marina shouted with surprising venom.

"Gerund, we need to keep it all for ourselves," Carmenta finally spoke. "You don't have to prove anything."

Gerund ignored them and still held out the water, nudging it slightly toward Ralteer's lips. The dying man seemed to soften ever so slightly. Then he closed his eyes and shook his head to decline.

"Anything to tell your people, then?"

"Not from you, no." His whisper was quiet and matter-of-fact—no malice left in his voice.

Within moments, Ralteer was completely still and his eyes didn't open again.

Carmenta collected Ralteer's discarded handgun and returned to the driver's seat of the mine cart. Gerund and Marina dragged Ralteer's body off to the side of the tunnel and unceremoniously leaned it against the wall. Gerund placed both sets of ID back in Ralteer's jacket. Carmenta started to ease the mine cart through, but Gerund motioned for her to stop.

"There's a lot of loose rock here and we don't know if there are other bombs planted. We need to continue very carefully."

Marina carefully walked to the front of the cart. "Fine. I can take point and walk the path ahead, that way the rest of you can conserve your energy."

"Let me take point. I'm more experienced," Gerund insisted.

"I know how to spot a mine, I've been at war for a while myself, remember?" Marina argued. "Besides, you're wounded."

"So are you," Lizby piped in. She raised her head. "I can lead." However, as she looked back at Ralteer's mangled body, her expression faltered subtly.

Gerund shook his head, and then Marina followed suit. Carmenta's furrowed face conveyed skepticism as well. Beyond Lizby's lack of military experience, they all had reservations about Lizby taking on any task, so fresh into her state of grief over losing Sabos. Lizby took in their reactions and seemed to sense their concern over her taking point. Her shoulders slumped slightly.

Finally, Marina broke the moment of quiet. "Gerund's got a leg wound, he needs to ride," Marina pointed at Gerund's bandaged calf. "I might be missing a couple fingers, but I can walk fine. I'm leading."

No one argued further, and Marina lit the path ahead with the lantern while scanning the floor for anything that looked man-made. Carmenta followed a few meters behind in the cart. Gerund sat in the passenger seat and Lizby struggled to get comfortable in the cargo basket.

The progress was slow and tedious, with Marina scrutinizing every loose chunk that had fallen off the rock shelf. But while Ralteer had been wandering through the dark, Marina's path was brightly lit and she was alert to the potential danger. After a while she became more confident in her sweep and walked faster. Gerund looked to the low ceiling ahead in case there was a bomb attached, but he kept this concern to himself to avoid worrying the rest of the group.

Unfortunately, their efficient pace lasted for only a few more minutes. The minecart's battery was not as fully charged as expected or perhaps wasn't designed to propel so much weight. The cart began to rapidly lose speed. It whined as it crawled up the incline and within another minute it came to a halt.

"Goddammit," Carmenta growled. "Some son of a bitch didn't charge the cart when they parked it." When charged, the carts could run for hours and travel up to 10 kilometers. "We walk from here."

Marina continued to lead and the rest followed in tight formation. Carmenta and Gerund had the guns. With her training, Marina would normally have been a better shot than Carmenta, but with her disfigured hand she was now useless for that purpose.

Despite the uncertainty of what lay ahead, the quartet's spirits lifted. Regardless of their contrasting origins, they were all united in their priority of survival. The war would wait. Relationships could be fully mended later. Proper mourning was to be postponed. Right now, they all wanted to see daylight. They had a lantern, a pair of weapons, and each other's backs. It would be enough. There was no more grumbling. There wasn't much talk at all, but they didn't need it. The occasional reassuring glance at each other confirmed their common purpose. The four were making steady progress and the tunnel continued to slope upward; a great sign.

At last, the lantern light reflected off something ahead. It was an overhead sign, which became legible after several more steps: PIT ACCESS LEVEL 2. Beyond the sign, a wide door loomed. The door looked old and heavy, with a dull pewter finish, and thick, grimy hinges that looked like they hadn't been opened in decades.

"We're back at the Pit! And we're at Level Two, which is over halfway up. We might be above all of the wreckage," Lizby hoped, with a brightness to her voice that belied her pallor of grief.

"It's a blast door. Its purpose was to minimize the risk of a blowout, back when OreLife's methods were a bit riskier," Carmenta explained as she flanked the sturdy metal door. "Let's hope we can open it."

"Or that we like what we find on the other side," Gerund warned.

"Only one way to find out," Carmenta said as she jerked the handle back and swung the door on screeching hinges.

Chapter 53

The quartet of survivors did not in fact like what they found on the other side of the door. They were greeted by several glistening rifle barrels and blinding flashlights. They froze in defeat, and Gerund and Carmenta had the presence of mind to keep their pistols down, and then slowly lowered them to the ground.

Gerund squinted through the glaring flashlights and tried to see who had gotten a jump on them. There looked to be at least a dozen people, each one pointing a firearm at them. No chance. Two men wedged themselves against the door frames, blocking some of the flashlight beams and revealing their smug expressions. Gerund was relieved at the sight of their familiar Coalition uniforms. *All right, all right. We can make this work.*

"Walk forward. Slowly. Hands raised," one of the soldiers ordered. "Who else remains in the tunnel?"

"No one else. Corporal Gerund Williams, Coalition 84th unit," Gerund answered confidently. "I'm escorting these civilians to safety."

The four survivors walked out the door with arms raised as the two soldiers rushed behind them and picked up their surrendered pistols. There were nine more soldiers in the greeting party. All brandished two-handed firearms; Gerund also spotted various blades, fragmentation grenades, flash grenades, and other gear strapped to them. They were armed to the teeth. All of them were Coalition regulars, no mercs; which was a good sign in Gerund's calculation. Maybe they could talk their way through.

Level Two consisted of a 10-meter-wide stone ledge that circled the rim of the Pit as far as they could see in the path of the flashlights. There were several suspended walkways, each ending with ladders that either rose into the darkness above or descended toward the depths of wreckage that must have been hundreds of meters below. The darkness stretched above them too; but there were many structures between them and the surface, plus he didn't know if it was day or night, so the lack of sunlight was not unexpected. He had heard that the Pit was mostly shielded from sunlight even on the brightest day except nearly at the surface. A thin cable railing encircled the stone ledge and each of the walkways. The stark contrast of the bright flashlights on the stone ledge against the vast dark backdrop of the mostly empty maw of the open Pit gave Gerund the sensation of being on stage during a performance. Unlike his embarrassing attempts at theater as a youth, this time he felt no stage fright.

Even as their new captors encircled them with raised weapons, Gerund remained composed, and if anything, feigned an expression of boredom as if the quartet was being merely inconvenienced.

"I'm Captain Valence," a woman with piercing hazel eyes announced as she strode forward. From the way the other Coalition soldiers deferred to her as she walked through, Gerund was certain she was their leader. Her uniform was smudged with dirt, but her cap still rested neatly on top of her short-cropped hair. She came to a rigid stop in front of Gerund and fixed him with one of the most intense stares he had ever endured. “Corporal Williams, there is no safety. The Sovereignty is in control of the surface. We have a path out but can’t breach their perimeter.” She ordered the soldiers to be at ease and the weapons lowered.

Gerund’s hope threatened to falter. The Sovereignty had control of the mine’s surface, but maybe only temporarily, he thought. Perhaps the Coalition would storm back. He looked around Level Two and saw another pair of Coalition soldiers posted around a huddled group of people against the wall. Sovereignty prisoners; three men and two women.

Captain Valence noticed his gaze and nodded at the prisoners. “We blew apart their squad yesterday. Killed four with a booby-trap and the rest surrendered. Cowards,” she leered at the forlorn captives. They stared down at the stone. “We will use them as leverage to exit the mine. That’s the plan, anyway.”

“Your group mined the tunnels?” Carmenta asked, aghast.

“You bet. Got to cover our asses. Why, did you find some?”

“The man who did this to me and her...” Gerund said as he pointed to his calf wound and Marina’s missing index and middle fingers, “...he stumbled upon what must have been one of your mines. Took his leg off at the knee; he died shortly after.”

“Oh, so we did you a favor,” Valence smirked. “One way or the other, a mine tends to find the enemy.”

“Hey, there are civilians in this mine,” Carmenta protested. She shook in indignation. “That is such a rotten thing to do—leaving mines for anyone to stumble upon. You are what's so wrong about this war." Incredibly, she spat upon the ground at Valence's feet.

Several of the soldiers leaned forward with malice. Valance glared daggers and looked Carmenta up and down. Her hands balled into fists several times. *She looks unhinged*, Gerund thought. *So does the rest.* He looked at the weary, hard faces all around. *They've seen some shit these past few days, that's for sure.* They were no longer professionals; if they ever truly were. But Gerund noticed far more than a lack of proper procedure. This squad felt feral, far less composed than Gerund's 84th unit or any of the other Coalition units he had interacted with. *This group is out to hurt people,* he realized.

Captain Valence's anger finally subsided and she clasped her hands behind her back. "The miners are not my concern. OreLife should have evacuated all of you. You guys keep getting in the way instead of staying put."

Lizby stepped forward this time. "Look, we're just miners and we'll take our chances at the surface. We're just trying to get out of here."

"I've agreed to escort them as far as I can," Gerund added, though no such agreement had taken place. But it rang true to him as he said it. "Let me get them out of the way."

"Less mouths to feed," one of the soldiers noted.

Valence nodded in agreement. "Yes. You and your little *harem* are free to pass through. But we need to requisition your rations and firearms for the cause."

Carmenta clenched a fist in protest but deferred to Gerund to respond. He looked at the Sovereignty soldiers again and knew from their fearful expression that they were wise to move on, away from this group. He also believed that protesting wouldn't get them far. "Fine," he agreed. "Which paths to the surface are accessible?"

"I don't recommend that at all. But it's your funeral," Valence said. She pointed at a pair of catwalks beyond the group of prisoners. "Those will both take you up to an observation platform much closer to the surface. From there, many of the walkways were knocked out during the crash, but you'll see several that lead to the surface."

The soldiers took their rations and their water and patted them down roughly. Gerund couldn't help but glance at Marina. If they pulled down her collar even a few centimeters, then her incriminating Sovereignty tattoo would be visible. Not only would she be taken into custody or worse, the rest of them would surely be held accountable for her deception. Marina tensed as they searched her jacket. Her mouth was a tight line and she stood rigidly. The soldiers took out her lighter, flicked it on for a moment, then tossed it back to her. They let her go, as they did with Lizby, Carmenta, and finally Gerund after frisking each one.

"Are there any mines we should be aware of?"

"Oh yes," Valence grinned cruelly. "Almost forgot. We *secured* some of the upper access tunnels."

"What? Where?" Lizby asked.

"Oh, they're all over on the upper platforms. You should be fine on the walkways, though. No one mined the walkways, right?" Valence turned toward the rest of the soldiers, who all shook their heads.

"We'll handle it," Gerund stated, and began leading the way toward the first walkway.

"I'm sure you will, Corporal," Valence began to walk them out. "Where will you go after escorting these civvies, assuming the Sovereignty even lets them through?"

"Not sure. I'll make my own path and keep my head down," Gerund said.

"Good. I don't think you would be a good fit with our squad, Corporal." *No disagreement there.* "Where did you find these women?"

"Gerund helped us," Carmenta asserted. "The four of us were lost and—"

"I didn't ask you," Valence glared again.

"It's true. We stumbled upon each other and agreed to help each other," Gerund said.

"Heartwarming. What about this one?" Valence pointed at Marina. "You've been awfully quiet."

Marina looked back attentively. "I, uh...It's been really awful down here. I guess I've been in shock over everything, is all. A little tired, too." *She sounds rattled after being singled out,* Gerund thought. *But then again, who wouldn't?*

"Hmm. Aren't we all?" Valence seemed to accept this answer, but then she pointed to Marina's bloody bandage that covered her pinky and ring finger stumps. "What happened to your hand?"

Marina examined her hand as if noticing the wound for the first time. "Oh, I cut it on some debris during the collapse. It was really bad before the bleeding stopped."

The captain seemed satisfied with this answer, too. She stopped at the base of the incline leading to the prisoners. The four guards leaned against the wall and stared at them suspiciously as they approached. Their prisoners looked up with looks that implored the newcomers for help, as if they could suddenly grant them release. Gerund didn't want to think about the captives' prospects. There were few scenarios through which they would emerge from this war alive. In the increasingly guerrilla nature of the war he had witnessed firsthand, POWs, if they were taken at all by patrols, often had a way of disappearing before they could be processed by the nearest headquarters. Two of the men were beaten badly, each with a swollen face with one of them cradling a swollen arm that suggested a bad break. The third man and one of the women had abdominal wounds. It appeared that they had been hit by shrapnel by the explosive that had killed the rest of their squad. Perhaps they would be used as leverage as Valence had said or in some type of prisoner exchange with the Sovereignty. Gerund knew that this was their only hope at survival. There would be no mercy from Valence's group if the prisoners couldn't be used as a resource. In his 12 years of experience, he could tell when a Coalition unit could be counted on to act honorably. He was certain this wasn't one of those units.

Gerund met the prisoners' gaze as he approached but said nothing. He could not help them. There was a 1-meter path between the prisoners and the railing. Gerund and his comrades had to walk through single file. Lizby led the way with the lantern, followed by Marina, Gerund several paces behind her, and with Carmenta close behind. Gerund brushed past one of the grinning guards who had made no effort to step out of his path. *Asshole. What is their problem with us?*

One of the men with the broken face squinted out of his eye at Marina as she passed and poked the uninjured woman next to him. Marina looked up and away into the openness of the Pit. It was a casual but too quick of a gesture; she clearly was avoiding the prisoners' gaze. The man poked the woman even harder and then whispered into her ear. *This isn't good,* Gerund realized. *We can't catch a break.*

Chapter 54

Marina struggled to maintain her composure. The sweat gathered inside her pores. She felt all the prisoners' eyes on her now. She picked up her pace as she walked past the gawking man with the beat-up face who had first noticed her. *Oh no....they recognize me.* Marina realized that the Sovereignty must have released an alert with her photo after she had deserted. *Please don't say anything. It won't help you.*

The man looked at her again. "That's the girl, I'm telling you," he whispered into the woman's ear.

The woman leaned closer and nodded. "Oh my god, yes."

Marina turned her head and met the woman's gaze. Marina widened her eyes and mouthed *no*. But the woman was already rising to her feet. "Hey!" she shouted. One of the soldiers came off the wall and threateningly raised the butt of his rifle toward the woman. "Wait, she's part of the Sovereignty! She's a deserter trying to pass as a miner. Check for one of our tattoos on her neck!"

Marina tried to keep going but one of the guards blocked her path. *Oh no. It's all falling apart, after coming so far.* The large guard leveled his automatic rifle at her torso. He was smug and overconfident. She could strike before he could react...go for his knees and push him over the railing with his high center of gravity...but then what? Marina flipped through the possibilities in her mind. They did not bode well for her and her companions.

Valence came forward. "Hold up—stop them all!" The guard stepped toward Marina and the two behind Gerund began moving up on him. The soldiers at the blast door raised their weapons. "Prisoner! You know this woman?"

The Sovereignty man and woman shared a knowing glance and both nodded. The woman, still standing, again leveled an accusing finger at Marina. "Not personally. But before the battle our commander circulated her photo. She deserted her post the night before. She abandoned us."

Marina scowled bitterly at the prisoners and imagined what deservedly awful fate awaited them. But then she relented in her ill will, admitting to herself that she might have done the same thing in their desperate position to gain favor. She empathized ever so slightly with their plight, and she wondered if she would have been so understanding before she had undergone her recent trials.

Marina looked back to Gerund and Carmenta. She wondered if she could count on them. They would have to put their lives to intercede for her at this point. *What would I do in their shoes?* she considered. *Probably try to save my own skin, to be honest...*

The guard looked back to his Captain for direction. Valence nodded grimly. "Check her for the mark." The guard stretched for Marina's hand.

Now or never. In one swift motion, Marina stepped close to the guard who confronted her so she was past his rifle's barrel. He tried to bring back the gun, but Marina had taken the combat knife out of his thigh sheath with her good hand. As he continued to fumble with his rifle, she swung behind him and pressed the deadly sharp blade against his throat.

As Marina was making her move, Gerund sidestepped toward the edge of Level Two where the Captain was walking. She shouted in surprise and tried to bark an order that caught in her throat. Gerund gripped her shoulder to spin her around. Valence went for her sidearm, but before she had cleared the holster, Gerund had a tight grip around her neck. *Don't let her go, Gerund,* Marina thought as she brought her own hostage under control. *It's our only play.*

Lizby hesitated at the top of the ramp. She began to walk down to help Marina, but with the Coalition soldiers taking aim, she decided to duck down for cover instead. *Smart move, Lizby.*

Valence continued to joust for control with Gerund while keeping a grip on her gun. She was losing strength quickly. "Stop," Gerund commanded calmly. "Rest your hand."

Valence's gun hand was pointed forward uselessly, and Gerund tried to wrestle the pistol from her sweaty hand. But she squirmed and the gun fell to the ground and then clattered under the wire railing to disappear into the dark abyss of the Pit below.

There were eleven soldiers down the incline, and Gerund had already passed two of the guards by the prisoners. Behind him, Marina continued to hold her guard by knifepoint. Lizby remained prone at the top of the incline. *Where is Carmenta?* Marina worried. Out of the corner of her eye, she spotted Carmenta crouched near the prisoners, between the Coalition soldiers and Gerund. They needed to isolate the threats. Gerund slowly backed up. "Carmenta, get beyond me. Go up to Lizby."

Carmenta squeezed by him and scampered up the ramp to lay by Lizby. To dissuade the two guards behind him from making a move to save their captain, Gerund held Valence close and walked to the side so that their profiles were close together at the thinnest angle for both the soldiers down the ramp and the two guards up ahead.

"What do you think you're doing? She's scum. Are you going to throw away our cause and your life for her? How do you think this is going to end?" Valence hissed, straining precariously against the knife blade. But Gerund held it tight. There was no backing down now.

"Tell your men to lower their weapons. Let my people through."

"Can't do that, Corporal. Just leave the deserter to us and we'll forget the rest of this happened."

"Nonsense," Gerund said. "You have no choice." Captain Valence didn't respond. Deadlocked.

I got to make them think we're capable and dangerous. Because we are. Marina took a breath, and twisted her wrist to dig the tip of the knife into the soldier's shoulder just a few centimeters. She felt a sickening *thunk* after the knife had built enough pressure to pierce the fabric of his shirt and then plunge into the meat of his shoulder, He yelped in surprise and wriggled to break free, but she held firm. "What do you have to lose?" she yelled, her voice quivering with adrenaline. "We want to leave. All you have to do is step aside." She spoke into her captive's ear. "I'll keep going deeper with this knife until your arm becomes useless. Then I'll start somewhere else on your body. Tell your Captain to let us go." The words crawled out of her dry throat with raw desperation. In truth, she felt appalled for hurting this stranger. He was a younger man, maybe under 20; practically a boy. Perhaps even an honorable soldier, probably just stuck with a rash commander. She hated every second she held the knife in him. But she couldn't let him know that.

"Captain," he stammered. "We don't need them. Let them go, worry about them later."

"Worry about us *never!*" Marina clarified, pressing her knife again into the fresh wound in the man's shoulder.

Her hostage gasped. "We don't need these people. Just let them go," he repeated.

But Captain Valence gave no order. She wouldn't have all her troops stand down. At least not long enough for them to be in the clear. One of her soldiers didn't warrant that. She was willing to sacrifice the life of one for the pride of the many. Marina knew this, and apparently so did Gerund.

Gerund pulled Valence away from the group a few steps, and then stepped out toward a gap in the ledge railing that led to an open catwalk that stretched out into the darkness and was suspended by thinly spaced wire over hundreds of meters of open mine. No handrails; nothing below as far as the eye could see into the darkness.

"What are you doing? This goes nowhere. Stop!" Valence shrieked.

And then Gerund stepped off the ledge onto the catwalk.

Chapter 55

Captain Valence continued to mumble objections to the deadly consequences of walking across the narrow catwalk, but Gerund dragged her onto the platform without the least bit of hesitation. He kept going even after she dug her fingernails into him. "What's the matter? Afraid of heights?" he asked.

"You're crazy," she whispered.

The catwalk was a half meter wide and Valence had no choice but to match Gerund's pace in case her struggle tossed them both over the edge. Gerund remained as calm as possible. He was not the least bit troubled by the stark contrast of the dense steel beams suspended over the nothingness of the open air below. His companions and the Coalition soldiers stood dumbfounded, shocked by his stoic resolve. *This is the best option for us. So I'm doing it. No regrets.* Gerund also took comfort in the feeling that this was their only choice that he could see. It strengthened his confidence.

Gerund steadily stepped backward across the beam as if in an out-of-body experience. He was in control despite all the opposition facing them. He didn't feel the slightest bit of fright at the prospect of falling. He knew how unnatural that was. During their trek through the tunnels, he had worried about how his complete lack of primal fear would manifest in civilian situations, but now its absence just felt empowering. Valence was of course unnerved by the great height and by this point, at 10 meters distant from the ledge, matched his pace without so much as a whisper of protest. Any unexpected change in momentum might send them tumbling into a fall with a brain-splattering conclusion. Their bodies would probably never be recovered.

"Stop!" One of the soldiers called out to Gerund. "I'll shoot one of your friends!" The soldier aimed his rifle toward Marina, but she had already flipped her squirming captive around as a shield.

Gerund stopped and very gradually begin to tilt sideways, all the while keeping a tight grip around the Captain's neck. She dug her nails into him again. "Tell him that would be a bad idea," he growled.

"Don't shoot them! Just...." Valene looked at the expectant faces of her men and women. They appeared conflicted. They weren't used to losing control and being without decisive leadership. "Just hold on."

Gerund was losing patience. The shock of his and Marina's move was wearing off, and the soldiers would try something out of desperation soon. Gerund glanced behind him. The steel beam was dimly lit by the soldiers' flashlights and seemed to connect with a network of scaffolding at the edge of his vision. It was time for a risky maneuver. He got into a wide stance. He twisted his body while maintaining his traction on the beam and let go of Valence's neck while thrusting her over the side. He grabbed her shoulder and kept her waist close to him. Her arms hung over the abyss limply, as did the rest of her body. She was frozen in fear and kept still so as to not fall forward another centimeter.

"OK, OK!" she whispered.

Gerund drew her back very slightly, only a few degrees, and left her front half hanging precariously over the open blackness.

Valence trembled with rage. Or fright. Or perhaps a mixture of both. "Let them through! Guns down. Just do it!"

The Coalition soldiers slowly complied. They looked shocked to have their hand forced in this way. Lizby and Carmenta each rose expectantly into a crouch. Marina maintained her grip on her hostage, the knife still flush with his neck, "Give us our weapons and supplies back."

"Come on, no way!" one of the soldiers protested.

"Do it!" Valence yelled. "Give it all back to them!" Marina was relieved, but kept an outward edge of lethal desperation. She kept her eyes wild and flicked her knife right across her young hostage's jugular. Marina prayed he wouldn't test her; she wasn't bluffing with the threat.

A soldier immediately hustled forward with the two pistols while another brought up the food and water. Carmenta met them in front of Marina and grabbed the items with a glare before running back up the ramp to rejoin Lizby and give her one of the pistols.

Valence slowly tilted her head to look back at Gerund. Her cap had fallen into the abyss, and she glared through her hair. "Bring me back, all right? You got your supplies. We're leaving you alone."

"One more thing," Gerund insisted. "Let these prisoners go. I'm concerned about their welfare."

Valence's eyes bulged. "Why? They're Sovereignty."

"I aspire to be a decent human being. This doesn't end well for them if they stay in your custody. That's five human lives—people who probably just want to go home and see their loved ones."

"And what about our lives? We need these prisoners as leverage to ensure our own safe passage. We are Coalition. We should come before them, if the cause means anything to you at all."

"I'm not arguing. Do what I ask. We won't be on our way until you do."

Valence fixed him with a stare of hatred, but she had nothing further to counter with. "Release the prisoners."

The guards exchanged bewildered glances. "Commander, repeat please?" One of them shone a flashlight more directly on Gerund and the Captain.

"I said release the prisoners—let them all go!" Valence screamed.

The Sovereignty prisoners rose on unsteady legs with sudden hope as the guards walked away with disgusted scowls. The newly-freed soldiers helped each other up the ramp to stand behind Lizby and Carmenta. Gerund carefully brought Valence to an upright standing position on the beam and began walking her back. When they were within a few meters of the safety of the ledge, he tightened his grip again. "I need to bring you up the ramp. Then you'll be free to go and do whatever your squad is plotting next."

Valence inhaled sharply, but didn't respond. Soon they were on the ledge again and protected by the cable railing. Valence's muscles relaxed slightly. They slowly backed up the ramp. They gave Marina and her captive a wide berth. Carmenta met him at the top of the ramp. Lizby had begun to follow the prisoners up a long stairway, lighting the way with her lantern like a shepherd among a ragged flock. The stairs led to a higher stone ledge, which was adjoined by a platform and other structures that Valence, before things had gotten hostile, had indicated as leading to the Sovereignty-guarded surface.

"Marina, come up here. We got it covered." Gerund said. Carmenta waved her gun in front of Valence to emphasize this point.

Marina let the young man go and he nearly collapsed before pressing his hand over his bloodied shoulder and rejoining his comrades. When Marina was safely away from the Coalition soldiers and atop the ramp, Gerund released Valence. The Captain sprung out of his grip and swiftly walked to her troops without another word. Gerund turned to join the others, who were already racing up the stairs.

Carmenta wished that Gerund had pressed the issue more. He could have demanded some of the group's rifles. All the weapons. And have them strip down to underwear, just because. But the situation had been so tense that Carmenta held her tongue. *He got us all out of there, didn't he? Without firing a shot.*

Lizby and the five former prisoners awaited on the next level and Carmenta bounded up the stairs on the heels of Marina. She could hear Gerund's footsteps closely behind her. They were all exhausted but pushed onward with renewed vigor because reaching the surface seemed plausible now. She ran up the last step and emerged onto a stone outcropping lined with a concrete layer. Another blast door on the wall of the Pit led back into the mine tunnels. 10 meters to the side, the ledge housed a utility building with conveyor belt systems connected underneath. A track snaked down the stone wall and connected to the shack through a large port. Inside, a trio of OreLife railbots hung idly in a corner; either without power or without the autonomy to attempt any of their programmed tasks. The building had a wall-length window that overlooked the open Pit. Marina shone a flashlight beyond the one-story building. Another narrow staircase, suspended by cables, faded upwards in the darkness. *What's the plan now?* Carmenta wondered. *We've traveling blind.*

Once they were all on the platform, out of range of the Coalition soldiers, Carmenta and her companions huddled together while the Sovereignty soldiers whispered to each other.

Marina grabbed Gerund's jacket and tugged him close to her face. "What's the deal? You had to drag them up here with us? They turned me in! What are we going to do?"

The man and woman who had exposed Marina's Sovereignty origin looked sheepish and skittish. But they were unarmed and had nowhere to hide. Carmenta sympathized with Marina's anger. The Sovereignty prisoners didn't have to point out Marina's desertion. But maybe because it was one of the few things they had control of, they decided to punish Marina, no matter what might happen to her. And no matter how vindictive the Sovereignty prisoners seemed, Carmenta could understand. Her cousin was a deserter. Despite her reasons for leaving, even if the Sovereignty cause was doomed or misguided, Marina would always have to live with the ugly label.

Gerund broke free of her grip. "Should I have left them with those brutes?"

Marina softened slightly and shrugged. "It's not our responsibility. I just don't see why they have to come with us."

"Did you ever think they might be able to help us break through the surface? The Sovereignty might let Carmenta and Lizby through, but they're not going to let me—the enemy, or you, a traitor—pass through alive. But with these five vouching for us, we have a chance."

The man with the broken face who had first spotted Marina stepped forward. "We'll definitely vouch for you. We'll convince them, for sure," He looked at Marina through his swollen eyes. "But truth be told, I'm not sorry for reporting on you. You abandoned us. You would have deserved anything those soldiers did to you."

Marina's face registered a volatile conflict of shame and rage. Carmenta was relieved that at that moment she and Gerund held the only two weapons. Marina surged toward the man. "We just saved your ass! I should throw you and that bitch over the edge for ratting on me! I just wanted to pass through, and you ratted me out to the enemy." Lizby put the lantern down and darted between the groups. She blocked Marina and held her in a wide but firm grip. Marina leaned forward but Lizby was determined to keep her back.

The Sovereignty woman who had also exposed Marina shook a fist and stomped within a meter of Marina. "Who's the bitch? You left the whole Sovereignty, all the people who depended on you. You put on a civilian's clothes—from a dead body no doubt—did you kill her too? Then you try to slink out of here like a coward!"

This has nothing to do with getting out of the mine and everything to do with pride, Carmenta realized. “Enough! Cast judgement later. The goal for every single one of us should be survival, yes? Let’s do just that.”

“Carmenta is right,” Gerund agreed. “Escort us past any Sovereignty defense at the surface and, on my honor, we’ll simply part ways. OK?”

The Sovereignty group of five looked at each other and nodded. The more grievously wounded of the bunch looked like they were ready to agree to anything. Marina relaxed enough that Lizby was comfortable to release her from the hold.

Carmenta pointed into the open doorway of the utility shack. “Through here. There are stairs on the other side leading upwards. We’ve got to be getting close to the surface.”

Gerund led the way followed by Marina, Lizby, and Carmenta. The Sovereignty soldiers trailed a few paces behind. The lantern and flashlights lit up the dead computer consoles underneath the window and the large idle gears that took up one half of the shack’s floor plan. The building rattled as they crossed. Gerund paused at the stairway exit. He carefully poked his head out to peer up the staircase. He angled his flashlight upwards. The stairwell stretched far ahead, beyond the light. It was suspended by long overhead cables.

Carmenta realized that if the Sovereignty was waiting in the dark, then the group would be sitting ducks with their lights, walking up a narrow path in single file. *Lambs to the slaughter*. Carmenta shook her head. *Valence said Sovereignty troops were in control at the surface. I’m sure they have sentries between here and the top.* “Gerund, wait,”

Carmenta cautioned. "I don't think we should all go up at once. Let's have one of their own lead the way. That way, the Sovereignty doesn't shoot on sight."

Gerund nodded. "Good idea. Who would like to take point?" he asked the Sovereignty group in the shack. He imbued the question with enthusiasm, as if offering a free vacation or an opportunity to be cast in a film.

One of the men stepped forward. "I'll do it. Just give me a flashlight," he said with weary resignation.

Gerund and Carmenta didn't volunteer their flashlights because they had the weapons and needed to see properly. And Marina was too bitter to compromise with the former Sovereignty prisoners. When no one made a move, Lizby reluctantly handed the man her lantern.

Carmenta and her companions let the man pass and began the walk up the suspended stairway. The aluminum stairs clanged noisily and echoed in the vast space above and below. There was no way to ascend stealthily.

"Wait, what is that?!" one of the four Sovereignty soldiers yelled behind her.

"Oh my god, I think—"

Carmenta was thrown forward by a powerful blast. She collapsed against the base of the staircase, which fell apart beneath her feet.

Chapter 56

Lizby knew the situation was bad from the force of the shockwave that had burst through the utility building. Gerund, Marina, and the Sovereignty lead crouched defensively in front of her. They were shocked but seemed to be intact. She quickly took inventory of herself. She was covered with dust and her ears hurt, but she felt like she was otherwise okay. She saw Carmenta out of the corner of her eye, moving; breathing; alive. *Thank goodness.*

However, when Lizby turned around on the swaying stairway, she saw that the remaining four Sovereignty soldiers were dead. The utility shack was a heap of twisted sheet metal, with gears and conveyor belts hanging over the edge of the stone foundation. *No one could survive that.* The railbots lay blackened and smoking in the wreckage. One hissed a plume of superheated gas from some internal rupture. But what Lizby noticed next took her breath away. Poking out from the sheet metal and tangled within the mess of loose gears were *chunks of people*. There were a few intact torsos with heads among the wreckage, but most of the tissue was horribly mangled and looked more like poorly cut bushmeat than part of the humans who had been banged up but very much alive mere seconds earlier. *What...who did this?* Lizby looked away and rubbed Carmenta's shoulder. Her sister-in-law was crouched at her feet. She had been closer to the blast than Lizby and seemed completely disoriented. The bottom of the stairs had disconnected from the ledge and the two cables at the base had snapped. Carmenta was on two unsupported planks that threatened to plummet into the abyss below with every creak.

Lizby looked to Gerund. He had been so unnaturally calm since she had met him; fearless, even. *Come on, you must have some solution.*

Gerund met her gaze and then quickly assessed the carnage. “Keep moving!” he urged.

“What?” Lizby said. *I have no idea what’s going on.*

As if in answer, a barrage of bullets screamed by from a low angle. Lizby eyes widened to their furthest extent. The entire Coalition squad was firing at them, all the way from Level 2.

“They must have had the shack rigged to blow and then detonated a charge once they saw us go inside.” Gerund started to run up the stairs and motioned for the others to follow.

The lone Sovereignty survivor tried to come back down the stairs. “They can’t all be dead...not all of them,” he murmured. Gerund pulled on the man’s arm to turn him around, but he slipped by and continued down the stairs. The bullets continued to pass over them, but closer this time. Several clanged into the stairs and Lizby ducked even lower. *I’ve got to make it. For Sabos.* She repeated this thought like an incantation.

Gerund increased his pace and the others struggled to keep up. Every moment was freshly disorienting with the swaying staircase, the roar of gunfire assaulting their still-ringing ears, and the dizzying swirl of the flashlights. When he was several meters ahead of the others, Gerund paused to fire a burst of rounds at the muzzle flashes that indicated the Coalition positions. In response, the Coalition return fire concentrated in his direction, but he had already moved on.

Lizby tugged Carmenta to her feet. "Come on! We've got to move!" Carmenta looked at her in confusion—still in shock—and tried to say something, but it was much too quiet to hear in the chaos. *Carmenta, you got to move or we both die. I won't leave you. You're all I have left.* Their eyes locked. "Just move your legs, okay?" Lizby maintained a grip on Carmenta's hand and began to run up the stairs. Marina had already climbed ahead 10 meters, but paused to shine her flashlight on their path as they caught up. Lizby looked back once more at the surviving Sovereignty soldier. He was crouched among the wreckage, weeping over the broken bodies of his comrades, unconcerned over his own fate. Lizby snapped her head forward; she could not bear the scene any longer. She and Carmenta hustled until the clang of the stairs ended and they found solid ground.

The gunfire ceased. Directly in front, they were shielded by a large overturned conveyor belt. Beyond that, the survivors found themselves on a wide, smoothed stone shelf that extended outward away from the center of the Pit. It was dotted with twisted wreckage from the crashed dropships and buckled steel columns. "Keep low!" Gerund yelled. "Make sure they don't have a line of sight."

Marina gasped. Her glossy eyes shone with wonder as she pointed straight up. "We are almost out! Look!"

Lizby couldn't believe her own eyes. Straight above, framed by a jagged outline of loose beams and toppled conveyor belts, the stars shone magnificently against a clear sky. She had forgotten what the surface could look like. She wasn't used to seeing the night sky from the mine during operations because the artificial lighting blocked any starlight.

"We must be close to the edge. Do any of you see a way out?" Marina asked.

"I know where we are, roughly." Carmenta said. She had finally regained some of her wits. She thought for a moment and pointed. Marina illuminated the indicated direction to reveal a slope in the rock 150 meters away, at the fringe of the flashlight's beam. Carmenta took a few steps in that direction. "Yes; we can climb out that way. I'm not sure where the main entrance stairs and bridges are, or if they are even intact. So we should try that slope."

"We got to be careful. If the Sovereignty is in control up here around the surface, then they've surely heard that explosion and the gunfire." Gerund said.

"What if they stop us? Gerund, they'll probably shoot you on sight. And Marina, they'll kill you too once they find out who you are. Are you sure you want to risk this?"

"It doesn't matter," Carmenta said. "They'll shoot at anyone beyond their perimeter in these conditions; you and me included, Liz. And none of us can go back. Not with Valence and those other assholes down there."

"Carmenta's right," Marina said glumly. "I'm going for the slope. This is my only shot to get out alive. Right now, tonight. And probably for the rest of you, too."

"Agreed," Gerund nodded. "We keep quiet and go dark. Once we make it up the embankment and past whatever perimeter the

Sovereignty has set up, we head for whatever cover we can find. Then we just put distance between us and the mine. The cover of darkness should protect us. Once we're away and you three are somewhere safe, I'm going to rejoin my battalion—as soon as I figure out where they are."

"Wait, you're going back to the Coalition?" Lizby asked.

Gerund looked into the stars. "I need to. I have a purpose."

"What are you going to tell them?" Marina asked.

"The truth, essentially. I helped some civilians escape and then rejoined my forces at first opportunity. I'll leave out some details."

"Be sure you do. They won't understand the truth," Marina said.

"We should refuel first. Eat all the supplies, drink all the water. It won't matter either way in a little bit," Lizby reasoned.

No one argued her point, and they were all famished and parched with thirst, so they divided the remaining supplies and consumed them completely. Lizby had second thoughts about running out into the darkness. Even if they made it up the embankment, what were their odds of evading armed soldiers in the surrounding plain? Part of her wanted to climb into a hole and hide for as long as she could. But if anyone else shared her reservations, they didn't reveal it. *We've come this far. Just a bit further, and we're gone. I'll try for Sabos.*

"It looks clear. Maybe we cover the distance without the flashlight, for stealth?" Marina suggested.

The other three agreed, and Marina clicked off the beam. They crouched in the dark for a few minutes to allow their eyes to adjust to the marginal starlight. They saw each other as vague shadows, but it was better than utter blackness.

"OK, on three?" Gerund prompted.

"Let's do it. Keep going no matter what," Carmenta said.

Gerund holstered his weapon. It wouldn't be much good in the dark, Lizby realized. "Three...two...one...let's go!" The survivors climbed over the conveyor belt wreckage and scurried across the exposed stone. Finally: escape...or death.

Chapter 57

Without a word, the survivors darted across the stone in under 10 seconds and reached the base of the embankment without incident. Carmenta couldn't believe her body was still pulsing with adrenaline at this point, after so many kilometers of being pushed to the limit over these past few days, but she was grateful for the edge it provided. *We're so close to escaping this hell.*

Their eyes had adjusted just enough in the starlight to silhouette each other's outlines and basic features, but they could not see the features of the slope clearly. On her left, Gerund had his pistol in his hand. On her right, Marina and Lizby huddled in a crouch. The concave embankment in front of them steeply rose at a 30-degree grade, but Carmenta felt enough pock marks and cuts in the surface that she was confident that they could scale it. They continued to listen carefully, but heard nothing. They hadn't been spotted.

In the relative serenity of the moment, this calm before the storm, Carmenta reflected on her life. She wasn't satisfied with herself and her choices. She didn't know if she ever would be, but she wanted the opportunity. Her relatively content childhood seemed so far away now, as did the memory of her parents and so many others lost on her homeworld. One distinct memory rose through the others now; her frail father, on his deathbed, a month after the solar flare had ravaged their planet. Weak with hunger and trembling through dehydration, he had clasped her hands in his bony fingers and implored her to endure and find hope, and seek truth. She was weak herself, as everyone was during the devastating famine, and she didn't expect to survive long. Her mother had just died and she merely nodded while sitting on her father's deathbed, not believing the promise in his gaunt eyes. However, his words had stuck with her every day since, driving her on as she fled north with Sabos, and echoing in her mind once they reached safety.

She wanted to forget the years of bitterness that she had shouldered since then. She hadn't fulfilled her promise to her father yet; she hadn't been living with much hope. Carmenta glanced up with glassy eyes. The stars themselves seemed to promise better days, if she could only survive long enough to experience them.

The group drew close so they could ascend the embankment together. The first hint of dawn was appearing behind them; they needed to take advantage of the cover of darkness now. Gerund led the way as they crawled up the hill. Carmenta could see the top edge silhouetted against the star-strewn blue night sky, but she couldn't discern how far away it was. The edge indicated the top lip of the mine complex before the endless plains began. Once they crossed the threshold, they would need to cross as much as the plain as they could before the dawn fully broke, because they would be entirely exposed and in anyone's line of sight for kilometers.

Their progress was slow as they sought traction in the dark while trying to minimize noise. But there was still no indication of Sovereignty soldiers, or the Coalition or anyone else. Had Valence lied?

Two minutes later, they were still climbing, and the top edge of the embankment seemed as far away as ever. Best case scenario, they were halfway there. By now, the stars had started to fade from the dawn sky. Ahead, the top of the hill glowed with a sliver of bright, white light—different from the emerging sunlight behind them. *Is it the Sovereignty?* Carmenta wondered.

The four survivors were totally exposed as they crawled slowly up the incline. If a shooter spotted them, he would have no trouble picking them off, as it would be minutes before they could reach cover. But they didn't see anyone as they continued, and the edge of the embankment finally loomed ahead.

They gathered at the edge. The dawn emerged rapidly on Sarabek, and within minutes the cloak of darkness would be completely gone. Gerund peeked over, and Carmenta joined him.

The sight astonished her. One hundred meters ahead, the largest spacecraft she had ever seen was parked on the open plain, just outside of the OreLife access road. The vessel had to be at least 300 meters long. It was shaped as two cylinders, each starting in massive engines. The body was lined with cargo bays and protruding bulkheads spaced unevenly apart. The vessel narrowed to end in a disc-like gun platform on the front-center of the craft, which held five massive gun turrets, each easily 8 meters long. A bulky bridge deck dominated the back quarter of the vessel. The craft's spotlights cast downward to illuminate the crowd of hundreds that gathered beneath the massive feet of its landing gear. Carmenta squinted to see what the people were doing. She saw floods of Coalition troops guarding columns of Sovereignty prisoners. She also saw hundreds of civilians, but surprisingly, only about a third of were dressed as miners. The rest looked like they were from Haast, the nearby mining town. By now, Lizby and Marina had also ascended to the rim of the Pit to gawk at the scene.

"What's going on?" Marina whispered.

"Valence was wrong. The Sovereignty no longer controls the surface. The Coalition seems to be loading everyone onto the ship," Carmenta said. *We meet the Coalition again: good news for Gerund. Still bad news for Marina.*

People were hastily moving toward the vessel's ramps. All the Coalition soldiers were fixated on their prisoners or hustling everyone on board through one of three ramps. There was no perimeter.

"Maybe we can just walk up. Over there—on the aft end of the ship—we should mingle with those civilians and find out what's going on. No one will stop us—not with all this logistical chaos."

"What about Marina?" Lizby said. "If they check her for the mark, then it's over for her." *And us,* Carmenta thought.

Gerund shrugged. "I don't know. She can take her chances staying behind here, or she can come with us and blend in as a civilian. No one is going to check her right away—not with all these people here."

"We're out of the mine; let's just get out of here. Head in the opposite direction across the plain," Marina said, pointing to the open expanse.

Gerund slowly shook his head. "This is my chance to rejoin my unit, and Lizby and Carmenta might be safe there. In the meantime, you'll blend in too. But you're welcome to leave on your own," he said with an indifferent tone.

"Fine," Marina growled.

Carmenta shook her head. "I'm staying with her. We're not going to split now."

Gerund visibly softened. "Look, I think something awful is coming. Let's find out what it is. We can stick together for now, and approach through the crowd of civilians. We'll find out why the ship is here, and then we'll figure out what to do next."

"Come on, Marina. We'll be careful," Lizby encouraged.

"All right, I'm coming." Marina stood. "Let's see what all this fuss is about."

Carmenta had ridden a space-faring vessel just once—during her homeworld exodus—but it had been a much smaller craft, perhaps one twentieth the size of this beast. She had never seen a ship even half as big. She couldn't imagine why it was on a frontier world like Sarabek, and why it would risk landing. However, her companions weren't going to speculate further—Marina and Gerund were already leading the way towards the crowd. They had placed their pistols in their belts and walked as casually as their haggard bodies were capable. Carmenta and Lizby scrambled to catch up.

Perhaps it was the low light of the emerging dawn, or the focus on the ship, but no one in the swarm of soldiers and civilians seemed to notice them as they approached. Because he was Coalition, Gerund led the way as they waded through a sea of men, women, and children. The civilians parted ways for Gerund upon seeing his uniform and no one challenged them. Now that she was closer, Carmenta confirmed that the civilians were her fellow Haast residents. She saw a few in their OreLife mining uniforms, but most wore the mismatched tunics and trousers that were typical of home life in the town. Most of the civilians carried nothing more than a backpack, and some of them were still in their pajamas. They were close the center ramp of the ship, and the group of civilians bunched up against a line of Coalition soldiers who blocked the path to the ramp. The Sovereignty prisoners were being loaded on the rear ramp, and the Coalition was loading its equipment and personnel on the forward ramp.

Gerund turned around to confer with the other three. "Obviously, this is some sort of rushed evacuation. These people are not prepared, but they seem eager to get on that ship."

"They all look like they're from Haast; I don't see anyone from the village," Lizby said, referring to the hometown where her parents still lived.

Carmenta tugged the sleeve of a nearby man who held a few meager possessions in his arm. "Hey, what do we know so far?"

The man was irritated. "About what?"

"Uh, about what the Coalition is doing. Where are they taking everybody?"

"They didn't tell us where. They told everyone to come here. A truck came through my neighborhood last night, and this Coalition officer with a loudspeaker said that if we wanted to live, we needed to be on that ship within 2 hours. So everyone rushed straight here."

"That doesn't make any sense," Carmenta said. "If they hold the mine, at least at the surface, why are they bothering with Haast? Or the people in it?"

"I have a feeling that the war is coming full-force to our doorstep—what happened before was just a skirmish. Otherwise, your guess is as good as mine." The man turned away and tried to push his way closer to the front of the crowd.

"I'm going to ask those men," Gerund said as he pointed at the line of five soldiers that had blocked off the ramp. "Hang back here. Hopefully I can get to the bottom of this."

"Gerund, wait," Marina implored. "I'm not sure you guys want to be on that ship. I'm telling you right now I'm not going. Even if they give you an explanation, I won't trust it."

"You might not have a choice, Marina," Gerund said.

"We should have fled in the opposite direction, when it was still dark. Whatever this is, it can't be good," Marina insisted.

"Once again, I'm just hoping to see what I can find out, and then we'll decide what we can do." Gerund looked to Carmenta and Lizby for validation.

"Agreed," Carmenta nodded. "The people seem to be here on their own free will, but I doubt the Coalition has told them much."

"Gerund, see if you can get us first-class seats." Lizby smirked, but her grin vanished as quickly as it had appeared. "Also, see what is going on in the village—I'm worried about my parents there. Everyone is spooked. Even all the soldiers."

"Will do. I'll be right back." Gerund broke through the edge of the crowd and approached the Coalition line slowly. He showed them his identification, and pointed back at the Pit a few times as he explained. The conversation went back and forth for a minute before Gerund went rigid, and made a motion to ask the soldier to repeat. Gerund ran a hand through his hair while shaking his head. *That's no good.* A few more sentences were exchanged, and Gerund thanked them before returning to the crowd. A few civilians accosted Gerund for explanations, but he batted them aside. His ashen face promised grave news.

"Well? What did they say?" Marina demanded.

"It's an evacuation, all right. The Coalition may have secured the mine surface, but the Sovereignty fleet has entered the system and are only a few hours away. The Coalition is pulling out." Gerund cleared his throat. *If stoic Gerund is so shaken, this must be bad.* "But not before detonating a hydrogen bomb over the mine. They're not going to leave an asset like that behind for the Sovereignty."

"What?!" Carmenta hissed. Further words failed her. *How can they do this?*

Marina's whole body shook incredulously. "That's absurd! It'll wipe out everything in at least a 50-click radius. And the nuclear blast would cause damage in a 100-kilometer radius."

"My parents, their whole village—they're only 60 kilometers away! What did the soldiers say about the village?" Lizby was devastated.

"They didn't even know about the village when I mentioned it. I don't think the Coalition has time to evacuate it too," Gerund explained. "Maybe it's a smaller hydrogen bomb..." he offered weakly.

"Fuck that, there's no such thing as a *small* hydrogen bomb. You don't detonate a hydrogen bomb unless you want to scourge as much of the land as possible." Lizby said through tears. "I can't leave my parents. They are probably still in bed, and I have no way to warn them about what's coming. Sabos is dead and alone—I'll never recover his body. I can't leave."

"You have to," Carmenta said gently, putting an arm around her.

"But everything I've ever known is here. And my parents are still alive, how can I leave Sarabek without them!?"

"It's out of your control, Lizby. It's not fair but you can't do anything except survive for their sake. Sabos wants you to be safe—to have a future. Don't you believe that?"

Lizby nodded weakly. "Yes."

"Just follow us, ok? I need you at my side, Liz. Can you do that?"

"Ok. Because they would want me to, I'll go."

Carmenta turned to Gerund. "How much time do we have?"

"He said that the ship is leaving as soon as they get their Sovereignty prisoners, their remaining troops, and as many of the civilians loaded as they can. He didn't know where they're going. The other Coalition ships have already left, and I don't think even this beast has room for all these people."

We're putting a lot of trust into what they told us, Carmenta realized. "You believe what those soldiers told you? The Coalition is not bluffing with this bomb?"

Gerund nodded. "I do. There is precedent for the Coalition using a scorched earth policy on abandoned territory. I've seen it myself; entire shipyards wiped out and cities set aflame. This hydrogen bomb might be overkill, but maybe it's the only thing they have immediately available that can bury the mine," Gerund said. "I don't know if they're going to fly the bomb in, or if it's already here. But we need to get on this ship. I'm not willing to call their bluff."

"So how do we get on?" Carmenta asked.

"I'll pull my Coalition rank to escort us to the forward ramp ahead of everyone else. Should work, I think...Listen, we need to get on the ship *now*," Gerund urged.

As if on cue, the ship's enormous rear engines began to roar. The clay soil reverberated beneath their feet. The civilians waiting in line for the ramp bunched up as the people in back pushed forward. The Coalition soldiers brandished their weapons to prevent the crowd from surging forward as one of their captains called for order. The last of the Sovereignty prisoners boarded the rear ramp and it began to close. The guards at the center ramp began to process the civilians as fast as possible. Another line of Coalition soldiers formed between the crowd and the forward ramp as some of the townsfolk drifted over.

"Hurry. Best to let me do the talking." Gerund trotted away from the center ramp and broke through the crowd where it was less dense. Carmenta, Lizby, and Marina followed close behind.

"If they inspect me, I'll be shot," Marina warned.

"You are dead meat if you stay here," Gerund countered.

"I know, I know; but they might stop the rest of you since I'm with you. Hold up," Marina said. The others halted. "I...I should try to get on the center ramp. Separately."

"No! I'm not leaving anyone else! Everyone I've ever known here will be dead. We stick together!" Lizby cried.

"Lizby's right," Gerund said. "Let's stick this out together."

"Gerund..." Marina began.

"No, it's settled. We're—"

"Okay, okay. But take my gun, would you? I can't try to walk on with that, can I?"

Gerund accepted her pistol. "Ok, let me talk to these guys up here, and then follow me through.

Gerund approached the line while holding up his crinkled identification papers. The other three followed ten paces behind. Both the soldiers ahead and the civilians behind them looked on suspiciously.

"Corporal Gerund Williams, 84th unit," Gerund announced, not waiting for a challenge from the nervous men. "I need to escort these three civilians on board."

"Wow, you look like shit, Corporal." the ranking officer remarked.

"Yeah, well, we've been in the tough spot, wandering our way out of the mine. Been a rough couple days to say the very least."

The men let him approach, and the officer checked his papers briefly and was satisfied, but held up a hand to stop Carmenta, Lizby, and Marina from coming any closer.

"You had better board now. But these civvies need to get in line and wait their turn at the center ramp. This one is for Coalition personnel only."

"What does it matter? It's the same ship." Carmenta interjected.

No one responded to her. The officer remained firm. "Corporal, you can hear the engines building up thrust. The Sovereignty fleet must be closer than previously estimated. I'm withdrawing the last of my men right now—you should come with us."

"Right, the ship is leaving and the bomb is coming. Why are you holding us up? These are more lives that can be saved."

"I have my orders. We need to maintain separation to prevent mass chaos."

"Fuck those orders. They're coming too." Gerund stated firmly. Carmenta wondered how far he would go for them. His hand hung dangerously close to his holstered pistol. *Just let us through, please. Don't make us kill you.*

The officer opened his mouth for a retort, but then his weary eyes conceded. "Hurry up."

They strode past the line with great relief, but as they did so, a pair of gunshots popped from behind. Carmenta glanced back to witness all semblance of order breaking down. The crowd was surging towards the soldiers who guarded the center ramp, who had abandoned their struggle to hold them at bay and now scurried up the ramp, which was rising. Others from the crowd ran toward the forward ramp—the last entry to the ship. She and her companions and the rest of the soldiers dashed to get inside before the swarm of humanity reached them.

To Carmenta's relief, the soldiers on top of the ramp extended their arms and helped them climb up into the crowded bay. The last of the soldiers ran on behind them as the ramp began to rise. The bay was filled with unsecured, hastily loaded weapons and crated equipment and nervous soldiers. She joined the others to stand against a wall. Gerund was exhausted, but perhaps relieved, too. Marina, however, was incredibly anxious; her Sovereignty mark would instantly misidentify her as a spy. Lizby eyed the ramp as it hissed shut; she looked beyond devastated. *I can only imagine. She lost Sabos, and for all she knows, her parents are about to be fried.*

"Why are we launching so soon? I thought we had at least a couple hours before the Sovereignty got here," a soldier huffed as he leaned against a bulkhead.

"Their fleet is approaching orbit right now," another soldier answered. "The bomb is on its way."

Lizby sprang off the bay wall. "Stop the bomb! There are a lot of people down there!"

"They should have left days earlier. And we got most of them on board, I think."

Most?! Carmenta was repulsed by this callousness but not surprised. "There's another town with range of the bomb. What about those people?" she cried.

"Take us to your commander!" Lizby demanded.

"It's not our problem, and it's out of our hands now, anyway. No, you can't see the admiral," he scoffed.

Marina tried a gentle hand on Lizby. "There's nothing we can do right now."

"Easy for you to say. You chose to leave everything you knew behind. Everyone I love is here," Lizby snarled through tears.

The soldiers had already turned away, and the ship shook as it lumbered off the ground, and then accelerated at a slight upward angle. Carmenta looked out a bay door window. The Pit began to slowly diminish in the morning light as they rose into the atmosphere.

Chapter 58

The giant Coalition vessel flew as fast as its massive engines were capable, bouncing its unsecured passengers where they sat, and threatening to crush them with loose cargo that skidded towards the back of the bay. Gerund and Carmenta tried to console Lizby.

Marina sat silently, staring vacantly at the floor, still processing their escape. She wondered where they were being taken and if they would be separated on the ship. She was terrified of being discovered as a former Sovereignty soldier. Most of the soldiers had made their way farther into the interior of the ship, while several remained to wrangle the cargo to the support beams with straps.

After 10 minutes of flight, there was chatter building from the interior of the ship, and more soldiers came into the bay to gawk through the rear-facing oval windows. Marina and Lizby found a free window. They could see the circular Pit outline only faintly from so many kilometers away. Haast wasn't discernible, but the village was—it was located about halfway between their ship and the mine.

Marina realized that the explosion was imminent. It was too far away to see any ship that might have delivered the bomb. She wondered if the bomb had a delayed descent or detonation that allowed the ship to escape. *Lizby...you shouldn't witness this.* Lizby breathed anxiously as she stared at the valley where her home village lay. *I don't know...the village seems so far away from the mine. Maybe they'll be safe...oh god, I hope so. Lizby has suffered too much already.*

An intensely bright fireball flared into existence directly above the mine as the atmosphere ignited. A fiery blast tore through the surrounding landscape, engulfing kilometers within seconds. The fireball engulfed the mine and Haast as a mushroom cloud thrust into the atmosphere. In a blink of an eye, the town was gone. *There goes Lizby's and Carmenta's homes*, Marina thought. Even though they were at least 40 kilometers away and 15 kilometers high, the combination of the size of the explosion and its incredible speed made it feel much more intimate. The fireball had reached its maximum size within seconds, 5 kilometers in diameter, and the cabin of their ship was inundated with uncomfortable heat. The fiery blast continued to roll through the surface, rapidly covering the distance between the bomb epicenter and Lizby's home village. Lizby gasped as the wave showed no signs of losing momentum. Then the shockwave finally reached them. It violently shook the ship, bouncing Marina and the others off the wall and causing its nose to tilt slightly downward before the pilot was able to recover. The blast reached the twin mountainous peaks that lay 30 clicks east of the mine. The shape of the mountains held firm, but all the foliage on the slopes ignited in a pair of bright flares.

Marina squinted under the intense light and perspired from the thermal pulse that continued to assault them from so far away. But she and Lizby remained pressed against the window for breathless moments as the blast continues to radiate across the kilometers, hardly losing any momentum as it closed in on the village.

"Oh my god—it's going to hit them!"" Lizby wailed.

She's right, Marina realized. *They don't stand a chance.* It had been only 20 seconds since detonation, but already the explosive force had reached the village, which was sixty kilometers from the mine. The village had few discernable details from their vantage point; just an arc of highway connecting to a maze of smaller avenues, dotted with mostly single-story buildings and a few warehouses at the edge. Marina wondered if the Coalition command had failed to account for the proximity of the village in their hasty planning, or if they simply didn't care.

Lizby bit her hand as a plume of superheated air and debris swept over the village. Though the bomb's blast had perhaps lost some force, it was more than powerful enough to plow over the entire village. When the dust swept through, they saw complete devastation. The village was instantly on fire. Roofs were torn off; some buildings were annihilated entirely. Lizby collapsed on the floor and covered her face. She wept almost silently, shaking slightly as she sobbed.

I can't imagine that anyone lived through that. Marina continued to watch the blast expand across the landscape. They were high enough that their ship continued to climb unhindered, even as the blast wave swept beneath them. Along its enormous circumference, the wave began to finally dissipate into rising clouds of dust. Upon seeing such force, Marina expected to hear the blast, but they were so far away that no sound had yet reached them.

The fireball had imploded and the heat had finally started to relent, leaving the ship uncomfortably warm. The hydrogen bomb's mushroom cloud dominated the horizon, rising all the way into the stratosphere. Marina slowly backed away from the window, careful not to step on Lizby, who remained grieving on the floor. Carmenta knelt beside her sister-in-law. She offered no words of console, but merely stayed with her. Gerund hovered nearby for the next few minutes, unsure of what to do.

Finally, after crossing 50 kilometers, the sound of the explosion roared through the ship, causing it to shake and drowning out all sound for 5 seconds, and continuing to rumble for another 10. Afterwards, the bustle of the ship seemed quiet in comparison.

They would have no rest in the aftermath of the explosion. An officer entered the bay and shouted for the remaining soldiers to finish securing the cargo, then turned his glare to the four companions.

"What are these civilians doing here?" None of the other Coalition soldiers answered him, so he narrowed his gaze to Gerund. *Can't they just give us a minute?* Marina thought.

Gerund straightened up as he answered. "They boarded this ramp right before take-off. It's been unsafe to move through the ship since."

"They need to be with the others. This is an active operation." He motioned for the three women to come forward. "Folks, follow me."

Carmenta helped Lizby to her feet. The widow—and now orphan—had stopped crying, but her eyes were glazed with indifference as Carmenta led her toward the Coalition officer. Marina hesitated. *What's going to happen to me now?* She looked at Gerund; he seemed only mildly worried. Maybe the situation did not pose much of a threat to them. Well, perhaps not to Carmenta and Lizby, Marina conceded, but a quick check of her neck, and she would be toast. If the Coalition was willing to sacrifice hundreds of civilians to prevent an industrial asset from falling into Sovereignty hands, how much more willing would they be to simply flush her out of an airlock if she was revealed?

Gerund leaned forward. "Go. Act natural," he whispered and patted her on the shoulder. "I'll follow up and try to see you guys when I get a chance. I need to report for duty right now, or else I might receive extra scrutiny for being AWOL for so long."

Marina followed Carmenta and Lizby out of the bay, stealing a glance behind before the automatic door snapped shut. Her last glimpse of Gerund was his forced smile, which was an uncertain twist of encouragement and apprehension.

Chapter 59

I'm wet and cold. Carmenta's first sensations as she woke caused her eyes to flutter open, and she rapidly gained consciousness along with panic. *I'm underwater!* She flailed her arms in the frigid liquid and connected with a mask firmly fixed over her nose and mouth. She instinctively thrust herself upward, but encountered a glass barrier and a tangle of hoses.

She wasn't alone. In the dim, green-tinted light, she saw motionless bodies floating to her right and left, adding to her distress. Like her, they were suspended from hose bundles. Unlike her, all their eyes were closed. *Suspended animation,* she realized. She had heard of the Coalition using this technique to transport troops across the vastness of space. Both men and women were packed around her, with minimal covering. She didn't see Lizby or Marina. *What have they done to us? How did I get here?* She tried, but couldn't recall. She remembered the ship leaving orbit and being herded into a corridor with the other civilians—but that was it.

Carmenta thought she heard a pair voices. Through the blurry water, she saw nothing but a tall bulkhead. She twisted around in the water to spot two observers on the opposite side of the tank. A man and a woman in fleet uniforms pointed at her. Their voices were audible enough, but warbled through the glass and water. She waved her arms wildly, but the crew didn't appear alarmed at all by her conscious state. Irritated, perhaps; but not concerned. The man pointed to her midsection, and she looked down to notice a large tag strapped to her belly; with large numbers printed. The woman tapped efficiently on her datapad, and then looked up expectantly at Carmenta. *Oh no, what are they doing?*

With a chilling *whoosh*, a rush of air filled Carmenta's mask, and her first breath immediately made her feel faint. *Gas.* She attempted to hold her breath as a futile defiance. *Where are they taking us?* she wondered. She lost her fight within seconds and exhaled, taking in more of the gas as the Coalition techs smugly smiled. *Shit, time to sleep…*

Her vision faded to black, and Carmenta's world fell silent.

"Why weren't the rest of us told?" Gerund demanded.

"It was a need-to-know basis, and you are not part of this ship's crew."

"What's going to happen to them?"

"For the next month they're going to sleep."

"And then?"

"Everyone is free to go once we make port. The Coalition may even give them some travel vouchers."

Gerund stood in an officers' lounge across from a lieutenant. Gerund had checked in with Coalition command, and was off assignment for the duration of the spaceflight. He had followed the lieutenant into the lounge, intent on getting some answers about his friends.

The lounge was sterile and empty besides five plush lounge chairs and an antique wooden table. However, it had one of the larger windows on the vessel; a gigantic rectangular view of the cosmos. On this side of the ship, it provided them with a spectacular portrait of the *Jurate* nebula. The aqua-blue, purple-tinged ribbon filled the window from top to bottom, encompassing millions of stars, and unfathomably, was millions of lightyears across. The stars outside of the concentrated nebula, although lonely, had their own stark, brilliant beauty. Although Gerund had seen Jurate before, the view never ceased to be majestic. In contrast, the stern, impatient face of the lieutenant irritated him.

"I hope they'll wake up fine," Gerund sighed. *I should have stayed with them—I would have intervened.* "Physically, and mentally. Hibernation should never be rushed with so many people. I know from personal experience that there are often awful side-effects."

"Sure, hibernation is not ideal. But they should all be grateful we didn't leave them at the mine. Staying alive is enough for them."

Gerund spun away from the officer, and continued down the hallway. He had just learned some disturbing news. Overnight, as the vessel shot away from Sarabek, all the civilians—men, women, and children—had been ushered into one of the aft holds, and then forced into hibernation by their armed escorts.

Marina, Carmenta, and Lizby had been among the bunch, and he hadn't had a chance to speak with them since their separation. He hoped the hibernation had been safely done, and they hadn't been too distraught. In particular, Marina could have been exposed by her Sovereignty mark. In the rush of the evacuation, perhaps she had been processed without any Coalition crew noticing. But if she had been revealed, she would have received the space justice reserved for suspected spies: an icy, lung-bursting trip out an airlock.

"Why did command feel the need to induce hibernation? I thought we were only a month away from our destination."

"We needed to ensure that the food and water would last the rest of the journey. We didn't anticipate taking on refugees."

Gerund could understand the calculation: they were at least 40 days from the nearest safe planet. Without forcing the civilians into the hibernation, the supplies would not last. Except, Gerund had already seen the ship's hold: mountains of grains, legumes, and freeze-dried meats—filling the large space almost to the ceiling.

"Bullshit. What's the real reason? I've seen the stacks of supplies in the hold—there's enough to last half a year."

The officer hesitated. "Uh, I don't know about that."

"Yes, you do. Now tell me what's going on," Gerund demanded.

"OK, OK. But look, you can't be telling anyone. We need to stick with the official line that there are not enough supplies."

Gerund twirled his hand impatiently. "Yes. Now out with it."

"The Coalition injected a gas into the civilians' masks once they were unconscious. It's not supposed to damage them. It sounds crazy, but it's...it's supposed to alter their brains—make them impervious to fear."

"What?! Impervious to *fear?*" Gerund was aghast. *What happened to me during my hibernation—that was no accident,* he realized. *I was just an early Coalition experiment.*

"Yeah, the gas supposedly affects part of the brain, the part that processes fear. If it works predictably, then I'm sure it will have many applications for our armies."

More than you can imagine. Gerund thought. *This will intensify the war.* "This is wrong. These people had no choice."

"Military necessity, and like I said, it's not going to hurt them. Plus, they're lucky to be alive at all. And you know, I could do with a lot less fear, after fighting in this war."

Gerund reddened with anger and he drew several sharp breaths before speaking. "Nonsense! You can't just wipe out someone's fear—it's not like surgery. There will be a void where an important part of them was."

The lieutenant furrowed his brow. "I don't know about that."

The man wouldn't understand. And neither would Gerund get far appealing to the Coalition for liberty. He turned to peer out the window. He placed his hand against the glass; the gray planet at the edge his view had dwindled to the size of his hand. *I need to help them. But how?*

"Thanks for the info," Gerund said flatly. He lingered to take in the starscape a few moments longer, then began to walk away.

The lieutenant spread his arms wide. "Hey, just enjoy the journey. We have over a month before we reach the front again. Relax."

Gerund didn't respond. He strode purposefully out of the lounge, though he didn't have a plan. *I can't wait a month to help them. It will be too late by then. Besides, who knows what the Coalition has planned for them next...I'm lucky I got lost in the shuffle after I woke.* Gerund considered whether any of the three would seek to free him if their roles were reversed. Lizby? *Surely.* Carmenta? *Probably.* Marina, after all we've been through? *I dunno.* But he decided it didn't matter. His friends needed him, and he couldn't go back to hell—the total war between the Coalition and the Sovereignty—without trying to save them.

THE END

Made in the USA
Monee, IL
24 January 2021

58507749R00256